AGAINST ALL ODDS

ANNIE HOLDER

www.annieholder.com

ONE

The text messages were puerile, obvious to the point of insulting. It seemed her husband liked his girlfriends' short on brains, long on patience. His replies were rare despite their persistence – unless availability collided with inclination, prompting a rush of hurried and clumsy sexting, culminating in an assignation.

Being forewarned enabled Grace to throw away fewer uneaten dinners. It had been going on for so long she now checked his 'phone as a matter of course, to give her half a chance when diary planning. No point agreeing to a meal with friends if Dominic had pencilled in a more tempting morsel for the same evening.

The regularity of his philandering had gradually rendered the reading of the 'phone a nightly necessity, just to keep up – like a devotee of a Dickens serialisation or an avid *Archers* fan. While he was in the shower or on the toilet, Grace would flick through the daily record with detached interest. She'd long since given up feeling anger at the women registered only as single letters in his telephone contact list. The anger she directed at herself, for her spinelessness. The tone of the messages made them seem young, keen; desperate to please with their promises and declarations. Perhaps Dominic's approbation was necessary for a promotion or pay rise, and doubtless none of them knew he was married, as he'd never worn a ring.

Once Dominic had departed for work, Grace tidied up the breakfast things, showered, dressed, and stared searchingly at her unresponsive reflection in the hall mirror.

Eventually, she slunk out of the flat, closing the front door diffidently, and taking the back stairs to avoid the neighbours. She crept as close to the walls as pedestrian traffic would permit, up the Clerkenwell Road to a coffee shop she'd never visited before. It wasn't that she was meeting anyone, or particularly wanted to sample their brand of coffee, but had decided an appearance in public would force respectable behaviour. Not that it mattered. If she was really about to go as mad as she feared, who in the middle of London on a normal weekday would even notice if she threw a cardboard cup with a plastic lid, and ranted an expletive or two at the drizzling sky?

She purchased a coffee, and hauled the heavy remains of herself to an alcove in the very back corner.

'It must be today. For our future.'

A regular contributor to the Inbox of Infidelity for over three years, and more articulate than most whose prose frequented the little on-screen boxes, the woman in question nevertheless entered as energetically as any of her peers into the demeaning displays of digital devotion. Did they realise they were competing, hawking their wares like market-stall traders with perishable stock and a limited time to shift it? By the tone of their words, each considered herself the only one. That was what made it so pitiful. None of them were the only one, because of her – the wife – the *only* 'only one'. But what did the long-ago-devalued title of wife matter here, when contrasted with such passionate urgency?　The vital importance of 'their future'; which it seemed would begin today, whatever his helpless, hopeless spouse felt about it.

Grace stared at the table top, her unseeing eyes picturing only the message encased in its jokey, over-designed little iBubble of quirky coolness, as if it was saying, 'Hey, don't mind me, I don't mean any harm.　How could I possibly hurt y'all, looking as cute as I do?' – all the while creeping up and slicing her in two like a battle-axe through the spine.

Could she really place all the blame at Dominic's door?　Their married life was now so routine, so one-dimensionally distant from its whirlwind beginnings, it was hardly surprising he was seeking excitement elsewhere.

Dominic liked life to sparkle and shine, to impress and entertain, to push his buttons and fire his imagination.　At first, boarding the rollercoaster beside him had been an adventure – a rush the like of which she had never experienced – but it didn't take long to become exhausting.　There was never a day off!　Dominic kept up the punishing pace until Grace found herself wishing for the ride to stop, the stress to dissipate, and the over-stimulating world to cease whirling on its axis.　The longing for quiet, predictable routine – time to catch her breath and shuffle her jumbled thoughts into order – became all-consuming.　She began to take deliberate steps out of Dominic's spotlight, so imperceptibly neither noticed at first, until one day Grace realised he'd gone out without her, and she was indescribably relieved to have been left behind.　Neither discussed the shift in the tectonic plate beneath their marriage, but both understood it had warped irreversibly.

Grace came to understand Dominic had married her money and social position; she, his dashing persona, the *idea* of him, the kudos of snaring and taming such a sought-after prize. If forced to tolerate his disappointing mate in exchange for the cash and the connections, Dominic Radley considered himself well within his rights to make his wistful little wife a less maddening encumbrance. He thrust her into the fly-trap clutches of Fenella Dalrymple, a past conquest. Worldly wise, suitably-connected, acerbically honest when the occasion required it, Fenella was just the person to whip Grace into suitable shape, stamping with stiletto-shod sharpness upon every one of her artlessly-romantic notions. Grace could admit she had learned some valuable lessons from Fenella, not least the efficacy of turning the other cheek. It enabled her to desensitise herself to the continued betrayals; preventing her from feeling anything more than a dull ache in her insides, like a slowly recovering muscle-pull, every time she discovered a fresh initial saved in Dominic's contact list. Fifteen years ago, she would have shared her anguish with anyone fool enough to enquire. Now, she understood if your own husband didn't give a shit about your feelings, virtual strangers at dinner parties definitely wouldn't. It was better to use occupational therapy to quiet the internal scream. She rearranged her wardrobe regularly. She ironed socks and underwear. She rotated the crockery sets so all got equal use. Whenever she felt as if she might toss each plate across the room at the far kitchen wall like a Frisbee as she emptied the dishwasher, she did deep breathing until the moment passed, and then concentrated on an hour or two of yoga. She found learning control of her body and mastery of her thoughts addictive; plus, standing on her head became an excellent distraction from the temptation of taking a tennis racket to the Wedgewood on the dresser. Grace would rather pretend everything was satisfactory than admit she had chosen unwisely, and seek to stand alone. At their age, in her situation, where on earth would she go, even if she had the guts to leave?

Grace sipped at her coffee. The oddly-shaped hole in the plastic lid released a large glug of near-boiling liquid into her unprepared mouth. She couldn't spit it out, so had to swallow it. At least the burning sensation seared all else from her mind for a second or two, and returned her to her surroundings with a muted gasp.

An expensively-tailored woman advanced towards her. Grace found her heart fluttering between anticipation and terror. Was the woman coming to speak to her? Might it be nice to speak to someone other than Fenella…but maybe not this instant, when she could think of nothing by way of small talk but, 'My husband has his future planned with another woman! Something's going to happen today! By tonight, I might not even have a husband – and then what will become of me?'

As a precaution against even accidental eye contact, she took rapid refuge behind a newspaper abandoned on the table by a previous customer, but of course the woman wasn't coming to initiate conversation with her – this was London, for God's sake! Besides which, she was invisible.

What the woman wanted was the table opposite hers in the alcove, and took her seat without even acknowledging Grace's existence, let alone passing the time of day. To prove she was as downright rude as everyone else in this town, Grace expended some effort in attending both to *Metro* and Macchiato, whilst in her mind's eye the green boxes of the text messages swirled over the top of the newsprint until she wanted to screw them up inside the paper, and hurl the whole bundle across the room.

The more Grace concentrated on not making an unhinged exhibition of herself, the more aware she became of the other woman and how distracting she was, slurping her drink loudly through the slot in the lid, and dividing her attention between tapping her false nails on the screen of her tablet, and flicking with exaggerated impatience through a glossy magazine. At length, as Grace was beginning to feel she would like to bunch up the newspaper and throw it at the woman instead, her 'phone emitted an ostentatious bleep. She snatched it up, let out an exclamation of annoyance for the benefit of her audience, and bustled hastily out, leaving the magazine. The lure of the glossiness proved irresistible to Grace. It was the work of a moment to spring up and pilfer it, charitably swapping it for the paper.

Across the cover was a wide stretch of white sand meeting a clear sea, rippling waves criss-crossing one another on the ebb tide, exposing only the odd stone or trail of weed to blemish the otherwise perfect expanse as the tide edged out. The sky seemed endless, colour deepening from near-white at the horizon, through grey, to pink, and finally blushing out to a rich lilac at the page's perimeter.

The whole image was so vivid she almost believed it possible to reach in a hand and trail her fingertips through the bubbling edge of one of those receding, inch-deep waves.

In that moment, she thought nothing of the text messages, or even of Dominic; nothing of the burnt roof of her mouth, the reprieved crockery, or her lifeless eyes reflected in the hallway mirror. She desired only to place one foot in front of the other into the smooth and sinking sand where shallow sea met exposed beach, adding her imprint across the otherwise untouched surface; leaving a mark somewhere in the world instead of fading away.

She would neither explain nor inform; no more would she leave a note exhorting him not to worry. In fact, she would extend him the same courtesy he showed her; namely, none whatsoever.

Wherever that beach was, she would go to it, and everything else that was supposed to matter could take a running jump.

TWO

The call was answered so fast Fenella must have been sitting on the 'phone, "I wondered when you'd join the party! Where the hell are you?"

Fragments of raised male voices stabbed between the clipped ice.

"What's going on, Fen? Is that someone shouting?"

"What's going on?! As if nothing whatever has happened in the world! Whom do you think might be shouting, Grace?"

"I don't…is that Toby shouting at someone?"

"Yes, he is, as a matter of fact, Grace. Yes."

"What – "

"Your husband is in my kitchen shouting at my husband, accusing us of being in on some conspiracy against him with his crackpot wife, who's decided to take herself off without leaving as much as a Dear John on the mantelpiece by way of explanation! Answer me this, Grace, what exactly are you trying to achieve? If you want him to pay you a bit of attention for a change, flouncing out in a sulk won't get you anywhere. I've always found a negligée and a blow job much more effective."

Grace was peremptorily silenced, as if Fenella's beringed and manicured hand had shot out of the receiver and slapped her across the face. She always did this, effectively neutralising all Grace's attempts at independence with a splash of acid, stinging with targeted accuracy. She was tempted to cut the call, switch off

Fenella and the discomfort of her judgemental, penetrating sarcasm...but what if something happened? She was the furthest she'd ever been from home alone. What if she were taken ill, or attacked, or murdered? If she told Fenella where she was, at least someone would be able to identify the body.

In a small voice, she stated, "There was a message, Fen, on his 'phone. Different from the others. This one was about the future; 'our future' it said. Done and dusted. He's leaving Fen, so – "

"So, you thought you'd steal his thunder and do it first."

"No, no...I didn't want the conversation! I didn't want to have to stand in front of him, hearing him say it, so I just decided I wouldn't be there. He can leave and I can just...not know..."

"Let me get this straight, you both respectively pack and leave, and your prime central London real estate is abandoned to the spiders while you each sit in hotels waiting for the other to make the first move...? Honestly, Grace, I'm not entirely sure you don't have a screw loose, darling. I don't know how you cook up these flights of fancy, but he's not going anywhere. He's beside himself because he hasn't seen you since yesterday morning! You do know the usual form is to have a plate-smashing humdinger of a row to leave him in no doubt of your departure and your reasons whereof – not creep out incognito like the Scarlet bloody Pimpernel and not tell a soul. He could have reported you missing! Half the Met might be out now turning the place upside down trying to find you, thinking you've been kidnapped or something. It's utterly irresponsible, Grace!"

"Oh, but having affairs left, right, and centre is perfectly ok, I suppose?" Wow, where had that come from? She'd never have the courage to say any of this to Fen's face. Thank God for the nine hundred miles separating her from the queen of the icy glare and pithy put-down.

Uncharacteristically, Fen let the retort go, instead crooning, "Sweetie, where's your common sense? Have you learned nothing these twenty years? You don't get mad, darling, you get even. Every time they do something you find less-than-acceptable, you hit 'em where it stings the most! The *Louboutin* shoes, the *Chloe* handbags, the remodelling at home, the very best schools for the children, the new car once a year. When you want something, you have it! The thirty pieces of silver; the price he must pay for having his cake and expecting to be able to eat it too."

"I'm sick of it, Fen! I don't want another handbag. I don't want my whole life to be a constant cycle of scheming and revenge. I want to be with someone who's delighted by my company, without it having to be some business transaction designed to pierce his wallet every time he pokes his mistress. I just want it to stop."

"Gracie, you're having a tantrum, that's all. You're doing something extreme so everybody notices you. It's childish."

"Fen, I rang you because…" Why? Why had she rung Fenella? Was it only so someone would know where she was, or had it been to obtain Fen's blessing for her actions, just to convince herself she hadn't completely lost all reason? What rational person left financial security, social status, undeniable comfort…for the urge to make the perfect footprint on an empty beach? Was that the act of a reasonable individual, or the hare-brained, half-baked lunacy of an idle dreamer with nothing better to do than navel-gaze her way into self-pitying depression?

Fenella treated the sudden silence on the line more as invitation-to-continue than cause-for-concern, reiterating, "Honestly, Grace, I've always thought you were a little bit 'out there', darling, but this takes the cake! Kooky is endearing. Ga-ga is not, frankly."

Grace could picture Fenella's lip curling as she passed judgement.

The ferry engine started up with a cough and roar which surprised Grace. She'd quite forgotten where she was.

As the boat began to move away from the dock, the motion and vibration set off several alarms on the open car deck below.

"Grace, where are you?"

She toyed with the idea of making something up, but knew she wouldn't. She had to tell Fen where…just in case…

"I'm on the ferry."

"To Calais?"

"To Orkney."

"Whaaaat?" Fen screeched, losing all poise in the face of such rank idiocy, "Well, that settles it; you have completely taken leave of your senses! What possessed you to go there? I don't think they even have Waitrose."

To Fenella, this one fact negated the requirement for any other proof to support her assertion of the total absence of civilisation. Grace felt her plan seemed even more insane when subjected to Fenella's withering scrutiny than it did within her own, reeling head. She began hesitantly, "I wanted to go to an unsullied place, to…erm…to make a mark…"

"Leave a stain, more like," Fenella drawled, acerbically. Fen was right, it was bonkers! She was standing on this dirty, windswept deck, freezing her arse off, spouting utter crap! Watching the Scottish coast recede made her even more unsure of herself. Perhaps she *was* just stamping her feet and flouncing out like a teenager in a huff, slamming every door on the way to ensure no one could ignore it.

"You know I'm going to tell Dom, don't you?"

"Fen, you're supposed to be on my side!"

"Says who, darling, the United Nations?"

Grace felt humiliated, hurt, alone, and very, very scared, so she snapped, "Oh, tell him what the hell you like, as you're so concerned with placing his welfare before mine! If...if...anything happens...I'm staying at a house called *Somerled* in a place called Birsay. I just thought someone should know, that's all...but don't worry yourself. I'm sure I can cope quite well without your kind concern!"

Grace whipped the 'phone from her ear and stabbed frantically at the off button. Denying Fenella the chance to have the last, scathing word was empowering, and Grace toyed with the idea of dropping the 'phone into the boiling, churning wash beneath her feet, but didn't do it. That was best left to heroines on gritty tv dramas. Terrified, overwrought women making grand gestures like leaving not only their husbands but mainland civilisation to boot, might be grateful for the practical application of a smartphone in their hour of need.

The strengthening wind buffeting insistently at her back made her glad of all the layers she'd elected to wear on rising from her B&B bed to the chill of the early Highland morning. Spats of November sleet persistently peppering her windscreen as she'd notched up the northbound miles made her wonder why she was sticking so resolutely to this stupid plan, the thrill of sticking a metaphorical pin in a map and discovering salvation at its zenith. If she'd any sense, she'd go straight to the return ferry queue as soon as she arrived, and dismiss the whole, sorry mess as a moment of madness…but she was tired of being the Grace who resolutely kept her seat on the ridiculous carousel of self-delusion. Foolish she may well be, but the humiliation of having to creep home and placidly accept the continuing disrespect was more crushing than pushing onward. Intentionally or not, by ringing her so-called friend, she'd ensured the die was cast. It had now become a question of pride to see this through, whatever it was.

THREE

The going became unsteady as the ferry hit choppier open water, and Grace was startled to be bumped against by another body. Her London senses barked 'beware!', and she clutched her handbag close – were there pickpockets on ferries like there were on the tube?

Instead of a hard-faced ne'er-do-well with five o'clock shadow and darting eyes, Grace beheld a young girl with vivid auburn hair falling in careless ringlets around drawn, pale cheeks. The girl's Scots accent was broad, but not unintelligible to Grace's untuned ear.

"Och, I'm sorry…I'm..." The girl staggered again, eyes glazing, freckles standing out prominently against the stark pallor of her pretty face. She swayed alarmingly, and would have fallen to the deck had Grace not instinctively lunged to grab her, easing her gently backwards onto the closest metal bench, and squatting in front of her, holding her knees to prevent her slipping forward, pickpocketing paranoia forgotten in the rush of genuine concern.

The girl slumped, hands to her temples, drawing the thick curls away from her face, and managing a few deep breaths. One palm pushed firmly against the knees of the girl, convinced even slightly releasing the pressure would see her slide from bench to deck, Grace managed to fumble a bottle of mineral water from her handbag, clumsily wrestle off the anti-tamper film, and use her teeth to tear off the strip of plastic to open the cap, "What a performance...here, have some of this."

The girl was too far gone for politeness, snatching the bottle and squeezing large glugs of the cold liquid into her mouth, swilling it around before swallowing, nostrils flaring. She took in gulp after gulp, and belched twice with no attempt at restraint, and no apology extended. Somewhere quite near the surface, in the shallow, Fenella-influenced part of herself, Grace found the primal nature of the girl's need rather distasteful, and decided she didn't want the water back.

Beneath that, where the essence of the real Grace still dwelt despite everyone's best efforts to eradicate her, swirled a maelstrom of curiosity and concern for this wild, Pictish beauty, with her curls of fire and air of desperation.

Quietly, as if she couldn't believe she was conversing so directly with a stranger, Grace managed, "Can I fetch someone for you?" waving an explanatory hand towards the steps leading to the warm interior seating area, where anyone with an ounce of sense would be. Only seasick, tragic heroines, lunatic women on the run, and determined whale-spotting tourists graced what had been optimistically christened the Sun Deck, as snow crystals whipped past them on the prevailing wind.

The girl belched again, and shook her head.

Grace took *Polos* from her pocket, and eased the first one away from its fellows, proffering the pack, "Mint? Very good for motion sickness."

The girl regarded her sharply, and Grace's hand wobbled hesitantly. What had she said? The girl's bottom lip trembled, and her mouth pulled downward, eyes blinking rapidly. She whispered, "How are they for morning sickness?" and fixed Grace with an anguished stare like a shout of pain. Grace gasped before she could stop herself, and whinnied a nervous, high-pitched giggle to cover her confusion, "Can't say I've tried them for that, personally..."

She remained holding out the *Polos* for what felt like months, too polite to withdraw them lest it be viewed as a judgement, until the girl put her out of her misery and inched the mint from the pack, pushing it cautiously between her lips as if she'd been ordered to ingest a cyanide pill. After a second or two of experimental sucking, she volunteered, "That is better. Takes the horrible taste away. You know, weeks now, I've had this taste...like metal in my mouth, and nothing I eat or drink'll get rid of it."

Grace again tried, "Isn't there anyone I can get for you? Someone sitting downstairs?"

A sudden potential sighting sent a surge of the cagouled binocular-wielders to starboard.

"Might be dolphins," said the girl, "Don't you want to see?"

Grace wrinkled her nose, "I've swum with dolphins in Florida."

The girl appraised her, nodding slowly, taking in her diamond earrings, *Omega* watch, thick *Barbour* jacket and designer handbag, drawing her conclusions.

"Nice."

Grace fidgeted, "Not really. It was all rather staged. I felt sorry for the dolphins, as if they were being used...which, of course, they rather were… I found I didn't like it. I felt guilty being there. My approach now is just to let nature be, and not try to impose myself upon it." She stopped abruptly, "Sorry…what do I sound like! Silly, pretentious, sanctimonious rubbish!"

The girl smiled, the rush of preconceptions blowing in all directions like the snowflakes round their faces, "Please can I have another mint?"

Grace pushed the packet into her hand, "Take them."

"Thanks. I don't feel so sick now."

Grace eased herself up onto the bench opposite the girl, straightening her stiffening legs. She could feel the cold of the metal through the fabric of her jeans.

"Look, I'll freely admit I don't know the first thing about being pregnant, but my friend who's had three says it's better to keep your tummy full to stave off the nausea. She used to eat porridge and custard…things that go down easily and don't burn on the way back up, or something…sorry…"

The girl was taking quick sips and deep breaths again.

"I shouldn't have mentioned eating…or being sick…sorry…"

Gulp.

Gulp.

In.

Out.

A sigh.

Another *Polo*.

Grace put her hand on the girl's arm, feeling responsible, "Is there someone downstairs who'll be worried?"

The girl looked at the floor, "No. No. You're very kind, but no…there's no one…" Her voice faded to a whisper, as if it had run out of energy on a long journey, and several tears dripped in quick succession onto the dark toes of her canvas pumps. Grace, hand still resting lightly against the girl's sleeve, squeezed the thin arm, and searched for a way to reassure her that everyone faced trials in their life, and she could get through this challenge if she was brave and resolute. It would doubtless have been very beneficial for the girl to hear the motivational speech Grace was rehearsing in her head. Unfortunately, when she opened her mouth, what actually tumbled out was, "I've left my husband," as if no one else in the history of the world had ever done such a momentous thing, "and my friend, whom I thought would support me, seems to have taken his side…and there's no family…no one with whom to…" except Fenella, and it turned out whatever she'd shared with Fenella was simply grist to the gossip-mill, "It seems they were all laughing at me behind my back, as if I never fitted in with their stupid herd…" Grace was shocked by how venomous her tone became at the sudden recollection of every humiliation suffered at the hands of Fen, of Dom, and all their ilk.

The girl nodded, offering back with feeling, "Believe me, I get it. I know how it feels not to belong anywhere. I know how hard it is to keep your head up when you're certain you're the local laughing-stock." She sucked in another *Polo* through pouting lips, and watched Grace intently with her vivid, green eyes; so bright they seemed to glow despite the insipid daylight.

Grace's heart began to flutter in her chest. She usually only had frank, open conversations with her reflection. She avoided prolonged contact with everyone else because their scrutiny made her feel awkward, foolish; worthless. Talking to Dominic was pointless, as he ignored everything she said. Talking to Fen brought either a salvo of supercilious scorn, or saccharine-coated sarcasm. Talking to strangers normally resulted in the embarrassment of mutual incomprehension. This was different, exhilaratingly so!

The girl crunched the *Polo* in her small, even teeth, tongue chasing the fragments around her mouth as she muttered, "I tried to make a good life for myself, but I just couldn't get it right. I ended up feeling utterly hopeless, as if everything I touched turned to crap. I'd always been sure of myself, convinced I could do things if I put my mind to them...and all that disappeared so rapidly I was floundering, afraid all the time. I felt as if I was being slowly suffocated, all this weight pressing in on me from every side, trying to squash me flat for being presumptuous enough to have a crack at making it in a world where I didn't belong. I had a basement flat, and I could feel the other three floors pressing down on me when I was lying in bed. I'd go on the tube and be convinced the tunnel would fall in and crush my carriage. I worked in this great big tower block, and I could feel all the floors above and below pressing together, so in the end I'd be squashed between them. I would get panic attacks and be walking the streets at five in the morning. I was too scared to stay indoors in case the house fell down."

That was it, exactly! Slowly suffocated, as if all the life was being squeezed out of her by a force she couldn't define, leaving her dead inside. It took every ounce of Grace's self-control not to leap from her bench and cling to the girl in a sudden embrace. She felt the same! Someone else understood!

She tried to suppress the delight in her tone as she cried out, "You don't realise how much better this makes me feel! I understand exactly what you're going through! I was married to this completely hyperactive guy who just wanted life to be a thrill-ride all the time. I'm not like that. I've discovered I greatly enjoy peace, calm, and solitude. I couldn't keep up, no matter how hard I tried. It wasn't the real me. I felt as if I was suffocating too, and losing sight of who I really was…who I'd been before I got married."

"Where did you live?"

"Clerkenwell – in London."

"Trendy!"

"A nice, top floor loft in a converted warehouse building, with big windows, high ceilings, a roof garden…I'm an artist, you see. I paint…" Grace thought if she said it aloud that might make it true. I'm an artist. Not, I'm pretending to be an artist, I've hardly created a thing since my degree and, given the universal derision of my husband and friends, now seriously doubt I'll ever have the confidence to do so ever again.

"I need the light. For my work."

Oh, she still sounded ridiculous – haughty, superior, full of herself! Fenella; I sound like Fenella.

The girl belched again, and took a shuddering breath or two, weathering another wave of nausea.

To distract her companion from her obvious distress, Grace exerted herself to continue the conversation. She'd attended enough tedious cocktail parties in her time to feel content with a banal enquiry or two, "You know London?"

"Aye. I lived there until recently."

"Whereabouts?"

"Pimlico."

"Ooh, a good area," Grace nodded like an estate agent touting for business. The girl responded bitterly, "Is it? Can't really comment. Never went out except to go to work. You know, moving to London I thought I'd have the kind of social life you read about in magazines or see on the telly. I imagined me and all my cool workmates meeting up for shots in trendy bars, sloping home laughing from clubs, watching the sun come up over the river…but none of that ever happened because I was Northern, and poor, and I hadn't gone to the right school or the correct University. My Dad didn't play golf with politicians or sit as a Director on the requisite number of Boards. He doesn't have time, you see. He's got sheep to shear, cows to milk, shite to shovel…"

Grace, whose own father had counted many politicians and peers within his social circle, and held more Directorships than Grace could tot up, found it wise to remain silent.

"It was just me, in my grubby pyjamas in my overpriced basement, trying to be something I wasn't, and making a conscious effort not to think about those floors above me, pressing down…" The wind blew a ringlet across her face. Irritably, she pushed it aside with a gloved hand. A couple of loose strands of glowing copper caught on the wool, and whirled away as the wind gusted again. Bewitched, Grace watched them for a moment, catching the light, contrasted against the unbroken grey of the sky. Isolated for so very long, Grace was impossibly fascinated by the tantalising glimpse into another life, as if she was peeking through the keyhole into an adjoining room, desperately trying to see beyond the limiting edges of the circular tableau.

Venturing far beyond politeness, Grace surrendered to naked curiosity, "What about…your baby?"

The girl scowled, "I screwed up there and no mistake…chased a fairy tale that turned out to be a horror story. By the time I came to my senses, it was too late. Och, I was so stupid! I'd tell myself I could finish it whenever I chose; I was the one using him and not the other way round. All bullshit, of course; all lies I told myself because I wanted to be with someone – anyone – rather than being alone. Does that make sense?"

"Of course. Perfect sense."

"I needed it to be real, because if it wasn't, what kind of a life did I have? No mates, naff flat, a job I hated with fake people I despised – but who I pathetically wished would like me anyway. I craved acceptance. I needed to belong. Prince Charming wanted Cinderella, and all she did was scrub the floor all day. Why did it have to be something that happened to other people? Why couldn't it happen to me?"

Grace cooed soothingly, "So you tried. You gave it your best shot. You saw the man for you and went for him. That's brave! A lot of women, me included, would wait for the man to come to them…and if he didn't, would let the chance go. Who can criticise you for having the guts to try?" Grace patted the back of the girl's gloved hand like a tiny puppy, "You didn't bury your head in the sand for twenty years, pretending your marriage was a roaring success when really it was a humiliating failure. You've done nothing wrong in my opinion. We all make mistakes. It's how we handle them that matters."

The girl managed a weak smile, "Thank you. You're kind. Somehow, I don't think my parents will view it in such a positive light, as a triumph against adversity. I think they'll consider it more a life-ending disgrace."

"So, you're going home to have your baby..." Grace was starting to understand, and responded encouragingly, "I think that's a very sensible thing to do. You'll need help. It's right to go where people can help you. You seem a very level-headed person to me."

"They don't know, that's the trouble. I just said things had turned bad down South and I needed to come home for a wee while. When it came to it, I wasn't brave enough to come clean. My mother thought I should've stayed at home and made a life in Orkney. She couldn't understand why I was so desperate to get away. She's always trying to fix me up with local boys I've known my whole life; boys who've been born and bred to croft like their fathers and grandfathers before them. Boys with no drive and no ambition beyond surviving on that stupid bit of northern rock...and I want more, I always have – but my stupid, overblown dreams have done for me this time. My mother's going to skin me alive for bringing disgrace upon the family. At least I won't be asking them for money as well as somewhere to live. The good thing about several years of decent income and no social life is you do a heck of a lot of saving up."

"See? You are a very sensible girl! You prepared yourself for whatever your future might throw at you. You might have made one naïve decision, but you've covered your back, haven't you?"

The girl scowled again, and didn't answer.

"It's your home...how bad can it be?" Grace pictured the now-deceased, doting parents no Disney Princess should be without, and couldn't conceive of a situation where returning to the bosom of your family could be anything other than a positive experience.

The girl fixed her with a knowing look, "You've never been to Orkney, have you?"

"Is it that obvious?"

"A bit. It's not like London. A single mum in London? It's no big deal in a place where the guy on the bus next to you has green hair and piercings on his piercings, but it's different here, amongst my super-conservative relations. Twenty-first century or not, when I come clean, they'll see it as life over, prospects pinched, hopes dashed! First, there's the disgrace. Then, there's the burden I'll become. No one else will ever have me because the entire West Mainland will know I'm soiled goods before tea time tomorrow. I'll have to move to Shetland to get a husband. Even that might not be far enough to escape the fall-out from my misdemeanour. Could be Norway or bust for me!"

Grace couldn't help giggling, "Surely not?"

"Don't even pretend to get it. If I thought I was persona-non-grata down South, you just wait until I get home and tell my deeply-traditional, churchgoing parents that I'm a soon-to-be single mum, and have expertly effed up both my future career and marriage prospects in one go, when they've spent most of the last decade boasting to whoever would listen about their world-beating daughter and what a success she's making of herself. The massive social climbdown this'll mean! The women my mother talked down to because their girls got married straight from school, and had three kids before their 21st! The humble pie she'll have to swallow cold in kitchens up and down the district! If I make it until tomorrow breakfast without being murdered in my bed, I'll almost believe I've got away with it. I can see the two of them conspiring to bash me over the head, bury me behind the barn, and just not tell anyone I ever came home…"

"You're exaggerating."

"Not as much as you might think. This is Orkney, not Clerkenwell."

"I bow to your superior knowledge."

"Why choose Orkney anyway, in November…it's hardly a cosmopolitan getaway for someone like you?" Grace wondered who 'someone like her' was, and stated cryptically, "Because of a beach, a picture; a stupid promise I made to myself to grow a pair…"

The girl looked pointedly – and with more than a touch of the Fenella Dalrymple's about her – at the grey skies, the swirling ice-flakes, "It's hardly beach weather!"

Something in her tone pricked Grace who, tired of being made to feel ridiculous, snapped before she could stop herself, "It's about pursuing an ideal! It's about not settling for things any more! It's about perfection and a sense of place!"

The girl guffawed, making the dolphin-spotters turn and stare, "Perfection? In Orkney? Like I said, you've never been."

Grimacing, Grace grunted, "You're making me dread it."

"Och, no! It's fine! I'm teasing you, is all."

"You'd better be!"

They exchanged quick looks, shy smiles, both simultaneously realising how much they'd shared, and how quickly, as if they'd only been searching for the smallest excuse to unburden their troubled souls.

"Where are you staying?"

Grace fumbled in her handbag for the email printout, "Had to do a bit of a last-minute-dot-com. All I could get with forty-eight hours' notice. Seems a great big place just for me, but looks very nice by the photographs. Bit Scandi-looking. Quite modern...somewhere called Birsay?"

The girl's nimble fingers were quick to snatch at the paper, hungry eyes scanning for information, "Scandi place you say? Oh..."

"Oh. Oh, what? Do you know it? Is it not good?" Grace hung on the verdict. The girl whistled. Grace's receipt was at the bottom of the printed sheet, "Pricey..."

Grace blinked, "Is it?" It wasn't ever a criterion she needed to consider, and was always a genuine surprise when brought to her notice. She stammered, "I'm not really sure what these things are supposed to cost…"

The girl tapped a knuckle onto the paper, "You can stay on these islands for probably an eighth of that price!"

Grace blushed, "Maybe they put the rental up because I did it in such a hurry?"

"No, I know that place. It's called *Somerled* after a Viking king. It's that expensive because it's really nice. You'll like it. It's the most incredible location, superb view, swanky house. If you're looking for perfection, you'll find it there."

"Have you stayed there then?"

"Erm…" the girl's reaction was interesting, frozen halfway between embarrassment she couldn't control and pride she couldn't conceal, "I have…yes."

Grace teased gently, "You're blushing…what's the gossip? You have to tell me, I'm going to be living there!"

"Erm…I…know…the person who owns it…"

"Know?"

"What?"

"The way you said 'know'…"

The girl's striking eyes alighted briefly upon Grace's face, before dancing away to the far horizon as she mumbled, "I had a bit of a thing with the man who owns it…a wee while ago now." She put a hand to each cheek as if absorbing the heat of her sudden blush into the wool of the gloves.

"If you wanted a fairy tale, why not stay on Orkney with the man you loved in his big, expensive, perfect house?"

The girl frowned, "Because I wanted him much more than he wanted me."

She unconsciously brushed a hand briefly across her stomach, and Grace longed to know whether this was the far-from-happy ending, but wasn't brave enough to ask.

"It was…complicated. He was much older than me. It was just a silly schoolgirl crush…"

"But you still hold a torch for him! The look on your face…"

"He's famous – a rock star! He used to sell out stadiums in the eighties and nineties…"

The girl spoke of the decades before her birth as if they were ancient history, and Grace rolled back the years to her teens and twenties with a secret stab of sudden longing to have her time over again, and live it very differently.

"Wow! What's his name? Would I have heard of him?"

"You might have done. His name's Vidar Rasmussen."

"Hmmm…it does sound vaguely familiar. It's unusual enough to stick in your mind. Unfortunately, I was never really that hip, even though I went to Art School! I wasn't one of the gang who was into all the cool groups. I might recognise him if I saw a picture. Was he in a band or something?"

"He had a band who performed with him, but I think he was the big name. It's quite a while since he's toured and stuff…almost before I was born! I guess it would have been a name of your youth. Oh, sorry, I didn't mean that in a rude way."

"No, no… No offence taken. I suspect I had rather a lot of 'youth' before you were even a glint in your father's eye!"

The girl smiled self-consciously.

"Will you see him when you get back?"

"He's in America, as far as I know. He can't be in Orkney anyway, because you're renting his house. It gets rented out for him while he's not using it. Yet another way to make him even richer."

"You sure the flame isn't still smouldering?" Grace teased, "Fancy rekindling it?"

The girl grinned, "You mean would I like to travel round the world from one fancy mansion to the next, melting his credit card? Course I would! When we were together, the bit I enjoyed most was the showing off. I could stick two fingers up to all the girls at school who'd picked on me. They were stuck on a croft, married to a moron, up to their knees in dung, with two kids and another on the way, and I was dating a rock star. Who was the loser now? He's a nice guy and everything, but he works all the time. I just had to fit in around what he was already doing. He didn't do it in a mean way, it's just that his job came first. I suppose you don't achieve what he has unless you're dedicated. I think he was entertained by me while he was here...but, once he left...? He went to do a project in London, and I thought it would be the cleverest idea I'd ever had to go there myself. We'd hook up, you know, because, obviously, everyone in London knows everyone else, don't they? Our eyes would meet across a crowded bar. He'd realise I was there and it was all meant to be! But stuff never works out like the movies, does it? My mother, needless to say, blamed him. Truth is, I just wouldn't leave him alone. In the end, he caved in – what bloke wouldn't? Some wee girly following them around offering it on a plate? She thought he'd led me astray, put ideas in my head. It took about two years for her to let him back over the threshold."

"You're still in touch? That's sweet…"

"He's our neighbour, when he's here. He buys eggs from my Mam. *Somerled* is up the lane from my parents' farm. You'll be literally less than half a mile away. If they do murder me and bury me behind the barn, you could be a witness! If you see them digging, you raise the alarm, ok?"

Grace smiled broadly, amused by the frankness of her manner, and intrigued by all she'd left unsaid. How exciting to share even a titbit of this interesting life! This girl was entertaining, quirky, forthright, and open – such a liberating antidote to the subjugating poison of life with Dominic that Grace was tugged towards her like a magnet to a pole. Even idealistic Grace was sensible enough to understand the exchange of a few clumsy confidences did not a lifelong friendship make, but it nevertheless felt as if she already had an ally here.

"Small world, eh?" The girl could see how cheered the woman was by the revelation they would be neighbours, and was flooded with gratitude. It had been so long since anyone had displayed obvious pleasure at her proximity. She pushed in another *Polo* between dry lips. The sharp taste of the mint suppressed the nausea. It was freezing on this deck, but the fresh air on her face removed the unpleasant sensation that preceded a fainting fit, and she needed to get used to the cold again. She was back in the land of Weather. No more fuggy city days, where the vagaries of climate barely made an impact upon the man-made, centrally-heated, artificially-regulated world. Here, the wind whipped hard and strong across the treeless landscape, cutting through all but the thickest layers, scouring even the hardiest cheek, and snatching away words the second they passed your lips.

She'd had to come home. There was no other option. She couldn't stay in London with no job – and the city had lost its sparkle, if it had ever had it in the first place. Perhaps it had only shone like a beacon of hope inside her own deluded head?

The steadily-worsening sickness owed its origin more to fear than physiology, knowing she'd have to face parents, siblings, relatives, erstwhile friends, and admit her naivety where once she'd lauded her superiority. Too soon she'd be plain old 'Ginger' Flett again, vilified for her self-importance, knocked right back down to size, and no one to blame for it but her stupid, stupid self.

To take her mind off the coast creeping ever-closer, the girl enquired, "How long are you staying?"

"I don't know. I haven't made any firm decisions…about anything."

"What are your plans while you're here? Birsay's dead quiet. The Wild West – just farms and wetlands, and a load of sheep, birds, rocks, and nothing but ocean until you hit Canada…and winter's coming."

"Don't become a tour guide, will you?"

"Don't get me wrong, it's beautiful in its own way, but it's empty, and it can be pretty bleak."

"And yet you want to have your child here?"

"I don't have much choice as I've nowhere else to go, and…it's home, it's what I know."

Grace turned and beheld the low, brown landmass in the distance. No obvious structure disturbed its undulating silhouette. Her mind had been wholly occupied with the monumental act of leaving Dominic. She hadn't given a moment's thought to what she might do upon reaching her destination. The sound of securing chains clanking on the open car deck below distracted Grace from her anxious observation of the approaching archipelago. Peering over the railing, she saw the overalled, hard-hatted deckhands starting to unchain the cableless lorry containers from their deck fixings.

"It's quick."

The girl shrugged, "It's only eight miles. In my opinion, it's slow – an hour to do eight miles? They should dig a tunnel."

Grace was petrified. They were here! They were moments away from docking!

"Are you driving to Birsay?"

"No, foot passenger."

"Is someone coming to get you?" Grace knew it was rude to ask so many questions that were none of her business, but her mouth seemed utterly disengaged from her brain, leaving her powerless to control what blurted out of it.

"No. They know I'm coming, just not the date. When it came to it, I wasn't brave enough to let on."

"Well, I think you're very brave. I think they're your family. I think it will be ok."

"I wished I shared your optimism."

The girl's face looked pinched and cold as she turned it away from Grace to observe the dockside of St Margaret's Hope fast-approaching.

Grace went for it, "I've got my car. I could give you a lift. That way, you could direct me…and I would have the peace of mind of knowing you got home safely, given you aren't feeling your brightest."

The girl sniggered, "You're so tactful. Do they teach you that at private school?"

Grace's expression darkened, and the girl quickly jumped in, "Sorry, that sounded bitchy. It wasn't meant to be. It's just you have a way of saying things that sort of…gets me out of jail. 'Not feeling my brightest' is the polite way of saying 'galloping morning sickness caused by your unplanned pregnancy'. I would never be able to put things as gently as you do."

"You're very hard on yourself."

"So would you be, if you'd screwed up your entire future."

"They might be so pleased to see you home and safe that nothing else will matter. They might be delighted to be grandparents!"

"I feel sick again. I think it's terror."

"Shall I take you home?"

"Yes…please. You're very kind to me. Thank you for not treating me like a pariah."

"No, no, not at all, don't mention it…"

A two-tone electronic bell sounded, followed by an announcement that drivers should return to their vehicles. Grace helped the still-unsteady girl to stand. She seemed weak, and grateful for the support of Grace's arm.

"It's none of my business, and I know you feel really sick, but you should eat because you seem very faint..." The woman clucked over her like a mother hen all the way down the two flights of stairs to the car deck, helping her carefully into the passenger side of a very smart four-wheel-drive as if she was an invalid.

She'd felt the familiar sensation again on the ferry, that she had to get outside before the decks above collapsed in upon themselves and crushed her flat. She'd been just about to fall to the floor under the weight of the burden she carried, when the surprisingly strong arms had caught and supported her. The girl sank gratefully onto the heated leather, wondered who this providential stranger was, and why Fate had decided to place their paths in such direct convergence.

****

It was easier than she'd foreseen to distract herself on the car journey, answering the woman's many questions about the areas through which they passed as they drove towards Kirkwall from the ferry dock. She directed the woman to the supermarket to stock up on provisions for *Somerled*, and elected to remain in the car, hunkered in the seat, coat hood up to conceal her distinctive hair. Mercifully, the cold wind kept everybody's heads down, and their progress to and from the store rapid and incurious. She recognised familiar faces, but they did not see her, which was all that mattered.

It was odd to be back after all this time away. If anything, the place appeared more desolate than she remembered it, the colours even more muted than memory had reproduced. The scouring wind thrust grey ripples of thicker cloud across an already-darkening sky. Even the green of the grazing pasture looked muddy and heavy with moisture. The brown slashes of dead heather cut across the low, rolling hills, as if reflecting the passage of the threatening ribbons of loaded snow-cloud above. Trails of shredded black plastic from the hay bales caught on the barbed wire fencing, gyrating crazily in the wind, desperate to free themselves. Wound alongside, in monochrome contrast, fluttered long strands of sheep's wool, bleached white by exposure. The girl's brain struggled to accept the emptiness after so long amongst hectic bustle, and wondered what the woman must be making of her choice of winter getaway.

"I told you it was bleak."

"It's striking," said the woman, uncritically, "It's the emptiest place I've ever been! Look!" She pointed from left to right, "There's just no one around! No people out walking, no one in their gardens, not another car on the road…"

"I did say it was the Wild West."

"I like it," decided the woman, "I like how different it is to everything I've ever known."

"Yeah, the novelty might wear off in a couple of hours when it's still freezing, there's no Wi-Fi, you're sick to death of the noise of the wind howling, and it's pitch black before tea time…"

"Stop being grumpy! You may not wish to be here, but perhaps I might find it nice to curl up before an open fire, catch up on my reading, and enjoy the peace and quiet of having no demands placed upon me but the onerous task of pleasing myself – seems quite attractive to me!"

The girl thought, when put like that, it seemed quite attractive to her too, but was too proud to admit it, "You need to take this lane left, by the Church."

"Ok."

"They're mostly single tracks here, with passing places, so you need to be careful."

The woman observed the narrow road meandering into the faded, watery landscape like a brush stroke in an Impressionist painting, "You can probably see two miles. If I can't prepare for an oncoming vehicle at that distance, I deserve to crash!"

The girl grinned, "At the end here, you'll get to a junction. Turn immediately right and that's my house. Next right is a gate and a track that goes up to *Somerled*."

"Look at all the birds here!" The woman craned towards the passenger window, trying to observe the many seabirds clustering on the islands of tufted brown grass dotted across the wetland.

"Twitcher heaven! Come proper breeding time, hordes of them descend on this dump, binoculars clamped to their faces..."

"Not a bird watcher?"

The girl wrinkled her nose, "You've seen one Puffin, you've seen 'em all...and their fancy beaks drop off when they finish breeding. Then they become very ordinary."

The woman narrowed her eyes suspiciously, "You're making that up!"

"No!" the girl declared, "Google it!"

"Can't," rejoined the woman with a glint in her eye, "No Wi-Fi in this dump, apparently."

The girl grinned despite herself, "All right, very funny! This is me here. You can drop me at the gate if you want."

The woman slowed the car to a crawl, took in the ramshackle farm buildings, rusting machinery, tumbledown cottage with aged pick-up parked outside, and said, "No, I think I'll see you inside, if it's all the same to you. For my own peace-of-mind, you know."

Initially relieved not to be abandoned, the girl suddenly realised what 'seeing her inside' would mean. The idea of this impeccably-dressed, elegant individual coming into direct contact with any members of her family, or the questionable hygiene of the cottage interior, filled her with apprehension, "It could all go banzai the moment we step through the door…"

"Exactly why I suggested coming in with you. Having a visitor in the house might keep everyone on best behaviour until the dust settles a bit. By the time I've been there ten minutes, the initial shock will have passed, and you should all be able to discuss it a bit more rationally. Just think of me as a decoy, drawing the heavy fire."

"Oh God…" The fear from the ferry resurfaced, along with the conviction she was about to be crushed by the roof of the car, or the weight of the heavy sky above. The woman placed gentle fingertips on her arm, distracting her enough to manage a much-needed deep breath.

"I don't think it'll be as bad as you envisage."

The girl smiled weakly, "And I know it'll be much worse than you 'envisage'..." She stopped herself, blushed; apologised, "Sorry, I get sarcastic when I feel threatened."

"Let's just give it a go, shall we?"

The woman drew the expensive car to a halt before the farmhouse. As the girl opened the passenger door she heard distant barking, growing louder by the second. As the woman stepped from the driver's side, she just had time to say, "You're ok about dogs, aren't you?" before the collies were upon them, leaping and turning in ecstatic, slobbering, mud-plastered delight, coating the two women in a scattergun pattern of paw-prints down their jeans and up their jackets. The woman, laughing, tried to stroke them as they bounced, with the inevitable result that eventually all four clustered around her, panting with glee at having made such a receptive new friend, enthusiastically chewing at her fingers, the tails of her coat, and the inviting leather corners of her designer handbag with soft, gentle mouths.

"Get off, get off!" The girl shoved them away with firm palms, "I'm sorry...it's hard to stay clean here."

"It's a farm...anyway, I'm washable."

The woman, trailing the curious dogs behind her, fetched the girl's small suitcase from the boot of the car, and wheeled it across to her, "Ready?"

"No..."

"Well, I, for one, am not standing out here in the freezing cold all afternoon! You've been so brave. Don't fall at the final hurdle." The woman gestured towards the farmhouse door. The girl advanced, stretching for the handle, the heaviness of dread settling in the pit of her stomach. It opened before she reached it, and she found herself looking directly into the emerald eyes of her mother.

FOUR

"Sonia? You never said you were coming back today!" Her tone was reproachful.

"No, Mam, I wasn't sure which ferry I'd get."

Sonia's voice wavered, and her mother's expression darkened, suspicious, about to unleash the barrage of questions she'd been saving up since Sonia's unexpected letter, when she caught sight of the woman standing a few paces behind her daughter. Long, glossy, chestnut hair swirled in the trapped breeze circling the filthy yard. Diamond earrings glinted. A wide, friendly smile exposed straight, white teeth. Her jacket was thick and obviously expensive. The blue of her jeans was rich and deep, not faded from many washes. Her shoes were unscuffed, and virtually untouched by the mud and slurry mix that eventually ruined all but the most robust footwear. She stood patiently in the centre of the farmyard, thigh-deep in sheepdogs, beaming with pleasure, and waiting politely to be introduced.

"Oh, Mam, this is my…friend…from London. She's staying here, and she kindly offered to drive me. That's why I came today." Turning to the woman, the girl's expression beseeched her to play along, "This is my mother, Margaret Flett. Mam, this is…" Here, Sonia stopped, realising she didn't know the woman's name. They'd already shared so much, and never bothered with introductions!

The woman rescued her, stepping forward with perfect timing and impeccable manners, "Grace. Delighted to meet you, Margaret. Your daughter is a darling. She's been so helpful to me. I must say it's lovely here. I'm so fascinated by what an elemental and wild landscape this is…"

Grace managed to propel them all into the welcome warmth on a wave of enthusiasm, gazing about her in genuine interest, artlessly-complimenting the rustic appeal of the vile farmhouse kitchen until the usually standoffish Margaret was so utterly charmed that Grace was gently divested of her jacket by reverent hands, and most-solicitously helped to a seat near the stove, a slice of cake, and a cup of tea. Sonia's teenage sister, Lorraine, wandered in to investigate the unusual voices, and beheld Sonia with some surprise, "What are you doing here?"

"And it's lovely to see you too, Raine."

"Lorraine," said Margaret, in her very mildest tones, usually reserved for Church, "this is Sonia's friend Grace, from London. Grace, this is my youngest, Lorraine."

"Lovely to meet you, Lorraine." Extending graceful hands towards the awkward, gum-popping, eye-rolling girl, Grace's left arm was nearly wrenched from its socket by Lorraine grasping and yanking her wrist towards her, "Oh. My. God. Is that an *Omega*, like Nicole Kidman advertises? Oh my God! It is! Mammy, look, it's got diamonds on it! Is that real or a fake one?"

"Lorraine!" Margaret was mortified. Sonia caught Grace's eye, and sniggered behind her tea cup. Grace winked at Margaret to reassure her she wasn't offended, and gently drew Lorraine to sit on the bench beside her, "It's a real one."

"Oh. My. God!" said Lorraine again, theatrically, "Have you got one of those, Son?"

Sonia eased back the sleeve of her jumper to display the unbranded watch purchased by her parents for her eighteenth birthday, leather strap battered, hole stretching out of shape at the place where she always fastened it, "No, Raine…have you?"

Lorraine looked Sonia up and down like the piece of crap she clearly considered her, took a large bite of her slice of cake, and airily questioned, mouth full, "What are you doing back here anyway? Thought you were supposed to be too good for the likes of us now?"

Sonia's eyes snapped down the table to her mother, who suddenly became very preoccupied with the strength of the tea, worrying at the bags floating in the pot with a stained spoon. That pronouncement certainly hadn't originated in Lorraine's empty head. Incensed, Sonia glowered at the table top, regrets at returning circling murderously.

The direction the reunion was taking seriously concerned Grace. An air of unspoken accusation hovered over the table, as if Sonia and her mother wished to say a great deal to one another that could never be articulated. Recrimination simmered like a forgotten pot on the stove, surface bubbling benignly, but blackening underneath. The silence lengthened, during which Lorraine chewed loudly, mouth open, Sonia stared fixedly at the table and gripped her mug in tightening fingers, and Margaret's eyes flicked nervously between the bowed head of her eldest, and the unreadable expression of her exotic, London friend.

"Margaret, I see Sonia has inherited your striking colouring. Such a beautiful shade – a rich copper. I've never seen anyone with hair such a vibrant colour that wasn't out of a bottle! Is that true Orcadian ancestry?"

Margaret flushed with pleasure at the compliment, patting her rather faded flame tresses – not as bouncing and shiny as Sonia's gleaming ringlets – and almost purred her reply, "Well, they say that red hair and green eyes is true Scottish colouring…but I don't know if it's Orcadian. A great deal of the ancestry here is Viking. Lorraine, love, you did a project on it for school a wee while ago, didn't you?" Lorraine, desperately trying to *Snapchat* the photograph she'd surreptitiously taken of Grace's watch before anyone noticed, glanced up, and beheld all eyes upon her. Shoving her 'phone up her baggy jumper sleeve, she ventured, "What, Mammy?"

Sonia sighed in undisguised exasperation, and the sisters locked eyes across the cake plate, Lorraine challenging Sonia to make that noise once more, just *once* more…and Sonia regarding her sibling with the contempt she felt her dimness deserved, turning to her new friend and explaining, "What apparently happened, Grace, was that the Vikings showed up, killed all the men and boys, co-opted all the women…so the female ancestry of the Shetlands and Orkneys goes back to the Neolithic, but the male genes are all Viking. God knows how they work that out after a thousand years of interbreeding, but that's the theory…ethnic cleansing."

"How fascinating. So, your lovely hair could be Viking in origin?"

"We're more like the Highland Scots – "

Margaret interrupted, anxious to be part of enabling Grace to understand the culture, "Several generations ago, my father's family came from Glencoe to croft here…and the family stayed."

"And thrived!" beamed Grace, encouraged by the exertion of both mother and daughter to shared conversation, "Speaking of thriving families – "

Sonia shot her a warning glance of such potency that her shining eyes blazed, casting a silencing spell upon Grace.

"What brings you to Orkney, Grace?" Margaret felt it wasn't too intrusive a question to ask, "Do you have family here?"

For the first time since their arrival, a chink appeared in Grace's impenetrable middle-class armour. She fumbled for a strand of her hair, and combed her fingers through it as if stroking herself to calmness with the gesture, "Quite the opposite, Margaret, I'm sorry to say. I'm afraid my marriage has ended, and I travelled here seeking an unspoilt, peaceful place to take stock. I'm not fortunate, like all of you, to have family around me. I had an older sister, but she was handicapped, and she died before I was born. My parents are dead. I haven't been blessed with the joy of children…" Here, Grace made sure she gazed pointedly at Sonia and Lorraine, who were engaged in trading venomous scowls of mutual dislike across the kitchen table.

"Very precious, family, isn't it Margaret?"

"Oh aye."

"I found so-called friends all took my husband's side, because they'd known him before they knew me, and I was left quite alone...apart, of course, from Sonia. She's a real credit to you, Margaret. Her kindness has been invaluable to me," Grace stated in her straightforward way, as if she and Sonia had been mates for months, not minutes.

Again, Margaret absorbed the compliment with quiet pride and, Grace hoped, regarded Sonia with a less disapproving expression.

"Did the two of you work together in London?"

"No, Mam." Sonia was quick to cut off that line of questioning, "Grace is an artist."

"Do you need any exams to do that?" 'Being an artist' looked lucrative from where Lorraine was sitting, if it clothed you in designer labels from head to toe, and rendered you as preened and perfumed as a footballer's wife. Grace turned to her, enthusiastically enquiring, "Are you creative, Lorraine?"

Lorraine popped her chewing gum in silent panic, and looked to her mother for assistance, while Sonia snorted sarcastically around the tiniest mouthful of cake she thought she could reasonably force down without puking, taking heed of Grace's exhortation to get something in her constantly-churning stomach.

"I'm not working on anything at the moment anyway," Grace clarified hurriedly, suddenly petrified her lie would be exposed, "I just need to come to terms with the last few weeks... It's hard to comprehend the enormity of beginning again in your forties, isn't it?" Grace fixed Margaret with a pleading stare, seeking her affirmation of the struggles of mid-life.

"I am sorry to hear that, Grace. Is there no hope of a reconciliation for you?"

"I don't think so…and I don't want there to be, really. He's been…unfaithful to me, you see."

"Ah, I understand." Margaret reached forward and patted Grace's hand condescendingly.

Sonia tried to ingest another morsel of cake, to divert suspicion about her uncharacteristic lack of appetite, but it wouldn't go down. She couldn't swallow. It was as if there was already a lump in her throat preventing it. In the end, she had to sluice it past the lump by dissolving it in her mouth with a glug of lukewarm tea.

"Where are you staying while you're here, Grace? Do you have some accommodation organised?"

Sonia was convinced her mother was about to invite Grace to stay in the croft! Where would she be expected to sleep, on the floor between their beds in the tiny room she had to share with Lorraine? Being the eldest boy, Bobby got his own room in the attic. Even if it was so narrow he could stretch out his arms and touch either wall, at least it was his and his alone. It had been Sonia's, of course, being the oldest of all, but she'd made the mistake of going away to University, and the vultures had descended in her absence, picking through the carcass of her room and possessions until what was left barely filled a shoebox. Alastair and Andrew had to share, but they were twins, so no one considered they deserved their own space. Lorraine, as the only remaining girl – as if Sonia had died some years before, leaving nothing behind but a graduation photograph on the mantelpiece that badly needed a dust – was obviously entitled to a room of her own, and would doubtless now resent having to share it with her big sister again.

At one time, as events progressed, Sonia had entertained hopes of being able to move into *Somerled*. Its owner was certainly not averse to her presence – but on his terms, and not on a permanent basis. It had made Sonia feel as if she wasn't really wanted anywhere, in the bosom of her family or the arms of her lover.

"Mammy, Grace is staying at *Somerled*," said Sonia, quietly.

"Oooohhh," Lorraine enjoyed the frisson of tension that rippled down the table as Sonia spoke the name of Vidar Rasmussen's house. Her mother sniffed, and drew herself up in her chair, "Alone, I presume?"

"Oh aye, Mam," Sonia reassured, "I thought I'd just bring Grace in to say Hello and then I'd show her up there…settle her in…"

"'Cos you know where everything is…" muttered Lorraine, not quite loud enough for her mother to hear.

Sonia didn't want to be in the kitchen a second longer. Remain, and she might just have to squelch this whole slice of cake into her sister's stupid, over-made-up face. How was she ever going to share a bedroom without smothering her maddening teenage sibling in the night?

"Have you finished your tea, Grace? I'll take you up to the house before it gets dark…"

Sonia pushed wearily to her feet, and very swiftly turned her back on mother and sister to fetch the coats, struggling hers on in the chilly porch to provide greater camouflage for her thickening body.

"It was so lovely to meet you, Margaret…and you too, Lorraine," said Grace, sweetly. "You have such a charming home, and such beautiful daughters." Here, she touched one slim-fingered hand to Lorraine's curly, dark hair, and the other to Sonia's shoulder, "You must feel very blessed."

Grace was unaccountably relieved to see Margaret extend an arm and draw her youngest daughter into a casual embrace. Lorraine rolled her eyes again, as if nothing was more embarrassing in all the world than to be loved, but made no attempt to pull away. So, Mrs Flett was capable of showing affection, and of having it reciprocated, in its own way. That boded well for the future, for Sonia, once she finally came clean.

"Oh aye, Euan and I are very blessed in our children." Margaret fixed Sonia with a look Grace couldn't interpret, but which made Sonia shoot quickly out onto the doorstep, "Come on, Grace, it's freezing!"

Grace clasped Margaret's hand in both her own, as if they were old friends, "Thank you so much for the tea, and the welcome. It's so generous of you."

"Any time. You must come to Sunday lunch once you're settled in…meet my husband and my boys…"

"That would be lovely. You're so kind…"

"Grace, come on!"

"Better go. Need to empty the car and see how everything works before it's pitch black!" Grace unlocked the doors, and Sonia clambered inside.

The big car purred powerfully away, leaving the newest two initiates to the Grace Fan Club waving adoringly from the farmhouse step.

Grace turned to Sonia, slouched sulkily in her seat, "Next right?"

"Next right."

The four-wheel-drive surged up the loose shingle track, rounded a raised bank designed to cocoon the front of the house from prying eyes and sea breezes, and swung onto a circular flagstone driveway with a double garage to the right, and the front door and low, larch-clad eastern elevation of the house directly before them.

"Ooh, Sonia, this is very nice!"

"Told you."

They parked, and Grace fumbled in her handbag for her booking confirmation, "There's a code…to a key box…"

She pushed in the provided code to the secure box on the wall, releasing the flap which held a door key and an infra-red control. Grace examined it, puzzled.

"Garage door," Sonia clarified.

"Oh, I see."

"If you leave your car out all the time, the salt in the air rusts the paintwork, and then it looks as crap as all the other cars here. Better to park it in the garage, particularly if you end up staying a while."

"Right. Now the alarm!" Clutching her piece of paper, Grace unlocked the door and bustled to the control panel, entering the code and silencing the beeping.

Sonia glanced around. It felt funny to be here. It even smelled the same – wood, polish, leather, the underlying hint of aftershave and washing powder…fresh, clean, familiar, evocative…and not a hint of cowshit.

Grace put down her handbag by the hall table, and dropped door key, opener, and car keys into the Celtic-looking pewter dish provided for the purpose, flicking on the lamp and collecting up the small amount of post spread across the doormat.

"Looks like mostly junk mail. Do you think we're supposed to hold onto it?"

Sonia shrugged moodily, suddenly irrationally jealous of Grace for being able to stay here when she could not. Not noticing, already turning away from her, Grace was through the hall door and into the living area beyond, exclaiming, "Wow! This is lovely!"

Well-aware of how lovely it was, tempted to collapse on the floor and kick and scream like a two-year-old, Sonia steeled herself against the disappointment, and followed.

Grace turned, beaming with delight, "This is very smart, Sonia. I can see why you liked staying here so much…"

Sonia sighed, and flopped onto the steps leading to the sunken seating area. Grace observed her utter dejection, and promptly sat down next to her, putting her arm around the girl and drawing Sonia's head to rest against her shoulder. Sonia, who hadn't been hugged for comfort in so long, couldn't resist the urge to relax against Grace. Grace's other hand stroked her hair gently, "I'm sorry. I didn't understand there was some unfinished business between you and your Mum, not until I saw you together."

"It's my fault. I should've warned you. I didn't know you were going to come in. Everything seems to be my fault these days!

Before I left, we both said some things we shouldn't have...and we didn't patch it up, so it's been there like a big boulder in the middle of a burn for five years, disrupting everything. She called me a tart, a whore, a spoiled princess, and a lot of other things I didn't want to hear from the mouth of my own mother. For my part, I said she was a thick bitch, that she was jealous of me because I could leave and she was stuck here in her shitty life...and then I went, and I didn't get in touch for five years – not as much as a postcard – until I wrote a couple of weeks ago saying to expect me back, and even then I never said when or why..."

"And you rolled up today with me in tow, and no one could say anything because we were all being on our very best behaviour! Aren't the British daft?"

Sonia smiled, enjoying the simple, sensory pleasure of the gentle stroking of her hair, "I'm jealous of you, being able to stay here."

"You can stay here too, you know. There's more than one bedroom, isn't there?"

Sonia sat up abruptly, before she was overcome by the temptation, gesturing in front of her with rigid palms, "No! I have to sort this out – patch it up with my Mum, prove to my Dad I haven't changed, find a way to get on with my brothers and sister, build bridges with all the people I was horrible to, accept it will be the single most humiliating thing I've ever had to do, and start again. This whole, stupid mess is about having to start again."

"We're both starting again, and you're doing it in a much more courageous way than I am. I'm rooting for you, and your baby."

Sonia felt her throat catch, and declared with a rush of feeling, "I know. I couldn't have walked through that door this afternoon if you hadn't been there, smoothing the way."

Grace took her hand, "Nor I through this one."

"Thank God for the ferry, eh?"

"Absolutely – a good job they'll never dig your tunnel…"

They sat for a moment longer, side by side, holding hands, treasuring the silent solidarity.

"Let me show you where everything is before it gets too dark."

Sonia stood and snapped on the switch by the door, bathing everything in the subtle glow of artfully-placed lighting. Grace looked around appreciatively, "It's so posh."

Quizzically, Sonia ventured, "Aren't you used to posh?"

Grace chortled, "Different kind of posh!"

"It's all way out of my league. Sorry about my tacky sister, by the way. She's not too subtle."

"She's young!"

"She's fifteen, and I don't think she's ever read a book in her life! All she cares about is make-up, hair, boys…"

"It's what they watch on the tv, isn't it? Don't be too hard on your sister. I know people three times Lorraine's age who consider little else. Perhaps she doesn't know any different? You and I might be the first to say caring about appearance is materialistic, that it's the definition of shallow…but did you notice how much better dressed we are than your Mum and Lorraine? How much glossier is your hair than your Mum's? How much better manicured are your nails? How much softer is your skin? That materialism we profess to hate so much is woven into the fabric of our existence to the extent we no longer notice it." Grace pointed at Sonia's clothes, "You're wearing labels."

Sonia nodded. She decided not to tell Grace they were factory seconds from an outlet store.

"So am I...and I was on my way to being offended when Lorraine suggested my watch might be a fake. What does it matter if it's a fake, if I like it and it tells the time? But that snobbery's within me – I can't help it. I wish it wasn't. I hope by being somewhere like this, where that rot doesn't matter, I will become the person I'd rather be. It's in you too. You told me you sought it out, you wanted it...so don't be quick to judge your sister for wanting it too. Every young girl desires her rich, handsome prince, doesn't she...and that fairy tale you chased all the way to London with such single-mindedness?"

Sonia acknowledged this truth pragmatically, "Aye, she does." She paused a moment, as if considering whether to share something, before saying, "Come in here." She beckoned towards a room to the right of the kitchen, "If nothing's changed, I'll show you..."

Intrigued, Grace stood and followed her.

The room in which she found herself was a large Master Suite, an American-style superking bed with huge headboard dominating the centre of the far wall. The view matched that of the living room, with a wall of windows looking down over fields to beach and sea. As in the living room, the floor level dropped away to take account of the hillside position of the property, and three shallow steps led from the raised area dominated by the massive bed, to a reading nook down by the window. Oversized reclining chairs and an arched lamp stood before shelves displaying not only an eclectic collection of reading material, but various unusual ornaments, quirky bookends, and framed photographs. Tripping lightly down the steps as if it was something she'd done many times before, Sonia urged Grace to follow, and held up a picture, "You're too polite to pry, but…here you are." She placed the frame in Grace's hand, hanging over her arm and pointing, "That's Vidar, who owns the house…who I…you know… Those two are his brothers; Ragnar, who you probably dealt with about the rental, and Jannick, the baby one."

Three tall, broad, ruggedly-handsome middle-aged men in dinner suits grinned from the photo. Ragnar, on the left, was the stereotypical Viking, with fair hair, blue eyes, and blonde beard – the tallest and broadest of the brothers. Vidar, in the centre, appeared older than the other two, with greyer hair, and more lines wrinkling around his eyes and across his cheeks as he laughed. The youngest, Jannick, was dark-haired, brown-eyed, a direct contrast to the Scandinavian Ragnar, but all were unmistakeably related; the same easy manner, laughing eyes, strong jawlines, and broad grins radiated from all three faces.

"Good-looking boys."

"Aye," Sonia lingered over putting the picture back on the shelf.

"Can't say I recognise him. He does look a bit old for you, Sonia."

She blushed, "He is basically Mam's age, but…"

"But?"

"He was famous! The idea of him was exciting…and I like older men, I suppose. They're just so much less dumb than fellas my age."

Grace thought of Dominic, and couldn't suppress an exclamation, "Ha! Don't you believe it! They're just dumb in a different way."

Grace was surprised to notice a world-weary expression crossing Sonia's face, temporarily ageing her youthful features, "I know what you mean."

"Are you all right?"

"What? Oh, aye…I'm tired is all…" Sonia didn't want to be inside *Somerled* any more. She had no desire to return to the farm either, but that didn't prevent her wanting to flee the comfortable warmth of the plush house, and the sudden sharp sting of memories, "Do you need me to show you how to work anything? It's all new and fancy and easy…you shouldn't have any problems with it, but if you do, you can text me. I'll give you my number. There should be a password for the Wi-Fi written down somewhere, but the speed's shite. No fibre-optic up here! Don't be in a hurry to download anything."

Grace laughed, "I'll be ok. I'm not very techy."

"Ok. It's getting dark. I'm going to go before I can't see to get back. I should've brought a torch."

"I could take you in the car."

"It's no distance!"

"If you're sure…?"

"Positive. I need ten minutes on my own to think. There's no privacy at home."

The two walked back through the house and out onto the driveway, exchanging 'phone numbers. Grace pressed the button to open the automatic garage door, which gradually lifted to reveal a Range Rover plugged in to a battery trickle-charger on one side, and space for her car on the other. A large stack of logs and kindling stood along one wall.

"Excellent! Could get snowed in and I'll be all right."

"There's always a chance…winter's nearly here."

"I love the snow," said Grace, dreamily.

"You're boring," said Sonia mischievously, "You just think everything's great."

Grace laughed, "I love the fact something new is happening to me. Nothing new's happened in so long."

"I hate the fact something new's happening to me!"

Grace stopped, horrified by her own tactlessness, turning and reaching for Sonia's hand again, "I'm sorry Sonia – that was insensitive of me."

"I'm joking!"

"Will you really be all right? You'll have to tell all soon. It's not a secret you can keep indefinitely!"

No, thought Sonia, not and share a bedroom with her eagle-eyed, image-obsessed baby sister, who would at first note gleefully how fat Sonia had become, and then how *localised* the weight gain…

She was heartened and emboldened by Grace's concern, "Don't worry, I'll get it done tonight. That's why I want to walk back. I want time to rehearse what my announcement will be over dinner.

They'll all be there – one explanation will do the trick, and then at least that bit's over."

"I wish I could do something to make it easier for you," Grace opened the car boot and lifted out her suitcase.

"You are doing something," insisted Sonia, "You're being on my side. You don't realise how long it's been since anyone has fought my corner.

Grace smiled warmly, "Yes, I am on your side. You know why? Because it's the right side to be on."

Sonia grinned back, gratefully, touched by the unconditional support, "Any problems with stuff not working, text me."

"I will. Thank you."

Both shuffled their feet awkwardly. The moment for leave-taking had come, and neither was sure how to approach it. Supporters to friends in the blink of an eye, the passage of a thought, the fall of a tear, the blurting of a secret…but still strangers to one another, norms of behaviour far from established.

"See you." Sonia turned slowly away, unwilling to leave Grace's reassuringly-optimistic company, frightened of having to sit amongst her own family and reveal her monumental mistake.

Grace's voice stopped her, fearful of the girl's departure, of being left alone without her indomitable new ally and the comforting distraction of her lively conversation, "Sonia, you won't just go down to the bottom of the hill and never come back up?"

FIVE

The handshake was as firm as ever, the smile as broad, but there was something behind the eyes... Stewart couldn't place exactly what about his friend's demeanour made him uneasy, but there was an unmistakeable difference in him.

"Thanks so much for getting me, buddy, it was a last-minute change of plan. Family ok?"

"They're fine, fine...you all right?"

"What? Oh yeah...ok..." Vidar smiled, but it was a weak facsimile of his normal wide, beaming, twinkle-eyed grin, which usually had the recipient of it helplessly gurning back like a baby in a bouncer within an instant of beholding it.

Vidar helped Stewart heft his two guitar cases and a suitcase into the boot of the doctor's Audi.

"Nice car, man! When did you get this?"

"Couple of months ago. Wee fiftieth present to myself. Went to Inverness and spent the day in and out of every dealership doing eeny-meeny-miney-moe until I'd made my decision. Better than the other one 'cos it's a wee bit bigger."

"Because, obviously, you need your car to be even bigger now your kids are away at College, and you only have to take one black bag and a teeny, tiny wife in and out of it," Vidar teased, a little of the usual sparkle returning as he climbed inside and turned to wink at his friend.

Stewart raised one unimpressed eyebrow, adopting the tone and expression reserved for his student sons when they ridiculed him, retorting, "Having a dig? Make sure you don't forget the ample room for two sets of golf clubs...and it's mighty handy when collecting disorganised friends with ridiculously bulky luggage from the airport at short notice..."

"Touché," Vidar chuckled, sighed, and ran a hand through greying hair.

Stewart didn't ever like to pry. Vidar enjoyed Orkney precisely because it provided the antidote to the intrusive chaos of the rest of his existence; pursued by the press, followed by fans, his time and energy endlessly demanded in quantities far beyond the reserves required of any normal life. That Vidar had the stamina to maintain it was testament both to his dedication to career at the expense of all else, and the conditioning of over thirty years spent travelling the globe, living out of his suitcase. It must take a toll – you'd have to be superhuman not to feel the strain once in a while – and Stewart had witnessed Vidar's exhaustion at first hand on more than one occasion, but his behaviour was different today from mere physical depletion. Stewart couldn't put his finger on quite what it was about Vidar, but if he had to give a professional diagnosis, he would chalk it down to nothing less than hopelessness, as if Vidar was sitting beside him in his comfortable birthday purchase and questioning the continuing point of it all.

As they drove out of the airport on the Kirkwall road, Stewart probed, "Things not go well in London?"

Vidar turned to him, surprised, "Why do you ask that?"

"You seem a wee bit out-of-sorts…"

Vidar tried a smile, but couldn't summon it, "It went fine in London. I just got sick of being trailed down the street by people with selfie-sticks. It just seems wherever you go now there's a camera in your face. I'm sure ten years ago it wasn't like that. People just want a piece of you whatever you're doing. They don't give a damn if you're choosing groceries or buying socks. They think they have ownership of a part of you, that they know you! Oh, ignore me, I'm just being grouchy and ungrateful. I don't mind people talking to me. I wouldn't be anything without that…I just…"

Again, the careworn sigh, the frustrated scrape of the fingers through the front of his hair.

Concerned, Stewart tried a change of subject, "It's been horrible here…so cold…and early snow."

"When I was done in London, I was planning to go back to LA…better in December than here, huh?"

Stewart grunted agreement, and waved enthusiastically through the windscreen at a doctor colleague waiting to pull out of the hospital car park as the Q7 surged past.

"That was Bob Turner. Recognise him?"

"He did look familiar…"

"You've met him at our place. You spent all evening buttering up his wife. Why didn't you go back to LA then?"

"You know, Stew, to be honest, I couldn't handle being in that massive place all on my own. Up there in the hills with those high hedges, big gates…I felt as if I would just disappear."

"Isn't that the point of it?"

"Well…yes…except…"

"Come on, mate, what is eating you?"

"I own eight properties, Stewart. Eight. All around the world. Whichever one I go into, when everyone has left, it's just me in a big, empty box surrounded by a lot of expensive stuff I didn't even choose. Half the time it's something the interior decorator put there a century ago and I've never had time to decide whether I like it or not, so it all just sits there, and the housekeeper dusts it, and I walk past it. None of it means anything, not really. It's not enough any more. The gloss has rubbed off. It's just me, staring down the barrel of fifty years old in an empty house with nothing to show for it – "

"But platinum disks on every wall, awards coming out of your ears, and billions in the bank?"

"Now who's having a dig?"

"Well, you're hardly failing, mate!"

"No, agreed, I have been a lucky boy…but I've worked for it. I've given up everything for my career since I was a kid…"

"Ah, I think I'm starting to get it! You're wondering what it would have been like if you'd done a bit less career and a bit more everything-you-gave-up, aren't you?"

"Perhaps… You don't go home to an empty house, do you? You go home to a smiling wife, healthy kids – "

"Now, this is Elaine we're talking about. The smiles aren't always guaranteed!"

Vidar grinned, "Scary Elaine…but she loves you, doesn't she? She's there for you, no matter what."

"Surely you aren't craving domesticity, with your opportunities to enjoy yourself? You've had more girlfriends than I've had hot dinners!"

"Yeah, and they're with me because they think latching onto me for a week or two will help them launch their career as a model or a pop star or an actress, whatever they've decided to become that month. Get their picture taken with me at some première or other and they think it opens a door for them. There's no feeling there, no regard, no care…"

"Still, can't be bad, eh?"

Stewart was beginning to feel really worried. He'd never seen Vidar like this, not in the fifteen years he'd known him. Usually, he was an upbeat, glass-half-full character who grabbed the chances life offered with both hands, squeezing the possibility out of every situation with infectious optimism.

"I never thought so…and then I'd see the pictures and it would be as if I was taking my daughter out for the evening. I looked like an idiot, so I knocked it all on the head. It was the right thing for my dignity, but it just makes the houses even emptier, you know?"

"I don't know what to say, mate."

"I'm just sick of being on my own…sick of it. I want some company. I don't mean being surrounded by the entourage of people who dress me and feed me and pounce to attention every time I open my mouth. I mean company! I mean Scary Elaine, who shouts at me if I don't wipe my feet, and goes nuts if I don't use a coaster for my coffee cup on her nice table."

Stewart smirked as Vidar, distracted by his own private frustrations, unguardedly described his friend's fierce little Glaswegian wife in all her combative, house-proud glory.

"I mean somebody to talk to, to share opinions with, to discuss and debate and joke and laugh. Not someone who says 'how high?' when I say 'jump', but someone who says 'you wanna jump, you get on with it your damn self'. Only now it's impossible to have that because the persona, the ego, the *fame*," Vidar spat out the word as if it tasted bitter, "precedes you into every room and clouds every judgement people make about you. There is no possibility of an incognito encounter with anyone because that's how life is, how it's been for so long I have no idea how to change it. I'm trapped in a situation of my own making."

"So, you've come here to hide for a while and feel sorry for yourself."

Vidar snorted, "Your bedside manner sucks, Doc, you know that?"

"I'm a GP, not a Psychiatrist."

"You saying I'm nuts?"

"No more than you've been for the rest of the time I've known you."

"I did think about going back to Denmark, to the lake house, but my whole family are right there on the doorstep. I know it sounds crazy, but the idea of that made me feel even lonelier…"

"Vid, you're just tired. You work yourself into the ground and then wonder why you're at a low ebb. You should cut yourself a bit of slack now and again. You're just at that time in your life when you start to feel a wee bit mortal, that's all. Bit of grey in the hair, bit of grey in the beard. Maybe a bit of flab where it never used to be – although the amount you pound the gym in pursuit of eternal youth, I doubt you've noticed that yet. I felt like shite as soon as I got the wrong side of forty-five. I got through it though, with the help of my scary wife…and fifty wasn't so bad once I decided I was going to treat myself to a big, shiny car when I got there. You should give yourself permission to enjoy the life you have…otherwise what are you endlessly working for, to be richer? It's not my business, but I hardly think you need to be any richer…and what are you now – forty-seven; forty-eight?"

"Forty-seven."

"How long are you going to keep pushing yourself like this with no let-up? Airport to performance to studio to interview to airport and on you go again and again. Are you still going to want to do that when you're fifty-seven; sixty-seven?"

"I haven't given it any thought…"

"Well, perhaps your down-time here should be given over to serious consideration of the latter half of your life. You have the luxury that you could never do a day's work again and still not spend all the money you've made. I think your problem might be that you're running out of reasons to get out of bed every day. The hole in your life isn't professional, it's emotional. Maybe you should be looking at a way to plug that, not pretending it doesn't exist by working so hard you can't remember your own name half the time…"

"You seem very concerned about it, Doc."

"You're my friend. You've been my friend for fifteen years. You're the most unassuming superstar I've ever met."

"Know a lot of them, do you?" Vidar prodded sarcastically.

"That's my point! You say the ego precedes you into the room and spoils everything, but it doesn't…it doesn't. No one would ever know who you are, what you've achieved, what you have. Who else would patiently teach my kids to play the guitar, or take them rock-pooling when they were little, or help round up sheep when they get out, or give neighbours a lift into town if you're going, or muck in and dig out the paths when it snows? I tell you something, none of the other rock stars I'm best mates with ever do any of that!"

Vidar smiled, "I like doing all of that. Makes me feel as if I fit in somewhere."

"As your doctor, let me give you some medical advice, for your own wellbeing. You don't need another hit album or an extra Grammy. What you need is a life…and you should be concentrating a bit of that legendary energy of yours on working out how you can get one."

"Is that your prescription, Doc?"

"Yes, it is – to work on yourself, not on your brand."

"Point taken. Thank you for your honesty."

"What are friends for?"

"People mostly tell me what they think I want to hear…"

"That's certainly not healthy, is it? Anyway, can you imagine that happening here?"

"Not for a moment. The very first time I put the trash out in my pyjamas, Mag Flett would appear telling me to have some self-respect."

"Ah!" Stewart thumped his friend's thigh, "This'll interest you! Speaking of the Flett family, little Ginger's back home."

The sweep of those flame-red ringlets across his chest, the softness of her pale skin pressing against his naked body, vivid green eyes gazing deep into his...

"Little Sonia Flett..."

Stewart chuckled, taking his eyes off the road briefly to observe with amusement the change in his friend's expression, "And you can wipe that look off your face. There'll be no chance of her warming your lonely nights because she's pregnant, by all accounts."

Vidar lurched in his seat as if he'd just been stabbed with something sharp.

"How? I mean...I know *how*...but...little Sonia-I'm-going-places-and-leaving-you-suckers-for-dust-Flett? It seems unfathomable...so uncharacteristically short-sighted of her!"

"Life has a way of biting you on the arse sometimes, doesn't it?"

"I guess..." Vidar seemed distracted, uncomfortable, as if the news was unwelcome.

"She hasn't come to see me since she's been back – too embarrassed, I daresay – but Elaine saw her mother in Dounby Co-op and the whole thing came out. As you can imagine, Margaret is scandalised. It seems wee Ginger's foray into the world of motherhood was an unplanned excursion."

"Poor little Son. Her family is out of the Ark. I don't imagine they're being too supportive of her. Makes you wonder why she came back at all."

"The impression Mag gave was that she didn't have much choice in the matter. Lost her go-getting job."

"Ouch... What did she say about the father?" There was more than a flicker of interest in the keen, grey eyes.

"Apparently, she's keeping that particular card very close to her chest, so I'd suggest sniffing around there offering a butch shoulder to cry on will doubtless bring the mother out with suspicions aroused and shotgun cocked. Do your thinking with your big head, not your wee one, eh?"

"Relax. There's nothing left between me and Sonia Flett. It was a bit of fun that ran its course. There's no unfinished business there. I told you, I'm laying off the young girls. I'm gonna act my age from now on. I can't deny I'd like to see her again, but only out of curiosity, not to cause her any more trouble than she's already in."

"Good. Keep it that way."

"It's going to be tricky lying low next door."

"Just don't let Margaret catch you 'consoling' her eldest in the farmhouse kitchen, that's all. Not if you want to make your own fiftieth birthday, anyway."

"Is that Doctors' orders too?"

"Yes, it bloody well is!"

Stewart squeezed the big car through the gate and up past the rear of the Flett family farm to the large timber lodge cut into the side of the hill overlooking the bay. The whiteness of the xenon headlights shone their bright beam in an arc around the circular driveway as Stewart turned the car.

"Want help unloading?"

"No, I'll take it in. I'm used to lugging that stuff around."

"Bit of washing to do?"

"You could say that."

Vidar swung his long legs out of the car. The cold of the evening swirled into the fuggy interior, and Stewart shivered.

"Thank you for getting me, I really appreciate it. You and Elaine should come up to eat sometime soon."

"Sounds good…and remember what I said. Spend some time here working out what it is you actually want out of life – and stay away from Sonia Flett!"

Vidar sarcastically stood to attention on the driveway, saluted, and crossed himself for good measure, "I promise!"

"Boot's open, smartarse."

"Thanks again."

"Any time."

Vidar shut the passenger door, popped the boot and removed his bags, and waved as Stewart disappeared down the hill, leaving him alone on his drive in the chilly dark.

SIX

Vidar stood for quite a while on the flagstones, listening to the roar of Stewart's big car as his friend enjoyed his own private race homeward along the empty lanes in his indulgent birthday present. Vidar smiled to himself. He was fond of Stewart and his family. The man had never been starstruck; never treated him with anything other than the straightforward openness of one friend to another, despite their very different life circumstances. Stewart held an influential position here as local GP, and his wife as a nurse. They self-evidently made more of a contribution to this close-knit rural community than Vidar ever could. That was why he enjoyed Orkney so much. It was satisfying to be anonymous, arousing barely a flicker of curiosity. Once his neighbours understood who he was and why he'd come, they delved no further. Hardly any tourists noticed his presence because no one would remotely expect him to be anywhere like this in a million years! He had to sign the odd autograph for a keen-eyed visitor, but found it was more of a novelty here than the nuisance he might be tempted to consider it in London, Copenhagen, or Los Angeles. Perhaps because being in Birsay caused him to forget what the rest of the world thought he was – his 'brand', Stewart had called it – and enable the man trapped behind it to have some room to breathe?

Vidar held his key in one cold hand, zipped up his jacket against the gusting wind, and stood with his back to the front door, watching fast clouds scud across the bright, full moon.

His stomach growled. He should have trespassed further on Stewart's endless kindness, and got him to stop at a Kirkwall supermarket on the way. He hoped one of the people his brother let the house out to on his behalf had left a tin of something behind in the cupboard that would see him through until the shops opened tomorrow morning.

Whichever home he chose to frequent, all were equally devoid of welcome. No homecoming hug, no special celebratory meal, no interest in where he'd been, no one to put the pretensions into perspective. Nothing but him, his mountains of dirty laundry, the threatening winter, and the frighteningly fast passage of time. However wealthy and successful he was, when the front door closed behind him a moment from now, he would simply be a single, ageing man; sitting alone in a cold house eating something out of a tin – and he knew without a shadow of a doubt such an existence was no longer enough.

Shivering uncontrollably now, Vidar steeled himself against self-pity, unlocked the door, and impatiently shouldered it open. He staggered into the hallway with his burden of heavy luggage, dumped it unceremoniously in the middle of the floor, and pushed the door shut behind him.

There was no post, which surprised him. Usually, if the house had no Lets, and the cleaner hadn't visited for a few days, there were at least a few junk mail circulars spread across the mat. He slipped off his shoes, and padded across the hall. The house seemed quite warm, and he shrugged off his coat, tossing it across the bags on the floor. He'd deal with all that tomorrow. Unpacking was a chore he couldn't face in his current dissatisfied mood.

As he approached the connecting door, he noticed a faint light shining underneath it from the living area beyond. That explained the lack of post. The cleaner must have been here. She'd obviously left the light on by mistake, or Ragnar had told her his big brother was coming home, and she'd kindly left a lamp on for him. It might explain the warmth too. Perhaps she'd decided to flick the thermostat up a notch to ensure he returned to a warm house? Maybe – his empty stomach growled again – she'd left him some food? He didn't care what.

Hopeful, he pushed down the handle and opened the door, utterly unprepared for what he'd find.

****

In. Stomach swells, filling with the breath.

Out. Stomach contracts, actively pushing out the tension along with the air.

Grace, sitting in the lotus position on the rug next to the sofa, opened one eye as if that would improve her hearing. She could have sworn she'd just heard a car...?

No, she must be mistaken.

She closed her eyes again, returning to her meditation. If at home, this would have been the time Dominic barged in from work, banging around disturbing her tranquil evening, demanding to be fed like a spoilt child when it was far too late and too bad for the

71

digestion. She had always already passed through the pangs of hunger; besides, his unnerving presence made her so uncomfortable any lingering appetite instantly fled like a spider in a spotlight. Daily, she'd wondered why she still bothered preparing such elaborately-complicated meals, as Dominic robotically forked in the food with barely a pause to taste it. Unfortunately, she'd established a benchmark of quality and could not dip below it without drawing attention to the fact she'd stopped trying. A Chicken Kiev simply would not do in place of Steak Diane. A rod for her own back, Sonia would call it.

Sonia.

Her friend.

What was more, the only proper friend she'd had in her forty-two years. Over these last few weeks, she'd come to realise previous encounters masquerading as friendship had never been anything of the sort. Real friendship was accepting without judgement, supportive without indulgence, laughter without reserve, opinion without censure, and adventure without end. If Grace wanted an honest, straightforward exchange of views with someone who would consider her opinion without shouting her down, share without expecting a return, and buoy her up when her confidence wavered, she walked the half-mile down the lane to the Flett farmhouse. She was welcomed into a haven of warm security, filled with laughter, banter, the smells of cooking and sooty chimneys, muddy shoes and damp dogs. Nothing was particularly clean, it certainly wasn't fashionable, and footwear other than wellies was out of the question, but there was unsurpassed comfort and conviviality. Grace could never understand why Sonia so despised it! It didn't matter that the dresser was covered with a layer of dust and paperwork so thick Grace assumed it had been some years in the making. It really wasn't important that the marks up the boot room wall probably came from something a cow had done. It didn't seem significant that she'd brought six different coats of varying styles in her suitcase, and had only worn one – her thickest, warmest anorak – which now had quite a lot of mud and other unmentionables up the front of it from the paws of the exuberant farm dogs, and a significant quantity of sand in the pockets from her beachcombing finds, now cluttering the windowsill in the guest bedroom she occupied at *Somerled*. She supposed she could have taken over the large Master Suite with its view down to the sea, but the family photographs and personal items occupying the shelves had made her feel she was intruding in private space. The guest room was clean, bright, and impersonal – more what she was used to in a room, given her whole London flat was a honed homage to minimalism. Her chosen bedroom had a large window which looked out over the circular flagstone driveway, and across the Flett's fields to the farmhouse and wetland wildlife reserve beyond. Grace loved that when the moon was out, it shone with stunning reflected symmetry in the waters of the reserve, and when she left the blinds open, she could see the farmhouse roof from her bed, which made her feel secure. The kitchen formed one corner of the large, square living space, with a dining table in front of it. A baby-grand piano occupied the lower-floor area in front of the window, facing onto a flagstone patio, and the vast lawn that curved down the hillside. The entire rear of the house was glass, providing an uninterrupted rural panorama. The ubiquitous ewes hunkered down within waving tussocks, trails of their wool caught on the barbed-wire fencing and blew horizontally in the persistent wind, like scudding clouds across a green sky. Rolling pasture eventually met shelving rocks and a beach of purest cream, with clear sea sweeping majestically across its expanse twice a day.

The bay was protected by a curve of rock extending out some hundred feet from the beach, to create a shallow lagoon at low tide, the stillness of which was only disturbed by the gusting wind rippling its surface, or the stately passage of a pair of swans who had claimed the stretch of silent water as their own.

A large double-sided fireplace divided living space from office and gym, with a sunken central seating area dominated by an enormous u-shaped sofa, curving around a huge coffee table, and a flat-screen television above the fire. The whole house felt roomy without being ostentatiously large. It was subtly well-designed, functional, and comfortable. As Grace relaxed into this new space, she started to leave things lying around, something she would never have done at home – a book on the end of the sofa, two or three mugs on coffee table, worktop, and draining board. She knew she was going to tidy them up eventually, but there was no pressure or hurry to do so. Instead of pathologically putting everything away the moment she no longer required it – in case Dom came home with a business associate in tow whom he was trying to impress – she left the bread out on the board, her slippers halfway across the room, and her handbag over the back of a dining chair. Her one concession to tidiness was to stand her undeniably filthy wellingtons on some newspaper, to prevent their vileness spoiling the hall floor.

She thought herself very lucky to have discovered this gem at such short notice. The added coincidence of such closeness to Sonia convinced Grace she had been supposed to see that magazine, intended to come here, meant to find exactly this house, and encounter the very person to bring her to it. Why else had all this happened so quickly, and so easily?

Thus, Grace's first few weeks passed in a blur of surprisingly happy self-discovery. She relished the previously unknown freedom of making all her own decisions. Instead of pandering to her husband's whims, the pattern of her day was now dictated by her own desires. She ate when she wanted to, and the time when she would have previously been disturbed into nausea by Dominic's demanding presence became her opportunity to relax, unwind, and practice her yoga. She still hadn't attempted a piece of art, but was confident this would come, eventually, if it was supposed to. Grace felt strongly that this place had a plan for her, and she must follow the course it indicated.

Sliding onto all fours, Grace clasped her hands before her in a fist, and pressed her forearms onto the ground. Lifting her bottom upward tipped her head to nestle into the thick pile of the shaggy rug before the fire. Clasped hands behind her skull, supporting her head and holding it still, she gently eased to tiptoes. Grace walked her feet out wide to either side of her hips, took a deep inhale, tightened her stomach muscles, and gradually lifted her legs; first to the splits at hip level, and then slowly and deliberately upward until her feet touched, and she stood on her head on the rug, staring at her reflection in the window to maintain her form, concentration, and balance. Content she was in control, Grace allowed her eyes to close, and surrendered to the sensation of floating produced by the pose. The freer she became, the suppler her body felt. The more confidence she unearthed, the stronger her muscles seemed. Powerful, unbreakable; she stood straighter, and walked taller. She was a butterfly emerging from long pupation, and discovering the liberating potential of her newly-grown wings.

As she opened her eyes again to check the straightness of her legs in the huge lounge window, she saw a figure reflected in the glass, standing motionless by the hall door.

SEVEN

Grace yelped in shock and tumbled sideways, trapping her body in the narrow gap between sofa and coffee table, getting a foot caught awkwardly behind the table leg, and her hips wedged painfully. The more frantically she struggled to free herself, the further her stuck limb slid, and the lower her trapped pelvis dropped, until she was left inverted, pointing only her shapely bottom upwards towards the intruder, panting and gasping in her ineffectual efforts to get free. Notwithstanding the possibly-perilous nature of her situation, an untimely fit of the giggles nevertheless ambushed Grace. The more she sought to control herself, the funnier her predicament became, and the weaker her bids for freedom as she laughed, and laughed, and laughed…

Eventually, there seemed to be nothing for it but to commando-crawl out into the centre of the rug, sniggering helplessly, and confront the intruder if he was still there. Grace felt surprisingly relaxed about being burgled. If he wanted her stuff, she'd probably let him take it. If he wanted anything else, she knew she was fit enough to make a run for it, and the Flett farm was only a scream away.

Once sufficiently free of her furniture prison to right herself, Grace popped up a rosy and breathless face topped with wild hair, and beheld the perplexed expression of Sonia's boyfriend from the bedroom photographs.

****

There was a woman in his house! Not just any woman, but one clad in skin-tight lycra, who was doing a very erect, unwavering headstand in the middle of his hearthrug. The reflection of her body in the large window showed the front was as delectable as the back, and that her eyes were closed, face serene, ribcage expanding and contracting gently as she breathed slowly and rhythmically in concentration. She was so deep in meditation she didn't realise he was there! Vidar knew the decent thing was to draw instant attention to his presence in some way. Instead, he stood with his tongue hanging out, knowing full well that if he as much as *breathed* the show would be over, and then the real trouble would start, like it always did with women.

He held his breath until his chest ached, and prayed for her to keep her eyes closed so he could keep his own wide open and fixed upon her body. She spotted him too soon, squeaking in alarm, and tumbling sideways, somehow ending up trapped between coffee table and sofa.

Horrified, Vidar couldn't believe how quickly this was turning from sweetly delicious to very, very sour. She'd be calling the cops on him if he didn't start explaining fast. He fixed his eyes on the floor in front of him, braced himself, and waited to be harangued. After all, it was his fault. His brother had obviously very practically and efficiently let the house on a last-minute booking, and because he was having a childish woe-is-me sulk about life, he'd decided he was above checking it was ok to change his plans. What an idiot...and he'd ruined the holiday of a paying guest, whom he'd doubtless now have to pacify with a refund and some alternative accommodation at his own expense. All for the sake of a 'phone call to Denmark he was too arrogant to make because he expected the whole world to oblige him! He was about to launch into the explanations and apologies she would expect to hear, when the giggling started. Bemused by the sound, he shot a wary glance down into the living area, and beheld the lovely, peachy behind sticking up above the coffee-table and wiggling with the giggles and struggles to get free. He was seized with the instant and highly-inappropriate desire to rush down and squeeze it. He couldn't, of course. He was probably already in enough trouble without adding minor sexual assault to the charge sheet, so remained where he was, enjoying the inviting warmth of her laughter and the titillation of the jiggle. He considered that, hunger aside, this evening was developing into an unexpectedly enjoyable one.

By the time he'd decided it was positively rude to leave her struggling unassisted, he was rescued by her success, popping up breathlessly to a kneeling position in the middle of the rug, eyes wide, cheeks flushed, and hair sticking out in all directions from a wonky topknot. Pieces of fluff from the thick rug were caught here and there amongst the tufts, giving her the appearance of a baby bird just hatched in a bundle of twigs and feathers. There was no fury, reproach, or indignation in her expression, only the residue of her laughter in bright eyes, glowing cheeks, and an open, frank curiosity as she regarded him with a flash of recognition.

****

The unapologetic directness which it seemed had become part of her personality since encountering Sonia on the ferry, permitted her to pant, "Ooh, you're Sonia's friend. This is your house."

The man seemed taken aback, perhaps by the absence of conventional politeness, or maybe by mention of Sonia? Perhaps Sonia had exaggerated the extent of their past connection to impress her? Grace was momentarily concerned she had spoken out of turn, or occasioned some embarrassment for her friend. Her brows knotted, and she regarded him earnestly, "I've made a mistake, haven't I? I'm not supposed to be here, am I? I've got a booking confirmation!"

Anxious not to appear any crazier than she already did, Grace's strong legs pushed effortlessly to her feet. She crossed the room swiftly with lithe strides to extract the sheet from her handbag on the dining table. Going over to where the man remained, stationary, a step or two inside the door, she proffered the paper insistently. He took it, but didn't look at it, instead stating quietly in a soft accent, "No...no...I'm not supposed to be here. I didn't check...I just came home. It's me who's wrong, not you."

Still shyly smiling, holding the sheet of paper as if he didn't know what to do with it; he gazed at her steadily, intently, drinking in the sight of her. When Dominic regarded her with any directness, it was usually intended to convey a rebuke. It made her feel instantly guilty and chastened, even when she didn't understand what she'd done wrong. This look was not the same. This look made Grace suddenly very aware her hair was a mess, she was wearing top-to-toe lycra, and no bra. With as much subtlety as she could manage,

Grace reached fingertips across to pluck her cardigan from the back of the sofa, intending to slide it on and feel less exposed to the transparent hunger of the unblinking stare.

Unfortunately, everything this evening seemed designed to demonstrate the utter unsuitability of her given name. Her cardigan tied itself in ever-greater knots of fabric as she scrabbled desperately to turn the sleeves right-side-out, struggle it on inelegantly, find the belt, fumble and chase it through the loops, and finally succeed in wrestling herself under cover with all the sophistication of a game show contestant.

****

He knew it was rude but he...couldn't...stop...*staring*.

It was imperative to fill his eyes and mind with as much of her as possible, before this awkward situation came to a head, and one of them left for alternative accommodation.

Vidar knew she was the most beautiful woman he'd ever seen, but didn't understand why he felt this with such conviction. She was certainly nothing like the sort of women with whom he usually consorted. Petite and curvaceous rather than willowy and thin; she wore no make-up, clearly did nothing to her hair, did not bear any of the hallmarks of a body rendered out of proportion by plastic surgery, was evidently not in the first flush of youth – as slight crow's feet cut tiny lines through the tan around her eyes – but she was slim, shapely, compact, and powerful; body and limbs obviously toned by frequent practice of the sort of gymnastic exercise he'd just witnessed.

Her countenance was open, and the animation of curiosity still shone in her eyes. The slight pink flush to her cheeks and décolletage, whether from embarrassment, exertion, or the residue of the laughter, made him wonder if that's what she would look like during sex – bright eyes wide, cheeks flushed, beautiful body on show to him alone…

Suddenly realising he was fantasising about sex when she was standing feet from him, and expecting him to do something with the piece of paper she held out, Vidar swiftly took it, but didn't trust himself to reply in case he blurted something inappropriate. The silence extended painfully, until he managed to burble some incoherent nonsense about it being his mistake. All he could picture with any clarity was how easy it would be to reach forward, slide a fingertip under the strap of her lycra top, and inch it off the smooth shoulder – first one side, then the other…

His expression must have revealed a hint of his yearning, because the blue eyes widened in sudden comprehension, and she reached to pluck a cardigan from the back of the sofa.

Ashamed he'd obviously embarrassed her, Vidar was nevertheless entertained by her struggle to get into the garment and preserve some modicum of propriety from his predatory gaze. He had to get his unruly imagination under control! Just because he'd been longing for someone to be here – and what a someone! – didn't mean he had any claim on her, or any right to discomfit her with his unconcealed desire. She wasn't anything to do with him, wasn't here to welcome him home – in fact, his presence was doubtless unwelcome – and, in a matter of minutes, he would either be abandoned here to a lonely evening, seeking a hotel suite, or settling into the spare room at Stewart and Elaine's. Wherever he ended up, he'd be alone once more, with only the precious mental images he'd managed to capture of this captivating girl to sustain him through another solitary night.

****

Now quite clearly suppressing mirth at her ineptitude, the man wordlessly passed back her paper. Grace took it and returned it to her handbag, mortified by her lack of sophistication. It was always like this! Dominic spent a lot of time rolling his eyes at her and tutting. She tried so very hard to behave correctly, but seemed to have some sort of hopelessness-gene inherently preventing her from ever getting things right. Even this patient man was laughing at her! She was less embarrassed at what a show she was making of herself with her back to him, but surprised to still be able to feel the heat of the stare. It tracked up and down her like a laser beam, and made her turn swiftly to face him again. If she looked straight into those unusual grey eyes, propriety would surely prevent them roaming all over her at will as they had been doing.

She sought something to say, "You can't be wrong! It's your house. You decide who can be here…"

She didn't feel threatened by him, that wasn't it at all – but he was impossible to ignore, despite his stillness. He remained just inside the door, but the aura of his commanding presence filled the whole room as completely as if he'd been preceded by a fanfare of trumpets, a military parade, and a troupe of high-kicking, ostrich-feathered, sequin-covered dancing girls. He was clearly accustomed to being noticed. Confident in his skin, he resonated amusement, curiosity, what Grace detected as stimulation of a disconcerting kind and, she suddenly realised…incredible weariness… Perhaps he was standing so still because he was too shattered to manage anything else with adequate politeness? Grace imagined how it would feel to arrive home after a long time away, looking forward to a quiet and relaxing evening, only to find your private space invaded by a stranger, and then be expected to courteously tolerate their inconvenient presence when all you wanted to do was fall into bed and sleep for a week. Ever-solicitous, Grace promptly forgot her awkwardness, and ventured conspiratorially, "While we decide which of us isn't supposed to be here, shall I put the kettle on and you can have a sit down…only you seem pretty tired, if you don't mind me saying?"

****

Vidar was well-aware his fame endowed him with mysticism, suggesting he was a greater individual than the next man, and would deliver accordingly for the right partner. He was a rich seam to be mined for every nugget of favour. Even little Sonia had used him to show off unashamedly at every opportunity.

Expected to be magnanimous, affable, approachable, smile on command, never get tired, cold, hungry, or bored, and perform like a captive monkey whenever his input was demanded, whether he gave a damn about what he was doing or not, Vidar's feelings were usually the last to be taken into account; riches and adulation were considered sufficient compensation for the smothering of true identity by public persona. Therefore, having someone notice something about him – the real him, not the famous facsimile –

touched Vidar more than he was rationally able to explain. Hopelessly enchanted, he radiated unguarded delight, and surrendered to the unusual temptation to admit his very human weakness.

****

If possible, the man regarded her with even more intensity than before, and the confused half-smile slowly crinkled into a wide-mouthed grin of such genuine pleasure that Grace found herself twinkling up at him, quite helpless against its magnetism.

"I am tired. I've been travelling all day. You know what else? I'm starving. You don't have any food, do you?"

"Ooh, I've got plenty," breathed Grace, characteristically eager to please, "What would you like?"

"I don't care. Anything. I'm so hungry, I could eat you!" The man waggled his eyebrows at her and she giggled like a schoolgirl, shooting into the kitchen. Blushing hotly, she dived head first into the fridge to hide.

****

He didn't deserve this; a stranger who had disturbed her evening and couldn't stop ogling her like the wolf preparing to devour Red Riding-Hood, and yet she pottered industriously about the kitchen preparing a tray of tea just for him. Watching her move her agile curves around his house with such ease, as if she belonged there, tugged at his insides in a way he couldn't explain…not purely the lust he'd been battling for the last five minutes, but something greater, deeper, indefinable, and unfamiliar to him. He only knew he would stand and stare all evening if he could. A shy glance over her shoulder from behind the safety of the fridge door suggested his continued observation was making her uncomfortable. He forced his unwilling feet down the stairs to the sofa and flopped onto it, facing away, delivering her a break from his constant gawping.

He had to distract himself from the temptation to turn immediately, instead grabbing at the paperback on the table, anything to divert his attention.

****

"Any good?" He was asking about the book on the coffee table.

Grateful for a way to diffuse her increasing awkwardness, Grace responded with her accustomed enthusiasm, "Yeah, it is. It's by the chap who wrote Jaws. It's an old one about diving on Bermuda, secret drugs on a shipwreck, baddies, and voodoo…"

"Sounds all right," he scanned the cover blurb absently.

"I'm enjoying it. Sonia's Mum leant it to me."

"Ah…Margaret Flett," there was an edge to the calm voice, "The Boudicca of the north east. The most intimidating individual to inhabit Orkney since the Viking hordes arrived!"

Grace sniggered, "Not a fan of Mrs Flett?"

"Let's just say I live in abject terror of her."

"Of Margaret?"

"Don't get me wrong, I have the greatest respect for the woman…but in the way you'd respect a sleeping lion or a resting cobra…with the healthy awareness that at any moment they could strike!" He slapped the book down hard on the table at the final word, and swung round on the sofa, settling down at the opposite end so he could watch her again.

Before her nerve failed her once more under the heat of the stare, Grace wheedled, "So, was Sonia telling the truth then…?"

"About?" he stalled, coyly.

Grace twinkled a cheeky smile, fluttered her eyelashes, and disingenuously enquired, "About the two of you having a bit of a thing?" It was easier to be flirtatious with him by placing the ghost of Sonia between his intense gaze and her inadequately-dressed body, like a protective veil.

"A 'Thing'? Yeah, I suppose you could call it that. It was a few years ago now, when she was quite young and I was…old enough to know better. Hence my pathetic fear of Mag Flett. She blamed me for it all…The Thing…"

"Because you were old enough to know better."

"In her opinion."

"So, you don't see yourself as responsible?" teased Grace, only half-judgementally, remembering what Sonia had openly shared about her persistent pursuit of this singular and handsome man.

"If you're suggesting I took advantage of little Son…well, yes, I did, of course I did. I'm a man! We're not sensible like women are! We don't think about the consequences of things before we do them! If it's right there in front of us, we don't possess the self-control to say no!"

Grace was brought up short by the abrupt image of the text message, destined to remain forever-imprinted on her memory. Dominic certainly didn't have the self-control to say no. Concerned at the sudden change in her expression, assuming she was offended by his words, the man backpedalled frantically, "She was over eighteen! I didn't do anything to her she wasn't willing to have done! I didn't dump her or break her heart or anything like that. It just ran its course. If I was anything to her, it was probably a rite-of-passage. Every young girl has to have a Sugar-Daddy once in their lives, don't they?"

Grace placed the tray on the coffee-table, and occupied the same stretch of sofa out of habit, without considering their physical proximity. It had become her chosen reading spot; the position affording the best view down to the sea, and the place most frequently touched by the rays of the setting sun, warming her as she curled like a contented cat on the plump cushions.

She laughed incredulously, "Do they? I never had one... Think I'm past it now. Perhaps I got married too young?"

"You're married?"

Was he fearful her irate husband was about to appear from an adjoining room? She considered Dom, thought of the fact her 'phone was always switched on, battery charged...and yet no conciliatory call came, no text message begging her to return. Fixing her eyes on the stream of hot, dark tea surging from the pot's spout, Grace mumbled, "I'm shortly going to be...unmarried..."

"I'm very sorry to hear that."

As Grace handed over the mug of tea, she discovered he was smiling broadly.

"You don't look very sorry."

He shrugged, unembarrassed, "I'm a musician, not an actor."

Flushing, Grace shoved a plate of buttered barmbrack slices under his nose.

"I could eat all that."

She pushed the plate onto his lap, and took one slice from it, "Eat it, then."

The irrepressible grin enlivened his features again, "Thank you!" chewing enthusiastically and mumbling with full mouth, "This is delicious, did you make this?"

"Yes...there's nothing to it..." About to explain what was in it, Grace came to her senses. Shut up! He doesn't want to know the recipe!

"It's really lovely. You're very clever. I can't even boil an egg without instructions."

Unaccustomed to receiving praise for her culinary efforts, Grace glowed with pride.

"So, you're best friends with little Sonia Flett, huh?"

"Yes," said Grace very firmly. That was the only thing she was sure of right now. Everything else seemed to be rippling underneath her like an earthquake.

"How long have the two of you known one another?"

"Only about a month, I suppose. I met her on the ferry coming over here. She was a bit...unwell...and I just kept an eye on her as she was on her own. We got talking, found out we'd be living close to one another and...just...got on. Between you and I, I think she needed a friend – and I certainly did."

"Unwell...?" Was there a hint of merriment behind the steady expression?

"Well, um, yes...she was unwell..."

"It's ok, I've heard from a friend of mine about Sonia's very particular 'illness'."

"Ah. Sonia said word gets around fast up here."

"It sure does. You can't keep a secret for long…"

"Did you try to keep your relationship a secret?"

"The 'Thing'?" This time the glee danced clearly in his eyes, "Not really. I didn't go out of my way to tell anyone, but Son made sure to shout it from the rooftops to ensure there wasn't a soul around here who didn't know."

"How did that make you feel?"

He shrugged, "Unsurprised. I'm used to a lot of my life being public property. In fact, my time with Son was a lot more private than any other girlfriend I've had. Ok, half of Orkney knew, but the rest of world didn't."

"Is that really your life – everything out there for public consumption?"

"It can be. It isn't my choice necessarily, but sometimes that's the way it goes. Chase fame, and you have to accept all that goes with it!"

Grace smiled, "Do you miss Sonia?" She was idly playing with the concept of him caring for her proud but vulnerable little friend in a rekindled relationship. Sonia needed someone to look after her, regardless of what she might say to the contrary.

He registered genuine surprise at the question, "I hadn't thought of her at all, until I got back here and my friend mentioned to me that she was home and pregnant."

"What about now you know she's less than a mile away?"

Instead of snapping at Grace to mind her own business, he gave the invasive question measured consideration, "I'd like to see her, to make sure she's ok. It would be good to show her she's not alone, and her baby is a happy event – because, knowing Son, she won't see it that way – but it's not going anywhere, if that's what you mean. She's a beautiful girl, but it was all just a rush of blood to the head…"

"Literally," said Grace drily.

Vidar's eyes widened in surprise before he noticed the glint in hers, and tutted, chuckled, shook his head, "Is she ok?"

"She tries to be very jocular and blasé, but she's petrified. I feel for her. She seems very young to be doing everything alone. I try to be supportive but I don't have children. I have no clue what it feels like to be in her situation."

"I don't think you need to know, I suspect you just need to be less judgemental than her mother."

"You really can't stand Margaret, can you?"

"She's too quick to criticise everything Sonia does – but what has she achieved for herself? She's got narrow horizons, low expectations, all these high moral standards she herself has failed to live up to. You know she only married Euan Flett because she was pregnant with Sonia? Not as pearly-white as she'd like everyone to believe, huh? Perhaps she resents Son for going full-throttle in pursuit of the kind of life she never managed to achieve for herself? Perhaps she's vindictively pleased every time things don't work out? I'm not saying I know what goes through her mind…but I've always suspected she's jealous of her daughter, because Sonia's a go-getter and she isn't."

"I can't believe that's true."

"She's not evil or anything…but she's not what I'd call 'kind'…"

"Perhaps just not to irresponsible older men, who engage in scandalous behaviour with girls young enough to be their daughters…?"

"She was in her twenties! Besides, it's over."

"And you really don't feel anything for her at all?"

"Not what you mean…only…pity for the mess she seems to have found herself in. It's a bit of a tragic end to all her grand plans. I used to encourage her to go for things, because it seemed to me nobody else ever did, but perhaps I pushed her too hard? Perhaps she wasn't ready to take it all on, despite her bravado?"

"I think she is quite brave really; braver than I'll ever be."

"She's proud! If she made a mistake, she'd never admit it. She'd just keep plugging on regardless. You need to be capable of admitting when you've screwed up, but Sonia could never do that."

"She certainly can nowadays! All she seems to do is take on the blame for everything, and beat herself up. Perhaps she's changed a bit since you saw her last – grown up, because of what's happened to her?"

"Superior Sonia? I don't believe it for a second!"

"You'll have a chance to see for yourself, she's here nearly every day."

He regarded her in frank amazement, "But surely you're not suggesting…? I need to go, don't I?"

Grace's confidence stuttered like a candle flame in a draught, but she persevered with her new-found conviction that if it felt right, it was. Perhaps it was irresponsible to suggest he remain, but only a fool would let him go so easily!

Vidar felt a billion butterflies pirouette around his lungs, through his stomach, and up and down his suddenly-weak limbs, as she offered in a small voice, "You might disagree with this, but the way I see it – it's your house; you have more right to be here than anyone. You've obviously been working hard, and you need to unwind a bit. If you have no objection to me being here – I have paid and everything – then I don't see why we can't, um…share…?"

It occurred to Grace her suggestion might be misconstrued. She gabbled immediate clarification, "I mean, I'm in the guest room; I haven't been in your room! Well I went in there when I first got here – for a look, you know – but the pictures and everything…I felt as if I was intruding… I'm much happier in the guest room."

He was gaping at her, astonished, "Are you sure about this? I'm completely at fault here! I'm supposed to be in LA, and I changed my plans at the last minute. I didn't check it was ok. I blundered in and disturbed your vacation – "

"It's not really a holiday, " Grace corrected, "It's…"

What was it?

"I'm not actually sure how long I'm staying," Grace admitted.

"Well, that makes two of us. Perhaps, if you truly don't mind, we can be indecisive together, huh?" Again, she was treated to the cheeky grin, which had such a tumultuous effect on her when combined with the unwavering directness of the grey-eyed gaze.

Seeking to further reassure him she wasn't as mad as she appeared, Grace burbled, "I won't get in your way, I promise! I've had years of experience at being invisible. I'm not throwing wild parties or practising my opera-singing. I'm just pottering around doing a bit of reading, bit of yoga, bit of baking... I'm remembering who I use to be...and I'm trying to look after Sonia a bit. If it's the last thing I do, I'm determined to convince her Mum that being a Granny is a good thing, ideally before the baby's born."

Vidar regarded her appreciatively, "I'm sure if anyone can move the mountain of Margaret's disapproval, it's you."

"I'd like to help Sonia. She's helping me, and I want to return the favour." Pondering what Sonia's friendship was doing for her battered self-esteem, and the reason for its bruising, permitted Dominic to invade her thoughts. Unable to instantly drive away his malevolent image, she shivered involuntarily.

Vidar sat up, concern in his eyes, "You're cold! Shall I light the fire?"

Grace wasn't cold. She was completely comfortable in this well-insulated luxury, but she didn't want to tell him what had made her shiver.

As he stood, Grace yawned unselfconsciously, and stretched languorously across the cushions, unguardedly allowing her cardigan to fall open and display her lissom figure to him once more. Battling the temptation to slide his arms underneath her, and lift her body to his, Vidar swiftly put the coffee table between them, kneeling before the grate and scrabbling in the bottom of the log basket to unearth some newspaper. He concentrated hard on the job in hand, dismissing with difficulty the image of her back arching, pelvis pushing upward as she stretched.

The paper flared and caught, tongues of fire licking to blacken and burn the kindling, until a healthy spurt of flame soared with a guttering roar. Vidar wedged three large logs into the grate and pushed the door closed on the wood burner, nodding with satisfaction as the initial hungry surge, tempered momentarily by the heavier wood, settled gradually to a crackling blaze.

At the kitchen sink, washing the soot and newsprint from his hands, Vidar watched her refill their mugs from the teapot, and tug absently at her hairband, pulling to release the untidy knot of hair. Free of its twist of tight elastic, the brown tresses slithered over her shoulders and down her back. She circled her head slowly, as if her neck was stiff, and the skeins of softness tumbled and swung. Vidar gripped the tea-towel in one fist, and the edge of the cold granite worktop in the other, wondering how far he could take this…and how quickly…

Usually, he would sprint full-pelt towards the goal of gratification. He never felt disappointment or sadness when a faltering relationship invariably ended; only regret at the wasted time and effort. There was something unmistakeably different here. This woman wasn't a self-centred, materialistic marionette, but perceptive, considerate, positive, and approachable. He couldn't sit and have an easy-going conversation with the usual women, because they never ceased talking about themselves long enough for a response to be required. They certainly never articulated optimistic determination to improve the welfare of a friend, expressed anxious care for the comfort of a stranger, or presented rich, dark, fragrant, homemade fruit loaf oozing with creamy butter, and generously allowed said stranger to eat it all.

Leg curled underneath her, face turned towards the fire, she watched the hypnotic dance of the flames…and Vidar watched her for as long as he dared, before deciding the only way he'd know whether this had potential was to test the boundaries a little.

Returning to the sofa, he sat much closer to her than before, and awaited her reaction.

She looked round at him, surprised, as if in her fascination with the fire she hadn't noticed his passage across the room. Her smile was shy, but she made no comment about where he sat. Vidar casually extended a hand and gently brushed dextrous fingers through her hair, easing out the tufts of white wool caught here and there between the strands, "You have half the rug in your hair."

"Oh…" Grace giggled and touched her head uncertainly, "Is it gone?"

Her hair slipped smoothly over the back of his hand and tickled his wrist, sliding between his fingers like ribbons of silk. He wanted to sink both palms into the softness, push back her head, and touch his lips against the hollow of her throat, but he knew it was too fast, not right…this was too significant to rush. Unwilling to do so, he nevertheless stroked through the ends of her hair a final time, and murmured, "Gone."

"I must look a right state!"

"I don't know your name."

"Oh…no…it's Grace. Grace…um…" She thought of the wedding and engagement rings zipped into a pocket in her handbag, and struggled out the maiden name it felt odd to utter after twenty years of marriage, "Hamilton."

He held out his large hand and grasped hers; not a handshake exactly, but a gentle squeeze, his fingers lingering against her palm, and releasing her with seeming reluctance, "Vidar Rasmussen."

What could she say? Her knuckles tingled where his long fingers had stroked across her skin. She wanted him to hold her hand again. She wanted the deft, strong palm to cup her skull, as it had momentarily when he'd stroked the fibres from her hair, "Unusual name."

"It's Danish."

"You Vikings get everywhere, don't you? The original pioneers!"

"Yes, we do. Yes, we are!"

"I know there's a Danish connection here from a long, long time ago – are you an archaeology buff? Why Orkney?"

"I could ask you the same question."

"But if I tell you, you'll think I'm barmy. Everyone I've told thinks I'm crackers, even Sonia!"

"I've done some certifiably nuts stuff in my time, so, try me."

Grace touched fingertips to her lips, holding in the secret and considering whether to let it escape, before blurting, "My ex was serially unfaithful to me. He was either unable to control himself, or he just didn't want to."

She stopped abruptly, and shot a glance at Vidar, assessing the effect of this admission. Vidar said nothing, nodding slowly, accepting it; awaiting more.

"He made no effort to hide any of it, as if it didn't matter whether I found out or not, because I'd never have the guts to do anything about it one way or another. I cooked, I cleaned, I did what I was supposed to do as the dutiful wife, but my opinions meant nothing, and my feelings didn't matter. I'd always been faithful! Twenty years of marriage, and I'd been fully aware of his infidelity for at least ten of those years...and I think I knew it was going on before that too, although I didn't have any proof until he started using his mobile 'phone to organise his complicated sex life. I know it's wrong to read another person's messages behind their back...but..."

"It's more wrong to disrespect your wife like that." Vidar spoke quietly, but with an edge of anger to his voice. Who was he cross with; her, for prying, or Dominic, for lying?

"You could argue if I hadn't looked, I wouldn't have known – blissful ignorance! My friend Fen says all men do it, and I shouldn't care so much...but I'm convinced my husband had screwed her too, so I could never say for sure who's side she was on!" Grace struggled out a high-pitched, slightly hysterical giggle she swallowed abruptly when it started to sound like a sob.

Vidar moved his body closer, but didn't touch her. He simply asked in his straightforward, placid way, "So, you put up with it for all that time, looked the other way and just kept going...what happened to suddenly change everything? What's intolerable today that was tolerable yesterday?"

The green text-message bubbles popped into her vision, and floated in the fire as she stared at the flames. Why didn't they catch alight and burn to nothing?

"He got a particular message…and it implied something much more serious than a bit of casual sex. It suggested he was preparing to start a new life with one of these women. Something inside of me sort of…cracked. All that time, all that patience; all that loyalty in the face of such blatant disregard, but I was going to be discarded all the same, like worn out shoes or broken glasses. I knew the time had come to leave, to make a grand gesture to indicate I'd had enough of his revolting treatment of me! So, here I am."

"This is your grand gesture – Orkney at the start of winter?"

"I got it a bit wrong," snuffled Grace, fingers pressing uncertainly against her lips again, regretting they'd let so much information out, "The thing to do, of course, would have been to kick him out, wouldn't it…but instead I kicked myself out! How very obliging of me. I just had to be where he wasn't. I couldn't spend another day in his company."

"But why pick Orkney? You could have 'obligingly' removed yourself to Bali, or Tahiti, or the south of France?"

"I didn't pick it. It picked me. I've forgotten how to make decisions…in fact, I'm not sure I ever knew how until I got here and there was no one to defer to. I was sitting in a café down the road from my house…not because I wanted to be there, but because I thought if I was out in public, I couldn't do myself a mischief. Someone had left one of those wanderlust-type trendy magazines on the table. It had the most beautiful picture I think I've ever seen on the cover – untouched beach, white sand, clear sea, lilac sky – and I just had this potty plan that the only way to prevent myself disappearing completely was to make a mark somewhere which would resonate with meaning for me. I so desperately wanted to press my bare feet into that sand at the water's edge, and leave a trail of footprints. I knew they'd be washed away with the next tide but I would know they'd been there! I would know I'd had the guts to see through something I'd decided upon independently and spontaneously! I could leave him and live, rather than just existing! I vowed I'd go – then and there – and it should be a vow I couldn't break. I thought it looked as if it might be Southern Europe, or the Far East…but when I opened the magazine and read the article…"

Vidar chuckled, "It was Orkney."

"Yep. Typical me! Devote wholeheartedly to something in a romantic waft of fantasy without checking the facts, and then realise I've stitched myself right up…sort of describes my marriage too. I commit, and then can't back out because it feels as if I'm cheating, letting everyone down. I get into all sorts of terrible messes by leaping first and thinking later…but this time I really had to come, because I knew if I didn't, life would convulse around me, and I would just vanish."

"If he had left you for another woman, you could have begun again, in your home, with all your familiar things around you. It would have hurt, but you didn't have to be the one to go."

"It's his world, not mine. Everything is the way he expects it to be. The pattern of my day is dictated by his. Nothing is my choice, my taste. I got married so young, and sacrificed so much of myself to trying to make it work, I wouldn't have known how to begin again, not there. I'm glad I came here! I don't regret it at all! It's done, dusted. This is a new life for me now."

"Hasn't he been on the 'phone, begging you to reconsider?"

"I told a mutual friend where I was, ages ago. She said she'd tell him. He hasn't called...not once. I'm not upset. If anything, I'm relieved. I want to concentrate my energies on starting afresh. This is a big thing for me. I was controlled for so long."

"How did you feel when you got to your beach? Satisfied?"

"I haven't been."

"But it's why you came!"

"I know – stupid, eh?"

"I can't believe you haven't been!"

"I just..." Grace tried to think of a good reason, couldn't, and slumped dejectedly, staring into the fire with an expression of such hopelessness Vidar felt compelled to rescue her, "Do you know where it is, what it's called?"

"It's called the Sands of Wright...or something like that."

"Yeah, I know it. It's at Hoxa Head, almost all the way down the other end of the mainland...big, wide beach."

In a small voice, Grace mumbled apologetically, "I don't really know why I haven't been..."

Vidar stretched his long legs out across the coffee table, wiggling his socked toes, "Well, that's tomorrow's agenda sorted then."

"What?"

"Forecast is good tomorrow. Cold, of course, but sunny. We'll have to check the tide, but I think we're going to the beach!"

"Are we?"

"Yep!"

"Oh…ok."

The mesmerising gaze alighted on her again, capturing her like an escapee prisoner in the beam of a searchlight, causing her to fidget mightily.

"What is the matter with you?"

"You're…" She moved the empty cups around the table, placed them on the tray, took them off again, "You're very direct. You make me feel a bit…a bit…"

"A bit…?"

"Flustered," confessed Grace, unable to prevent the hot blush spreading, jumping as she accidentally clinked the mug clutched in her shaking hand against the obstacle of the teapot.

Grace had quite forgotten what it was like to feel anything but ignored. Directed at her, Vidar Rasmussen's very rapt attention was therefore both exhilarating, and terrifying.

Vidar slid even closer. She could feel the radiating warmth of him. Still he didn't touch her, "Want to know a secret?"

Grace held her breath, and trembled with thrilling trepidation, "Um…"

"You make me feel pretty flustered too."

"Ohhhh…."

Playing distractedly with a section of hair, twisting it around her finger, Grace peeked at him from beneath downturned lashes, and mumbled, "I feel even more embarrassed now."

The engaging grin reappeared, along with another low, slow chuckle, "You've nothing to be embarrassed about."

"Hmmm..." Grace flicked her hair with pretended nonchalance, but couldn't answer.

"Look, I'm dead on my feet," he gestured behind him with a thumb towards the Master Bedroom, "If you're really sure it's ok for me to be here, I'm gonna turn in..."

"Oh, of course, yes! You were shattered when you got here, and then you had to sit and listen to me harping on about my mess of a marriage!"

"Don't be silly. Divorce is a huge upheaval after such a long time with someone. When life gets turned on its head, you need to offload some of the stress. If you explain it to another person, it helps make sense of your own feelings about it."

"You're very kind...very patient."

"You don't understand how nice it is not to come back to another cold, dark, empty house. It's a real privilege to be fed. and looked after; to sit, relax, and talk to someone openly about their life. It's something I never get the chance to do, so thank you for being here, and for not calling the cops on me."

"Why would I do that?"

"I'm not supposed to be here."

"It's your house," insisted Grace, forcefully.

He winked at her, "It's *our* house."

Grace's whole body instantly turned to cooked spaghetti, and she feared sliding off the sofa into a soggy heap on the floor.

Vidar yawned, "I'm going to bed. Big day tomorrow. We've someone's epic life-changing journey to complete."

Grace began to pile the crockery onto the tray. Vidar touched her arm lightly, barely at all, "Leave it. I'll do it in the morning. You've done everything."

Accustomed to doing as she was told, Grace promptly ceased tidying and stood abruptly, at the very same time Vidar eased to his feet. Turning, Grace discovered her body was centimetres from his and, paralysed by awkwardness, stared fixedly at his broad chest, and frantically mined her blank brain for a suitably polite way to bid him goodnight.

Vidar bent his head close to hers, and Grace was convinced he was about to kiss her. She felt alternately hot, then cold, tilting back her head, and fixing her wide eyes on the beams of the ceiling, holding her quivering body in check by counting the knots in the planks of wood. She tensed, anticipating the pressure of his lips against her skin but, mouth close enough to her ear that she could feel the warmth of his breath, he simply whispered, "By the way, I don't think you're invisible at all. I'm very aware of every delicious inch of you. See you in the morning."

His body passed her, missing by millimetres, and was behind the barrier of his bedroom door before Grace recovered her composure sufficiently to drop her eyes from the ceiling. With shaking hands and shuddering legs, she tottered towards her bedroom, fumbling with her paperback, already knowing she could spend all night reading, but wouldn't take in a single word.

EIGHT

It had taken Grace a long time to settle, and what sleep she'd managed had been fitful, disturbed by erotic dreams. The vivid picture of Vidar's handsome face crinkling into his captivating smile; the feel of strong, directing masculine hands sliding into her hair, cupping her head, powerful arms supporting the weight of her surrendering body; a naked male torso illuminated in flickering firelight, reaching her fingers out to touch, before raising her head and finding she was looking not into Vidar's kind, grey eyes, but into the face of her husband, whose mouth twisted in a spiteful smile, delighted to have confounded her bubbling hopes.

She lay on her back in the centre of the large bed and stared up at the sloping ceiling, listening to the unfamiliar early-morning sounds of Vidar moving about the house beyond her bedroom door.

Her Orcadian routine consisted of pottering in her dressing gown, absently spooning in mouthfuls of cereal while she waited for the kettle to boil.

However, given yesterday evening – the 'every delicious inch' declaration that had awoken such tumult within her – perhaps popping out in just a robe wasn't the most sensible course of action? Potentially, she shouldn't risk an appearance until showered, dressed and looking both more presentable than yesterday, and better-protected from the efficient penetration of that searching gaze.

A soft knock at the door made her gasp, and lurch bolt upright.

"Grace? You awake?"

Naked, oblivious to the chill outside the covers, Grace crawled on hands and knees to the end of the bed, and stared at herself in the long dressing mirror behind the door. Her worst fears were confirmed. Messy hair and pale skin; squinting, puffy eyes – she'd needed the hours of settled sleep that had eluded her.

"Grace…?"

The door handle edged downwards, and Grace frantically scurried back up the bed and under the covers as Vidar cautiously entered, preceded by a breakfast tray.

Grace tugged the layers of sheet, blanket, and eiderdown around her body as tightly as she could, clamping the bunch of covers under her armpits to hold them in position, and hastily pushed a hand through her hair, trying to make herself look less like a scarecrow.

"Good morning. Did I wake you?"

"No…no…I was awake."

"Sleep ok?"

Confessing a night of semi-sexual desires about one's host doubtless wasn't wise when only protected by three layers of bedclothes. As Grace suspected the shrewd eyes could read her every thought, she opted for economy with the truth rather than a blatant lie, "Tossed and turned a bit. How about you?"

"Crashed out within ten seconds of my head hitting the pillow. It was probably my snoring that disturbed you."

Grace demurred, "I couldn't hear you snoring."

"Good. Well, we'll battle the wind this morning, and you can spend all afternoon dozing in front of the fire…catch up on the sleep you missed."

He placed the tray next to her on the bed, and sat down on the far corner of the mattress without asking permission, keen eyes fixed on her, "Are you sure it wasn't because you were disturbed by the idea of me being here? I can always get a hotel. Just say. I won't be offended."

How could she explain it was exactly because she was disturbed by him being here! Unable to answer his question in a way that wouldn't betray her thoughts, Grace fell back once again on indisputable fact, "It's your house."

Vidar smiled, "Ok. Up to you. If you change your mind, just say."

"It's fine."

"Good. I'm glad, I can't deny it."

The serious, steady, direct eye contact turned her well-exercised limbs to bits of wet string. Discomfited, she was unable to do anything but blush beetroot and look anywhere but into those soft eyes, silver as moonlight on the wetland water, "You delight in embarrassing me!"

"No, that's not it at all…you just get embarrassed so easily."

"I'm not used to people being as…upfront with me as you are."

He shrugged, "I've always said what I think. Maybe it's a Rasmussen family thing, maybe it's a Danish thing…maybe it's just a 'me' thing? Whatever it is, I can't change now. I just struggle to see what you have to be embarrassed about, that's why I find it kinda funny."

Grace sighed, washed over with futility. She was the wrong side of forty, discarded by her husband, the best years of her life behind her. What did she have to offer any man, particularly such a man as this, "The scruffy way I look? My complete lack of sophistication in every situation?"

He shook his head firmly, "It's not really such a huge surprise your self-confidence has been undermined after twenty years of disrespect by the one man who's supposed to value you above everything else. It'll come back though...and, in the meantime, you should stop worrying so much. Be who you are...because who you are is just fine – more than fine."

Grace smiled shyly, gratefully, and whispered, "Thank you."

He gestured at the tray, "Eat your breakfast. I didn't know what you'd want, so I guessed."

Grace thought about an early morning in her London home, Dominic shovelling in food she'd arisen specially to prepare for him, observing him as they silently sat feet away from one another at the table, her husband not even lifting his eyes from the newspaper to acknowledge her effort; escaping from the house as soon as he was physically able, abandoning her to the monotonous emptiness of a day alone, nothing to look forward to but the careful preparation of yet another unappreciated meal, resignedly weathering the sting of neglect like a paper cut across her heart.

"I've never had breakfast in bed before!"

"You're kidding?"

"No..."

"I'm not sure it'll meet high expectations."

"It will," said Grace, with childlike earnestness, "It definitely will."

Stirred by the simple affirmation, Vidar distracted himself from the instant desire to kiss her by pouring two steaming mugs of tea from the pot on the tray. Grace forked a square of syrup, fruit, and cream-covered pancake into her mouth and nodded, "Yummy."

"I checked; low tide is tennish, so if we go soon you'll have acres of beach to play on before it turns."

Grace giggled, unsure, "You're not messing about, are you?"

"No. You've come here to make a point, so make it! This is where we're going," Vidar picked up an Ordnance Survey map from the tray and unfolded it across the bed, pointing with the end of his fork, "This is where we are, and this is your beach."

"My beach..." Forgetting her vice-like grip on the bedclothes, excited at finally seeing one of her secret dreams come true, Grace leant forward to study the map and didn't notice the steady downward slide of the covers across her breasts and past her waist to settle at her hips. Several seconds elapsed before she became aware of the chill, and happened to look down. Horrified to behold the bare skin of her own stomach, Grace gasped aloud and hoiked up the blankets, making the crockery clink together loudly as the sharp tug on the covers disturbed the tray. Vidar, occupied by the map, glanced up, registered the shock on Grace's face, noted her exaggerated clutching of the covers, and crowed, "I can't believe I missed that! Do it again!"

Amazed at how relaxed and confident she sounded, Grace heard herself laugh aloud and shake her head firmly, "Oh no…that was a one-time-only unveiling!"

"And I was reading the stupid map…" Vidar shook his head in pantomime regret, and stabbed at another square of pancake, a caricature of utter dejection.

Grace took a sip of her tea, and hid her smile behind the safety of the mug as she murmured, "You'll have to be quicker than that to catch me!"

Vidar grinned and scooped a dollop of syrup off his plate with a forefinger, "Stop flirting, I'm trying to be on best behaviour. Eat up. Let's get moving while it's low tide. Wear everything you own – it's gonna be freezing on your beach."

****

The wind blew so forcefully off the sea that Grace struggled to push open the passenger door of Vidar's car, wrestling against invisible pressure to ease the door sufficiently wide to wriggle out. The moment her feet touched the grass, a gust snatched the handle from her gloved fingers and slammed it shut again, "Oh!"

Vidar shot around the side of the car in response to her shout, "You ok?"

"Yeah. The wind got the door. I just wasn't expecting it."

She shivered, jogged on the spot, and swung her arms back and forth, "It's so cold!"

"It's Orkney. It's December. Right," Vidar held her shoulders and gently rotated her to face the full force of the north-easterly wind, "This is your beach. This is what you gave up your old life for."

The wind was so strong it stretched her skin slowly across her cheekbones. She tugged her bobble hat down more firmly over her ears. The exposed ends of her long hair whipped and danced, "I am a nutcase, aren't I?"

"No comment. Come on."

Taking her hand as if he'd been doing so for decades, Vidar led her down the sand dunes, the wiry grasses dipping and rising rhythmically like the necks of courting swans. Halfway down the dune, a section of missing bank dug out by the violence of another winter's battering presented a more-sheltered hollow, protection from the severity of the driving wind. Vidar curled himself into it. Without thinking it was a small seat for two people, Grace wriggled in beside him and found they were pressed together, leaning shoulder-to-shoulder, hip-to-hip, knee-to-knee. The rounded, grass-covered edges of their shallow cave directed the wind across them rather than full into their faces, as they snuggled in companionable silence watching fluffy, white clouds scudding across the blue sky as the low winter sun slowly climbed.

"It's actually very nice," said Grace, with characteristic positivity, "Out of the wind, it's pretty pleasant – sun's out, white sand, nature, peace…"

"Oh yeah, it's lovely. I can't feel my face," teased Vidar, deadpan.

Grace rolled her eyes in mock frustration, "Well, you live here!"

"Yeah, but not all the time. I live in California too."

"You Vikings are supposed to be used to the cold – hardened to it!"

"Nearly thirty years on the West Coast has softened this Viking up a bit."

"If you don't like the cold, why come here in the winter?"

"Something told me not to go to LA. I felt pulled to Orkney instead. I must have known you were here."

That look again – and Grace thought her rapidly-beating heart might burst out of her chest and roll down the dune into the fine sand at the bottom.

"You're kind to me, you know…bringing me here, making me do this. It feels right, yet I never would have done it on my own. I suppose you already knew that? You knew I wouldn't come unless you brought me?"

Vidar shrugged non-commitally, and concentrated very hard on the horizon. Grace's curiosity was piqued by his reluctance to engage, "Why are you on your own? You seem to me to be a fundamentally good person…and yet you're alone. The pictures on the shelves are of you and your brothers with little kids – nieces and nephews?"

"One niece, two nephews…my middle brother's children. My little brother's gay – no children."

"Right. You and your brothers look quite alike."

"I always think we're very different! I'm a lot older than them. There's ten years between my middle brother and I, and fifteen between me and my baby brother. I'm the mixture between my parents, sort of nondescript. Ragnar is like my Dad – a proper Viking – gigantic and tough-looking; blonde, blue eyes, big beard! Jannick is like my Mom – little and slight; dark hair, brown eyes…but Jannick's the butch one."

"I thought Jannick was the gay one?"

"Yeah, but he's the butch one as well. It's funny. Ragnar the fearsome giant is a Geology professor – just stares at rocks and gives lectures all day. I basically show off for a living…and Jannick lives in South America with his very macho boyfriend Diego, and breeds cows, and rides horses. He's a proper, tough cowboy!"

"That's not conforming to stereotype, is it?"

"I don't know…but he's very happy with his life. All those men's men in leather trousers camping out together…it's the gay equivalent of locking me in a strip joint for the weekend. His eyes must be out on stalks the whole time."

"Except when Diego's watching."

"Right! Actually, they have a good relationship. Jannick went travelling after college, met him, and they've been together ever since. They're solid. They're in love. I kind of envy him the ease with which he found The One. Of the three of us, Jannick has the secure, successful relationship. Ragnar's been through one marriage already and is on to the second…and as for me!"

"That's what I was going to say…there's not even an old picture of you with a woman, a past wedding photograph, nothing…"

"My so-called relationships last twenty seconds. There isn't time to get a camera out and take a picture before it's all over."

"But why? I just can't see why it wouldn't work out. You're kind, approachable, you do breakfast in bed, you're very direct so they'd never be in any doubt about where they stood! You're good-looking, you're obviously successful – there should be a queue around the block!"

It was Vidar's turn to blush, uncharacteristically embarrassed by the fervour of Grace's outburst. Bashfully averting his face, he tugged distractedly at a tuft of hardy grass with his gloved hand, "I have a lot of baggage. Perhaps my reputation precedes me? Maybe they don't want to get too involved?"

"When you get to middle-age, everyone has baggage!" Grace again pictured Dominic shoving food into his mouth and staring fixedly at the FT next to his breakfast plate, as if even accidentally catching her imploring eye would turn him to stone.

"No, I've got proper baggage – airport carousel's-worth of it!"

"Like what?"

Vidar screwed up his face and didn't look at her, eventually offering in a quiet voice, "If I tell you about my past, you'll swiftly revise your much-too-kind assessment of my character."

"Tell me anyway," urged Grace impulsively, turning her body fully towards him in the confined space. Vidar felt how impossible it would be to refuse her anything.

He moistened his lips, nervous of having to speak, fixed his eyes on the waving grass beyond his outstretched feet, and stated unemotionally, "I was a drug addict when I was younger. It's well-documented. My antics were all over the press at the time; maybe not here, but certainly at home in Denmark, all over Scandinavia, Northern Europe, the States…every bit of my dirty laundry got an airing at some point. I started travelling and performing when I was still a teenager, so by the time I was into my twenties, my reputation as a hellraiser was well-established. I had too much money and too much freedom. I was bad for the sake of it. I used to do outrageous stuff just to get a reaction. I guess I thought if people were talking about me, it made me important."

He sighed, sounding exhausted, "I had a kid with some girl who was as messed-up as I was. I was so wasted I didn't even remember the act! I denied it was anything to do with me. When the baby came, it was drug-dependant. The DNA test said it was mine – irrefutable – and I'd been all over the media for six months or more denying my ass off, protesting my innocence, bleating I was being targeted because of my fame…when in fact I was just too screwed-up to remember who I'd had sex with. Talk about shameful! I saw the baby in the hospital when he was a couple of hours old. They let me hold him. He was tiny, really sick. He had all these tubes coming out of him. I'll never forget how terrible he looked. They told me he was unlikely to last the night. I went to a bar in LA, got completely out of my face, and waited for the call to come. It never did. He made it through the first night, and the next, and the next; a month, three months, a year. He's twenty-eight now."

"Wow! He's a survivor then!"

"He is."

"Do you see him often?"

"I've never seen him…apart from that one time…"

"I don't understand."

"I was a teenager – I was nineteen – I was an addict; a disgusting mess. I couldn't look after myself, let alone care for a child. My lawyer dealt with it all. My company bought them a house, gave his mother an allowance, put her through rehab umpteen times, paid for the Nanny, the school fees, his college, bought him a condo when he was twenty-one…"

"What does he do? Is he married or anything; are you a grandad?"

"I don't know. I know nothing about him except his date of birth, and that his mother named him Zachary. I've deliberately kept my distance, for my sake and his. I don't know where he lives, what he does, if he's married or a father, gay or straight. Legally, I stopped paying for him when he was twenty-one, so my company's involvement with him ended there…same as the allowance to his waster of a mother. She never really quit the booze or anything, and she used to sell made-up stories about me to the newspapers. The way to shut her up was to stop her allowance until she retracted the story. Not the most decent way to carry on, but it used to do the trick."

"Weren't you curious about him?"

"No…at the time, all I was curious about was where my next fix was coming from."

"And now?"

"Now, insurmountable guilt destroys any hint of curiosity. Any amends I might wish to make would be too little, too late. He's a grown man with a life to live. He doesn't need to waste his time pandering to his selfish, absent father. He needs me in his life like he needs an audit from the IRS. I feel for him. It can't have been easy – your mother's a skank and all you know about your playboy Dad is what you read in the papers. He must hate me, and I don't begrudge him the right to do so. I deserve it."

"But that's the past. You don't do that stuff now, right?"

"Nope. Seventeen years clean and sober."

"See! That's half his lifetime! You could build a bridge – "

"I don't think so, Grace. I think it's too late…too much has happened for me to ever be able to look him in the eye. Can you imagine how lame an apology would sound, after all he's doubtless been through because of being related to me?"

"It's a start…" mumbled Grace.

"No." Vidar's voice was quiet, but the firmness in his tone brooked no argument, "I think that's why there's no queue. People look at me and they think I'm still the old Vidar – the naughty kid – and I am that guy, of course. I just have a lot more self-control than I ever had when I was young. Life's taught me a lot of hard lessons, and I've tried to learn from them."

"So, what was the final straw that got you off the drugs?"

"I nearly died…I got locked in secure rehab, like jail, and I just had to stay there until I got better. When I got out, I had to change my life, so I stopped all the months holed up in tour buses killing time between gigs with girls and booze. I bought a couple of houses instead of living in hotels all the time. I put some roots down, and tried to stabilise myself. I started doing a lot more writing, producing, composing; much less travelling, fewer live performances…it made it easier to get into a routine, keep my mind occupied, not look for mischief because I was at a loose end. I've made a life I like, and I've rebuilt my trashed reputation. I get respect for my work now, and recognition. The only thing that's not great is my post-drugs life is pretty lonely."

"You're a survivor too," stated Grace, simply, "Your son must get it from you – the Viking invincibility gene!"

"Perhaps." He didn't like her mentioning the child. He flinched every time she alluded to him.

"You strike me as a strong-willed person – that's why you're so successful. You're very determined."

"Or too pig-headed to know when I'm beaten."

Grace rested against him, and tilted her head towards his, whispering, "I like determined better."

Vidar smiled and nudged her with his shoulder, the weight behind the push making her body rock away and fall back against him again, "Speaking of determined…take your shoes off."

"What?"

"Take your shoes off."

"It's December!"

"You wanted to walk on a pristine beach, leave your footprints, make your mark. This is the beach. It's empty…no one will see you being crazy…go right ahead."

"It's freezing!"

"I'm not saying get naked, I'm saying take your shoes off."

"I'll get all sandy!"

"You come all this way, and turn your life upside down because of one picture in a magazine. You embark on this whole, big adventure to change how you feel about yourself, and yet you won't do the one thing that brought you in the first place? You have to do it…otherwise, why are you here?"

"Are you going to do it with me?"

"This is *your* odyssey, not mine. If I do it with you, it will take all the significance away. No, I'm going to sit here in my thermal socks and my nice, warm boots, and watch you freeze your toes off in the Pentland Firth. You're the lunatic here, not me!"

"I can't believe you're wimping out!" Grace baited, suddenly afraid of being on the huge expanse of sand without him.

"It's not my crazy idea, I told you. You picked a beach in Orkney to run away to at the start of winter. I would have made sure to choose a beach in the Caribbean."

He was teasing her, challenging her, issuing a dare she couldn't back away from.

"Get on with it," Vidar tapped the dial of his expensive watch with a gloved finger, "I'm waiting…" Waiting. Not going anywhere. Observing, protecting, supporting…but without declaring any of that aloud, so he could deny he'd been doing any such thing, and she could kid herself she was doing this alone. Perhaps because of the chaos of his past, mellowed, empathetic Vidar realised one sometimes needed a little encouraging shove in the right direction.

Before she had time to consider the wisdom of paddling in the sea north of Scotland three weeks before Christmas, Grace wiggled out of the security of their sandy cave and into the constantly-surprising force of the wind. She tugged at the laces of her trainers, loosening them and sliding her feet free, breeze whistling through the fabric and chilling her toes as she pulled off her socks and pushed them into the tops of her shoes, "Look after them for me."

Standing and rolling up each leg of her jeans to just below the knee, the frigid air whirled around the exposed skin, making it tighten until each hair follicle stood to attention, prickling with cold.

With one delighted, toothy beam in Vidar's direction, Grace turned and surrendered to the hill, gathering momentum as her bare feet skipped from sharp, scratchy seaside grass to soft, fine sand. Eventually, she landed with flat fleet on the unyielding surface of the beach proper, and used the grip of the firm ground to drive power through her strong legs and flexible feet, speeding full-pelt towards the far-off sea. The sprint warmed her body but, as she got closer to the water, the sand, corrugated into hard ripples by the driving wind and receding tide, whacked unevenly against the underside of her feet, and disrupted her stride pattern. Feet hurting as they slapped over the ridges, making her stumble, she eased her brisk pace to a jog, and became aware of the shock of the cold water every time it splashed across her feet and up her calves. The constant wind raked the flat sand until her legs and feet began to burn with the extremity of the chill. Paddling into the first few inches of sea was a relief, the water giving her chapped skin some respite from the unforgiving blast.

Looking down at her barely-submerged feet, Grace could see they were white with cold. The skin seemed tight, and each individual toe appeared pinched and small, not chubbily rounded as they usually were. Fumbling off a glove and pulling her 'phone from her jacket pocket, Grace took a picture of her frozen feet in the ice-cold, clear water, then padded out to the water's edge, relishing the throbbing of her skin as proof of the reality of her experience. A metre or two from the gently-lapping waves, head-down, Grace became totally absorbed in the task of creating the perfect trail of footprints across the creamy-grey sand, photographing them on her 'phone with the vague determination that an artwork lurked behind the images, when she felt brave enough to ride out any ridicule and create something that could do justice to the promise of this new beginning. Deciding she would make a film of the panorama, Grace upturned her 'phone screen, beginning her scene with the low-angled winter sun blinding the camera lens in the unseasonably-vibrant blue. Gradually lowering the 'phone to take in the horizon, the headland, and capture the stretch of truly-deserted sand, Grace turned gradually back towards the hollow and the waiting figure of Vidar, suddenly consumed by the excitement of possessing him on film. Smoothly running the camera across the bank of dunes, pleased the film captured the wildly waving grass and the authentic howl of the perpetual wind, Grace stared fixedly at the screen, thrilling to the anticipation of seeing him appear at any moment. Unease swirled in her stomach as he failed to materialise in the little square. Not wanting to ruin the otherwise pleasant rhythm of her film, Grace continued panning, but now with beating heart and churning guts, past their hollow and further along the dune. Had he left her; a spiteful judgement upon her childishness? Was she being derided as thoroughly here as she'd ever been at home? Distressed, Grace instantly felt foolish, freezing, sick, and miserable. Dismayed she'd read it all so wrong, as usual, Grace was about to abandon her movie and rush back up the beach, when her peripheral vision caught a movement on the top of the dune. Slowly directing the camera further, Grace couldn't suppress a delighted gasp as she spotted him. He hadn't left her! She zoomed in until his body filled the screen. He was fetching something from the car. As he closed the boot and turned, Grace realised it was a towel. He looked up towards her, beheld her filming, grinned, and beckoned. She noticed her trainers sitting on the vehicle's roof and felt a rush of something within her, but didn't understand exactly what it was; a catching of breath in her mouth, the constriction of her throat, the exaggerated pounding of her heart. She wanted to throw herself on the sand and sob until spent, but at the same time desired to run in circles, faster and faster, jumping and whirling and screaming with ecstasy.

She could do this! She was doing it! And she was doing it because of the man standing at the top of that dune with a towel for her wet feet, waiting for her to return to him.

It ceased to matter to Grace that she hadn't filmed full circle around the bay and back to the winter sun. She'd reached Vidar…and nothing beyond mattered as much as getting back to him as soon as possible. Stopping her film, and shoving her 'phone into her pocket, Grace pelted up the beach as fast as she could, powerful onshore wind at her back propelling her along. She scrambled energetically up the dune, the feeling returning to her numb feet and legs as a burning, grating heat like the itch of a chilblain.

Arriving in front of Vidar breathless, beaming and windswept, she appeared to him exactly as she had last night – flushed cheeks, dancing eyes, happy countenance.

"I thought you'd frozen solid."

"Was I ages?"

"Yeah."

"Oh…sorry…"

"It's fine, you don't have to apologise to me. You were having fun, jumping about, making your footprints…"

"Oh God," Grace groaned and buried her face in her hands, "I'm forty-two. I need to get a grip, don't I?"

"I'm forty-seven, and you should see the pranks we all play on each other when we're backstage at gigs. I can act my age when it matters, but I'm damned if I'm doing it all the time! How many toes fell off in the sea?"

Grace curled her feet, "By the feel of it, all of them."

"Come here."

He reopened the boot and indicated Grace should sit on the tailgate, wrapping the towel around her feet and resting them against his thighs as he rubbed off the wet sand.

"Ohhhh…they're burning now!"

Vidar reached up for her shoes and socks, "Put these on – at least you'll warm up a bit and then you can wash off the rest when we get home."

He held one small, chilled foot in both his big, warm palms as Grace bent the other leg and wrestled an unwilling sock onto her salty, sticky, alien-feeling extremity.

"You're so cold! I didn't expect you to be that long."

Despite the dull ache in her foot, Grace loved being securely cupped between his fingers.

"I thought you'd run down there, get a millimetre into the water, scream, and run straight back again, but you were over half an hour..."

"I wasn't! It felt like two minutes!"

"You're much tougher than I gave you credit for...and you certainly squeezed as much from that as you could."

Grace jumped to the ground, wincing, "God, my feet are agony!"

Laughing, Vidar shut the boot, "Come on, let's go home and warm up."

****

As they drove across one of the Churchill bridges, even Vidar's big car wavering in its lane as the relentless wind pushed powerfully against it, Grace stared wonderingly at the rusting hulks exposed by the low tide, weighing up whether to blurt out what was uppermost in her mind, feeling the need to share with him as he had been so prepared to do with her. Turning from the majesty of Scapa Flow to contemplation of Vidar's chiselled profile, she murmured, "For a minute, I thought you'd gone."

"Huh?" Vidar turned down the radio and glanced at her, "What?"

"When you went to the car, I looked back at the dune where I expected to see you, and you weren't there. I was suddenly afraid you'd left me...to teach me a lesson for being so stupid..."

Vidar gaped at her, realised he wasn't concentrating, and snapped his attention back to the narrow road, "Grace, why would that even cross your mind?"

In a small voice, Grace breathed, "It's the kind of thing my husband would have done. He used to leave me places when he said

I was being an embarrassment. I think he believed a short, sharp dose of abandonment-panic would bring me back into line…"

Vidar shook his head in astonishment, "An embarrassment? What the hell kind of a way is that to treat your wife? Grace, I'm aware you don't know me, and I don't know you…but you should understand one thing – whatever I am, I'm definitely not your husband. I would never dream of treating anyone that way!"

"No," said Grace, distantly, gazing across the wind-rippled water, "You didn't leave. You got me a towel. You dried my feet and tried to warm them up. You encouraged me to pursue my scheme. However daft you might have thought it, you entered into it with me. You showed me I should go for things instead of being too frightened…and I felt free for the first time in as long as I can remember. No, Vidar, you're definitely not my husband…and, from where I'm sitting, that's a one hundred per cent good thing."

****

When they got back to *Somerled* and peeled off their layers of coats, scarves, and hats in the hallway, Vidar shivered and said, "I feel freezing now too, and I didn't have my feet in the ocean!"

Grace smiled sheepishly, "It was stupid, wasn't it?"

"But you did what you said you would…and that's not stupid, is it? I'll light the fire and we can have some lunch. This time of year, the days go so quickly."

"I've been sleeping so much," confessed Grace, "because it's pitch black by four."

"That's why when the sun does come out, you should go and make footprints on the beach – otherwise you could go nuts…oh, wait a minute!"

Grace poked him in the ribs good-naturedly at the implication she was already quite crackers enough, and shoved past him into the living room. Vidar pretended to stagger at the force of the push, limping into the room hamming up the jab in the chest for all he was worth.

Grace rolled her eyes at the antics, but couldn't stop the smile that pulled at the sides of her mouth with invisible determination to prevail.

Vidar straightened up and looked pointedly at her damp trouser legs, "How are your feet now?"

Grace tried to waggle her toes, but they felt leaden, heavy, and thick, "Sandy, sticky, cold…"

"Go and wash the salt off. I'm gonna get the fire going."

Grace padded into her bathroom and peeled off her sticky socks, shoving them into the laundry basket. The bottom third of her trouser legs were also stiff with salt from her splashing sprint across the wet sand. She took them off too, filled the bidet with water, sat on the closed toilet seat, and eased her feet into the delicious warmth. As her chilled skin touched the water, Grace recoiled at the burning sensation, her white toes instantly turning hot pink and roaring with fiery discomfort. She bit her lip and persisted, inching in past her ankles, and circling her feet to acclimatise them. Dangling her feet in warm water produced the same urge it always did; a wish to slide the rest of her body into the liquid isolation and float blissfully. She relaxed for a moment, mind blank, hunched forward, chin resting on her bent knees. Reaching and scooping handfuls of the water, she trickled it down her shins and calves back into the bidet, before pulling out the plug, swinging her legs onto the bathmat, and patting them dry with one of Vidar's fluffy towels. Everything here was luxurious, from the gorgeously-thick bath sheets to the satisfyingly soft bed with its oceans of cosy covers, the deep pile of the hearthrug, and the comfortable, wide sofa, perfect for lounging over a good book, a mug of tea, and a slice of something homemade and hearty. Vidar's house was like the man himself, understated yet beautifully put-together; welcoming, bright, interesting, and surprising. Thinking of Vidar made Grace realise she was in the bathroom with no trousers on, and the wardrobe containing her clothing was the length of the bedroom away, the other side of the open door. Wrapping the towel around her waist, Grace shot across the bedroom and grabbed the first item from the nearest drawer; a pair of her yoga leggings, which she struggled on with difficulty under the towel, feeling like a character from a 1970s sitcom. It just felt rude to shut the door on him after what they'd shared on the beach, and what she'd said in the car. A boundary had been crossed, and return passage was impossible. The shadow of pain crossing his face as he described the harrowing first and only sight of his infant son, clearly still so raw in his memory! Grace felt the same rush of determination to be of use that assailed her when she thought of Sonia. If it was within her power to ease the hurt he felt, she vowed to do it. It was the least she could offer in return for what he'd given her today, an empowerment she'd never expected to experience.

Hanging up the damp towel, Grace pulled on a pair of thermal socks, and padded to the kitchen.

The log-burner was already cracking loudly, and spurting energetic sprays of sparks against the door as the chunks of wood settled into one another.

"I hate clearing it out," Vidar pushed a newspaper-wrapped bundle of ash into the kitchen bin, "but I like sitting in front of a real fire. Everyone in the States has these gas-effect ones…it's just not the same – no smell, no crackle, no pictures to watch in the flames."

Vidar washed his hands, and admired Grace's bottom with the same appreciative focus a portrait enthusiast might lavish upon a Rembrandt, as she bent over in her yoga trousers and inspected the contents of the fridge.

"What shall we have for lunch?"

"Whatever you want."

"Shall we just have a sandwich? The rest of the bread needs using up. That's the thing about homemade, it doesn't really keep."

"But it tastes so much better. You baked the bread too?"

"Yeah…"

"You are clever. Can you teach me?"

"Course! It's not hard. If I can do it, anyone can."

"I'm not so sure about that."

"Honestly, it's simple. We'll make some tomorrow. I'll show you how easy it is. If you knead it enough and give it time to rise, it pretty much makes itself."

"Says 'MasterChef'."

Grace shook her head, laughed, absorbed the teasing compliment with a flush of pleasure and pushed the bread board towards him, "Please can you slice up what's left of that loaf? What would you like inside? There's some eggs from Margaret's hens…I know it's meant to be for breakfast, but we could have a sort of an Eggs Benedict, couldn't we…and there's some watercress we could have with it?" Grace turned to seek Vidar's approval, unsure whether what she'd suggested would be good enough. Knowing if he'd been alone, he'd be chowing down on shop-bought bread, possibly only augmented by a smear of butter, Vidar stood in the centre of the kitchen and nodded like a novelty car accessory, amazed at his good fortune, "Yes please, that sounds fantastic."

Grace radiated delight at his response, and deftly plucked ingredients from the fridge, chatting with perky enthusiasm as she competently whipped up a dressing, slapped a thick layer of butter on each slice of bread Vidar cut, and generally did three things at once whilst making it seem effortless. Vidar relished it all; the happy chatter, the clonk, clink, bubble and rustle of the lunch preparations, enjoying the fact she was so obviously in her element in his kitchen.

"Can I do anything? You're doing it all again."

"You made breakfast," reminded Grace, expertly cracking eggs one-handed.

"I opened a packet and chopped some fruit."

"And it was lovely," said Grace firmly.

Vidar smiled, "It's not quite in the same league as 'I'll just whip us up Eggs Benedict in thirty seconds flat', is it?"

Grace laughed, "You can make the tea."

"What is it with you British and tea?"

"It goes with everything in any situation! Having a crisis? Put the kettle on. Bit of good news? Share a cuppa. Visitors? What's more welcoming? And it's an excellent way to warm up when you've been for an ill-advised winter paddle…"

"But can I be trusted with such an important job?"

"You've got to start somewhere."

Vidar placed the mug next to its fellow on the tray, and carried the kettle to the sink to fill it up, standing as close as he could to Grace as she rinsed watercress under the tap. He could smell the fresh fragrance of her perfume, and detect the scent of the shampoo she used on her hair, "You would make cardboard taste good."

"We'll have that tomorrow, cardboard casserole…and you'll be eating your words!"

Grace pointed to the stacked tray, "I'll let you carry that, it's heavy. Knowing me, I'll go head-first down the steps, fling it everywhere, and we'll be picking mayonnaise off the rug for a week."

****

Grace knelt before the fire and dished out the items from the tray onto the coffee table, pouring the tea, while Vidar laid another large log on top of the glowing embers in the wood burner and immersed himself in the unexpected contentment of his domestic situation. If Stuart had demanded he explain yesterday's indefinable longing on their car journey from the airport, Vidar would have described exactly this, down to the very last detail. Acceptance, kindness, care, stimulation, sanctuary; bucketloads of *Hygge* being dumped on him by invisible sprites, giggling their little heads off as they doused him in serenity. He sat down across the table from her, leaning back against the side of the sofa, and stretching his long legs towards the hot fire, "That's good now."

"Lovely…cosy…"

Vidar admired the repast spread across the coffee table, "Ten minutes in the kitchen and you come up with this. It's superb, Grace. I've done very well out of this 'let's just share' arrangement, haven't I? Delicious food, wonderful company, interesting conversation…"

"Because, of course, I'm having an utterly miserable time by comparison."

Vidar's gorgeous grin lit up his features, "Well, I'm obviously trying my best to make it as torturous as possible."

Grace giggled and chomped into her sandwich, filling oozing out onto the plate, "It's ok…bread's getting a bit chewy…"

"It's perfect, Grace…delicious! I've never had anyone make wonderful food like this for me without it being their job to do it."

"None of your five-minute girlfriends do any cooking?"

"No way! Might have accidentally ingested one too many calories, or broken a nail peeling something…not worth the risk just for me! I had this one girlfriend who was a model. She used to eat Kleenex, because it filled your stomach up but there were no calories."

Grace licked mayonnaise off her fingers and gaped, "You are joking!"

"Wish I was. Apparently, they all did it. She thought it was quite normal. They'd rather eat tissue, feel sick all day, and be a size zero, than be healthy and fit and feel good. See why it never lasted? They were all completely nuts...it used to drive me crazy. The idea of any of them cooking something incredible like this is laughable!"

Grace frowned, "Bleurghhh, sounds disgusting. I like cooking. It...occupies my mind when I can't think straight. It used to give my boring life some structure. I couldn't exist on a tissue diet. I might last a day...then I'd cave in and have to make myself a pie."

Vidar chuckled, "Very wise. Women are supposed to be curvaceous. There's nothing sexy about these emaciated girls. It's like trying to cuddle up to a pencil."

Grace almost spat out her mouthful of tea, swallowed hurriedly, and squawked in delight, continuing to giggle as she eased up on her knees and leant across the table to reach for the cake tin.

Once again, Vidar was seized with the inappropriate urge to squeeze a rounded buttock, or run his hand down a yoga-toned thigh. Grace's seeming preference for wearing lycra to kick around the house was proving quite a test of his self-control. To prevent himself misbehaving until he considered the time was right, Vidar sat on his hands until she returned to her cross-legged position on the rug opposite him, tin on her lap.

"What's in there?"

"Pudding."

"Which is?"

"Rock cakes. Margaret gave me loads of eggs. I'm struggling to think of ways to use them up."

Vidar leant forward and peeked into the tin, "Mmmm."

"Want one?"

"Yes…probably more than one."

Grace put the tin on the rug between them, "Go for it."
"Thanks."

One big bite and a mumbled exclamation, "Grace! These are lovely too! There isn't anything you can't make!"

Grace bit into her own cake, and winked at him as she chewed.

Vidar regarded her steadily, "Thank you."

"For what?"

"For not making your excuses, packing, and running away as fast as your legs could carry you after what I told you this morning."

"It's the too-much-too-young rock star thing, isn't it? You don't have a monopoly on it. It's you, and half the people on my iPod."

Vidar watched her warily, waiting for more, "And that's it?"

"You turned it around! You said yourself you made mistakes and you learned from them. Sheer force of will has brought you to the place you are today, by the sound of it. If anything, it makes me more admiring of you, not less."

"Wow…I don't know what to say…"

"Well don't say anything, then. Shut up and eat your cake."

"Yes, Boss."

Vidar tried to not ogle her as he ate – he knew better than anyone how creepy it was to be constantly observed while you were going about your daily life – but it was so difficult not to. All his eyes wanted to do was look at her. There was nothing else as worthy of his notice in all the world as this beautiful, bright, bubbly, engaging woman…and she was in his home, sitting happily feet away from him, smiling and drinking her tea, talking as if she had no plans to leave any time soon. He made a mental note to call his younger brother and find out when *Somerled's* next booking was due. Usually, the house was empty for the coldest months, when even the hardiest bird-watchers or history enthusiasts struggled to find much to fire their passions in the dreary Orcadian winter. If a guest arrival was imminent, he'd generously compensate them to cancel their booking. Nothing could be allowed to disturb the rightness of this. That way, she could stay as long as she wanted to. Forever might be nice.

Stewart would be so proud of his adherence to doctor's orders! Look how well he was getting on with forgetting his 'brand'. He'd done nothing even approximating work since getting off the London flight yesterday afternoon. By Vidar's own exacting standards, he was practically retired!

Grace was lying on her back on the rug, flicking to find her place in the dog-eared paperback. Vidar reached to pluck two cushions off the sofa, "Here."

She glanced up gratefully, "Thank you."

"You warm enough?"

"Toasty."

"Good."

Was she warm? Was she comfortable? Dominic never asked those kinds of questions. He cared only whether he was warm and comfortable. As far as her husband was concerned, everyone else could shift for themselves.

Grace lifted her head, and Vidar slid the pillow gently underneath it, "Thank you."

"No problem." He stretched out on the rug next to her; close, but not enough to make her tremble at his nearness as she had last night when he'd bent to whisper in her ear. Thinking of it made Grace feel jittery again, fidgety and unsure of herself.

Vidar yawned hugely, "I could doze off now."

"I know – stodgy food, cosy room, getting dark – it's terrible! I sit down to read and wake up two hours later!"

"The coercive stress you've been under for years and years, it's no wonder you're tired." He rolled onto his side, propped himself up on one elbow, and queried anxiously, "You know it's safe to relax here, right? You know nothing bad's going to happen?"

NINE

Sonia thought she'd go quite mad if made to watch another episode of whatever home improvement show her mother had fixated upon this week. Dinner in the oven, table laid in preparation for the boys' arrival, her mother sat in her accustomed chair, half-finished blanket across her legs, and crocheted with nimble-fingered precision, eyes on the screen, passing occasional derogatory comments on décor, price, and location. Lorraine curled on the floor before the fire, knees up, balancing a magazine through which she flicked lazily. Meg, the retired collie, stretched out next to Lorraine and licked the fingers of her free hand persistently, until her sister resumed her absent tickling of the dogs' head, home-manicured nails sinking into the curly black and white fur, rubbing in slow circles as the old dog snuffled happily.

As Margaret glanced up and made a particularly sniffy remark about the state of someone's kitchen, Sonia shot to her feet, "I think I need some fresh air! I might wander up to Grace's for an hour before dinner."

"Don't go bothering her Sonia! She doesn't want you there every five minutes."

"I'm not there every five minutes! I haven't seen her for a few days…"

Mam hitched the half-finished rug up her legs with a sharp tug, and muttered darkly, "Of course, there's no requirement for you to listen to me…I'm only your mother…"

Sonia didn't have the energy for another argument. She merely said, "I'll be back for dinner, Mam."

"See that you are…and don't be late, we won't wait for you! And ask Grace if she wants any more eggs."

In the boot room, Sonia pulled on her wellingtons with panting bursts of effort. Bending was becoming trickier as her middle swelled and tightened.

Taking the shortest route to *Somerled*, up across the grazing fields, Sonia hefted her increasingly-heavy body over the stile, and tramped the steepness of Far Field. Copper and Jess, the two ponies, were sheltering in the lee of the barn, awaiting feeding time. She detoured, to stroke their soft noses and rest from the exertions of fighting wind, terrain, progressing pregnancy, and mounting frustration. At the top of the hill, she carefully eased a leg at a time over the low barbed-wire fencing, taking care not to catch her tights, and crunched across shingle path and flagstone driveway to the front door of *Somerled*.

Levering off her boots using the iron scraper, Sonia stood them in the shelter of the porch, and let herself in, as was her custom, calling a cheery, "Helloooo!" to announce her arrival.

Vidar lay in the middle of the rug before the fire, body curled against Grace's, arm tight around her waist, pulling her securely to him. Both were fast asleep, their breathing slow and rhythmic. Grace's head and torso tilted backwards to rest against Vidar. His face was buried in her hair. Sonia had long ago ceased to feel jealousy at the sight of Vidar with other women. The internet feed of said images altered with such regularity that anything other than a pragmatic acceptance of her position as purely another notch on a well-vandalised bedpost was pointless fantasy. Vidar went through girlfriends quicker than he wore out socks, swiftly disabusing Sonia of any notion she retained a special place in his head or heart. Therefore, as she stood at the top of the steps processing her surprise at this most-unexpected sight, it wasn't resentment that assailed her, but the pleasantly perplexing combination of mild amusement, curiosity, and the conclusion it was all rather sweet. They looked utterly content and totally at ease with one another. Sonia was impressed by how fast Grace moved. She'd only visited *Somerled* three days ago, and there'd been no sign or mention of Vidar then. Sonia supposed she should just tiptoe out and return home, but it was impossible not to want to know every detail.

Slamming the hall door hard, Sonia folded her arms, shoved her tongue firmly in her cheek and, channelling her mother, demanded loudly, "Just what exactly is going on here?"

****

Vidar opened one eye, beheld Sonia's petite (and now rather barrel-shaped) figure at the top of the stairs and grinned lazily, as unembarrassed and unapologetic as ever.

Lifting his head, he observed Grace still slept soundly, and put a silencing finger to his lips. Reluctantly easing his body away from hers, he tiptoed up the stairs to his former girlfriend, clasping her in his big arms and hugging her tight, whispering, "Hey Son. Ok?"

He placed a gentle hand onto her protruding tummy, communicating his knowledge of her situation. Sonia could feel its warmth through the wool of her dress, and for a moment her cheeky confidence wavered as she hissed, "No, of course I'm bloody not!"

He held her against him, and planted a soft kiss in her hair.

Noticing the absence of Vidar's warm body at her back, Grace wriggled onto her side on the rug, her head rolled off its cushion pillow, and the sudden jolt woke her. She sat up, rubbing her eyes, and beheld Sonia and Vidar standing together, his arm protectively around her shoulders.

She beamed at Sonia, "Hello you – haven't seen you for days! Are you all right?"

"Yeah," Sonia felt as if she probably shouldn't be standing this close to Vidar, but Grace seemed unconcerned.

"Good!" Grace stood and came over to her, taking her hand, "Your fingers are freezing! Come down here and sit by the fire. How did you find out Vidar was here? Shall I go for a walk so you two can have a reunion without me being a gooseberry?"

Confused, Sonia directed a questioning glance back up the stairs to Vidar, who deliberately avoided eye-contact. Sonia suspected she understood what was going on here, even if guileless Grace did not.

"Och, no!" said Sonia, boldly, waving an airily dismissive hand in the direction of the globally-renowned multi-millionaire, "I've come to see you, not him."

Grace shrugged laughingly at Vidar, "Well, in that case, have a cake, Sonia, I've got millions."

"Oh, Mam wants to know if you want any more eggs."

"God, not yet! I haven't got rid of the last batch!"

"Well, she knows you bake a lot."

"Yes, but only to get rid of her sodding egg-mountain! Those hens must be shattered."

Sonia sniggered, and plonked at one end of the sofa without further invitation.

"Here," Grace shoved the cake tin into her hands, "Eat as many as you can. Are you staying for dinner?" She looked round at Vidar in the kitchen, as if checking it was all right to invite her. He nodded enthusiastically, and Sonia felt crushed by disappointment, "I'd love to stay, but I promised Mam I'd go home. She says I bother you."

"Rubbish," said Grace in a clipped, disapproving tone Vidar hadn't heard before, like a schoolmistress from a black and white movie, "but you'd better go home if you said you would. Anyway," Grace sat down next to her friend, curling her legs underneath her and leaning towards Sonia, "Are you feeling all right? Have you been poorly the last few days?"

Grace paused to look up gratefully at Vidar as he put a fresh pot of tea on the table in front of them, and a clean mug for Sonia. With great amusement, Sonia detected the mutual delight passing between the two of them as their eyes met. Once Grace's attention shifted away from his face to pouring the tea, Vidar gave Sonia a conspiratorial wink. She narrowed her eyes and regarded him suspiciously – what was the crafty sod up to?

"I've been fine. Mam just doesn't like me coming up here all the time. She says I must get on your nerves."

"Nonsense, Sonia! You can come whenever you want – you know that."

"Yes, I do know that, but Mam's convinced I'm in the way and you're only being polite…"

"No, no, no! 'Polite' was London. I don't do 'polite' any more, I do 'genuine' now. Nowadays, if I don't want to do something, I don't do it. If I didn't want to invite you in, I wouldn't. You do tell your Mum that, don't you?"

"Oh, aye, repeatedly…but because she doesn't want me in her house, she can't believe anyone else would want me in theirs either."

For a moment, Sonia's cynical mask slipped, and exposed the uncertain young girl hidden behind it. Her vivid green eyes alighted on the jumping flames, sudden moisture gleaming within them. Grace exchanged a worried glance with Vidar, before reaching across and waggling the tin on her friend's lap, making Sonia jump, "Come on, at least have one with your tea, for the sake of the continuing goodwill between your mother and I…"

Sonia giggled and selected a cake, "Mmmm, delish Grace."

Vidar, sitting beside Grace and observing the interaction between the two women with interest, held out his hand, demanding the tin, "Give me another one before you eat them all, fatty."

Sonia pretended to be offended, picked out a large cake, and tossed it straight at his head. Vidar caught it deftly but showered himself in crumbs, causing both Grace and Sonia to squeal with laughter.

Sipping her tea, equilibrium restored, Sonia looked cheekily from one to the other, "Are either of you ever going to tell me what's going on here?"

Vidar flashed her a warning glance.

"What's going on where?" murmured Grace distractedly, picking escapee currants off the front of her jumper.

Vidar enacted a swift cautionary mime behind Grace's back for Sonia to keep her silence about the cuddle she'd witnessed. Had Grace not known she'd been snuggled up to Vidar? She'd certainly looked comfortable enough for Sonia to assume an explicit level of physical intimacy between them.

"The two of you here? Together? When Grace arrived last month, unless she's a very good actress, she'd no real idea about you. Now, here you are, behaving as if you've known one another for twenty years!"

Yes, that was it! Sonia had summed it up succinctly. Watching Grace bustling in the kitchen or sitting companionably next to him on the sofa, Vidar experienced the conviction he'd always known her; that when she moved with relaxed ease around his home, it was as if she'd forever been there, and eternally would be. That was why he'd been pulled back here after such a long absence – because this woman was his destiny, and he; hers!

Oblivious, Grace explained, "There was a bit of a mix-up with my booking. Vidar came home believing the house was empty. I was here thinking my booking was all confirmed. It wasn't fair to chuck him out of his own house, and I didn't have anywhere else to go at short notice…so, we discussed it and decided to share."

"Is that what you call it?" teased Sonia.

"Yes…?" Innocent Grace was puzzled by her friend's suggestive tone.

Vidar made further frantic faces, urging Sonia to shut up.

"So, what does this 'sharing' entail?"

Vidar rolled frustrated eyes at Sonia, and mimed throttling her.

"I dunno," said Grace, breezily, "Whatever's going on that day. Ooh, guess where we've been?"

Sonia couldn't help herself, "I can't possibly begin to guess where 'we've' been…"

"My beach! Hang on…" Grace went into the hall to fetch her 'phone from her coat pocket. Vidar took his chance to scoot across the sofa and bump his body firmly against Sonia's, "Quit it, you."

"What?"

"Shelve the stirring. Listen, Son, this is important to me. I'm trying to do it right, ok? Don't you dare get in the middle and start meddling for entertainment or petty point-scoring, you understand me?"

"All right, keep your wig on! I was just having a wee bit of fun, that's all. Whatever you're up to, you don't need to worry; Grace doesn't look at the world the way you and I do. She's much nicer than we are. I don't think she's on to your evil plans yet."

"They're not evil – they're honourable! That's why I'm trying to be a good boy…and your contribution is not helping."

"Ok! I was only messing."

"Well, stop, all right? Otherwise I won't be so pleased to see you any more."

Sonia didn't like the idea of that, so snapped defensively, "Like I'm bothered what you think – "

Vidar's smooth voice cut effectively across her, "Seems to me, Son, you need all the friends you can get right now."

Sonia glared at him, stung both by the retort and the insight. Grace's reappearance prevented any reply, "Stop arguing, you two." She leant over the back of the sofa, wriggling her shoulders between Sonia and Vidar, and holding out her 'phone, pointing at her picture, "See, the perfect footprint!"

She unfurled the battered magazine, and placed her 'phone next to it, "Not a million miles away…"

Vidar tapped his knuckle onto the glossy page, "It looks warmer in this one."

Sonia grinned, "How cold was it?"

Vidar grimaced, "Well, freezing, of course…unless you're Iron Woman, here…"

"You never went in!"

"Who else made the footprints?"

Sonia flicked through the other pictures Grace had taken, and found the one of the pinched-looking white toes in the glacially-clear sea, "I thought I was barmy! What were you thinking?"

Grace nudged Vidar, "Told you she'd say I was mad."

"It's December! You'll catch pneumonia!"

"No I won't," said Grace, adopting the same tone of solemn certainty with which she'd attested to the perfection of Vidar's breakfast before tasting it, "I won't catch anything, because I was meant to go there. It was supposed to happen. It's closure on my old life."

"You are. You're mad. Completely cuckoo!"

"I'm not mad," insisted Grace, "I think what I am is free."

Again, Sonia watched their eyes meet, and both nod gently to one another, reinforcing their faith in Grace's new-found liberation. Sonia couldn't suppress a smirk. It was…cute…there was no other word to describe it. She wanted to reach up to the two of them – grown adults almost twice her age – and ruffle their windblown, sleep-mussed hair.

Vidar caught sight of her sniggering, "Charming though Son's constant mocking is, it's just a tactic to prevent us discussing the real elephant in the room. Let's talk about the thing we all want to know and Son isn't telling…"

Sonia pouted, and glared at him, "Which is?"

Vidar reached out his hand and ruminatively rubbed Sonia's swelling stomach, already round and obvious in her fitted wool dress. There was comfort in the gentleness of the touch stroking back and forth across her firming belly, but she knew that to relax would be a mistake.

"I'm no PhD, but I seem to recall it takes two to Tango…and yet here you are, just you, and no sight or sound of the proud father…?"

Sonia flicked his hand away irritably.

Grace pointed at Vidar across the table, "Regardless of what happened between you two in the past, whatever is going on now in Sonia's life is her business, Vidar! If she chooses to keep elements of her life private…well, that's her right. We all have that right, don't we? You of all people must understand the value of privacy – how precious it is!"

Vidar regarded Grace admiringly, "You continually surprise me. You can front up when you want to, can't you Grace?"

Grace faced Sonia apologetically, "Sorry, sweetheart, but I'm going to talk about you as if you aren't here for a minute."

Grace turned back to Vidar, exuding surprising aggression, "She's young. She's on her own. She's going through an emotionally-difficult event with, as far as I can tell, very little understanding from those closest to her of the enormous life-changes being forced upon her. All of us have failed relationships behind us. Some more than others, Vidar." Here, she paused, and looked pointedly at him, "If it didn't work out for Sonia, you can't judge her for that. She needs our support, not our censure!"

Grace finished this outburst breathless, indignant, inflamed by the passion of defending her friend at all costs. Vidar thought she'd never looked more beautiful. He put his arms around Sonia. His embrace was claustrophobic. Although he addressed the younger woman, his eyes were on Grace.

"I hope you realise what a wonderful friend you've found in that lady over there, Miss Sonia Flett. I hope you understand what a sense-talking lifeline she is for you."

Sonia tried to extricate herself from his powerful grip, "I do, yes. You don't have to tell me."

"Perhaps you should consider being more open with your friend at least…?"

Grace interjected, defending Sonia, "What's past is past. We're friends now, supporting each other through life as it is, not as it was."

"You're lucky, Son. You could be being forced into full disclosure. Your friendship could be conditional upon it. I mean, does he really deserve your protection, Son? What do you get in return for such loyalty? We all know how you like a bit of glitz and glamour. Is it someone well-known? Has he paid you to keep your mouth shut?"

Incensed, Sonia spat, "Why, Vidar, is that what you'd do?"

"Right!" Suddenly, Grace was between them, hand on Sonia's shoulder, other palm pushing Vidar in the chest, "Stop! Get over there! Stop intimidating her! Sonia, you are pregnant. You need to keep yourself calm and quiet. You'd need a chainsaw to cut the atmosphere in here now. How did the two of you ever have a relationship? All you do is argue! Would you like another cake Sonia; a fresh cup of tea?"

"No, no…I need to get back…" Sonia wobbled upright on leaden legs. Recently, weariness washed over her with no warning, like a wave breaking across a rock. Grace's strong arms steadied her friend, and she flashed an exasperated glance at Vidar, "Don't feel you have to leave because of him picking on you."

"It's not that. I told Mam I wouldn't be long, and it seems to take an eternity to walk anywhere now. My body feels so heavy."

"Are you sure you're eating properly?" Grace stroked a stray ringlet from Sonia's face, and Sonia was overwhelmed by a rush of affection for her friend's genuine concern.

"I am eating enough to keep the whole island going…I'm fine! It's nothing to do with him, I just need to go. Don't worry about us," she reassured Grace, "we've been fighting for years...we're really good at it now, aren't we?"

"Brilliant," acknowledged Vidar with mock pride, "I'm just concerned for your welfare, Son, that's all."

"Well, try to express your 'concern' a little less forcefully, will you?" admonished Grace, ushering Sonia towards the front door. Vidar shook his head and appeared annoyed, but blew Sonia a kiss once Grace's back was turned.

In the hallway, Grace helped Sonia on with her coat, and watched with mild anxiety as she struggled on her boots, huffing and puffing, "You are all right, aren't you Sonia?"

"No, Grace, I'm bloody pregnant!"

Grace touched gentle fingers to Sonia's hand where it splayed on the front wall, balancing herself as she tugged on her boot, "There's no issue with Vidar, is there?"

"No, don't worry. It's always been that way and it always will be. That's how we treat one another."

"How did you ever manage any romance between all the sparring?"

Sonia's smile was regretful. She didn't answer the question, but rejoined, "Grace, he's totally preoccupied with making goo-goo-eyes at you, it would appear."

Grace stiffened, "Oh, shut up Sonia! No, he isn't! We're house-sharing."

"Oh, really? I give it less than a week before you're sharing way more than just living space. He always gets what he wants, and I've never seen him look at anyone the way he looks at you."

"Oh, I've never heard so much rubbish in my life!" Grace was purple with mortification from polo-neck to hairline, "Go on! Go home! Stop teasing me and making me embarrassed! It's so dark, can you see to get back?"

Sonia smiled sweetly at her friend, "Oh aye, I know the way well enough."

Grace kissed her cheek, and chided, "Be good, stop laughing at me, take care of yourself. Come whenever you want, but please don't bring me any more eggs for at least a week."

"You be good," teased Sonia, "and try to keep your knickers on…"

"Go home now, Sonia Flett!" Grace was laughingly shocked at Sonia's cheek.

"See ya."

"Bye."

Grace watched Sonia across the driveway and over the bent and broken barbed-wire fencing. Sonia turned and waved as she disappeared below the curve of the hill. Grace returned the wave, closed the door, and went back inside to Vidar.

She sat on the sofa next to him, scrutinising him lengthily, trying to give him a taste of his own medicine. Vidar, naturally not the least unsettled, looked calmly back.

"You pick on that girl!"

"Bullshit. Son can take it. Believe me, Grace, she gives as good as she gets – always has."

"So I understand," said Grace, drily, "but she's been through a lot."

"She's no fool, Grace. That is a mess of her own making. Why she did it, I don't know, but that pregnancy was no accident. She's protecting someone who doesn't deserve it."

"You speak as if you know who it is."

"I do."

"What?!"

"It's an older man with money; someone she thinks can get her away from farms, cowshit, sheep, wind, cold, and being ordinary…"

"I think Sonia's far from ordinary!"

"And she thinks the same about you. That's why you're friends. She needs you, Grace, to keep her hope alive."

"And I need her. She's showing me I am still the same person I've always been – inside – and now I can be that person on the outside too. It's ok not to be ashamed of myself any more."

Vidar interlaced his fingers with hers, held her hand in his lap, and smiled lazily, "There's nothing about you to feel ashamed of! Going anywhere with you would make me want to burst with pride! I don't know what happened to you within your marriage, and it's none of my business…but understand that you're safe here, ok? This is a place where you can relax and be who you are – for as much time as you need. If you have dreams you've been waiting half your life to fulfil, I say go for them! Make them happen! Now's the time to change your life – make it what you've always wished it could be! I believe passionately in going for what you want; I've always done that. If you want help, I'll help you. I'm here for you, as long as you need me."

Grace felt a fluttering in her stomach and slid her other hand on top of Vidar's, sandwiching the warmth of him between her palms.

How would it be if Sonia was right?

TEN

Vidar tugged his hat down over his ears and mentally prepared himself to step out into the cold, calling, "Bye!" opening the door, and almost walking straight into Sonia, who was at that moment reaching for the exterior door handle.

"Aah!"

"What?"

"God, you scared the life out of me!"

"I didn't know you'd be there, did I? Perhaps if you rang the bell and waited to be let in like normal visitors...?"

Sonia pouted, "Where're you going?"

"You're so nosey!"

"Shouldn't you be spending all your time strutting around flexing your muscles and trying to seduce your wee 'housemate'?"

"Oh, give it a rest. If you must know, I'm going down to Dr Kirkbride's."

"You're walking?" Sonia was amazed.

"Yes, Son," said Vidar, sarcastically, "There's this thing called exercise. Have you heard of it? It's supposed to be really good for you."

Sonia rolled her eyes, "Very funny. Have you seen that?" She pointed behind her at a large bank of threatening cloud advancing from the open sea, "It's going to piss down any minute...you'll get soaked."

"How sweet of you to be concerned for my welfare."

"Is that part of your dastardly scheme – get sick so Grace has to mop your fevered brow?"

Vidar sniggered and observed the approaching squall, "It's a way out yet. I'll make it. If I don't, I'll have to dry out in front of their fire, won't I? A Registered Nurse can mop my brow instead."

"Very practical, but it won't get you anywhere with Project-Dive-In-Grace's-Knickers, will it?"

"What did I just say? Give it up!"

Sonia smirked and regarded the weather with the sage eye of a farmer's daughter, "I'd drive if I were you."

Vidar patted his stomach, "Maybe, but you don't have your own bodyweight in cake to burn off."

Sonia frowned uncertainly, stroking her bump, "If only it were that easy to get shot of unwanted weight, I'd have walked the length of the mainland five times over by now!"

Vidar stroked a gloved finger affectionately across her cheek, "Never mind, Son. I presume you're not here to see me?"

"Och, no!" said Sonia breezily, confidence revived by his touch.

Vidar grinned, "Didn't think so." He inclined his head towards the house, "Grace is inside; cooking, naturally…"

"Does she cook all day?"

"No," said Vidar brightly, "Sometimes she stops and does yoga."

What are you up to?"

"Nothing, regrettably."

Sonia fixed him with her bright green eyes, "I don't believe you."

Vidar shrugged, the picture of innocence, reopening the hall door, and shouting, "Grace, Son's here!"

Sonia hissed, "If you won't dish the goss, I know someone who will!"

About to reply that he could do without Sonia's interference, Grace's appearance silenced Vidar. Out of the corner of his eye he could see Sonia laughing at him, but couldn't stop himself pausing at the front door to savour the sight of Grace. Every time he looked at her, he was struck afresh by the near-irresistible force of his desire to possess her, and never let her go.

Grinning at them both, he drawled, "See you later girls," and with a last, lingering look at Grace, set off briskly down the track seeking to outpace the coming storm, swinging his carrier bag, humming to himself, and feeling as if everything was just about perfect. Life had been predictable for so long, he couldn't remember the last time he'd felt this excited about anything. The future fizzed with potential like unopened champagne…and he was controlling the twist of the cork.

****

Grace helped Sonia off with her coat and watched, concerned, as she struggled out of her boots with a grimace of discomfort.

"Trouble with your feet?"

"It's bending down…it's impossible now! It feels as if I'm going everywhere with an inflatable ring round my middle."

"Come in and have a sit down. I'm just getting the lunch on."

Grace bustled back to her preparations and Sonia followed, privately amused it was mid-morning and her friend was already in the kitchen. For whose benefit could it possibly be but Vidar's?

Sonia wriggled inelegantly onto a stool at the breakfast bar, glad to take the weight off her leaden legs, swinging them gently and feeling her feet tingle with pins and needles, "Smells nice in here. What you making?"

"Just a quick thing for lunch…" Grace proficiently folded thin sheets of filo pastry across a filling, "Want to stay to eat?"

"What's in it?" Sonia already knew she was going to say yes.

"Salmon, leeks, mustard, dill, bit of cream for a sauce, bit of cheese on top to make it crispy."

"Yes please. I would like to stay."

"What about earache from your Mum?"

Sonia shrugged, "This is me we're talking about. I can't be a dutiful daughter all the time – what would she have to whinge about?"

Provoked by Sonia's attitude, Grace grated cheese liberally over both the filo parcel and the worktop as she chided her, "You revel in discord! It's as if you enjoy the bickering – like you and Vidar!"

"It's sport," Sonia reached over and plucked curls of creamy cheddar from the work surface, licking them off her fingertips, "There's nothing else to do here, is there?"

"Except wind up your Mum?"

"Trust me, she annoys me just as much," assured Sonia moodily.

"Your poor Mum…"

"No, 'poor Mam' nothing! You don't know the latest."

"Which is?"

"She only made me go to church!"

"I didn't know you were religious?"

"I'm not!"

"Why'd she make you go then?"

"To humiliate me! She made me wear my smart coat which is, of course, rather tight nowadays in certain places. We were fashionably late – again, doubtless on purpose, so the entire place was rammed by the time we got there. Then she made me walk through everyone to a seat down the front! Just another fallen woman, prostrating herself before a higher power to beg forgiveness. Bless me, Father, for I have sinned…"

Grace sniggered behind her hand, "Oh Sonia, you say things that make me laugh, and then I feel guilty – as if I'm enjoying myself at your expense."

"It's all right," Sonia squidged more trails of cheese between her fingers and sucked them into her mouth, "I don't mind you finding it funny, because the whole bloody thing's ridiculous. If it wasn't happening to me, I'd be finding it hysterical!"

"Perhaps she did it for a good reason?"

"Aye – to teach me a proper lesson."

"No, to do you a favour."

"How d'you work that one out?"

"Well, she knows half the place is gossiping about you. Why not kill two hundred birds with one stone, and present you in public? 'Make the announcement' as it were, without either of you having to say a word! Quite clever, really, because no one would dare to be bitchy or judgemental in church – God's watching."

It was Sonia's turn to chortle, "Good ol' God, saving me from the less-than-Christian snidey comments!"

"No doubt they're all now gossiping about you at home...but you don't have to sit and endure that, do you? I think your Mum helped you out there, Sonia."

"I thought she was shaming me...here's the harlot!"

"Think about it, sweetie! She walked in beside you – she didn't make you do it alone. That's a show of solidarity in my book. She protected you from the bitching by displaying you in a place where decent people wouldn't dare say anything less-than-supportive, and she's neutralised all the speculation in one fell swoop. Yes, she's home. Yes, she's pregnant. Anything else? No? Well, wind your necks in then! See?"

"I s'pose..." Sonia was unwilling to admit her much-maligned mother might have curled a peachy touch into the back of the net from well outside the penalty box, but Grace's theory had merit.

"There is one thing Mam's 'announcement' didn't include, though."

"What's that?" Grace wiped up the cheese Sonia hadn't eaten, shaking the cloth over the sink so the crumbs fell like snowflakes onto the stainless steel.

"Who the father is," said Sonia quietly.

Grace flicked on the kettle, and fetched two mugs from the cupboard, "That's no one's business but yours and his." She thumped each mug firmly onto the worktop in time with her words, "You stick to your guns on that. You don't want him with you because he's not a nice person, right?"

"Right."

"He's never going to be a part of your baby's life, is he?"

"No!" said Sonia firmly.

"Let them wonder, then. Tell a different story every time and you'll drive the gossips nuts! Perhaps he came out of the closet, or he's missing in action? Maybe he signed up for a one-way trip to Mars the moment you broke the news? Perhaps he's lost at sea, locked in Broadmoor…or he ran away to join the Circus!"

Sonia lolled across the breakfast bar, giggling, as Grace's suggestions for the whereabouts of the elusive father became ever-more outlandish.

"Remember, Sonia, it isn't anyone's business but yours."

Grace stacked the cooking utensils into the dishwasher, gesturing with a sauce-coated wooden spoon, "Don't feel you have to tell a soul, not even your Mum, if you don't want to."

"I definitely won't be telling my Mam I've been passed over again. She gave me a hard-enough time about Vidar. When he moved on, she did a lot of that sniffy, tutty, I-told-you-so stuff."

"She's your Mum, Sonia! However much you two annoy one another, it is her goal in life to protect her children from unnecessary pain…but you're a stubborn little madam, so if she tells you not to do something, you do the complete opposite to prove her wrong. You always think you know better! I'm prepared to concede that in some areas you might have greater life experience than your mother. I'm guessing she doesn't have many exams or a degree like you do? I'm guessing she hasn't lived far from home?"

"She's never left Orkney!"

"But she's a wife, a mother. She's raised five kids on a low income in a challenging place…she knows a lot she keeps to herself, and you don't give her any credit for that. She may not be book-smart, but she's a savvy woman, she can get things done and," Grace pointed behind her, down the hill towards the farm, "she rules that roost, doesn't she?"

"Aye, she certainly does," Sonia grudgingly admitted.

"When she was a lot younger than you, she had more than one child, a husband, a business to run…and she's made it work. I see her in a different light than you do. She's only seven years older than me! She's my generation, Sonia, and I consider she's done a great deal more with her life than I have. Don't write her off as incompetent just because she doesn't have letters after her name!"

Grace carried the mugs over to the sofa. Smilingly absorbing Grace's gentle scolding, Sonia eased herself off the stool and trooped after her on tingling feet, relishing the opportunity to sink back into the supportive softness of the plump cushions.

"I'm not saying Mam's a complete idiot – "

"You sure? And as for your Dad, do you even remember he exists?"

"Dad doesn't really get involved…never has done."

"Leaves it to your Mum, does he?"

"He's got a farm to run. The way he sees it, the child-rearing thing is Mam's job, and the stock-rearing thing is his job."

"What you're saying, Sonia, is that she's a single parent in a lot of ways. Perhaps she understands what you're in for much better than you realise?"

Sonia shrugged petulantly, picking fluff off her tights with snatching fingers.

"Whose opinion do you respect, Sonia? Anyone's, or only your own?"

Sullenly, "Yours...Vidar's..."

Grace smiled sorrowfully, leant forward, and touched her arm gently, "Darling, thank you sincerely...but are you sure? Take a long, hard look at us. I'm jobless, homeless, middle-aged, with a failed marriage behind me, and no idea what I'm going to do with the rest of my life. Vidar is a recovering addict with – by his own admission – a selfish and irresponsible past, and an apparent inability to remain with the same woman for more than a fortnight. Your Mum and Dad have been together through thick and thin – probably quite a lot of 'thin' – they own land and property here, they've got a business that supports seven people (soon to be eight), and they've been successfully married for the best part of thirty years! It might not be the epitome of romance, but it works for them. And yet you'd place mine and Vidar's opinions before those of your parents? Why, Sonia, because we have money?"

Sonia fidgeted awkwardly, because that was exactly why.

"Sweetie, believe me when I say money does not equate to a successful life. My rich husband treated me like crap for twenty years. I sat in my fancy, London loft hating every bit of my life with a passion, too scared of having to go without to stand on my own two feet. Money controlled me, it didn't liberate me. Look at Vidar! I believe he's very wealthy, yes?"

Sonia nodded.

"Ok, but his life is really lonely, Sonia, really isolated... He sits up there on his celebrity pedestal, all alone, getting worshipped by everyone, and unable to interact in a genuine way with a single soul. I'm sure, if you asked him, he'd swap with your Dad tomorrow."

Sonia grinned, "To live with my Mam? I'm not convinced that'd go so well..."

"I meant, to live an ordinary life! They're not super-fond of one another, are they?"

Sonia wrinkled her nose, "Not so much," she regarded Grace slyly, "You, on the other hand, he can't seem to get enough of."

Predictably, Grace blushed instantly, as she seemed to every time Sonia alluded to Vidar's attraction.

"Don't be silly, Sonia!"

"I am not 'being silly', and you know it. He's got the proper hots for you! Have you just not noticed the way he looks at you, or are you deliberately pretending it's not happening?"

Grace touched nervous fingers to the hollow of her throat.

"The look..." she muttered, as Sonia chuckled, feeling confident. This was one area of life where her experience definitely outstripped that of her older friend.

"I did warn you, didn't I? I did say he was up to something. Sex?"

Grace jumped, staring at Sonia with wide eyes, both horrified and hopeful, "What? No! Do you mean have we had it?"

Sonia couldn't stop herself laughing openly at Grace, "Now who's being funny? You were married for twenty years, and yet you act as if you've never done it in your life! It's sex, not splitting the atom! It's hardly difficult to do. Even my thick, ugly, stinky brothers manage to get a wee bit now and again..."

Grace held up a hand to stem the teasing torrent, "We haven't had sex, Sonia."

"Yet."

"Sonia!"

"What? This is Vidar we're talking about! It's not if, Grace, it's when."

"It's not like that – "

"Oh, bollocks," stated Sonia, disparaging Grace's reticence, "It's Vidar. It's always 'like that'. What's he done?"

"What?"

"To you – what's he done?"

****

"Vidar! Come in!" Elaine's smile was warm, her body language instantly flirtatious. Stewart had quite a few friendly, approachable chums, but none of such universally-acknowledged gorgeousness as the ruggedly-handsome, mouth-wateringly-muscular, meltingly-attentive Vidar Rasmussen. She stood on tiptoe, proffering a soft cheek to receive a kiss, deliberately not stepping back quickly enough to avoid some brief body contact with him as he entered the hall.

Vidar took off his gloves and hat, and shoved them into his coat pocket, "It's freezing out there, and I was racing the rain that's coming! How have you been?"

"Very well, Hen. How are you?" She touched his arm – any excuse – concern briefly clouding her features, "Stewie said you weren't your usual cheery self...?"

Vidar laughed and patted her hand, "I wasn't last week, but I'm better now."

He held up a carrier bag, "This is for Rory. Apparently, he wanted some specific record from the States for his DJ stuff. He messaged me and asked if I could find it for him. I didn't want to ship it to him at college because I figured it would get broken. I thought he could have it when he comes home for Christmas."

"Want to see the old man while you're here?"

"Why not?"

Vidar followed Elaine into the living room, where Stewart snoozed in his accustomed chair, "Is he ever at work?"

Elaine laughed, and ruffled her husband's hair with gentle fingertips, "Stewie…"

Stewart grunted, and opened his eyes to see Vidar sitting on the sofa opposite him, "Hey, 'Stewie'."

Stewart pointed an aggressive finger, "Watch it, you."

Vidar chuckled, "Look at him, dozing through the day like a pensioner…"

Elaine giggled, and perched on the arm of Stewart's chair, brushing his hair off his forehead, as if soothing him. Stewart eased an arm comfortably around her, and rested his head against her hip, "I'll have you know I was out to an emergency in the middle of the night. While you were no doubt snoring in your leopard skin pyjamas, some of us were working hard."

"I'll let you off just this once, then."

"Very big of you…what you got there?" Stewart gestured to the carrier bag beside Vidar on the sofa.

"Oh yeah, I was telling Elaine – it's that vinyl Rory wanted for his superstar dj-ing."

"You got it?"

"Yeah man…I know people!"

"Great. Straight from the States. He'll be chuffed to bits with that 'cos no one else'll have it!"

"Yeah…you need to tell him though, because he doesn't know."

"Right. He's home Friday anyway."

Elaine leant forward and slid the record from the bag, "A proper old record! What's Rory want with that?"

Vidar nudged her elbow, "Vinyl's back, Elaine! Didn't you know?"

Elaine shook her head in wide-eyed incomprehension, "I have absolutely no idea what you're talking about now. All I know is that everywhere you go, it feels as if you're being sucked into some time-warp. Honestly, I was in Stromness the other day and there were these little girls walking down the street dressed like *Bananarama*, all the youngsters wear those massive headphones…and now Rory wants LPs! Talk about back to the eighties!"

Vidar grinned, "I can't remember."

"Oh, shut up! You're only two years younger than me!"

"No, I literally can't remember," Vidar knocked his knuckles against his skull, "There's at least ten years missing from up here…"

Elaine patted his knee, "I don't want to know any more. Will you stay for coffee, Vidar?"

"Yes please, Elaine, that would be lovely."

Elaine got up, and was almost out of earshot as Stewart grunted, "Notice she doesn't ask me if I want one."

Elaine stopped in the doorway, and rose predictably to the bait, "Well, you do, don't you?"

"Aye."

"And I knew that, so there was no need to ask you, was there?"

"No, Hen, you're quite right, as always..."

Elaine tutted, raised her eyes heavenward, and stalked from the room.

Stewart grinned sheepishly at Vidar, "I'm in trouble."

"You bring it on yourself, man."

"Scary isn't it, the way she can read my mind?"

"She's not reading your mind, she's controlling it. She knows what you're thinking before you do, my friend."

"What hope is there for me?"

"None, you lucky bastard. You're well and truly caught."

Stewart chuckled lazily, but it swiftly turned into a protracted yawn, "Christ..."

"What did you have to go to?"

"A dying man. There wasn't anything I could do for the poor old bugger except palliative pain relief and a wee bit of bedside manner – more to reassure his daughter than anything else. He's half-potty, well on his way. He might see Christmas, but he won't see much past it, I daresay."

"That's not a good thing to have to do on a cold winter's night, is it?"

"Not my favourite. I don't mind if it's a situation where you can administer some treatment, and go home again feeling you've done something towards making them better…but there was no making that better. There was nothing I could do but commiserate – there, there, chin up, be over soon. If he was a dog you'd put him out of his misery, but because he's a human, he has to go on suffering in pain and confusion until nature eventually takes its course. Daft, really…"

Stewart sat staring into space for a moment, before gesturing to Vidar, "Obviously, that's off the record."

"Absolutely, Doc. I won't let on that you're going around euthanising half the mainland."

"Oh, sod off. Even if I could get away with it, I wouldn't do it. It goes against everything I believe in. My goal is to preserve life, not take it."

"I'm only kidding!"

"I know…it's just sights like that make you question who'll be with you when you really need them – right at the end."

"Your little mind-reading buddy'll be there…"

"I hope so…berating me about very inconveniently dying without putting that shelf up like she asked me to, or not timing my collapse for after I'd mowed the lawn…"

"Like I said, you lucky bastard."

Elaine's muffled voice floated from the kitchen.

Stewart cocked a thumb, "And so it goes on…"

"What's she saying?"

"I dunno, I can't hear her."

"You can't expect her to keep flitting in and out, dancing attendance on us like some member of waiting staff. Let's go see what she wants."

Vidar stood, and Stewart reluctantly complied, yawning once more, stretching his tall body so his hands almost touched the low, beamed ceiling of the croft, "You know, mate, your overly-chivalrous behaviour has a tendency to make the rest of us look bad."

"Yeah, 'cos I'm such a success with women," rejoined Vidar sarcastically, as the two sloped down the passage to the croft's bright, airy kitchen extension, with its glass atrium roof upon which the December rain now battered insistently.

"We heard your dulcet tones, my sweet," said Stewart, squeezing one of his wife's buttocks playfully, and avoiding the swinging arm with practised ease.

"There you go, Hen," Elaine placed a mug of coffee before Vidar.

"Thank you, Elaine," Vidar treated her to his most endearing, boyish grin.

"Biscuit?" All other visiting friends got the family biscuits. Vidar got the expensive ones for important guests, that she hid behind the spice rack so her boys wouldn't find them.

"Do you mind if I don't?" Vidar patted his washboard stomach, "This last week I've done nothing but eat...I need to exercise some willpower."

"Oooh, what are these biscuits?" Stewart crammed one into his mouth whole before Elaine had time to snaffle the pack and return it to its hiding place, chomping and exclaiming indistinctly around his mouthful, "These are nicer than the ones we usually have!"

Elaine wrestled the pack from her husband's reaching fingers, "That's 'cos they're four times the price – get off!"

"But it's all right for him to have them!" Stewart whipped another while his wife's attention was diverted to Vidar, who watched the pantomime with obvious enjoyment.

"Vidar has self-control! He'll eat a couple and no more! You'll keep going until they're all gone!"

"He doesn't have self-control! He just has a narcissistic obsession with not looking fat in photographs! Anyway, they're open now…I have to eat them before they go soft."

Stewart reached for number three, and Elaine threatened his knuckles with the teaspoon, "Get off! Do you want a stomach like that, or a stomach like that?" She pointed from the oft-photographed, delicious definition of Vidar's toned abdomen to her husband's emerging paunch. Stewart considered, head on one side, "On reflection, I think I'll take a stomach like this, because only you see it – and you have to put up with it – and it's a lot less work than his. I'd rather keep my top on and be able to have the odd treat with my morning coffee."

By now, Vidar was giggling helplessly behind his coffee mug, as Stewart attempted a fourth assault on the biscuits, and again got a teaspoon to the back of the hand for his trouble, "Ow! How many sit-ups do you do a day?"

"Two hundred or so…"

"Two hundred sit ups a day…every day…even weekends?"

"I don't only do crunches…I do other exercises as well."

"But every day?"

"Every day. Even Christmas."

"See!" said Elaine, not for the first time secretly wishing her husband would take a leaf out of Vidar's book when it came to keeping himself in shape.

Stewart shook his head, "I'm the first one to advocate a healthy lifestyle…but, everything in moderation, mate! You should relax a bit."

"I am relaxed!"

"I must admit you seem a lot happier than last week."

"Yeah," there was undisguised cheekiness in Vidar's grin, "Life's all right."

"Is it?" said Stewart suspiciously, "If you won't eat one wee biscuit because it might give you a millimetre of stomach, why've you been stuffing your face for a week?"

Vidar tried to keep his expression neutral, failed, and grinned like the Cheshire Cat, "Because the food's been heavenly."

"You haven't done what I told you not to, have you?"

"No, Doc, cross my heart…although I have seen her. She's got a big bump already."

"Oh," Elaine twigged what the boys were discussing, "Wee Sonia…"

"Aye. Still hasn't been to see me! I can't make her attend check-ups but I'd like to think she'll swallow her pride sooner rather than later and make an appearance."

"Och, I wouldn't worry, Hen! Margaret'll talk her round in good time."

"I wouldn't bet on it, love. You know, if it was the twins or Lorraine I'd be inclined to agree, but Mag seems to have a blind spot when it comes to the older two. Look at Bobby with that abscess! In the end, it was Euan who brought him in in agony, saying 'there's something not right with the lad'...half the poor little sod's face was twice the size it should have been! I don't think Margaret had clocked it at all! It seems she only realised she had to do something with her kids once the twins came, and Lorraine's over-indulged, if anything."

"Well, she is the baby. Andrew gets a bit of that from your mother..."

Vidar drew in sharp breath, "Careful where you go with this, buddy...wife versus mother."

"It's going nowhere, because I have no wish to change the subject. You can't cook to save your life, wee Ginger's not known for being a domestic goddess, so where's the 'heavenly' food coming from?"

Vidar's grin widened until it seemed to stretch from ear-to-ear. Slowly, he reached into his pocket, withdrew his wallet, extracted a fifty-pound-note, and placed it teasingly on the worktop, "Go to the movies, Elaine. I need to talk about women in a highly-offensive, men-only kind of way."

Elaine regarded Vidar in some surprise – she'd never heard him say anything remotely like that before – and was rewarded with particularly-lengthy contact with his unblinking gaze, the optical equivalent of a caress down her naked spine. She luxuriated in it, before recalling her husband, and snapping playfully, "Well, if you're going to be smutty, you can do it in the bothy."

She flicked Vidar's fifty back across the worktop to him, "Thanks, but I'll go to the movies on you another day..."

"Any time. Just ask."

While Vidar looked at Elaine until she thought her legs might give way, Stewart, oblivious to the effect his friend was having on his wife, topped up their coffees from the cafetière, and glugged a rich swirl of cream into the top of both, "Come on, I'm dying to know what you're going on about."

As Vidar sprinted in the driving rain across the patio to the ancient bothy Stewart had lovingly restored, Elaine tugged on her husband's arm, "I'm expecting the edited version later. Ask lots of questions – you never ask enough questions!"

"Ok!" Stewart put his hand over his coffee cup to keep the rain out, and followed Vidar as quickly as he could without spilling his drink.

As they let themselves in to the tiny stone bothy with its sod roof, Vidar inclined his head towards the kitchen, "What was that – did I upset her?"

"No, she wants the highlights later."

"Of course...I don't mean to exclude her, but I can't say half the stuff I want to without using language I think a listening woman might find offensive..."

"I'm even more desperate to know now."

"It's freezing in here!"

"Yeah, let's get the fire lit. Chuck us some of that kindling over…"

Within five minutes, Stewart had a gentle blaze crackling into merry life in the pot-bellied stove, and Vidar had manoeuvred two of the battered armchairs to take advantage of the already-radiating heat. At one end of the little bothy, a workbench, lathe, and various shelves of tools and implements frittered away many pleasant, pottering hours. The central stove, when roaring heartily, gave off enough heat to warm the building, and was topped by an old-fashioned hotplate.

The far end of the room housed pool table and dartboard, and had been habitually crammed with the Kirkbride boys and a collected assortment of local teenagers for much of the preceding decade.

Standing their cooling mugs on the hotplate to rewarm them, Vidar sank into an armchair, "I'd forgotten you don't sit on these chairs…they sort of absorb you…"

"That's a proper armchair, that is! It's the furniture equivalent of a warm hug with a fat girl." Stewart propped his feet on the log pile.

Vidar looked down the room to the end gable by the pool table, "I'd never shout about my pointing, but that wall's still up, so it can't be that bad."

"Did you do that bit?"

"I did that whole wall, and it's still standing! That's gotta be, what, ten years at least?"

"More…the boys were just changing school. It's frightening how fast the time goes…"

"It was hot that summer, wasn't it? We got really burnt doing the walls."

"Yeah, it was roasting! Don't you remember, once word got around that you were helping me, how all Elaine's mates kept showing up on flimsy pretexts, just so they could check out your pecs?"

Vidar laughed uproariously, "Are you sure? I don't remember that!"

"Oh, I do. Every five minutes another one'd appear..."

Vidar chuckled, "I do remember people coming round, but I just thought they were interested."

"Aye, in your torso."

"I'm not sure that's true. It might have been your torso – the dashing young doctor!"

"In a 'torso-off', you'd win hands down. Even my own wife thinks so!"

"Depends what you're after, doesn't it?"

"Aye, and they were all after you, mate."

Vidar grinned, shook his head, and passed Stewart his warmed coffee. Stewart was on the verge of standing up, going to the secret bottle stashed under the workbench, and suggesting his friend might fancy a nip of something more warming in his mug...when he remembered this was Vidar he was talking to – the man who, nowadays, didn't let as much as a headache tablet pass his lips. Stewart had read the past headlines like everyone else. Suggesting a nip of Scotch, and revealing where it was hidden, might be a step too far even this many years after his 'recovery'.

"Are you going to get to the bloody point, or are we going to sit here reminiscing about decades-old bricklaying all afternoon?"

"No, we're definitely not!"

"Come on then, what's making you strut like a peacock? It better not be a thing to do with Ginger Flett."

"Not a thing, buddy, I promise."

"Right. Good. Well?"

"You know the night you dropped me home?"

"Aye…and I did wonder about leaving you on your own. I'd never seen you so…low."

"You went, I let myself in…and there was a woman in my house."

"What?"

"Yep – a real, living, breathing, beautiful, lickable, fuckable woman."

"Wow! Who was she? I mean, were you expecting her? Had she been…laid on?"

Vidar laughed knowingly, "Laid on?"

Stewart was embarrassed at his own lack of personal experience of the seedier side of life, when compared with Vidar's well-documented worldliness.

"You know…"

"Yeah, I know! No, she wasn't 'laid on', as you so politely put it. It was a booking mix-up. I checked with Rag a while before I wanted to come here, and he said *Somerled* was empty until May…because no one wants to come over winter, right? I looked at the forecast, saw you'd already had snow, and thought 'screw that, I'll go to LA'. I said to Rag I was going to the States instead. About a week before I was done in London, I started to think about Christmas in LA; how I'd have to go to particular places, see people I wasn't bothered about, act a certain way…and I just couldn't face it. I thought about Denmark, but I knew I'd have to sit across the table from my parents at Ragnar's for Christmas dinner, and the idea of that put me off going. Despite wanting to see Rag and Jess and the kids – and I know I don't see enough of them – I felt as if I couldn't watch them being happy together. How screwed up is that? I even rang Jannick, and he said he had a big breeding programme going on. I was very welcome to visit, but he and Diego were spending the whole of the season with their arms up cows' privates, and I would hardly see them. There didn't seem much point flying to Argentina to be alone in a pile of cowshit. I felt so irrationally jealous of them all making plans and having people to do things with that I thought – forget this, I'm going to Orkney. I can sulk up there for weeks on end and no one will interrupt me or tell me to snap out of it. I don't have to see a soul, and I won't have to feel jealous of the people I love for having a much better time than I am."

"So, you came here in a huge strop, basically."

"Oh yeah, I was mad."

Vidar finished his coffee, and snuggled down more into his chair, nodding at the stove, "You need another log on there."

"Yes, your Lordship."

"You're nearer! You have your feet on the damn things!"

Stewart chuckled, leaning forward and using his jumper sleeve to inch open the now-red-hot stove door to wedge in two more logs, "You cold?"

"No, it's good now."

"It's bloody brilliant, isn't it? I do love it in here."

"We did a top job on this place."

"We should build a man-cave in that massive garden of yours, a little bolthole for you to escape to."

"I don't need one. I haven't anything to escape from! Well…"

"Well…?"

"Where was I?"

"You walk in, there's this lickable, fuckable woman…"

"Oh yeah – Rag's clearly had an enquiry and Let the house, because the last conversation I had with him, I told him I was going to LA."

"Right."

"So, I walk in and there she is, doing a headstand in the middle of the rug – "

"A headstand?"

"Yeah, she's a yoga nut."

Stewart pulled a face."

"No, Stew, it's amazing! It should be a spectator sport. I've no idea what I used to do with my afternoons before I had Live Yoga to watch. The things she can do with her body! She's…bendy…"

"How did you find that out?"

"By observation!"

"Righto…"

"Anyway, I'm standing there, just inside the door, not daring to breathe, move or anything…and she's doing this headstand, eyes closed, hasn't noticed me…and she's in head-to-toe lycra, man!

There's so little left to the imagination, it took no time at all to fill in the blanks. I was romping ahead. In my mind, I was halfway through something seriously erotic on the rug, when she opened her eyes and spotted me – and got the shock of her life, obviously. I was expecting her to go nuts, call the cops...but there was none of that, none at all."

"What do you mean?"

"Turns out she's a friend of Son's."

"You told me you were laying off the young girls – "

"I am! She's forty-two."

"But she's a friend of Sonia's?"

"Yeah – they seem really close."

Stewart stared at Vidar, as if in sudden comprehension, "That's why Sonia won't say who the father is! He's a sperm donor! They're lesbians!"

Again, Vidar dissolved into gales of laughter, "Oh, Stew, you do make me laugh..."

"What?"

"They're not lesbians."

"How do you know?"

"I know. I've...done...things to Sonia Flett. I can assure you, she's no lesbian...and this new lady we're discussing is getting divorced after twenty years of marriage to a man."

"Plenty of people live in long-term denial about their sexuality. You've been in free-and-easy California for too long."

"She's not a lesbian."

"You hope."

"She's not."

"You say that with a great deal of confidence for someone who's just 'observed'. All hypothetical; no practical…"

"I know she's not a lesbian."

"With no good explanation for that certainty."

"Who's telling this story?"

"Get on with it, then?"

"Well, stop interrupting! I keep losing my thread…"

"How do you handle an international, multi-million-dollar, jet setting showbiz career – you struggle to string a sentence together?"

"I have a team of people who are paid obscene amounts of money to put me in the right place, at the right time, in the right outfit, so I don't have to remember…mostly because I can't. Where was I?"

"Oh Christ! You thought she was going to call the police, but she didn't because she's Sonia's lesbian lover…"

Vidar sniggered, "Whatever… She recognised me!"

"You are slightly famous, you know."

"Not 'showbiz-me'! Thankfully, I don't think she has a clue about him. Son had pointed me out in pictures around the house, and obviously told her a bit about our past. She was fine about me being there. She was surprised, obviously, but she just said – oh, you're Sonia's friend…and then she was taking all the blame – I've made a mistake, I obviously shouldn't be here blah, blah, blah… She was trying to show me her booking confirmation, and all I could think was how I wanted to get her naked and do all kinds of dirty stuff to her! She was standing two feet away from me in nothing but this tiny lycra, and I was thinking 'all I've gotta do is reach forward and whip your top down'…but I didn't do it, Stew. I was a good boy."

"What happened then? How did you get from that to a week of her cooking you dinners?"

"Before I knew what was happening, while I was still standing there with my tongue unravelling across the floor like some cartoon character, she was asking me whether I was tired, or hungry. I was, of course, and I found myself being sat on the sofa, fed, watered…and it felt like the most natural thing in the world! She's lovely to talk to. It was an unalloyed pleasure to sit and interact the same way I do with you. Obviously, Stew, it was a bit different. No offence, but you don't have the body of a goddess – "

Stewart patted his stomach, "Too many biscuits; not enough sit-ups."

Vidar nodded wryly, "I also don't think you'd look as hot in lycra…and, you'll be relieved to know, I'm not fantasising about chucking you on the floor and screwing you senseless, but I felt the same as I feel here, as if I could sit all day and just let life be what it is – no calls, no timetable, no one demanding my input, my money, my skill; no plane to get on, no place to be. It's very unusual, and a precious luxury for me. When I get to do it, I really appreciate it. Sharing opinions, confidences, laughter. There it was, in the comfort of my own home! Totally unexpected, particularly when I'd been preparing myself to be alone and miserable. It was…incredible!" Vidar shook his head as if he still couldn't quite believe his luck.

"When did you swoop?"

"What?"

"Well, you must've done something to accelerate things from that to…this…a week later."

"You're getting the wrong idea, Stew. I told you, I'm being a good boy."

"I don't get it."

"You're quite right; I started off, even when we were sitting on the sofa talking, thinking 'any minute now, I'm just going to get you naked' – "

"You make it sound so easy!"

"It is easy! You tell them what you're going to do and, if you say it with enough authority and conviction, they just yield to the inevitable."

"But?"

"I found I was steering away from the idea of sex, because I didn't want to spoil what was already happening. I was thinking how much I was enjoying myself, and how easy it was to be with her. We were both relaxed, there was no agenda…and I realised it had never been like that with a woman before. In my life to date, women have ended up being for two things: fucking and fighting. When one stops, the other starts. The only way to stop one is with the other, until you lose track of where one ends and the other begins, and which was meant to be the good bit, 'cos it's all gone bad! This felt nothing like that."

Stewart felt like a fifteen-year-old, leaning forward and demanding, "What happened when it got to bedtime?"

Vidar waggled his eyebrows, which made Stewart crack up, but answered, "Another shock. I was expecting to have to call a cab, find a hotel, but she said – I don't have anywhere else to go, I've paid to be here, but it's your house and you have more right to be here than anyone. I'm in the guest room, not in your room...shall we just house-share for the time being?"

"Bloody hell – just like that?"

"I know! I nearly fell off my chair! I was thinking 'I'll share whatever you want, baby'."

Stewart chortled gleefully, "You are a bastard, aren't you?"

"I haven't said any of it to her face, Stew! I've been really behaving myself. It just feels too good to mess up, as if it's got phenomenal potential if I can get it right. That's what's stopping me leaping in with both feet. I'm such a screw-up with women. All I can do is the sex bit! Everything else is always a complete disaster...but that night, it didn't feel like that. It felt as if I could do the normal, nice, domesticated bit as well as the next guy."

"So, you haven't done a thing...sexually..."

"No."

"My God. I'm amazed! That is so unlike you it's rather comical. You're reduced to sitting on your hands with a pillow on your lap, pretending it's all jolly platonic!"

"Not quite..."

"I knew it!"

"What's that supposed to mean?"

"This is you we're talking about – the walking todger."

Vidar guffawed, "Is that my nickname? I never knew!"

"If it's not, it should be! If you're not 'just friends', what have you done?"

"I haven't used my 'todger' – that's a great word! – for anything yet…but I have been testing the boundaries a little, to see how far she'll let me go before she puts the brakes on."

"So far?"

"No brakes."

"How far's so far?"

"No touching…well, I've held her hand when she was talking about her horrible ex, and I touched her hair when she had something caught in it, and I've dried her feet – "

"Her feet?"

"Yeah – she was in the sea."

"The sea?"

"Never mind. What I mean is I'm doing the whole 'get close enough that the air between you smoulders and see who ignites first' thing…so I'm standing as near to her as I can but I'm not letting our bodies touch. I'm putting my mouth close to her skin but I'm not kissing her. That way, if she doesn't want it to go further, it doesn't have to – but if she does, I'm right there. I'm trying to ramp up the sexual tension."

"How is it?"

"Humming… I'm trying to manipulate her into being the one who cracks first. That way, it's her decision…but it's taking every ounce of my self-control not to put my hands all over her. Her body's beautiful, Stew. She's in superb shape for her age…and she's got big blue eyes, happy smile, lovely, glossy brown hair…she's just…stunning. I can't screw this up, Stew! Something tells me this is what I've been looking for forever, but how do you know for sure? How did you know with Elaine?"

"As you so rightly pointed out earlier, Elaine knew, I didn't. She was on her Fresher's Week and she marched up to me, slumped over my subsidised pint in the Union Bar, and went – Oi, Blondie, you're asking me out."

Vidar crowed with delight, "Go Elaine!"

"I was too scared to argue. I still am. It's fantastic! I was a nerdy, bookish boffin from a remote, tiny island, and she was this brash, streetwise city girl. She was younger than me, but she showed me things I had no idea about. I'd be thinking – how d'you know how to do that? Do it again!"

Vidar creased up against the side of the bucket-like armchair.

"I've been at her mercy ever since, but I don't care about that. I knew she was right for me. She brought me out of my shell, gave me self-belief. She used to badger me like hell about stuff – getting off my arse and going for things…but if anyone had a pop at me, she'd come down on them like an Exocet. No one had ever had my back like that before. Unconditionally, you know? She still fights for me, every day, in a million tiny ways. I'd crawl over razor blades with my flies unzipped for her…and then turn around and crawl back the other way."

Vidar was still laughing, "I love you two. You're my benchmark of a perfect relationship."

"It's not perfect. Nothing ever is."

"No, but it's enduring, and that makes it perfect in my eyes. That's my problem, I can pick women up without thinking…it's keeping them I have trouble with. I need to figure out what I'm doing wrong."

"You're such a wee goody-two-shoes with girls. You notice their hair and their outfit and suggest they've lost weight…it's sick-making, especially as we all know you don't mean it."

"Works though, doesn't it?"

"But it's fake! It's all Superman and no Clark Kent. You need to let a wee bit of both come out…so they get swept off their feet by Superman, but Clark gives them a project to work on. Women like a challenge. If you show a wee bit of vulnerability, they're hooked! Not only is he handsome, ripped and rich, but…he needs me! Women were put on this planet to nurture, so let 'em do it!"

"That's what I'm saying – I've never experienced that from a woman before…"

"Not being rude about your previous choices, but I wouldn't say you'd ever dated what I'd call a normal woman. Models, actresses, popstars – all so petrified of looking fat they'd never eat a dinner in a million years, let alone cook one for someone else! It's like you with the biscuits. With your punishing fitness regime, what difference will one biscuit make? It's paranoia! It just makes you miserable for no good reason. All it feeds is your vanity! Look how much you've obviously enjoyed a week of cramming lovely home-cooked food in your chops! I take it she's a good cook?"

"The best."

"Relax a wee bit. Stop trying to be perfect all the time. Bit more Clark Kent; bit less Superman."

"I did tell her about the drugs…in case she Googled me and saw my whole, disgusting history spread out before her in tabloid headlines."

"How was it when you told her?"

"Fine. Better than fine. I was…embarrassed…but she was really nice about it."

"Case rested, m'lud."

"So far, she's nice about everything. She's easy-going. The only thing she seems to take seriously is Sonia's welfare."

"What did I tell you? They all need something to look after, mate. It's nature – you can't fight it."

"Are you saying I have to be really needy?"

"No, you have to be you! You're still doing it! You're still putting your image before your happiness! If you don't pack it in, another chance will pass you by. Treat her like you treat me, Elaine, our boys, your brothers, their families…with respect and care and genuine affection. We all know it, and we feel it – and we know it's the real you. Display trust, and you'll get it back. Treat her the way you want to be treated, and she'll reciprocate. If you treat women like it's all an act you're putting on, they know your heart's not in it. They're not stupid. They know when they're being 'handled' and they use you right back."

"Yep – that is what normally happens."

"Do as you would be done by. Be honest with her, and she'll be honest with you. If it's got the potential you think it has, it'll blossom in its own time. I'm no relationship guru, but it's common sense to me."

Vidar absorbed Stewart's advice with thoughtful concentration, "I ask you because you have a successful and loving marriage, and I'm both admiring and envious of it."

"There's no reason, just because you're in the public eye, why you can't have something equally successful and loving. You put as much effort into this as you've traditionally invested in your job, and the sky's the limit!"

****

"Come on, Grace! What's he done – kissed you, groped your arse, stuck his tongue in your ear…?"

"What is it about this place?"

"What?"

"Everyone has to know the minutiae of your business!"

"Welcome to life in a tiny rural community."

Grace tutted, and tossed her hair back over her shoulder with an irritable flick of the wrist, "I'm not used to discussing stuff like this with anyone!"

Sonia watched Grace keenly, convinced she wanted to talk but didn't know how to begin, "Listen, how about if I start and you join in?"

Grace stood stiffly, "I need to check the lunch."

"Och, you've just put it in!"

"That oven doesn't cook evenly! I need to check it's not catching on top. You won't want to eat it if it's burnt, will you?"

"You're not escaping from this, Grace!"

Grace ran up the steps to the kitchen, examining the pie through the glass door with an intensity it didn't warrant, and taking an eternity to turn the oven down to her desired temperature.

Sonia basked in the warmth of self-assurance, wriggling up onto her knees with some difficulty. She felt like a balloon animal from a children's party; limbs puffy and odd, body pinched in at the joints and swelling uncomfortably outward, skin stretching, flesh tight, ready to pop. Leaning over the back of the sofa, she repeated, "I'll start. You mustn't be embarrassed. It's only sex...it's not weird or anything. The best and most memorable sex I've had has been with Vidar. If you do get the opportunity to do it with him, you should. I guarantee you'll enjoy it. He's very good at it. All those girlfriends...he's spent a lot of time perfecting his technique!" Sonia shoved her tongue in her cheek, and winked suggestively at her friend.

Despite her extreme embarrassment, Grace couldn't help giggling at Sonia's expression. Giving in, she sighed, abandoned the rocket-science of the oven controls, and padded back down to the sofa.

"There've been...signs that something might...but I could just be getting it all wrong! Oh, Sonia, he just exudes confidence and control and...power! He's used to people doing what he wants, isn't he? Half of me is terrified of something happening with him, and the other half is desperate for...I don't know! His presence is compelling, but it's intimidating as well. It's good being here with him, and I feel fine, completely relaxed – talking to him and knocking around the house with him – and then he says something in particular...or he looks at me! That's probably the worst bit," Grace peeked shyly at Sonia, "and the best. There's something predatory in that look, as if he's a hungry lion and I'm a passing antelope. It's…as if he wants to consume me!"

"I have experienced 'The Look', but I'm not sure it ever had quite the effect it seems to be having on you. What's he done?" probed Sonia again, more gently this time, in light of Grace's extreme agitation.

"Nothing," admitted Grace, unsure whether she felt relief or disappointment.

"Explain. Why are you getting your knickers in such a twist if nothing's happened?"

"He gets really, really close to me…so close I can feel him, the heat coming off his body. It makes me tingle from head to toe with what must be anticipation, I suppose…but he doesn't touch me. He puts his mouth millimetres from my skin, but he doesn't kiss me. I think he's going to, and I find myself leaning towards him just to make some contact happen by accident, but he must be hyper-aware of that because he's always near enough to make me flustered, but far enough away for me to wonder if I'm getting the wrong end of the stick. Am I reading into this something that isn't there? Am I clutching at straws because I'm feeling vulnerable, or lonely, or scared of having to start again as a middle-aged woman?"

"No. He's winding you up for it, Grace! This is what he does. When he makes his move, he'll seem like a super-stud when he hasn't done anything. He's made you do it all inside your own head. It's foreplay, Rasmussen-style! You'll be in such a state by the time he does touch you, you'll just melt in a wee puddle of orgasmic goo."

Grace covered her eyes with her hands, and groaned, "Oh, Sonia, the things you say!"

Sonia cackled, "He's got you right where he wants you, hasn't he? You need to take control of this, pronto. Don't let him dictate it, otherwise he'll keep toying with you for his own amusement. He knows exactly what he's doing…"

Grace chewed her lip pensively, "I don't have your self-confidence, Sonia."

"I bet you actual, real, rustly money he's feeling as randy as you are. Pick your moment, and pounce!"

Grace was mortified, "I can't! I've never pounced in my life!"

Sonia threw back her head and laughed in a way that made her seem a lot older than her twenty-six years, "Grace, he looks at you like you're an oasis in the desert! He's not going to object if you slake his thirst outside his pre-determined timetable, is he? I can't picture him holding up a staying hand as you prowl towards him peeling off items of clothing…" Sonia did her Vidar impression, "Sorry Grace, hold it there. I had this down for a week next Tuesday…put your knickers back on, babe."

Grace had a hand over her mouth to hold in the giggles, like a schoolgirl who's just been told her first dirty joke.

Both women jumped in unison at the sound of the door, upturning shocked and guilty faces to Vidar, "It's terrible out there now. Stew brought me back 'cos it's raining so hard. You two look really shifty. What are you up to?"

"Nothing," said Sonia mildly, "Just chatting…"

"About?" Vidar was suspicious.

"Gynaecology," said Sonia, seriously.

Grace snorted and buried her face in a cushion.

Bemused, Vidar directed an interrogative look at Sonia, who shrugged as if Grace's outburst was nothing whatever to do with her.

He'd been gone a dangerous couple of hours – quite long enough for Sonia, sweet little pain-in-the-arse that she was, to do his cause some real damage if she chose. Unable to resist being near Grace, Vidar walked down the steps and sat on the sofa in the space between the two women. Grace had recovered her composure sufficiently to cease giggling, and sat wiping the tears of laughter from her eyelashes and cheeks with thin fingers.

Turning to Sonia, Vidar asked one of his characteristically direct questions, "Have you been badmouthing me to Grace?"

Sonia's expression was coy, "Far from it!"

Vidar narrowed his eyes, "What does that mean?"

"I was actually telling Grace what a stud you were…"

Vidar gawped at Sonia, who relished the fact she'd so easily managed to perturb the usually-unflappable Dane.

He turned his shocked face to Grace, who shook her head reassuringly, and muttered, "The things she comes out with! She makes me feel like such a prude!"

"Unusually, me too!"

Sonia winked at him, and gave him a double 'thumbs-up'.

Grace looked at her watch, "Are you ready for lunch? I think it's done." She lifted the deliciously-aromatic pie from the oven and carried it to the table.

Vidar smiled at Sonia, and whispered, "Nice here, isn't it?"

"Aye...not bad..."

"You could do a lot worse than follow her example, you know."

"What, follow my Mam's, you mean?"

Vidar shrugged, "Well, whatever you do, make sure you don't follow mine, huh?"

Grace pulled out her chair and was just about to sit when Vidar leant close to her and kissed her cheek gently, "Thank you, Grace. This is lovely," before busying himself doling out plates and cutlery, and pouring drinks. Frozen in place, Grace's wide, shocked eyes sought Sonia's, who did a quick impression of someone melting in a puddle of orgasmic goo, which, of course, set Grace's giggles going again.

Sonia hefted up her heavy body and waddled stiffly to the table, slumping onto a chair as if exhausted by the effort, trying not to grin as Grace fought to control her laughter and successfully cut the delicious-smelling filo parcel with a wobbling hand.

Vidar looked from one to the other, "I have no idea what's going on here, but I feel really outnumbered."

Sonia leant back in her dining chair and stroked her hands gently down both sides of her bump, "You wait...if this one's a girl too, you really won't stand a chance!"

ELEVEN

"Hey Stew, what's happening?"

"Everything, as usual! I'm just ringing while I've got five minutes, before I forget again. I was supposed to ring you the other day and it slipped my mind. What are you doing this evening?"

"Nothing special," Vidar tried to keep his voice light. Nothing special meant the usual evening tying himself in knots of desire and indecision; longing for Grace, and petrified of getting it wrong.

"Bob Turner's having Christmas drinks at his house. You know, along the lane a bit from me."

"Is he the guy whose wife is a music teacher?"

"Aye."

"Yeah, I know. The house with the blue door."

"That's the one!"

"Why are you telling me? Your two hardly need a babysitter these days…or do you need me to tuck Elaine in?"

"Steady on, old son, don't give her ideas, will you?"

Vidar laughed richly. Grace glanced up from the steps by the kitchen, where she sat painting her toenails, mouthing, "What?" at him. Winking, Vidar shook his head, and questioned, "What's it got to do with me?"

"I was supposed to invite you. I forgot. He told me to, days ago! Big fan, apparently. I don't know how it cropped up in conversation, but I told him you were here for Christmas and he practically wet himself! I said I'd ask you to his drinks, and then I forgot..."

"I don't know, Stew. When you say drinks, you mean drinks, don't you?"

"Well, I do...but...it's not like he doesn't know. He won't give you a whisky, mate...he'll give you a lemonade."

Vidar sighed, agitated, scraping a hand distractedly through his hair.

Stewart could detect his friend's distress, the hesitation on the other end of the telephone line, "Mate...if it's too much...? I just thought it might be nice for you to have an ego boost, that's all...as you're having a wee 'wobble'. I also thought it might be a pleasant stroll home on a chilly evening with a new friend, if you see what I mean? And, obviously, if you bring her, we all get to have a good look at her and gossip about you all evening."

"You're an asshole."

"I'm thinking of you, mate! How's it going being Clark Kent?"

Vidar glanced across at Grace, who was absorbed in applying a second coat, pink tip of her tongue protruding from between her lips as she concentrated.

"I don't know."

"Anything happened after what you told me last week?"

"No..."

"Who are you, and what have you done with Vidar?"

Vidar chuckled cheerlessly, and admitted, "I've reached a point where I don't know what to do."

"Hmmm...romantic stroll on a frosty night, I reckon."

"You're not going to give this up, are you?"

"No...'cos I promised him I'd get you to come. You wouldn't want me to look as if I'm full of shite about my showbiz connections, would you?"

"Don't tempt me, 'cos I'm feeling manipulated."

"Please. I promised him! He's a massive fan...he's been to loads of your concerts! You wouldn't want to disappoint a genuine admirer, would you?"

"Oh, all right!"

"Fantastic! There was one other thing..."

"What?"

"I wondered whether you might fancy bringing your guitar...?"

"Oh, Jesus, I'm the free cabaret!"

"Vid, please...I'll owe you one."

"You'll owe me more than one, you crafty bastard!"

"Thanks, mate. I really appreciate it, honestly I do. Bob'll be over the moon! Half-sevenish, yeah?"

"Give him the heads-up, Stew. No booze, not even for a joke, right?"

"He wouldn't dare. You going to bring her?"

"I'll ask."

"She'll need keeping warm on the way home – guaranteed!"

"Will you stop? I think you need more bromide in your tea."

Stewart sniggered, "See you both at seven-thirty..."

"What's the dress code of this thing?"

"You're the free cabaret, mate...wear what you like!"

"Asshole."

"Tatty-bye!"

Vidar cut the call with a sigh of exasperation.

Grace looked up, screwing the top on her varnish, "What's up?"

"Stewart Kirkbride, everyone's favourite Super-Duper Doc has stitched me right up!"

"How?"

"By saying I'll be the free entertainment for his friend's Christmas drinkies tonight!"

Grace laughed at his scowling face, "Well, it gets you out of the house, you miserable old sod."

Vidar grinned, got up from the piano stool, and walked over to sit on the step beside her. Grace extended fingers and toes, all painted the same deep cherry-red, "Christmassy, right?"

Teasingly, "Absolutely."

Grace rolled her eyes in mock annoyance, "I don't know why I bother!"

Vidar glanced at her, an encouraging thought occurring, "Did you do them on my account?"

Grace looked embarrassed, mumbling, "I did them on a sort of making-an-effort-not-to-let-things-slide account…"

"Good job you did, because you're going out this evening."

Grace pulled a face, "They don't want me! Have you heard my singing?"

"Oh, that's what it was! I thought you'd stubbed your toe or something…"

Grace whacked him in the chest, before squeaking in alarm and minutely examining her nails in case she'd smudged them.

Enchanted, Vidar put an arm round her, pressed a firm palm against her hip, and slid her along the step to bump against him. Lowering his head to hers made Grace upturn her big, blue eyes to him, and Vidar felt the now all-too-familiar stuttering in his self-control. Should he just do something, right here, right now?

"Thing is, Grace, I need your help. These events...they're fine, you know, nice people and good atmosphere...but there'll be a lot of booze sloshing around all night, and I find it...difficult..."

Grace regarded him intently, a frown of concentration producing a little wrinkle between her eyebrows. He wanted to kiss it away.

"The merrier everybody gets, the more drinks start to flow in my direction...and I want to drink them all, but I know I can't...I mustn't..."

Vidar closed his eyes briefly, and rubbed at his temples with his left hand, subconsciously hugging Grace closer with the right. Sympathetic, she stroked a palm lightly across his thigh, painted nails bright against the black of his jeans. The lightness of her touch made his skin tingle. Yearning, desperate, his hand gripped tighter, fingers threading through the belt loops of her jeans, tugging her closer still, before he mastered his longing and relaxed the tension in his enveloping arm.

"This guy, Bob Turner, is a bit of a fan, which is lovely...but if I'm supposed to make his party go with a swing, I need a wingman to protect me from the alcohol. I was kinda hoping that could be you. Will you help me?"

Grace's eyes twinkled mischievously, "Course I will! Goose to your Maverick. Slider to your Ice-Man. Muttley to your Dick Dastardly."

Vidar, working hard to appear vulnerable, got the giggles and failed in his attempt to resemble a puppy left out in the rain, "Thanks, Muttley. I owe you one."

Grace patted his knee, "No you don't. You're letting me stay in your house."

"*Our* house," he whispered insistently.

Grace enjoyed the little shiver that ran up her spine at the featherlight touch of Vidar's lips against her ear, "What do I have to wear to this thing?"

"Whatever you want. It's only up the lane. We'll walk there…so something warm enough to walk in, I guess."

"Not my hot pants then?"

Vidar was accosted by a vivid image of Grace bending over the oven in nothing but hot pants, and fidgeted with uncharacteristic discomfiture.

"Some of the neighbours are a bit elderly. They might keel over if you rock up in hot pants."

"Horror?"

"Joy."

"'Tis the season to be jolly…" Grace reminded.

"Bottom line – no pun intended – you put hot pants on, we won't make it out of the house, so I'm vetoing the hot pants. Of course, if you really want to wear them, you can always put them on when we get back…"

Laughing and blushing, Grace tapped her still-drying fingers against his cheek in good-natured admonishment, and bounced to her feet, "Right, if you won't let me wear my special occasion hot pants, I'll have to go and see what else I've got that's suitable for a collection of whisky-sodden pensioners I've never met!"

She strolled off towards the guest room. Vidar lay on his back on the floor, legs stretching down the steps, watching upside-down as her body moved away from him, wondering if he should follow, knowing he wouldn't. He wanted this, and he thought she wanted it too, but when was right? When would mean the difference between success and failure?

TWELVE

"Oooh, it's bitter out here!"

"See how the 'no hot pants' directive was a good call?"

"Very practical," Grace fiddled with her scarf, tucking it tighter inside her jacket, plugging the gaps around her neck against ingress of icy air.

Vidar swung his guitar case across his body with a practised movement, and turned to pull the door shut, "Got keys?"

Grace fumbled in her pocket, and a set of keys jingled in her gloved fingers, catching the moonlight.

"Cool," Vidar closed the door.

Grace took a deep breath, already anaesthetising herself to the critical scrutiny of a new company of strangers, wondering how long she would have to stand alone in the corner of the room at this gathering, false smile fastened to aching features, clutching her half-full glass as if it was her final link to self-control.

Vidar took her hand as he had that first day on the wind-raked sand dunes, as if he always held her hand whenever they walked down the road to parties. When she went anywhere with Dominic, he strode off ahead impatiently, and she was forced to scuttle after him in her too-high heels.

Her nervousness dissipated at Vidar's touch, and they set off down the steep shingle track. The earlier wet snowfall – a blizzard of fat, sticky flakes driven on a harsh north-easterly wind – had partially-melted prior to sunset, when the sky had cleared and the temperature plummeted, freezing the residue of the snow into a thick layer of gleaming ice crystals that crunched noisily underfoot. Grace skidded on the treacherous shingle, and nearly fell. Vidar instinctively slid his arm around her, turning swiftly and causing his own feet to skate, making Grace spin to grab his shoulders and prevent him falling too, again slipping herself, yelping in alarm, and gripping onto the front of Vidar's jacket. Eventually, they stilled, clinging to one another, gasping.

"Are we gonna make it?"

"High heels and ice don't mix."

"Knew I shouldn't have worn mine," Vidar glanced at his watch, "Wanna go back up and change shoes?"

Grace shook her head firmly, "No, it's a party. You can't go to a party in flat shoes."

"Ah, that's where I've been going wrong all these years, obviously. Are we carrying on then?"

"Won't get there by standing here! I might just have to tiptoe gingerly down to the bottom of the driveway."

"If you fall, I'll catch you, if I'm not already on my ass. Either way, one of us will have a soft landing."

Grace grinned, hooked her arm through his without asking permission, and held onto his bicep with both hands more firmly than she needed to, enjoying the feel of the moving muscles under his coat.

"It's amazing here, isn't it? One minute blowing a gale so you can hardly stand up, the next so still your breath just sits in the air in front of you. Look," she exhaled a cloud of moisture that hung before her face as if imprisoned within an invisible bubble, "One extreme to the other."

Vidar regarded her thoughtfully, "You know what's unusual about you – your ability to find fascination everywhere, to be pleased and entertained by everything around you."

"Is that a good thing?" Uncertainty churned within Grace. She could hear Fen's derisive snort, 'Darling, are you five? When you talk like that, quite honestly Grace, you sound simple.'

Vidar's reply was unequivocal, and Fen's sneering face vanished as if Grace had extended an arm and pushed her over, "Of course it's a good thing! It's making me appreciate stuff I never would have noticed before. Most people look to criticise, not to wonder…"

Grace beamed, and clung on tighter.

****

At the cottage with the blue door, a Christmas tree sparkled in one front window, and strings of fairy-lights in the hedges marked the footpath like an airport runway. The chimney smoked persistently, a heavy peat fire already well-banked and warming the interior.

Vidar opened the gate. It creaked as it swung. He turned, as usual, to see Grace through before him, and looked up in surprise as she hesitated. The Fen of her imagination recovered from the earlier shove, got up, dusted herself off, and regarded Grace with fresh horror – 'That's what you're wearing, is it? And do those silly, showy earrings even go? You look as if you've made no effort at all. You haven't done anything with your hair – have you even brushed it? What do you think you look like?'

"What's up?"

Grace whipped off a glove and touched a hand to her hair, relieved it felt smooth. She had remembered to brush it. "Do I look a fright? Do I look as if I haven't made an effort?"

"What's brought this on?"

"Something made me wonder whether I was a bit 'underdressed'." She didn't want to tell him Fen was standing right next to him, watching it all, "I mean, I'm just in my jeans."

"So am I."

Grace smiled dismissively, as if Vidar was missing the point, "Yes, but you're...you. You could turn up to a Royal Wedding in your jeans and everyone would forgive you. Me, they'd take to the Tower." Fenella nodded vigorously, as if it was quite right and proper that this should be so. Grace tried not to look at Fen, so Vidar wouldn't realise she was there, and pleaded with him, "Do you see?"

Vidar's lazy grin creased his handsome face. He reached out to take her hand, "Grace, you look...beautiful. You always look beautiful to me, whatever you're wearing, whatever you're doing. You're so beautiful, I can hardly take my eyes off you..."

Stunned into silence, Grace stood outside the gate with mouth open and eyes wide, gawping at Vidar until the sound of the opening front door distracted him, "Someone said there were people outside and...it's you!"

Although prepared to feel well-disposed towards Bob because he was both a fan and a friend of Stewart's, Vidar could quite happily have thumped the man for the timing of his appearance. Something had been shifting in the still night air between he and Grace, moulding and shaping itself into an opportunity to alter the nature of their relationship. Vidar tore his gaze from Grace with extreme reluctance, and switched on the showbiz charm. Flashing the trademark grin, advancing up the path pulling the still-thunderstruck Grace behind him, extending a hand, he exclaimed expansively, "Bob! We've met before at Stewart's, I think? I was talking to your wife about her music teaching."

Bob, hopelessly gratified by this exalted being remembering such a miniscule level of detail about him, was too overcome for any reply except an enthusiastic, double-handed pump of Vidar's proffered palm. Easing Grace gently forward, and placing a possessive arm around her shoulders, Vidar said, "This is my friend, Grace Hamilton. Grace, Bob is a colleague of Dr Kirkbride. No one can get sick tonight because this whole house will be full of the entire Orkney NHS, all drunk as skunks!"

Grace turned a dazzling smile upon Bob, gushing brightly, "Don't listen to him teasing! So lovely to meet you. It was ever so kind of you to let me come..." Bob was so instantly entranced by Grace he almost forgot Vidar was still there. He welcomed her in with alacrity, ushering her into a living room packed to the rafters with curious acquaintances, who might have given it a miss on a cold Christmas Eve were it not for the tantalisingly-dangled carrot of Vidar Rasmussen. Vidar grinned broadly at Grace's effect on Bob. She had the same ability as he to effortlessly enrapture everyone she encountered, but where Vidar knowingly-leveraged his charisma to get his own way, Grace seemed utterly unaware she possessed any.

Shrugging off his coat and adding it to the jumble already on the hooks, Vidar hefted up his guitar case and followed Bob and Grace into the lounge. The buzz of chatter increased in volume as every eye in the room alighted upon Grace. Each man momentarily wished he'd popped down unaccompanied. Each woman was suddenly convinced she'd arrived overdressed for a simple, neighbourly get-together. In jeans and a fitted white shirt, Grace exuded classic, relaxed style, as if she'd got up off the sofa, thrown on a jacket, and wandered down the road for a social drink. Her concession to the season was to dress up the simplicity of her outfit with high heels and long, costume earrings that dangled amongst the glossy, chestnut hair, and occasionally flashed a diamanté twinkle to the curious female onlookers. They noted the expensive watch, the berry-red manicure, the merest touch of lip gloss to otherwise naked features, and simultaneously hated her, desired her favour, and wished to metamorphose into her upon the instant.

The excited babble became reverent hush as the second visitor entered the room. Vidar, used to causing a stir, grinned amiably at the assembled throng of gawking faces, and bent to kiss Bob's mousey wife on the cheek and ask where she wanted him.

Elaine Kirkbride, jubilant at the chance to show off in front of so many people at once, elbowed her way through the awe-struck gathering to stand before Vidar and be treated to a proper bear-hug and generous kiss – in front of everyone! Stewart wasn't far behind her, shaking Vidar's hand warmly.

"Grace, these are my very best friends in the whole of the UK, Stewart and Elaine Kirkbride. Guys, this is Grace, who I think I mentioned...?"

Vidar winked at them both over Grace's head, a secret sign not to reveal how much they already knew.

"Hello," Grace twinkled a delighted smile.

"Lovely to meet you, Grace." Stewart couldn't argue with the accuracy of Vidar's description of Grace. As Grace turned to shake hands and exchange pleasantries with Elaine, Stewart's eyes met Vidar's, and a nod of affirmation passed between the two friends.

Vidar was distracted by Bob's wife, Susan, directing him to a corner of the room near fire and Christmas tree, where he could sit with his guitar. Vidar tugged at Elaine's hand, pulling her with him. Elaine was not unwilling to go, perceiving how much notice people were taking of her because of her obvious closeness to the guest of honour. Tonight would do her reputation no harm at all.

"Elaine, take care of Grace for me, will you? Get her a drink, don't leave her on her own...you know."

"Of course I'll look after her, Hen. It will be my pleasure," glowing with pride at being specially selected to babysit the second most fascinating person in the room.

"Can you get me a drink, too? Don't let them give me any booze, no matter how much they insist."

"Don't worry! What would you like?"

"Glass of water will be fine for me." Vidar lifted his guitar and pushed the empty case under the nearby dining table. Swinging the strap over his shoulder, he sat on the corner table and put his foot up on the chair Mrs Turner had expected him to sit on, instantly assuming the position and persona of the self-assured wandering minstrel.

Stewart leant down to whisper in Grace's ear, appreciating the subtle citrus scent of her perfume, and the soft brush of her hair against the knuckles of the hand that tapped her arm and gestured towards Vidar, "Have you seen him in action before?"

"He plays at home…just practising…"

Stewart noticed she'd called *Somerled* 'home', and vowed to retain that nugget to share with Vidar later, "You watch him work the room. Five minutes and, even if they're way too cool for a singalong, they'll be eating out of his hand, crooning away with all the rest." Grace smiled happily up at Stewart, and he momentarily experienced a flutter of desire, a sensation that tightened his chest and somersaulted his stomach; a hint of what Vidar must be feeling in the constant company of this engaging, alluring woman. No wonder it was driving him to distraction!

His friend was speaking. A solitary man in the corner of a packed room with just a guitar and no microphone, his low voice nevertheless cut commandingly through the hubbub to effortlessly achieve pindrop silence, "Hi everyone. My name's Vidar. Bob and Susan very kindly let me come over tonight, and they said it might be nice for us to have a little Christmas music."

Here, Vidar played a few chords on the guitar, as if warming the room up to the idea, "We can do Christmas crooners, carols, folk songs, ballads, rude songs – once everyone gets a little more drunk…" Laughter rippled. Grace noticed all conversation had ceased, and every eye was on Vidar. She thought if a crowded room looked so keenly at her, she'd want the ground to open up and swallow her, but Vidar appeared completely comfortable exceeding the critical expectations of strangers.

"Just shout out what you might like, and I'll give it my best shot. If I don't know the words, I'll make 'em up..." Louder laughter, and Vidar launched, as if he'd rehearsed it a million times, into a smiling, rich-voiced, cleverly-accompanied 'Chestnuts roasting on an open fire, Jack Frost nipping at your nose...' A few people in the room began to quietly sing with him, growing in confidence as more joined in.

"Smooth bastard, isn't he?" said Stewart to Grace, who didn't seem to hear him. She was staring at Vidar with unconcealed admiration; this evening her first glimpse of the professional, skilled, and versatile performer.

"Come on, Grace," Elaine slid her arm through that of the glossy beauty, "Let's get you a wee dram and you can meet some people..."

****

Vidar sang for over an hour to uproarious audience participation, happily observing the Kirkbrides circulating Grace around the room, introducing her to neighbours and colleagues. Vidar watched in satisfaction as Grace shook hands, beamed with characteristic enthusiasm at the loveliness of everything, universally bewitched the company, and generally appeared pink-cheeked with pleasure and a tot or two of whisky; laughing, joking and chatting inamongst

Elaine's roistering friendship group of what he and Stewart teasingly called 'The Naughty Nurses'.

When Mrs Turner whispered in Vidar's ear that there was buffet in the kitchen, Vidar nodded, and shared with his admiring audience, "Our generous hostess says there are snacks in the kitchen. I'm gonna have a break and a mince pie or three…and then we'll see if you can still sing in tune." Generous applause, and an exodus of bodies towards the little kitchen, creating a chatting bottleneck in the doorway through which Stewart wriggled, bearing a steaming mug of coffee and a plate of mince pies. He made a beeline for Vidar, passing him the cup, "There you go, mate."

"Thanks buddy. I think they're having fun, don't you?"

"They're loving it."

"Good. Bob satisfied?"

"You could autograph one of your snotty hankies and Bob'd frame it."

About to report what he gleaned from Grace, Bob appeared at Stewart's side, brandishing a CD, "Saw you Unplugged in Berlin in 2000…superb! I wondered if you'd mind signing my CD?" Bob waggled a 'Sharpie' under Vidar's nose. Smiling expansively, as only a professional entertainer can, Vidar drawled, "'Course Bob!"

Relieving the man of his pen and CD, and extracting the inner booklet, Vidar inclined his head teasingly, "You absolutely sure, Bob, only you know it'll instantly devalue it by twenty bucks?"

Bob grinned, spellbound, "I'm sure."

"Ok." Vidar scribbled a message and scrawled his signature with a flourish, "My handwriting's terrible, but it says 'Here's to great Christmas parties'. Is that ok?"

If Bob could have done so and lived it down, he would have thrown himself to the floor and kissed the man's feet – a personal message on an autographed CD, making it not only priceless to Bob, but valuable to a collector too!

"Fantastic..." he stammered.

"Righto, Bob," said Stewart, impatiently, "Go and put that somewhere safe."

Bob looked as if he was going, before turning back, and mumbling, "Your...er...friend. She's very...engaging...isn't she?"

Vidar winked at him, "Yes Bob...very."

Bob blushed, and Stewart sighed with exasperation, "Will you bugger off, Bob? I need to have a quiet word in my pal's ear."

"Oh...right...aye..." Bob gestured with the CD, "Thanks for..."

"No problem. Thank you for letting us come to your party."

Bob stumbled off, undeniably a happily-married man, but nevertheless ever so slightly in love with Vidar Rasmussen.

Stewart rolled his eyes, "Bloody hell! I thought he'd taken root!"

"It's his house, he can stand where he wants," Vidar pointed out, ever-reasonable, "but his timing does suck. I thought I was making some progress earlier with my 'engaging friend'. Thirty seconds more out there in the dark and I think something would've clicked...but, no, Enter Bob Stage Right, so I had to switch on the showbiz and forget the rest of it."

"It's surprising, really," explained Stewart, "'cos he's an anaesthetist. You'd think, in his line of work, timing'd be everything."

Vidar laughed and reached for a mince pie, taking a generous bite and chewing with an increasingly-dissatisfied expression, before dropping the uneaten half back onto the plate. Dry, glutinous pastry; measly, flavourless filling...not a patch on Grace's, with flaky, buttery pastry dissolving on the tongue, and a rich pop of mincemeat bursting in the mouth. Grace's pies were twice the size of Susan Turner's, and were always served warm with a hefty mound of clotted cream atop each steaming, sweet-smelling, mouth-watering treat.

"No good?" Stewart chewed his way through the other half of Vidar's pie. Ok, bit dry...sort of like Elaine's efforts, "Just a mince pie."

"Grace's are much better. Have one of hers and you'll never be able to eat crap ones like that again."

Stewart smiled privately at Vidar's partisan favouring of Grace's cooking over anyone else's.

Vidar washed away the taste of the very-average pie with a swig of coffee, "What did you want to tell me anyway?"

A few people were drifting back from the kitchen with standard plates of party-fare, all trying to have some interaction with the star in their midst – eye-contact, a nod, a smile, a raised glass in his direction. Vidar made sure to smile at all of them, whilst still appearing to give Stewart his undivided attention. It was an uncanny skill; one which Stewart wished Vidar could teach him, as it would enable him to concentrate totally on the Rugby whilst appearing to listen devotedly to every word his wife uttered.

"I asked if she'd ever seen you play before...and she said only when you practice at home..."

"At home?" Vidar's head snapped up, registering the significance.

"Aye...at home."

"Oh..."

"And then, when you went into smooth bastard mode," Vidar began to chuckle, "she just stood there gaping at you, unable to believe her eyes."

"Oh yeah?" Vidar was trying to keep it low-key, but his excitement was palpable.

"I think you impressed her, mate. She hasn't seen 'Showbiz Vid' in action before, has she?"

"No, I guess not."

"Well, every other woman in the room fancies you after that display, so why should she be any different?"

"What do you think of her, Stew?"

"I'm spoken-for, so I obviously don't have opinions about other women – "

"Oh, come on!"

"But, if I did, I'd think she was bloody gorgeous and you're a jammy sod."

"She is gorgeous, isn't she? I just wanted a second opinion in case I'd gone a bit nutty by going without for so long..."

"Oh, no, she's the real deal all right. If I wasn't a happily married man, you wouldn't stand a chance, pal! I'd be pinning her against

Sue's Aga right now, impressing her with my extensive physiological knowledge."

"You keep your goddam qualifications to yourself!"

Elaine snaked an arm around her husband's waist, "God, I'm rat-arsed…what are you two grinning about like a couple of naughty schoolboys?"

"Stewart's comprehensive medical training," replied Vidar, nudging Stewart, "She's pissed, Doc. You need to get her home and give her a thorough physical examination before she sobers up."

Elaine extended a wavering finger, "Shut it, you."

Vidar squeezed the end of her finger between his own, and Elaine giggled drunkenly.

Grace appeared from the kitchen, and Stewart was amused to observe his friend's utter enchantment as she advanced towards them. Smiling warmly at the Kirkbride's, she reached to press her fingers to the back of Vidar's hand, "I was going to get you some buffet, but it all looked a bit…" here, she glanced left and right before leaning forward and whispering, "out of a packet."

Stewart chortled, "You said that as if it was blasphemy!"

Grace blinked at him, nonplussed. In her world, it was blasphemy! Vidar elaborated, bridging the gulf between the lives of the Kirkbrides and the rarefied air Grace had breathed until a couple of months ago, "Grace, if you had a little soirée in London and you needed to do canapés, what would you do?"

Grace frowned, as if it might be a trick question, "Make them…?"

"Completely?"

"Yes…?"

"From scratch?"

"Yes…?"

Vidar turned back to Stewart, triumphant, "See? That's why those mince pies taste like shit!"

"Are they not good?" asked Grace.

"No," said Vidar, "They're as terrible as Elaine's."

Stewart creased up, and Elaine, dozing drunkenly against her husband's chest, roused sufficiently to squawk, "What?" as Grace gaped, unsure whether he was joking or not, "You're so rude to her!"

"She's drunk! She won't remember I even said that tomorrow, once Stewie's given her a good, festive seeing-to."

Shaking her head, laughing, realising she was being teased, Grace shoved his shoulder, gasping, "Stop it, Vid!" as both men grinned at each other.

Stewart gazed indulgently at Elaine, cuddled up against him, eyes closed, beatific smile on her face, "I had better take her home while she can actually walk. She may be a midget, but I still don't want to have to carry her all the way up the lane."

"Was Rory happy with that record, by the way?"

"Off the chart, mate! He thinks the sun shines out of your arse now."

"Well, that's because it does…"

"Right, we're off before she keels over." He shook Vidar's hand, "Have a top day tomorrow. Enjoy your doubtless-gourmet lunch, eh?" Stewart winked at Vidar, turning to Grace and planting a kiss on both cheeks, "Lovely to meet you, Grace. Sorry about my inebriated wife."

"Not at all, she's great fun. Good to meet you both."

"Merry Christmas."

"You too."

"Better find Bob and say bye."

"See you later, buddy."

Stewart hefted his wife across the room to the general amusement of the closest onlookers, before calling back, "Mind how you go on your way 'home'…"

Vidar absorbed the teasing dig with a knowing smile, "We will…"

"What's he talking about?" asked Grace, suspiciously.

"I said we were falling about like Bambi on the way down."

Grace smiled.

"I need to do Part Two. Can you get me another glass of water?"

"Certainly."

"Thank you, sweetheart," Vidar treated her to the steady gaze and lazy grin she'd begun to realise were for her alone, before switching on the professional persona, hooking his guitar over his head, and turning his attention back to the room, "Ok everybody, I hope you've all had a chance to nibble something of Susan's…" A raise of his eyebrows, met with laughter, whistles, shouts, "Let's see if you're all in as fine voice as earlier, shall we?"

Grace peeked around the kitchen doorway, taking an extra moment to watch Vidar before she took him his glass of water. He seemed the same as with her. The slow, easy, accented drawl. The teasing manner. But he was different too – with a job to do; reading his audience and evolving his performance with the ebb and flow of their enthusiasm; carrying all with him; holding them rapt in the palm of his hand. Impressive, confident, masterful, sexy; the superstar.

Small wonder he was permanently unfazed! He was an expert in crowd control by force of personality alone. She wondered whether it scaled up easily. Could he charm a stadium as proficiently as he controlled Bob Turner's heaving little living room? She suspected he could, and admired him for it.

She felt self-conscious carrying his water to him, knowing every eye would briefly divert from him to her. As Vidar finished singing, she placed the water down next to him, "Thank you." He nodded to the room, "My glamorous assistant." Grace was treated to an enthusiastic round of applause, and plenty of wolf-whistles. Surprising herself, she managed to make a joking curtsey and sashay off confidently into the kitchen to hide, as Vidar began a maudlin blues song, and the largely-tipsy gathering joined in with a lyrical mournfulness only the Scottish can do true justice to.

Grace felt content, involved, confident in her outfit, her reason for being there, and her accepted position amongst the assembled gathering as Vidar's partner. Given the universal adoration exhibited by every person in the room towards her companion, it was a source of considerable pride to be so closely associated with him.

Grace poured herself another small whisky, dropped two large ice cubes into it, and slipped back into the living room to watch Vidar work.

THIRTEEN

"Bye! Thank you!"

Waving and smiling as the front door closed, they were left alone on the lane, illuminated only by the whiteness of the moonlight. Vidar sighed with relief as he swung the gate shut and they began to walk, side-by-side, "Phew! Think that went ok."

"It was great! Everyone loved it."

"You weren't too bored?"

"I wasn't bored at all!" Grace was just realising she'd been to the first social gathering since before her marriage at which no one had been derogatory, sarcastic, or rude to her, "People spoke to me all evening! Everyone was friendly, kind, interested...it was lovely."

"Good, 'cos I couldn't really pay you any attention."

"It's all right. Elaine did that."

"She's gonna have a headache tomorrow...and a lunch to cook for three hungry guys. You can take the girl out of Glasgow, but not Glasgow out of the girl..."

"She's full of life."

"She certainly is!"

"Were you really worried about this evening?"

"I was nervous about the booze and about...oh, it's hard to explain! Big things are ok because you're unreachable. Stuff like tonight is nice, but it brings an extra pressure. You're right there, they can see you warts-and-all...no lights, no set-dressing, just how you are. For some people, it's a disappointment. It shatters the illusion. It never used to bother me when I was younger, but now it gets in my head and I can't make it leave…"

"Mid-life crisis?"

"I guess… I find myself questioning what I actually have to offer – and who still wants to hear it after all these years."

"Vid, are you joking? You made that party! If you hadn't been there, it would have been a load of stuffy professionals making stilted small talk about work, and forcing down iffy microwave snacks to the accompaniment of a Bing Crosby CD! Believe me, I've attended umpteen similarly-agonising events. People go because they're expected to, not because they want to. You've presented poor old Bob with a proper problem, haven't you?"

"I have?"

"Yeah! How will he ever top that next year, unless he has you back? It was truly staggering to watch you. Within ten minutes of getting going, you got a disparate group of people with very little in common, apart from passing acquaintance with Bob, to sing loudly and with gusto, to laugh more than they probably had all year, to top up one another's drinks, to make friends with strangers, to bond and unite in an outpouring of…joy…and you did that, just you, all alone, with your guitar, your skill, and your innate ability to touch people's lives and make them magical! You shouldn't doubt yourself. You might well be approaching fifty but, whatever you had, you've still got…and everybody in that room knows it, felt it, and is probably going home now to download every album you've ever made."

Vidar put his arm around her shoulders as they crunched back along the icy road, the frost on the tarmac glittering, "Thank you. I'm very flattered by what you're saying."

"It's not flattery, it's truth. Whether it's naturally within you or down to tireless practice, you have a true gift for touching people, for making their hearts sing. I stood and watched you, and the cleverest bit about it was how you assessed the mood, transfixed the room, made it seem to each person that you were singing just for them."

Vidar stopped, turning her to face him. The bright moonlight accentuated the outline of his features – high cheekbones, long, straight nose, defined jawline, the slight cleft in his chin.

"Surprising really, because I was singing just for you."

He slid his hand into her hair, cupping the back of her head as he had that first night so tantalisingly briefly, lowering his mouth onto hers, kissing her with increasing urgency, other hand pushing into the back pocket of her jeans, cupping her buttock, squeezing, pulling her against him.

Grace reached for him, feeling the strength and thickness of his neck beneath her exploring fingers, sighing, surrendering, wondering why she'd been nervous of him kissing her when it felt so natural.

Unsure how long they remained in the centre of the deserted, icy lane, locked together, lost in one another, Grace suddenly shivered violently despite Vidar's embrace, "Oh, I'm cold!"

She felt Vidar's lips smile against her neck, "Yeah, this isn't the best place to make out like a couple of teenagers, is it? Not when we have a home to go to."

Grace shivered again, and Vidar put his arm around her waist, drawing her against him, "Come on, let's get back."

****

They didn't walk anywhere in silence. Usually there was lively banter, frequent laughter, yet neither uttered a word in the ten minutes it took to get home. The absence of interaction unnerved Grace. She started to feel ashamed of exhibiting such wanton behaviour in the middle of a lane where anyone could have seen her, convinced Vidar was also privately regretting his haste.

Standing opposite him in the lamplit hallway of *Somerled* made Grace feel awkward, tongue-tied, gawky, as she struggled off her coat and took two attempts to get it to stay on the peg, missing completely with her scarf, which she then had to retrieve clumsily from the floor. She nearly fell over unzipping her boots, tottering and bashing her shoulder on the wall.

A smirk crossed Vidar's face as he propped up his guitar case and shrugged off his coat, "You ok, Grace?"

"Fine!" squeaked Grace, trying for breezy unconcern, instead hitting a note more like burgeoning panic.

Smiling to himself, Vidar went to put his guitar in the office.

Grace shot into the kitchen, snatching up the kettle and surreptitiously checking her hair and general appearance in its stainless-steel body before filling it up, switching it on and turning to ask Vidar if he wanted tea or coffee, almost jumping out of her skin as she realised he was right behind her, inches from her body.

His wide hands grasped her, thumbs hooking into the indentation of her pelvis; long, dextrous musician's fingers stretching around her hips, squeezing powerfully, tugging her to him, shoving the small of her back against the worktop with the insistent pressure of his lower body. His mouth first touched just above her cleavage, where her shirt was unbuttoned, and her skin seemed to burst into flames with each fresh brush of his lips across the top of her breast, above the lace of the cup of her bra, back along her collarbone to the hollow of her throat, and slowly up her neck into her hair. He murmured in Danish, more to himself than her, "Min smukke engel."

She didn't understand.

His strong fingers still gripped her hips, maintaining the pressure of his pelvis against her own. She could feel his erection. She was suddenly terrified, distracted by her fear. Ridiculous, but she had no idea what to do with her hands! One had instinctively clutched the handle of the oven door as Vidar had thrust against her; the other splayed rigidly across a cupboard front to hold her upright. She didn't resemble a woman in the throes of passion; she looked as if she was attempting to avoid being flattened. Why was she being so passive? It had been the same with Dominic. She'd submit, turn her face away, and permit him what he considered his conjugal right, even though his touch revolted her. Allowing Dominic into her head effectively chased away every residue of desire, leaving her clasping the oven, head uptilted to the ceiling, eyes squeezed tightly shut, until she became aware that the forceful pressure of his body had relaxed.

Cautiously opening one eye, she saw he was watching her calmly, with no hint of annoyance in the kind, steady gaze.

"Am I torturing you? Tell me. I can stop…?"

Grace blushed, and couldn't look at him.

One of Vidar's hands slid from her pelvis to her buttock, and patted it gently, "If you don't want to do this, it isn't compulsory. I guess I got the wrong impression from the lane. I thought maybe you wanted to, but if you don't, that's ok."

He eased away from her, and Grace instantly felt cold, scared, and abandoned. Panicked, she instinctively reached out, clutched the front of his jumper, held on, gabbled, "It's not that I don't want... What I mean to say is I'm not...um...I don't... I can't..."

Subsiding into agitated silence, Grace allowed Vidar to envelop her in his arms and gently press her head against his chest, stroking her hair, "Well, that was a little barrage of negativity, wasn't it? 'I don't, I can't, I'm not'..."

Grace wanted to cry. On the lane, she hadn't felt like this! She hadn't thought about anything but how natural it was to be touched by Vidar, and to reciprocate that intimacy. Now, here, in warmth, comfort, and privacy, she couldn't recapture that sensation because she'd allowed bloody Dominic into her head!

Vidar whispered, "Shall we just forget it...pretend it never happened?"

Grace put her hands over her eyes. Vidar was magnificent, gorgeous, spellbinding, and he desired her! Now, he'd be convinced she didn't feel the same. His feelings would be hurt or, worse for a man, his pride. He might be sufficiently insulted never to try again.

"I'm sorry Vid. I can't explain. There's such confusion inside me."

Vidar sighed with what sounded like exasperation, shook his head, hugged her to him tighter, "I am not going to make you do something you don't want to, ok? I read it wrong. I made a mistake. We're still friends, aren't we?"

Grace nodded emphatically, placing a flat palm against the firmness of his chest.

"That's all that matters to me..."

Grace smiled distantly, enjoying the feel of him, the rise and fall of his breathing, the slowing of his rapidly-thudding heart, the warmth of the secure embrace. Vidar played with strands of her hair, drawing it across the back of his hand and feeling it slide away, "I love your hair. It's so soft."

Grace wittered anxiously, relieved he was still prepared to talk to her, "My friend Fen was always saying it was ratty and I should brush it more, but I read somewhere that brushing too much makes it greasy..."

"Perhaps she was jealous of you? It's not greasy; it's silky. Look, it just glides across your skin..." Vidar brushed his hand through to the ends of her hair, and let it fall from his fingers.

"I'm sorry, Vid," said Grace again, quietly.

Vidar put his fingers under her chin, lifted her face to his, and kissed her softly on the lips, "Let it go. We're fine just the way we are. Let's have a hot chocolate, chill out, turn in...it's Christmas tomorrow..."

"Mmmm..." For a moment, Grace forgot everything but the sensual gratification of closeness to Vidar, stroking a fingertip across his cheekbone, gazing up at him, before his words about Christmas sank in, "Shit! I forgot to take the joint out of the freezer!"

Galvanised into instant action by the horrifying knowledge that not defrosting the meat would ruin her meticulous planning, all awkwardness was forgotten in Grace's desperation to rectify matters, clattering around with dishes and platters, muttering to herself as her busy hands worked deftly.

Disregarded in her flurry of frantic activity, Vidar made them both a hot chocolate, shoved another log onto the almost-dead fire as he passed it, hoping enough heat remained to rekindle a flame, sat at the piano, and looked at his own face reflected in the black window. What had he done wrong? In the cold of the night time lane, she'd melted. In the warmth of the cosy kitchen, she'd turned to ice. Vidar ran his fingers over the keys, and settled to a little Rachmaninov, trying unsuccessfully to expend his pent-up passion on the powerful pieces.

Maybe it wasn't meant to be, no matter how convinced he was of the rightness of their union? Perhaps she simply didn't feel the same? The first woman ever to refuse him, and the only one he truly wanted! Merely because he craved her didn't mean he had an automatic right to possess her. She hadn't asked him to arrive and impose himself upon her solitude. This house-share might be Grace's attempt to make the best of yet another bad situation involving an intimidating man. Perhaps the kindest thing for them both would be to leave...but he didn't want to. Even imprisonment in this torturous limbo was better than being without her.

He jumped as a soft hand touched his shoulder, "Taking out your aggression on that?"

He looked up at her, tried to smile, couldn't, "It's Rachmaninov. You're meant to go for it."

"It's phenomenal."

"He was a genius."

"I'm going to bed."

"Ok."

"See you in the morning."

He nodded, starting to play again.

Grace, nervous, ventured, "'Night, then."

"Søde drømme." His fingers continued to travel powerfully up and down the octaves.

"What does that mean?"

He stopped playing abruptly, but didn't turn to look at her, "Sweet dreams."

"Thank you...you too..." said Grace meekly, but he'd begun to play again, and she wasn't sure he'd heard her.

She left him at the piano, and went to bed with sudden tears brimming in her eyes.

FOURTEEN

Grace awoke slowly, opening bleary, swollen eyes to the beamed ceiling. Rolling onto her side, she stared at the closed blind, sunshine already bright around its edges.

She'd cried for a long time last night as Vidar had continued to play, forceful fingers driving across the keys with more power than she'd have thought the instrument could withstand. His anger at her had been palpable...and unsurprisingly so – talk about send the poor man mixed messages! I will, I won't. I do, I don't. I could, but now I can't. I might, but now I shan't.

And on Christmas Eve, of all occasions, after they'd had one of their characteristically companionable, relaxed days, and an evening full of pleasant surprises for Grace; understanding more about her fascinatingly-complex new friend in a couple of hours than she'd managed in the preceding fortnight. She'd observed the affability that entranced his audience, and contrasted it with the intensity bestowed upon her alone.

Desperate to urinate, Grace squirmed, sensing the cold in the air. The warming radiator under the window ticked and clicked as it fought to chase away the night time chill. Reaching for her watch, she saw it was only just past seven. Lying still for a moment more, Grace decided she couldn't hold on – she'd have to go. Wriggling out from under the covers without disturbing them too much, Grace hoped to preserve some vestige of body heat for her return, whipping speedily to the toilet, shivering despite her thermal pyjamas. On the way back to bed, the lure of the sunrise proved too tempting. She opened the blind and stood in front of the window, pressing her thighs against the radiator to keep them warm. Ice crystals of hoar frost glinted from each blade of grass, stone, and clod of mud, caking everything in crisp whiteness as comprehensively as any snowfall. The low angle of the rising winter sun glanced sharply off the glittering driveway, making Grace's heavy eyes squint in surprise at the brilliance of an Orcadian Christmas morning.

Notwithstanding the pale, cloudless blue of the sky – still run through with dawn's blush-pink brush strokes like a watercolour canvas – it looked bitterly cold. Grace's upper body felt the draught as the air of her bedroom hit the glass and tumbled down the pane to the sill, tipping itself like an overflowing bathtub onto the warmed currents rising from the radiator, beginning the circulating journey upward once more. The volume of colder air was winning the battle, and Grace was driven from the stark beauty of her view back under the blankets where it still felt warm. Wiggling down the bed into a comfortable position, Grace lay on her side, generous covers bunched around her, and enjoyed the feel of the sun shining through the window onto her face, closing her eyes against its intensity. Settled, warm, a residue of Bob Turner's whisky still in her system, it didn't take long for sleep to reclaim her.

****

"Grace…" A low voice, the soft lifting of her hair off her face with gentle fingers, and Grace awoke with a start, jerking and staring, "Sorry…I knocked and called but you were fast asleep. I didn't want to wake you, but I read your notes in the kitchen and I wondered if some meat had to go in the oven...?" Vidar's hand touched her again. Grace was very tempted to reclose her eyes and remain in her warm cocoon with Vidar stroking her hair...but it was Christmas! There was a lunch to prepare!

Struggling to her elbows with difficulty, lifting her head as if it weighed a tonne, Grace mumbled thickly, "What time is it?"

"Eight-thirty."

"What time did it say that meat had to go in?"

"Nine."

"Ohhh..." Grace flopped back onto the mattress, "Ughh, I feel so foggy...must've been that whisky..."

"Ah, the demon drink. I don't miss that 'morning after' feeling."

Grace touched a hand to her forehead, rubbing at a threatening headache, "Good job I did it all last night. I've literally just got to put the oven on and bung it in...and then baste it in a couple of hours."

"Do you want me to do anything so you don't have to get up?"

Grace considered, never having relinquished control of meal preparation to anyone before, "Please can you put the oven on 150° fan, so it starts to warm up...then I've got half an hour to stir my stumps..."

"Sure...you want some breakfast?"

"Mmmm..." Grace smiled, eyes closed, hair spread across the pillows, gleaming like polished walnut in the bright morning sunlight flooding onto the bed through the open blinds.

Vidar sighed, swallowed down his longing for her, and went to the kitchen.

****

Returning shortly after with his customary breakfast tray – the novelty of breakfast in bed had yet to lose its appeal for Grace – Vidar found she was curled up once more, snoring quietly.

He put the tray down on the end of the bed and glanced at his watch – 8.45am. He didn't want to wake her. She looked sweet, burrowed into the nest of covers like a hibernating dormouse, but he had no idea what he was supposed to do with the meat.

Lying down next to her, he rested an arm softly across her body, and extended a finger to massage her upturned palm in slow circles, "Grace, wake up honey…breakfast time…"

She murmured. The relaxed fingers of her tickled palm fluttered. Detecting the solidity of his enveloping form, Grace stirred. Unwilling, but considering it the wisest course of action after last night, Vidar reluctantly slid away from her. By the time she awoke fully and blinked into the sunlight, he was sitting cross-legged at the end of the bed, smiling and pouring the tea.

"Good morning. God Jul."

She pushed her hair from her face, "What?"

"Merry Christmas."

"Oh…oh yeah…" She smiled, "What is it?"

"God Jul…or you can say Glædelig Jul."

"Right."

"Here." Grace struggled clumsily upright, propping her pillows to support her, and reached both hands to receive the steaming mug with a grateful smile, embarrassed to be so close to him despite no alteration in their morning routine.

Vidar tugged the tray across the covers between them, "Breakfast."

"Do I deserve any, after last night?"

"I thought we'd agreed to forget about it?"

"Yes…we have. I just…feel bad. I think I led you on and I shouldn't have done."

Vidar shrugged, "And I got horny, and pushy, and I shouldn't have done."

He selected a triangle of buttered toast from the plate and gesticulated with it, crumbs tumbling onto the bedclothes, "Now, that was an occasion where I should have acted my age!"

Grace smiled hesitantly, "So, we're good?"

Vidar grinned and mumbled around his mouthful, "We're peachy, Grace. Just forget it."

He reached behind him, producing an elaborately gift-wrapped box, holding it out to his wide-eyed companion, "You can't have Christmas without something to open. I guess even your horrible husband would have gotten you a gift?"

Grace held the impressively-beribboned box in both hands, staring at it wonderingly, "He would have instructed his PA to buy me something. I never met her, but she had super taste…never chose anything I didn't like."

"How do you know he didn't tell her exactly what to buy?"

"He had no taste in presents at all! He thought ostentatious and blingy equalled nice, whereas she used to choose some lovely, imaginative, and unusual things. My friend Fen said they all got their secretaries to do the Christmas shopping – much less bother than having to get off their backsides and do it themselves."

"I've never sent anyone out to buy a present on my behalf. The whole point is that you make the effort, think about it, and put a little of yourself into it. It shows you're bothered about whether the other person likes it or not. If you don't choose, then you don't care…"

Grace nodded, stating matter-of-factly, "Well, he didn't care." She stroked reverent fingers across the top of the box, "Can I open it now?"

"No, you just have to look at it all day," replied Vidar, cheekily.

Grace gave him a jokingly-stern stare, and placed the box to one side, "I need to go and put the meat in, don't I?"

Vidar glanced at his watch and nodded, chomping his way through another triangle of toast.

"I'll do that and then come back and open my present."

"Ok."

A couple of minutes' clattering of roasting dishes, rustling of tin foil, thudding of cupboard, fridge and oven doors, and Grace returned, smiling shyly, with a hand behind her back, "You know how you can't have Christmas without something to open?"

She produced a chunky, rectangular parcel, holding it out to him, "It's only a little something…"

Vidar stared, so overcome he couldn't speak. No one bought him presents, not even his little brothers. Fans sent him home made offerings and souvenirs, but that was different. They went to the office, his staff opened them on his behalf, and thank-you letters were dispatched without his knowledge or involvement.

"Grace...I've never..." He stopped for a moment, collected himself, tried again, "No one usually buys me gifts. What do you get the man who has everything?"

"Penicillin?" quipped Grace, rendered uneasy by the strength of Vidar's reaction to the token, "It's just a little thing. It's definitely not as posh as yours...and my wrapping's not up to your standards."

"What, that?" Vidar pointed to her present, "I didn't do that – the gift-wrap girl in the store did it."

"You big cheat!" Grace shoved his shoulder, and was surprised by how cold the fabric of his pyjama top felt, "You're really cold!"

She bounced into her side of the bed, making the crockery on the tray chink loudly, "Get in under the covers and we can open our pressies!"

Needing no further encouragement, Vidar settled himself comfortably next to Grace under the blankets.

"Right," She looked up at him, blue eyes twinkling delight, "Who first – you or me?"

"Ladies first."

"Ok." Grace's nimble fingers unpicked the diaphanous bow encircling the box, drawing aside the fabric and easing off the lid to expose a thick, hardback, coffee-table tome, nestling on a bright cushion of tissue paper. An embossed black Celtic dragon curled strikingly across the matt-white cover, leaping into glossy relief as if writhing across a snowy landscape. Fascinated, Grace snatched it up, drawing a fingertip across its bumpy surface, and opening the book to similar imaginatively-displayed pieces reflecting Orcadian art from Neolithic to present, interwoven with explanation, fact, and folklore; rich and mysterious as its island history.

"Wow!" breathed Grace, "What a beautiful book!"

Turning to Vidar, clutching the present to her chest, she gasped, "Thank you so much – it's amazing!"

"Thought it might give you inspiration for some Orcadian art of your own…as you seem to spend all of your time sketching and screwing it up."

Grace frowned, "I suppose it's a confidence thing. I used to be quite proud of the stuff I produced – a long time ago – but I doubt myself now. Like you said last night, you wonder what you have to offer…"

"You do know I rescue them all out of the trash and unscrew them, don't you?"

"What?"

"I'm trying to flatten them out between the books in the office."

"Seriously?"

"Yeah. They're good! They're part of your process. You're feeling your way towards something and you've got to let whatever's inside of you come out, so you can get your juices flowing again. Otherwise, you'll never get to where you're going. You've been repressing your real self for so long. Just stick the pedal to the metal and go for it! What are you afraid of?"

Grace blinked, stunned, "I don't know."

"You draw like this," Vidar tapped a finger on the dragon, "It's abstract, but it's natural, evolving, curling, swirling, spreading out across the page. It's very organic…it's not a picture of anything, but the more you look, the more you see within it. It just starts to take shape, grow, adapt…and you screw it up and throw it in the trash!"

Grace stared at Vidar in open amazement. She hadn't realised he'd taken notice of her sketching; much less that he rescued her discarded efforts, and took time to admire and interpret her work. Dominic set no store by creativity, except as a commodity to enhance wealth, his one true passion. Sharing her living space with another individual who understood the creative process was a revelation. Tentatively, nervous of a Dominic-style derisive reception, Grace began, "When I was at Art College, I used to do massive canvases – big as that wall – with all these travelling black and grey ripples across them…and then I'd overlay with silver, so if you looked at it in a certain way, it became 3D."

"Sounds cool…"

"Yeah… I was proud of those… I did a whole series of them. You can convey a lot with the manipulation of the line."

"What happened to the pictures?"

"Not sure. I sold most of them at the end of that year. There used to a be a student exhibition and quite a few of them went, but a couple were left. I suppose they must be in the attic of my parents' old holiday place in Suffolk…the one I rent out…"

"I'd like to see them."

Grace wrinkled her nose, "Twenty-odd years ago? They'd probably be crap. I expect I'm remembering them with the rose-tint of nostalgia. I was young."

"And fearless!"

Grace laughed, "Clueless!"

"Before you got married and that asshole took your soul…"

Grace gasped involuntarily because, of course, Vidar was right.

Vidar detected the gasp and thought he'd overstepped the mark, "Sorry, I said that aloud, didn't I?"

Grace smiled wanly, "Don't apologise…you're not wrong."

Vidar tapped the book again, "Consider it food-for-thought…and stop putting your sketches in the trash. If you want to, you can paint in the office. There's plenty of room for a massive canvas or two. Don't be afraid to try…"

Grace smiled at him and stroked her fingers across the back of his hand where it rested on her new book, "Thank you."

"You're welcome."

"Your turn…it's not as smart as your present."

"It is, however, the first Christmas gift I can remember receiving in my adult life."

"Just because you're successful, doesn't mean you can't have presents!"

"Try telling that to my family."

"Open it."

"Ok." Vidar pushed a finger under the edge of the wrapping and peeled it open with a satisfying tear of rustling paper to expose the cover of a book of his own. He turned happily to Grace, "Ever get the idea we just lounge around reading all day?"

She grinned back at him, expectant eyes on his face. Vidar tugged the book free, releasing a smart hardback on the history of the Vikings in Orkney.

"I did check to see if you were mentioned, but…" Grace smiled bashfully and shook her head. Vidar laughed heartily, flicking through it, taking in the pictures, the maps, "Grace, this is a cool book."

"When they print the next edition, I'm positive it'll be updated to include you, now the most famous Viking in Orkney."

"My brother Ragnar is named after a Viking king…and *Somerled* was a Viking king."

"You'll know all about it, then."

"Thank you, Grace," Vidar leant over and kissed her cheek, "I love it."

She squeezed his hand, "And I love mine too."

Vidar scooted down the bed, settling himself comfortably, "How long before you have to check the meat?"

"Hour and a half? Why?"

"I vote for a Christmas lie-in," Vidar propped his new book on his chest and began to read.

Grace smiled at him, reached across to the bedside radio, and found a station playing Christmas oldies. She snuggled contentedly next to Vidar, sipping her tea, and gazing in delighted absorption at the glossy pages of Orcadian art, allowing her previously-fettered imagination to take flight.

****

An hour later, Grace's head rested on Vidar's shoulder, his face nestled in her hair, their books were dropped amongst the disordered bedclothes, and Christmas classics accompanied the soft sounds of their slumber.

When something hammered on the window, Grace awoke with a start, "Oh!" shooting upright to search for the source of the unfamiliar sound, thinking a seabird might have flown into the glass, blinded by the sunlight.

Instead, she beheld Sonia, grinning knowingly and pointing at the two of them, gesturing towards the front door to be let in.

"Oh my God, what's the time?" Grace pulled up the sleeve of Vidar's pyjama top to look at his watch and discover it was after ten.

"Oh! Vid! Wake up! Sonia's here!"

FIFTEEN

Vidar grimaced, opening one eye, "What day is it?"

"Christmas day! We went right off to sleep! Sonia's here. I need to check the meat…"

Dishevelled, frantic, Grace threw back the covers and leapt out of bed, grabbing her dressing gown and pelting to the front door to admit a giggling Sonia and a rush of frigid air.

"Saw ya! I bloody told you! Was it all right? I bet it was!"

Grace groaned, pushed her sleep-tangled hair from her face, and helped Sonia off with her coat, "Nothing's happened…"

"I saw you!"

"We went to a drinks thing last night. I had a whisky too many and Vidar had to do the entertainment…and then I had to get the joint ready. It was a late night, ok?" Grace was irritated by her own pathetic need to explain. Even though everything she said was true, she could feel Sonia's disbelief radiating from her along with the warmth of her now-rotund body, "We were opening our presents this morning, and then we were reading and we just…dozed off…"

"Must be your age."

"And a very Merry Christmas to you too!" Grace kissed her friend's cheek, and gave her a good-natured shove towards the living room, "Go and see if he's managed to haul himself out of bed. I've got to have a wee, and then I need to check how the meat's doing."

As Sonia entered, she observed Vidar wandering blearily from the guest room, clutching a book and searching for his slippers.

"Morning, Son. Merry Christmas."

"And the same to you. Nice evening?" Sonia teased. Vidar was too foggy with recent sleep to take the bait, merely grunting, "Had to do the free cabaret at Bob Turner's NHS Christmas whisky-fest..."

"You never had a drink!"

"No, course not! But I was late to bed...and I was awake half the night..."

Vidar didn't know Grace was behind him in the bedroom doorway. Sonia noticed a pinched, tight expression cross her friend's face, vanishing as Vidar extended his book proudly, "Look at my gift, Son!"

Sonia examined it, as underwhelmed as only a twenty-something can be with a non-fiction hardback, "Fascinating..."

"It's interesting! It's the intermingled history of my people and yours. Where d'you think you got that hair, Sonia Flett? From the Danes, that's where!"

Vidar relieved Sonia of his present possessively, "You don't deserve to look at my nice gift. Your mind's not open enough."

Vidar placed the book on the coffee table as carefully as if it was made of china, before settling to his detested daily task of clearing out the wood burner.

Grace placed a hot chocolate in front of Sonia, topped with a crown of cream that melted down the sides of the cup, and a stack of marshmallows threatening to topple at any moment.

"Oooh!" Sonia stuck a finger into the sweet, gooey topping, and licked it delightedly. Grace, marshmallow bag in hand, stopped before the tall tree, flicked on the lights, and watched them twinkle for a moment, "It's lovely, isn't it? Proper Christmas..." She ate a marshmallow and, on her way back to the kitchen, popped one into Vidar's open mouth as she passed him.

Sonia was both amused and puzzled by the level of physical intimacy displayed by the two of them, while Grace so continuously and vehemently denied any sexual contact had occurred. Either Grace was a consummate actress with a fine grasp of the ingenuous, or Vidar was exhibiting Olympic levels of self-control, given how constantly enthralled he seemed by Grace. He was demonstrating his obsession right now, completely ignoring his task and gazing after her in adoration as she returned to the kitchen to continue lunch preparations.

Sonia waggled the bag she'd brought in, "I've got presents."

"Oh, Sonia! You didn't have to do that! You should save your money for the baby, darling."

"It's only wee things," said Sonia.

"Well, we've got presents too," said Grace, peeling potatoes.

"Yeah," Vidar pretended to sound gruff, "The whole goddam office is full of 'wee things'."

"I got a bit carried away," confessed Grace, "Can you get them, Vid, 'cos I'm all covered in potato now?"

"I'll do this, then I'll get them. Sonia will just have to wait ten seconds."

Sonia sniggered, "You two are funny. You sound like my parents, the way you talk to each other! Like an old married couple…"

Usually, when Sonia made such an allusion, both squirmed with embarrassed delight and pretended not to like the idea. Today, however, the tense, uncomfortable look reappeared on Grace's face, and Vidar coughed and rattled the grate unnecessarily. Sonia wondered what it meant.

Vidar began to transport bags and boxes of gift-wrapped presents from the office, until the hearth rug was full.

Sonia gazed in awe, "Is all this for me?"

"No," said Vidar, pointing to Sonia's stomach, "Most of it's for him."

"Or her!" shouted Grace from the kitchen. She opened the oven door, lifted the edge of the tin foil, squinted at the meat, and closed the door with a nod of satisfaction. A deliciously rich, succulent aroma wafted down to Sonia and Vidar on the rug. Both sniffed, breathed, grinned, "That smells fantastic already, Grace."

"It's cooking nicely," Grace turned the oven down to allow the meat to cook more slowly, and nodded across to Sonia where she knelt on the rug amongst the parcels, "Start opening!"

Vidar, reclined on the sofa, drawled lazily, "Quick, or we'll be here 'til next Christmas…and I've got a lunch to eat."

Bubbling with childish excitement, Sonia set to, unwrapping babygrows, cot sheets and blankets, a night light, a smart change bag with added accessories, a quilted winter suit, little knitted hats and mittens, socks and bootees, a basket full of expensive creams and potions for new mothers, a book on weaning, teething and baby food and, most awesome of all, the largest box contained the Rolls-Royce of pushchairs, which gave Grace twenty minutes of entertainment as Vidar and Sonia faced-off on the hearth rug, squabbling about how it fitted together.

Eventually, Sonia sat on the sofa, scooping the dregs of melted marshmallow from the mug with her finger, and gazing at the jumble of gifts spread across the rug, "Oh my God, you two… Thank you so much. I don't know what else to say…"

Grace beamed, wiping her hands and bounding down to the sofa, "Don't say anything. Babies are expensive. We're just helping you out because we can."

Sonia hugged them both as hard as she could, unspent tears balancing on her eyelashes.

She raised her bag sheepishly, "My stuff seems a bit lame now."

"Don't be daft."

Sonia extracted two flattish packages from the bag and gave one to Grace and one to Vidar, who grinned in delight, "Second present!"

Vidar ripped it open in excitement, revealing a light grey sweater that Grace noticed perfectly complimented the unusual colour of his eyes.

"That feels nice – soft material. It's great, Son. I'm going to wear it today. Thank you."

"That's ok."

Vidar turned to Grace, "Come on, let's see what you got."

Grace tore off the outer paper to unearth a tissue-wrapped packet from which she lifted a delicate cream top, crocheted in fine wool with a pattern of such complexity it resembled lace.

"Wow, Sonia, that's beautiful!"

"They're made by a local lady. She crochets them from lamb's wool. I just thought, you wear loads of that kind of slouchy top with little tops underneath…it's sort of 'your style', so I thought you'd like it."

"I do. It's gorgeous!" She looked round at Vidar, "I'm going to wear mine today too. Obviously, not when I'm cooking, 'cos it'll get ruined…but later. Oh, thank you, Sonia!" Grace kissed and hugged her friend, "Such thoughtful, appropriate presents. You're obviously very good at picking for people. What are you doing about lunch?"

Sonia looked at her watch, "I need to go home, really. Mam's doing turkey and everything. She's not as in control as you. The kitchen's like a bomb's hit it. I pleaded morning-sickness to get out of having to help."

"You're so naughty!"

"How am I going to get everything home?" Sonia looked despairingly at the mounds of presents. Grace frowned, momentarily at a loss, "Short of loading up the car…?"

Vidar rolled his eyes, "I thought women were supposed to be resourceful? Put the presents in a bag, put the bag in the stroller, push the stroller."

"Ooh, top plan!"

"Rocket-science."

"Shut it, you."

****

Vidar and Grace waved Sonia off from the door and watched her down the drive, her new pram piled with presents.

"She looks quite at home pushing that, doesn't she?"

Vidar closed the front door, "I bet she ends up having loads of babies, like her Mom did."

Grace looked rueful, "The problem, Vid, is that a lot of men won't take on another man's child, which might limit her options, beautiful as she is."

"Someone'll have her. There's something about little Son. A guy with a fire in his belly who likes a challenge!"

They padded back into the delicious-smelling warmth of the living room, "When you break down the barriers, she just wants someone to look after her."

"Isn't that what we all want?"

Grace considered, "Yes, I suppose it is."

"What time's lunch, chef?"

"Half-one, two-ish?"

Vidar looked at the clock, "Half eleven…it's sunny…wanna get dressed and wander down the beach for a bit?"

"Why not? I need to be back just after one to put the rest of the veg on."

"Right, let's shower, put on our new clothes, and get some air before lunch."

****

Vidar stood under the powerful deluge and tried to stop his thoughts straying to last night. The more he sought to dismiss them, the more potent the images became.

What had he done wrong? He'd tried nothing that hadn't successfully seduced regiments of past women. He'd had some bad sex in his life, but he'd never made a girl turn to stone as surely as Grace had in the kitchen.

In the cold, dark lane, he hadn't held back. He'd revealed his physical hunger for her, and she'd responded with equal passion. He'd done nothing different in the kitchen but carry on where he'd left off ten minutes before…so what had changed in that time? Had he been too urgent, too forceful? But on the lane, she'd clung to him as tightly as he'd gripped her!

Vidar shook his head violently, frustrated, droplets of water flying in all directions from his soaking-wet hair, seeking to empty his mind of the memory of Grace tensing to endure his touch.

Perhaps she'd suffered physically at the hands of her husband? She certainly betrayed fear whenever she alluded to him. Maybe she was uncomfortable with any sexual contact? But that didn't explain the lane, the tugging at the waistband of his jeans, pulling him closer…

He dried himself irritably. He'd followed Stewart's instructions to the letter, and was no further on than he'd been a fortnight ago!

Vidar stood before the open wardrobe door and pictured Stewart, slumped in the armchair before the bothy stove, dispensing his sage advice.

What's your prescription for this mess, Doc?

SIXTEEN

"You ready?"

Grace nodded, so bundled up against the anticipated cold only her eyes were showing. Subconsciously preparing to weather the sharp slap of the driving Orcadian wind as she rounded the driveway's protective bank, Grace walked a few steps down the hill before realising how still it was, "No wind."

Vidar, locking the door, pulling on his gloves, trooping across the wet flagstones to catch her up, asked, "What?"

"No wind. Perfectly still. Like last night."

Vidar stood for a moment, waiting for a gust, "Weird, huh? Spend any time here and you mentally prepare to get buffeted around the moment you step outside the door. It's freaky when it doesn't happen."

Grace stood on tiptoe, trying to see the beach hidden by the hill, "Can't see what the tide's doing."

"I think it should be on its way out."

He took her hand, of course, and Grace felt the now-familiar flutter of delight at the gesture...even more precious after last night.

"Do you think we went over-the-top with Sonia?"

"Course we did! But no one else is going to, are they?"

"It was a master-stroke of yours to get that pram. She was overwhelmed by that."

"If the rest of the family club together to raise enough for a packet of diapers, I'll be amazed."

"You really don't think much of the Flett's, do you?"

"I don't think they appreciate one another enough. I know the situation is different and we aren't in each other's faces all the time, but I'd like to think I'd never take my brothers for granted in that way. I think we see the value in one another…but I'm not sure the Fletts do…"

"Perhaps they just aren't as openly-demonstrative of their feelings as you are?"

Vidar looked across the open farmland towards the beach, "I can see a bit of sand. Hopefully, tide's going out."

"We seem to spend a lot of time on the beach in the freezing cold, don't we?"

"Well, you're a nutcase and I'm just keeping an eye on you…"

"Hey, going to the beach is always your idea!" Grace dug him in the ribs with her elbow, and used the excuse of the movement to link her arm with his, so her body could press against him.

Smiling to himself, Vidar pushed both hands into his pockets to better pinion her arm to his side. She'd obviously forgiven him for going too far last night. The awkwardness, lingering past breakfast, had vanished.

The fresh, moist air magnified the detail of the landscape, and Vidar picked out the wheeling, circling outline of a bird of prey, at first camouflaged against the brown of the hill, then contrasted with the washed-out blue of the December sky as they dropped lower down towards the beach.

"Look at that!"

"Amazing! It's good terrain for them here though, all this open farmland."

"They're incredible, the way they zone in on a tiny mouse from forty feet up, or whatever it is."

"That's nature. Mind you, I'm the same...I can spot a packet of *Jaffa Cakes* at a thousand yards. It's about survival, you see."

Vidar grinned, and nodded sagely, "Right...the miracle of evolution..."

"I am highly-evolved. Thanks for noticing."

Vidar chortled joyfully, suddenly hugging her to him, "You make me laugh."

"Do I?"

"Yes, you're very funny – the things you say, the way you say them."

"I don't mean to be. I'm trying for sophistication. Obviously falling a bit short..."

"What gives you that idea?" Vidar pirouetted her away from him, as if they were dancing in the middle of the deserted lane. Grace wondered whether he sensed music around him all the time, in the same way she saw pictures in everything.

She stuck out her tongue and blew a raspberry at him. Vidar responded with a teasing blown kiss, before drawing her back into his embrace, "I'm having such a lovely day. Usually, I'm alone in a hotel room for Christmas, or an empty house. While everyone else has time with the people they love, I'm just getting frustrated at having to wait days for the world to return to normal so I can go back to work."

"Scrooge."

"Seriously, where is the enjoyment in spending enforced days alone because everyone else has someone to be with?"

"I understand. I was married and I still used to spend most of Christmas Day on my own."

"This year it's different, right? Laughs, company, gifts, food… Can't wait for the food!"

"You haven't tried it yet! You've got a lot riding on this lunch. If you hate it, it's going to ruin your day!"

"Grace, admittedly I haven't known you very long, but every single thing you've ever cooked me has been superb. Why should today be any different?"

"Do you think maybe your standards aren't very high?"

"No, I think you're an exemplary cook."

"It's easy to be confident and really go for something when you know whatever you do is going to be appreciated."

"You have a flair for it. I appreciate it because it's delicious, not because I'm sparing your feelings!"

"Good. I'd hate to think you were forcing it down out of politeness."

"I hope you've hung around with me enough to realise I say what I think about things."

"Yeah, you do."

"Is that bad?"

"No. I'm sick to the back teeth of being lied to, so it makes a refreshing change. It's probably fifteen years at least since I felt excited about Christmas…but this year, while I was deciding what to make, I felt a proper little flutter about it, as if I couldn't wait to get stuck in. I'm trying something new to me, something I haven't made for Christmas dinner before, so I hope it'll be all right."

"It'll be perfect."

"There you go again! No pressure…"

Vidar shook his head, hugging her tight. Grace liked being so firmly squished against the padded front of his jacket, "It will be perfect. It always is."

"My past Christmas dinners have always had the potential for perfection, but never turned out that way. However, in my defence, I don't think it was necessarily all my fault. Dom would go to the pub as soon as it opened, or that's what he'd tell me anyway. He'd get home about eight at night, roaring drunk, and dinner would be ruined. He'd be snoring on the sofa by nine, and I'd have been on my own all day knowing the one thing I'd made an effort over would be wasted, because it'd be all dry and horrible and he'd be too plastered to even taste it…but still we'd go through the charade, year after year, because I never had the guts to stand up to him and demand he got home at a decent time."

"He's insane, I'm sure of it! He had you, and all that goes along with you…and he took you for granted. Now, that's pretty crazy in my humble opinion."

"I should have stood up to him."

"You shouldn't have had to! He should have wanted to spend the holidays with his wife. It's a no-brainer from where I'm standing."

Grace looked up at him, "I don't deserve a lovely friend like you."

Vidar blushed, and blustered, "We going to the beach or just standing here all day?"

Smiling, Grace allowed herself to be tugged briskly by the hand along the remainder of the lane to the just-exposed sand. Stopping to look left, along to Marwick Head, Grace turned back and beheld Vidar stepping down onto the shelving flagstone gradually being revealed by the receding tide, bending to peer into the rock pools. She hurried to join him, Vidar pointing out the tiny, gyrating crustaceans, little fish darting from weed to weed, and the crabs that scuttled out of sight of their looming, leaning human shadows, intruding upon the secret world.

By the time they reached the far end of the beach, Grace had removed her hat and gloves, and Vidar was unzipping his padded winter coat, "I'm getting hot now!"

"It's nice in the sun."

"No wind. Tropical!" Vidar stood on the highest shelf of rock and looked out from his vantage point across the calm, flat lagoon. He was big, broad, muscular, handsome; hands in his pockets, watching the water, paying no attention to her. Without thinking, Grace crossed the remaining feet of stone to reach him, slid her arms right around his body, and hugged him as tightly as he'd held her on the lane, resting her head against his chest and looking up the hill towards *Somerled's* glass rear elevation. The big windows reflected the landscape so effectively the building was all-but-invisible, apart from the grey smudge of woodsmoke escaping the central chimney and staining the otherwise empty sky.

Vidar tensed at her touch, surprised by the well-meaning ambush, but instantly reciprocated the embrace, closing his eyes, feeling the warmth of the determined winter sun on his face and the woman on his body. He felt calm; at peace. If he could have nothing else but this, then the simple, rewarding close-companionship of this caring, beautiful individual was more than he could ever have expected. He should be – would be – satisfied with it, and cease to yearn for something he had no right to assume could be his.

"What's the time?" murmured Grace.

Vidar looked at his watch, "Just after twelve-thirty."

"I need to do the veg."

"Come on. Lunch time."

Hand-in-hand, they balanced one another back across the shifting pebbles to the lane.

SEVENTEEN

Vidar sat back, replete, rubbing a hand across his swollen stomach, "Ohhh...I've eaten too much."

Grace picked at the smaller pieces of crackling calling temptingly from the platter next to the remains of the pork shoulder.

"When you said you were trying something new, I didn't realise you were doing traditional Danish Christmas Dinner."

"I fancied doing something different. I've made turkey and all the trimmings every year since I can remember. Did I get it right?"

"Of course you got it right! You, plus cooking of any kind, equals perfection."

Grace glowed with satisfaction.

"I wish I could eat it all over again...but I'll explode."

"There's pudding yet!"

"Ohhhgggghhhh...." Vidar groaned in mock agony, "I can't! My lack of restraint in the face of your cooking could kill me!"

Grace giggled, "How about I roll you over to the sofa and you just lie there like a walrus on a rock for a couple of hours, and then we have pudding?"

"That sounds like a good idea."

"You'll want to have it. It's ris-a-l'amande."

"I love that stuff...haven't had it for years..."

"Traditional Danish Christmas Dinner...it said in the book that's the pudding you're supposed to have."

"You've really done this properly."

"We aim to please!"

"We succeed in pleasing…" Vidar reached across the table to take her hand, thumb rubbing softly across her knuckles, "Everywhere I go when I'm not working is just a building with some stuff in it – but a place with a Grace, that's a home."

"It's only lunch, Vid – "

"Lunch is the tip of the iceberg!" He fixed her with his disconcertingly-direct stare. Although she was becoming used to it, Grace wasn't yet immune to its penetrative power, "It's about having the best three weeks of my life…and what that feels like to me. The reason life's so good is that you're here, making everything right the way you do."

Grace blushed, unsure, after last night, what reception she should give this latest fervent utterance. Too enthusiastic, and they might be back in the fumbling, embarrassing quagmire of yesterday's mixed messages and confused signals.

"I just need to feel as if I've got a purpose. My big sister died before I was born, and it made my parents treat me like a *Fabergé* egg, which is why I was so desperate to get to Art College and try to make myself, rather than being their creature – but I never followed it through properly. I got married instead, and I believed, truly I did, that my purpose in life was to make my husband happy…but I failed at that as well. Now I'm left with no idea what I'm supposed to be for. If, while I'm figuring it out, I can do something good for someone else, well…I'm not wasting my time, then, am I? You appreciate what I try to do for you."

"Wanna beach next to me on my walrus-rock and watch a Christmas movie?"

"That sounds nice."

"Ok...why don't I clean this up and you go pick something to watch?"

"How about I clear up and you play something nice on the piano?"

Vidar squeezed her hand, "You always end up doing everything. It isn't fair on you."

"But you'll just throw the rest of the food away, and I want to save the leftovers to make something for tomorrow."

Vidar shook his head, amazed, "You're thinking about tomorrow's food already..."

"Anyway, I like listening to you playing."

Vidar stood up, lifted her hand, kissed it, "If you want me to play, I'll play...if my stomach will let me get close enough to reach the keys..."

****

Vidar spooned in the deliciously-creamy Danish dessert, "An hour after that gut-buster and I'm eating again! What are you doing to me, woman? Are you fattening me up for next Christmas?"

Grace teased, "I'm planning on having the Fletts round. I thought there'd be enough meat on you by then to feed all of us."

"Mag'd love that. She'd be begging to carve!"

Grace grinned, enjoying every almond mouthful, "This stuff's lovely! I'd eat it for breakfast...except it's a bit bad for you..."

Vidar chuckled and put his empty bowl on the coffee table, watching the film for a while, "I can't believe you made us watch *Gremlins*."

"It's a Christmas film!"

"In which they kill everybody and trash the town!"

Grace sniggered, "I can't abide the usual schmaltzy rot you get at Christmas. Whose life is like that? At least you get a laugh with *Gremlins*, instead of being nauseated by the levels of cheesy cheer exhibited by hordes of insincere, self-satisfied Americans... Sorry, just having a pop at your adopted country, there!"

Vidar yawned, "No, I quite agree. Most of their Christmas movies are terrible."

He wriggled round on the sofa until his head rested on Grace's lap, yawning again, closing his eyes, and sighing, "I think I have to sleep for a little while."

"On me?"

"Where better?"

Grace was determined not to be embarrassed, even though this contact with him was the most disconcerting yet. She stroked Vidar's hair off his forehead, as if it was normal for him to lie with his head in her lap, and she was completely unperturbed by it.

Drifting swiftly towards sleep, Vidar pictured Elaine doing the same to Stewart as he dozed in his armchair, and smiled to himself. Grace was touching him with the soothing, protective gesture of a wife caressing her husband; Vidar couldn't help but feel encouraged. There was something so irrepressibly cheeky in his expression that

Grace momentarily forgot her awkwardness, tickling his ear lightly with her finger, "What are you grinning at?"

Vidar replied softly, "I was just thinking about Stewart the other day. He gave me such a hard time about being a narcissist because I wouldn't eat one cookie – too afraid of getting fat. He'd be rolling up if he could see me now…something I'm incapable of doing because of my massively-distended gut."

Only just mistress of herself, Grace spiralled into fresh turmoil when Vidar turned onto his side, resting his face against her stomach, and wrapping his arms around her hips, cuddling her to him as if she was a pillow, murmuring, "I feel so good, so happy… There's this Danish word called *Hygge*. It doesn't really translate, but it's a sort of mental hug. A sense of serenity; of completely belonging to a time and place where you're totally at peace with who you are, where you are, who you're with, what you're doing with your life in that moment. My brother used to say he got it if the kids fell asleep on him when they were little and stuff like that. I never really knew what he meant until recently…but these last few weeks I've had it all the time, washing over me in waves. It's you, ladling out vast quantities of contentment the way you do; building a little nest, and making sure everyone's warm and safe inside it."

Vidar's breathing steadied and slowed as he fell asleep.

If only she possessed one iota of Sonia's inherent cockiness! Her brash little Orcadian buddy would be brave enough to try something if she desired it enough, and to hell with the consequences! What Grace wanted to do, more than anything, was lift Vidar's new Christmas jumper, and run her fingertips across his skin. She'd

Googled him, seen the interviews, the articles, the promotional pictures; the semi-naked, sculpted body. It was hard to explain why looking at pictures in the public domain made her ashamed, as he'd obviously used his physique as a promotional tool, but ogling him without his knowledge made her feel seedy, as if she was peeking at him through a crack in a door.

Fingers trembling, unable to believe she was really going to do it, she plucked uncertainly at the hem of his top, inching it up to expose a centimetre of California-tanned stomach above the waistband of his trousers. She slid a tentative finger a couple of inches across his hip, hardly daring to apply any pressure. Vidar grunted in his light doze, stirring as the touch tickled. Grace snatched her hand away, heart thudding, and sat stock-still, expecting his eyes to open.

They didn't.

Vidar mumbled, and hugged her tighter.

Too scared to try again, Grace placed her hands to either side of her on the cushions with deliberate care, lest she brush against him by accident. Flicking off the tv, Grace sat like a statue on the sofa, looking from Vidar's sleeping profile to the exposed slither of tanned temptation, cursing her cowardice.

EIGHTEEN

Vidar slept deeply for nearly an hour, until Grace was so desperate to urinate she was forced to wake him, "Vid…I really need a wee!"

"Hmmm?"

"Sorry, you've got to move. I'm going to wet myself!"

"Oh…"

He loosened his encircling arms and rolled away. He was snoring lightly again, mouth open, before she'd even reached the door of the guest room.

It was an inexpressible relief to pee. Afterwards, Grace spent some time in the bathroom, scrutinising her appearance in the mirror, cleaning her teeth, brushing her hair. Even as she did so, she inwardly berated herself for such feminine foolishness. What does it matter what your hair looks like, you're just sitting around indoors? Who cares if you taste of Christmas dinner? Who's getting close enough to you to notice?

She applied a smear of lip gloss, stared at her piteous expression in the mirror, growled at the reflection, and wiped her mouth irritably on her towel. She'd seen the photographs during her Google trawl…no matter how maddening he implied they were, why have a forty-something disaster area when you could have a twenty-something underwear model?

Deciding she might as well continue to be useful if nothing else, Grace tiptoed to the kitchen, emptied the dishwasher as quietly as she could, flicked on the kettle, and wandered down to the fireplace to push a couple of logs into the dying wood burner. She closed the metal door slowly and it squeaked agonisingly, worn hinges grinding abrasively together. Vidar snorted and awoke mid-snore, blinking in confusion at the harsh sound.

"Sorry," Grace whispered, "I was trying extra-hard to be quiet…failed miserably…"

Vidar focused, beheld her, grinned in unconcealed happiness, and drawled, "Hey baby, what's for dinner?"

Grace gaped, "Seriously?"

"No…definitely not."

Grace smiled, relieved, "You had me going there for a minute!"

Vidar yawned, stretching, writhing his body across the sofa cushions. His new jumper rode up further, exposing more tanned, toned tummy.

Grace became aware she was arching forward on hands and knees like a predatory animal detecting a scent on the air, fingers gripping the thick pile of the hearthrug, toes curling and pushing into the wool. What was the matter with her?

Vidar rubbed his eyes, yawned again, sat up, "I don't need any more food until about March! What I do need is a pee, a drink, and to go on a ten-mile run."

"It's dark!" Grace gestured at the early evening winter blackness beyond the window, standing as she spoke, and drawing the thick curtains to keep the room warm, "Shall I put the lights on?"

"If you want to. I think it's nice with just the tree and the fire."

"I'll leave it, then."

Vidar rolled himself reluctantly off the sofa to unsteady standing, "I really am tired. I was awake a long time last night."

Grace plonked dejectedly back onto the rug, mumbling, "I'm sorry about that…"

Realising his unguarded words had been interpreted as criticism, Vidar sought to diffuse the sudden atmosphere, "I'm not having a go at you, Grace. You want a drink?"

"Ok. Kettle's just boiled."

He padded off to the toilet, returned a couple of minutes later and made them both a cup of tea, while Grace knelt before the wood burner, concentrated on the flames, and tried not to think of the strip of skin she'd stared at for an hour but been too afraid to touch.

Vidar put their teas on the table and knelt next to her on the rug, "You look miles away. You ok? Thinking of Christmas past?"

She glanced over Vidar's shoulder at the kitchen clock, "He'd still be in the pub now, and I'd be sobbing over the turkey, frantically trying to stop it getting any drier than it already was…having to keep it warm in case he walked through the door at any moment…" Grace was shocked at how much her voice shook with remembered distress.

Vidar spoke in his mellow, reassuring tone, "That Christmas is over, forever…but this one's not quite done yet." Reaching into the back pocket of his jeans, he withdrew a pink box tied with a striped, brown ribbon.

Grace stared, "What's this?"

He shrugged, "Just something small. I forgot it this morning, what with getting my book, and Sonia showing up."

Grace looked worried, "I only got you one thing."

"That doesn't matter. I didn't expect you to get me anything."

Grace untied the ribbon and opened the hinged lid to discover a delicate silver choker with two tiny interlocking hearts.

A sharp intake of breath, "Oh, Vid, that's so pretty!"

"You sure?" His eyes raked her face for signs of insincerity.

"I'm sure," Grace breathed, "It's lovely…"

"Jewellery's always a bit of a gamble," Vidar confessed, sounding relieved.

Grace felt a rush of certainty; he hadn't forgotten the gift at all. After last night, he'd probably shoved it in the back of a drawer and elected it wasn't a gamble worth taking. What had she done since yesterday to make him change his mind?

"I'd like to wear it now," Grace lifted it eagerly from the box, unclasped it, and then fumbled with the brand new, stiff catch, "Oh, I can't do it up. Can you do it?"

"Sure," Vidar's hands brushed her skin as he held both ends of the chain and fastened them, running fingertips from the back of her neck, across her collarbones to the hollow of her throat, where the entwined hearts rested, "Looks nice."

She tingled where he'd touched her. Hiding her blush, Grace leant over the glass table to see her reflection, screwing up her nose at the flamboyance of the diamanté costume earrings she still wore, "These don't go. Too showy with my pretty new necklace."

She took them off, putting them on the table and turning back to admire the necklace again, "That's better."

Vidar looked at her for a long time in silence, not moving. Grace was surprised at her ability to meet and return the look with self-assurance, not having to drop her eyes at the intensity of his gaze as she usually would.

Eventually, Vidar whispered, "In that case, this doesn't go either."

He reached out a hand and unclipped the matching diamanté clasp which secured her hair, freeing the glossy curtain to unroll over his hand and tumble down her back.

Something *released* within Grace. Whatever it was that had held her in check was suddenly gone. It had undone with as little fanfare as Bob Turner's garden gate, or her own hair clip.

With total confidence, Grace knelt up, leant forward, and kissed Vidar hungrily, as if he was what she'd really been waiting all day to consume. Vidar responded instantly, reaching decisively for her as he had last night, sliding her firmly against his kneeling body with one powerful hand on her buttocks, and the other in the small of her back.

As their bodies pressed together, Grace rested her elbows on his shoulders, and cradled him between her forearms, sliding her hands into his hair, supporting his head as it tipped back into her splayed palms.

Vidar chuckled. Uncertain, Grace raised her eyebrows, "What are you laughing?"

He ran exploratory fingers up her back, under her t-shirt, unclasping her bra as he remarked conversationally, "I was just thinking – trust you to make me do this when I've had my own bodyweight in roast potatoes..."

Vidar pulled off her jumper and t-shirt as one, and hooked a finger into the front of her unclasped bra, slipping it off, bending his head, and sliding his tongue across the sensitive underside of her breast, flicking casually across the nipple.

Grace shuddered and arched her back against his supporting hands, warm and firm on her shoulder-blades.

Enjoying the titillation, Vidar bantered, "I could just flake out from overexertion, like those fat people who never make it to their apartment on the thirty-seventh floor because the elevator's broken and they have to take the stairs…"

Cupping his face in her hands, Grace kissed him again, and demanded good-humouredly, "Will you shut up?"

Vidar grinned, abruptly gripping her thighs firmly beneath her buttocks, making her gasp in surprise. He flexed his arm muscles, lifted her off her knees, and slid her onto his lap.

Grace wrapped her legs tightly around him, and leant back against the strength of his arms.

"One more thing."

Grace rolled her eyes and tried not to smile, but was unable to stop, "Yes, what?"

"I just want you to know, before you get me naked, that my stomach isn't usually this round. Someone forced me to eat a massive lunch."

"Oh, forced you? Like you're going to be forced to have sex in a minute?"

"Exactly," Vidar kissed her neck.

Abandoning all pretention to sophistication of any kind, Grace just giggled more.

Vidar couldn't believe how content he felt, how calm, how convinced of the rightness of this happening in just the way it was, at exactly the moment it was supposed to. Usually he had sex with women because…what else was there to do with them? Vidar employed sex as a tool to fill an awkward silence when there was nothing left to say.

For him, sexual contact had never before occurred to enhance existing intimacy, more firmly cement an already-strong connection, or convey an emotion more powerfully than any words.

Vidar tipped her backwards, resting her gently on the rug, lowering his body on top of hers, leaning to kiss her again, pulling away before their mouths met.

"What?" Grace's stomach tightened in apprehension. Was Vidar about to get his own back for last night and declare he'd changed his mind?

"You sure about this now?"

Grace decided to brazen it out, "Who started it?"

"You did, you vixen!"

Grace sniggered, fears forgotten, "Well…what does that tell you?"

She put her hands against Vidar's chest, confessing earnestly, "I made a mistake yesterday, a big one…and I created a load of awkwardness that didn't need to be there."

Vidar gaped in mock horror, "You mean, I could have done this yesterday, when I was thin?"

"Oh God – shut up!"

Chuckling, Vidar kissed her tenderly, cradling her body to him with an arm around her naked waist.

They remained close to one another for a moment, before Vidar rocked his body away to gaze wonderingly as he ran his free hand from the softness of her hair, across her cheek, tracing her jawline, lightly touching his fingers under her chin to lift her face and kiss her again, before moving away so he could look at her once more. Stroking languid fingers across her neck, around her bare shoulder and down her half-naked body, he cupped her breast briefly, and drew a tickling thumb over her ribcage, before stroking across her stomach, round her hip, and down her denim-clad thigh to hook his hand into the crook of her bent knee, pulling firmly upwards. The hand underneath her wiggled down her back to her buttocks, pushing hard to hold her against him, until she was being squeezed like an apple in a cider-press between the unceasing pressure of his palm, and the corresponding downward thrust of his pelvis.

"I've wanted to do this since the first moment I saw you, doing your headstand on my rug. Could you see it in my face, because it's all I was thinking about?"

"I was so embarrassed…"

"You were so beautiful. You still are so beautiful."

Grace brushed her hands up Vidar's clothed chest, and realised she could have her wish. She didn't have to settle for fantasising over a picture on a screen, or an illicit inch of exposed skin. She could take his clothes off and see all of him, touch him, and revel in it.

Pulling urgently at the front of his jumper, Grace tugged it upwards, over his head, and flung it behind her. She dared to touch, first with questing fingertips, then with flat, rubbing, relishing palms; joyfully experiencing the unbelievable firmness of his chest and stomach, the muscles slabs of delicious definition under the skin.

Seeking to hold himself in check, not try to force too fast as he had last night, Vidar took his time unbuckling her belt, undoing her jeans, searching eyes fixed on each other as they inched the material down over her hips. Vidar pulled at the ankles of both trouser legs to slide them off and free each limb in turn. Fighting the desperate urge to rush, Vidar instead trailed his fingertips lazily across her lower stomach, just above the lace material of her knickers, before hooking under the elastic and pulling those down too, in one determined motion.

In his confident way, he immediately ran a hand up her inner thigh and probed his gentle fingers straight inside her. Grace's blue eyes opened very wide, and she exhaled a shuddering breath, fingernails of one hand digging into the flesh of his chest, the other gripping the waistband of his trousers and yanking him sharply to her.

Mesmerised by one another, it took only seconds to struggle off Vidar's jeans and his underpants. Body taut, muscles quivering with the effort of restraint, Vidar gripped Grace's hips and rubbed himself against her, prolonging the anticipation until he could wait no longer, sinking his face into her hair and sliding inside her, feeling her body rise to meet him, "Min kærlighed..."

He held her against him for a moment, bodies still, savouring the sensation he'd never thought to experience, whispering, "Don't expect feats of athletic prowess, will you...I've had too much lunch."

266

Grace smiled dreamily, eyes closed, head thrown back, "I just want to be close to you, Vid...as close as I can get. I don't care about anything else."

Vidar kissed her hair, "Did it hurt?"

"What?"

"When you fell from heaven?"

Grace winced, "Too cheesy!"

Vidar laughed, pushed his mouth onto hers, kissed her hard, and Grace responded to him, flicking her tongue across his lips as he eased away.

Enveloped by velvety-warm softness, Vidar held himself in place, resisting the compulsion to move, enjoying the potency building within him.

Touching his forehead to hers, he grinned in his lazy way, "You're the best thing that's ever happened to me."

Grace opened her eyes, and stroked a berry-red fingernail down the cleft in his chin, "Are you a mind-reader?"

"Why?"

"Because I was thinking the exact same thing..."

They kissed again, irrepressibly-smiling lips brushing, meeting, pressing, parting, and Vidar surrendered to his longing, moving inside her body, holding her as tightly as he could, cherishing their connection.

Grace hooked her legs over his hips, and wrapped her arms around his neck, closing her eyes and losing herself in the bliss of total trust.

****

Later, they lay naked on the rug before the warmth of the fire, Grace's body curled to Vidar's back. Her fingertips touched the pattern that twisted from hips to shoulders, "Tell me the story behind this massive tattoo."

Vidar sighed, half-dozing in the firelight, "Not a clue. I can't remember a thing about it."

He shivered and smiled as Grace's tickling finger traced the abstract black swirls traversing his skin.

"You don't remember?"

"Nope. Just shows how wasted I was. It must've taken five, six hours in the chair...maybe more...and I have no memory of it, no idea why I had it done, or where."

"How old were you?"

"Again, not sure exactly...but about twenty-two, because in pictures before that there's no tattoo, and suddenly, it appears!"

"Very rock and roll."

"Very dumb..."

"You don't like it?"

"Course I don't like it! Not that it makes any difference, because I'm stuck with it, and I suppose it's become synonymous with me – my 'brand' – but I can't think what possessed me to have it done. I suppose I wasn't known for my clear thinking and good decision-making in those days. The worst thing about it is the Fan Forums, where people proudly post their pictures of having the same tattoo. Women as well as men! Breaks my heart to see it, and it's so tied up with the image that I can't come out and say how horrible I think it is!"

"So, you'd get rid of it if you could?"

"Oh yeah, definitely."

Grace's fingertips stroked a line down Vidar's spine from the nape of his neck to the cleft of his buttocks, making him shiver again, "I think it's sexy."

"Do you? I think it's stupid, and big, and black, and...inescapable...but thank you anyway. I can always rely on you to make me feel better about myself."

"Pleasure," Grace kissed his shoulder blade, and snuggled her body closer to him, wrapping an arm around his chest. Vidar held the hand that touched him, and leant back against her, "You know I said I was happy earlier?"

"Mmmm..."

"Well, I'd like it on the record that I'm even happier now."

Grace sighed contently, and kissed him again, before a noise distracted her, "Was that...the front door?"

"Fucking Sonia! I have told that girl a million times to knock, and not just let herself in!"

"Do you think we should, you know, put something on?"

"No," said Vidar firmly, "I'm comfortable. If she walks in here and gets the shock of her life, it serves her right! My house, my rug, my sex life...I'm not moving."

Grace put a hand over her eyes, "I'm embarrassed already and she's still taking her shoes off!"

"Relax. We are supposed to be here. She isn't. She won't be here long, trust me."

When Sonia bowled in, all wild hair and cheery manner, it took a second for her eyes to adjust to the barely-lit room from the brighter hallway. Only then did she see the two naked bodies entwined on the thick rug, illuminated by the intermittent light and shadow of the flickering firelight and twinkling tree. Comprehending her error, Sonia brought a trembling hand to her mouth, "Oops..." holding up an explanatory pack of cards and venturing, "I don't suppose you fancy Canasta, do you?"

Grace erupted into a fit of giggles against Vidar's back as he turned and pointed an aggressive finger at Sonia, "I have told you before about just barging in. You have ten seconds to get out of here, Son, without uttering another word!"

Grace did a little wave at her and mouthed, "Bye darling."

Sonia, with one wary eye on Vidar, winked, and mouthed, "Bye!" before making herself scarce as fast as her little pudding of a body would permit.

Finally – it had taken them long enough! Sonia smiled to herself as she struggled her wellies back on, thinking of Grace's infectious giggles, and Vidar doing his best to pretend to be annoyed, despite the smile that played at the corners of his mouth. Disappointed to be returning home so swiftly to more rowing about what to watch on the family's one television, Sonia nevertheless felt quiet satisfaction that her newest and most valuable friend had looked so content. If she liked her new life on Orkney enough, did it mean she'd stay? Selfishly, Sonia wanted this more than anything. If Grace and Vidar were properly together now, surely it couldn't help but make all their futures a little bit brighter?

NINETEEN

The doorbell rang shrilly in the peaceful house. Vidar, halfway through an immensely boring contract, dropped the folder with alacrity, easing himself gently out from underneath the dozing Grace. She stirred as he moved, "What is it?"

"Sorry – doorbell."

"Who is it?"

Vidar pinched her nose teasingly, "I don't know 'til I go look, do I?"

Grace rolled onto her back, squinted into the sunlight flooding the room, couldn't focus, and poked out her tongue at the only large shadow blocking the light. She wriggled sleepily onto her elbows on the sofa cushions, "Are you expecting anyone?"

"Nope." He opened the connecting door and padded down the hallway, remarking over his shoulder, "It's probably Son. It's usually Son."

"But she lets herself in...?"

Instead of Sonia, Vidar discovered a tall, well-dressed, dark-haired man, who absorbed the obviously unexpected sight of him with a consternation he was unable to conceal as the big Dane swung open the door. The visitor had to readjust his line of vision a good foot higher than his original point of focus when he found himself staring not into the eyes of an average-height woman, but straight at the broad chest of Vidar's commanding physique, a t-shirt with the Danish flag upon it stretched by the bulging muscularity beneath.

Despite his surprise, the man spoke clearly-enunciated English in a deep, smooth, confident voice accustomed to being heeded. This area didn't attract door-to-door salesmen, given there were very few doors a large distance apart, and his debonair appearance suggested something far more threatening to Vidar. As the man began to talk, Vidar realised he already knew what was coming, and fought to maintain a neutral expression as each perfectly-pitched syllable penetrated his heart like a freshly-whetted blade.

"Good afternoon. I'm looking for my wife."

Vidar gripped the interior door handle until his fingers started to ache. He pulled the angled edge of the door against his pelvis, ribs, and collarbone, and prayed it would prop him up, otherwise he knew his legs would give way.

"A Mrs Grace Radley? This property is *Somerled*, I understand?"

Vidar stonewalled, pointlessly, "I don't know a Grace Radley. I know a Grace Hamilton."

A pained expression flitted across the man's face, as if someone had just stepped on his toe in a crowd, "Hamilton is her maiden name."

"I see."

"If you don't mind, she's returning to London today. I've come to collect her."

"Yes," said Vidar, slowly and with polite control, "Of course you have."

He was suffering the searing agony of his heart shattering into a million tiny shards, scattering themselves on the Orcadian breeze. He wanted to explain in his quiet way that he did mind; he minded very much indeed – but what difference would it make? This man was Grace's husband. How could he compete with that? The implication within his tone was that this return was prearranged.

Both men regarded each other aggressively, Vidar unwilling to placidly surrender to the inevitable and admit the visitor, Grace's husband equally determined not to plead to see his wife, but too proud to leave without achieving his objective. A sardonic smirk briefly crossed the features of the other man as he detected a hint of Vidar's distress.

Admitting defeat, Vidar muttered, "Come in," standing aside and holding open the door to allow Grace's husband into the hall. The visitor looked around with unabashed curiosity as he stepped over the threshold. Vidar pushed the front door shut on the fresh spring day, and said, "After you," indicating the man should precede him into the living room.

Grace, who must have heard it all, was wide awake now; standing motionless and hollow-eyed in the middle of the rug, painted toenails peeking through the thick pile. Her arms were folded defensively across her ribcage, each hand gripping the opposite elbow as if holding the pieces of her body together.

Vidar felt a five month separation from Grace would occasion swift progress across the room to take her in his arms and not let go...but her husband stopped at the top of the steps to the living area, and regarded the tense woman in front of him with apparent equanimity. Was he waiting for his wife to rush to him instead? Vidar hung back out of a sense of decorum, and tried to make himself as invisible as possible against the wall. Grace's blue eyes flicked from Vidar's face to her husband's, and back again. Vidar couldn't escape the conviction she was making a comparison. He stood, barefoot, in frayed jeans, worn t-shirt, with unkempt, greying hair, and knew he would be found wanting when contrasted with this sharp-suited, polished, slick individual, patiently commanding all the attention in the centre of the room.

Grace said not a word to her husband, nor he to her, and no one moved for several seconds, until Vidar realised nothing would happen until he made himself scarce.

Eyes fixed on Grace – for Vidar, there had long ago ceased to be a point in looking anywhere else – he muttered, "Apparently, you're leaving, Grace?"

She didn't react. Not even a twitch disturbed her stony expression.

Certain he didn't have long before all semblance of self-control evaporated completely, Vidar managed, "I'll get out of your way."

She looked directly at him with a flat, empty stare devoid of life or meaning. Vidar strained to extract some comfort from it, but failed to find any. The light that had twinkled so brightly within the rich blue from the very first moment he'd beheld her had been extinguished. Feeling like an intruder in his own home, Vidar turned and left the room, shutting the hall door with more violence than he'd intended behind his departing back, and quitting the house before he lost all command of himself.

****

Grace flinched as Vidar slammed the hall door, as if he'd shut it on her fingers. After a moment or two, Grace heard the now-familiar sound of the electric mechanism that opened the garage. She closed her eyes as the sound of Vidar's car grew fainter.

Her husband looked openly around him, and nodded grudging approval, "All very pleasant. You didn't let the grass grow under your feet, did you?" He gestured to her hand, "Off with the wedding ring, on with the maiden name, and straight back in the saddle!" He smirked sarcastically, and raised an eyebrow, as if challenging her to justify her behaviour. Grace wrapped her opposite little finger around her left hand, where her wedding and engagement rings had used to be, and thought how odd it now felt for something to be around that digit; lumpy and alien, a relic of the past.

"You're suggesting I should in some way feel ashamed...is that it?"

Dominic shrugged, "I'm not suggesting anything. You're the one who brought it up."

"You don't really do shame, do you, Dom?"

"Do you think I have something to be ashamed of, Grace?"

She pictured the green bubbles of the text messages, and realised she hadn't thought of them for months. At one time, they'd occupied her mind so completely there'd barely been room for anything else, but they hadn't mattered for so long!

Dominic was still spouting supercilious, hypocritical rot, "I'm not the one who abandoned my husband and home without the slightest explanation, and pelted straight into the arms of another man under false pretences. He doesn't know a Grace Radley, apparently...but he knows a Grace Hamilton. If that's not being duplicitous, I don't know what is!"

Grace thought of the neatly-equidistant, thoroughly-dusted, expensive crockery displayed on the dresser in their London flat, and suddenly wished she was standing in front of it with Dominic's seven-iron. She had a desire to smash every single precious piece of it to smithereens, and then start on the glass shelves in Dominic's study, and maybe the walls of mirrors in the bathroom she'd had to polish every day to get rid of the water stains...

Taking a deep breath, Grace battled for self-control. She wanted to tear at her hair and scream the injustice of him being here aloud. She wanted to turn the clock back ten minutes and tell Vidar to ignore the doorbell, press her warm body to his, and convince him whoever was out there didn't warrant his attention as much as she did.

"Five months, Dominic. More than five months, in fact. Not a call to check I was still alive, even! Do you think perhaps I was justified in assuming our marriage over? I told Fen on the very first day where I was going, and why. She made it quite clear she was going to tell you everything...and yet...nothing, Dominic. Not a two-second text message. Nothing."

Dominic screwed up his face as if he'd been forced to smell something unpleasant, "You could have extended me the courtesy of explaining face-to-face, instead of sneaking out like a coward and expecting Fenella to do your dirty-work – "

"That's your speciality isn't it, marshalling the considerable dark arts of the redoubtable Fen?"

Dominic ignored the sarcasm, instead countering, "Did you expect me to chase after you like some lost sheep? Pardon me, Grace, but desperation isn't exactly my style! I'm a busy man. I haven't time to tear around the country every time my spoilt little wife throws a tantrum – we're not establishing that precedent. Your parents may have indulged your childish whims, but I'm certainly not going to tolerate that crap."

"This isn't about who cracks first! It's not a test of your mettle, Dom! It's our life; our marriage. If you'd wanted me back, you would have called…you wouldn't have been able to tolerate all that time without me in your life. The fact you didn't make the slightest effort to get in touch indicated you were no longer interested in being married to me, so I…I…"

"You glued yourself to some clueless chump instead. I understand, Grace. I see what's going on here. You are manipulative. You use people. I'm afraid I've known you too long for you to be able to get away with this ridiculous behaviour. You need to snap out of it. You have a place to be, a home, a role to fulfil. This…whatever this is…it's not real, Grace. It's based on lies…lies you told. He's stormed off in a huff, hasn't he? Do you think perhaps that's because you used your maiden name and never mentioned your oh-so-inconvenient husband? Do you think he might be slightly pissed off at being treated like a fool, Grace? Can't see him tolerating that, can you? You'll be out on your ear by dinner time. What a shame, as this is such a lovely place…"

Grace pushed her clenched fists into the back pockets of her jeans, and pressed one bare foot firmly down onto the other, to prevent her rushing forward and beating Dominic about the head.

She pictured the nights curled in Vidar's protective embrace, whispering hints of her humbling past into those understanding, grey eyes.

"Why didn't you call me, Dom? Why didn't you ask me to come back?"

"Oh, for God's sake, Grace!"

"Why, Dominic?"

"I was waiting for you to come to your senses, of course! We all need a little break from the routine sometimes. I was quite prepared to give you the space to have just that, but, being you, it had to be more dramatic. Most women'd just bugger off to Monaco for a fortnight, shag whichever suave European picks them up in the hotel bar, come back with a tan and a satisfying memory or two, and get on with it – but not you! You had to make it some big mystery, do something 'alternative' and go AWOL for half the year! I've had to put everything on hold at home to come to this godforsaken dump to fetch you back, only to find you playing house with some scruffy chancer! It's simply irresponsible, Grace! I've got big deals going through. I need to be there, not here. No one in their right mind needs to be here."

Grace thought of the wind whipping Sonia's marvellous hair into a maelstrom of flying fire around her face, as the two of them gossiped, giggled, and followed the happily bounding dogs down through the snow from Far Field to the farmhouse for tea and buttered rolls, still hot from the oven.

She pictured beautiful Vidar, sitting at the piano, glasses on the end of his nose so he could focus on both the keyboard and the composition-in-progress spread across its top, frowning in concentration until she placed a cup of tea next to him and got treated to the gorgeous gift of his grateful grin.

Dominic had never been grateful for anything she'd done for him...and she'd done so very much, including sacrificing every ounce of her own dignity to perpetuating their ugly excuse for a marriage. She needed very much to be here, not there, and if that meant she wasn't in her right mind, then she never wanted to be considered sane again.

"Do you think perhaps you've got your head together now, Grace...if that is remotely possible for you?"

"Yes, Dominic. You'll be pleased to know I've done just that."

"Well, good. About bloody time." Dominic glanced at his watch, "Right, get packed, because we need to catch the late-afternoon ferry, otherwise we'll be stuck here another night."

Grace gawped, "I'm sorry?"

"Come on. Get moving."

"Do you seriously think I'm going back with you?"

"Of course you are!"

"What?"

"I get it, ok? You've made your point. You've stuck two fingers up at everybody and had your rebellious teenage holiday. I hope you've got it out of your system because now it's time to unhook your knickers from the Viking's bedpost and get back to being an adult again...if you can manage that."

Insulted by his glibness, Grace snapped, "And what if I haven't 'got it out of my system'?"

"Grace, you've had your fun. Time to pack in the Neanderthal and return to civilisation. You've got obligations to fulfil."

"Oh, have I, Dominic? And what are those?"

Dominic shook his head irritably, and straightened his shirtsleeves with the characteristic tug of the cuff and snap of his long arm. The thick, good-quality fabric of his jacket sleeve made a sharp sound in the silence, like a gust whipping an unfurled sail from slack to taut.

"However you may feel about it, the fact remains you are still my wife – in law – and your place is in our marital home a thousand miles away, not shacked up here with some hippy foreigner you've known for five minutes! You are obligated to come home, Grace. At some stage, despite your penchant for romance, it's necessary to cut the bullshit and get on with what you're supposed to be doing."

Grace folded her arms and lofted her chin aggressively, refusing to play along.

Legendarily phlegmatic in every situation, a ruffling in Dominic's usual smoothness was becoming apparent. Had he imagined she would just placidly pack up and leave, bobbing in his confident wake like a newly-hatched duckling?

"Seriously, Grace, wake up! I'm sorry but this is not reality. Reality is our home in London, my job, our friends, our connections, our life together. That's real. This isn't. You've pissed off Conan the Barbarian by lying to him, so that's a row you'll have to have when he eventually slopes home, isn't it? Why not just avoid all the crap and get out now?"

"There won't be a row, Dom. Rowing is what people who don't like each other do. You and I, for example."

"Oh, Grace, just leave the attitude now. There's no one watching who'll be the slightest bit impressed. This isn't about what you like and don't like. This is about normal standards of proper behaviour. This is about what's expected of you. If you don't start behaving rationally, I'll be forced to tell people you've taken leave of your senses and abandoned me for another man. How is that going to look when it all tumbles down like a house of cards and you eventually come creeping home? It's going to be bloody embarrassing for you, isn't it? All I'm trying to do is preserve the integrity of your reputation…whereas you seem hellbent on destroying it. There are consequences to your actions, Grace! How long do you think I'm going to continue covering for you?"

"Forever, Dominic," stated Grace, simply. "I'm your wife, as you keep saying. You're supposed to have my back forever."

"There's a limit, Grace."

"To a lifelong commitment?"

"There are some things one shouldn't be asked to tolerate."

"Like infinite infidelity?"

Dominic didn't miss a beat, "Fen said you kept harping on about affairs! I don't know where you get these stupid flights of fancy from! I think you'll find you're the one screwing here, not me."

Grace roared, an animal sound building from deep in her throat; not a scream, but something much deeper and more primal – an outpouring of hatred, hurt, and frustration. She rushed forward with flailing arms and kicking legs. Despite her fitness, Grace was a small, slight woman, and her husband a well-built man. Not the immense, powerful size of Vidar, but certainly faster and stronger than his diminutive wife. Dominic Radley still played competitive hockey twice a week, and had done since his schooldays – not to mention the other athletic aerobic exercise he very frequently enjoyed – and he swiftly and easily gripped his wife's swinging arms, dragging her bodily backwards across the rug to dump her helplessly on the sofa. She struggled upright, but he pushed her onto the seat again with firm pressure on her sternum.

"Enough! I'm not going to hit you, Grace…but you're not going to hit me either!"

Grace covered her face with her hands, and started to sob uncontrollably. Dominic regarded her without sympathy, simply waiting for the rush of agitation to pass. After some moments, Grace's sobbing eased to shuddering breathing, and she raised a tear and mucus-covered face to stare up at him, hopelessly. Annoyed, Dominic extracted a pristinely-pressed handkerchief from his pocket, and tossed it at her. Grace wiped her face without delicacy, sniffing loudly. Voice thick from crying, she mumbled, "I'm not going anywhere with you. I'm staying here."

Dominic rubbed at his temples. He needed a Scotch, a cigarette, and a bit less bloody drama. Exasperation decided him. He could stand here all night trading insults with Grace, or he could deliver an ultimatum and remind her who was boss.

"Right. Fine. If that's the way you want it, I'm not going to waste my time exchanging verbal blows with you. I'm leaving tomorrow. Tomorrow…understand? And I won't be coming back, ever. I am still prepared to overlook your little…indiscretion. We'll just forget this whole, embarrassing episode ever took place, but it's your last chance. You come home with me tomorrow and life will go back to the way it was. It will be as if this never happened. If I come here tomorrow morning to fetch you and you still insist on acting like a spoilt child, that's it. I'm not prepared to keep pandering to it, Grace. You come with me tomorrow or you're stuck here, or wherever you end up when your rebound relationship turns sour. You can kiss goodbye to your lovely, expensive home, your fancy car, all our friends, the holidays. I shan't maintain you, Grace. You left me, not the other way round."

"I don't need you to maintain me. I have my own money – "

"And no idea how to take care of yourself."

She didn't answer.

"Tomorrow morning, Grace. I expect a considered response…and if you've got any sense, we'll be straight on that ferry!"

"You can come back tomorrow, Dom. The answer will be the same."

"He doesn't want you, Grace. Not now he knows you've lied to him."

"You can go now, Dominic."

"Tomorrow morning, Grace. You've a lot of thinking to do, I would imagine."

"No, I haven't. I did all my thinking before I left London."

"This is not real, Grace! I am real. Our marriage is real. This is la-la-land…it won't last."

"Leave me alone, Dominic. Haven't you done enough?"

"If you happen to grow a braincell before tomorrow, I'm staying at the larger of the hotels in town. We can leave whenever you're ready; the earlier, the better."

Grace pulled her legs up against her chest, dropping her forehead onto her knees, "You can show yourself out, Dominic."

He left the house without another word, the tinny sound of his hire car engine rattling faintly down the uneven shingle driveway towards the road.

Grace tried to cry again once she was sure Dom had gone, desperate to release some of the pressure inside her, but the tears wouldn't come. She wriggled down onto her back on the sofa, dry eyes fixed on the sun's travelling shadow across the beamed ceiling as the afternoon wore on, listening fruitlessly for the sound of Vidar's car.

TWENTY

Vidar made it less than half a mile down the road before he couldn't see to drive any more. Torrents of tears he couldn't control poured into his eyes and across his face, like driving rain down a windowpane. Lurching to a stop, car angled across the fortunately-empty layby beside the wetland's wooden bird hide, Vidar surrendered fully to his anguish, sitting with hands flopped uselessly in his lap, unfocused eyes staring blankly, and broad shoulders heaving with the force of his sobs.

He knew without doubt it was over. Whatever fantasy future he'd secretly been planning would never now come true. All those early mornings waking to the first fingers of light reaching around the edges of the curtains, when he would remember Grace was next to him, and she wasn't a figment of his imagination! There was no greater pleasure for Vidar in those secret moments than pressing himself against Grace's sleeping body, feeling the rise and fall of her ribcage as she breathed, detecting the gentle beat of her heart, being able to stroke his fingertips across her warm skin, and hear her murmur in her sleep as the touch tickled and disturbed her shallow slumber. He'd spend that heavenly time picturing what their life would be like, travelling from one home to the next as his peripatetic career drove him across the globe, consciously slowing the pace of his professional life to devote time and attention to…his wife…

Might it be time for Vidar Rasmussen, the world's number one confirmed bachelor, to contemplate the ultimate commitment?

A clear image of Grace's suave, self-assured husband hit him with the force of a blow, and Vidar snarled in fury, punching the steering wheel with all his might, furious at his own credulity, making himself jump as his fist depressed the car's hooter. It blared sharply in the silence and he glanced around, suddenly feeling foolish and exposed. Leaning over, he fumbled in the glove compartment, extracting some tissues, wiping at eyes and nose. He appraised his appearance in the rear-view mirror, noticing the wrinkles around his eyes, and lines etched down the sides of his mouth. His hair was almost completely grey now. Unshaven, there were definite traces of white in his beard. He looked like a tramp when compared to Grace's polished husband, with his Savile Row suit, shining black hair, clean shave, square jaw. All he was missing was the kiss-curl on his unlined forehead, but otherwise he was goddam Superman. The coldness in Grace's eyes had said it all: Marry you, Vidar? Why would I do that? You've been amusing while it's lasted, but, as you can see, I already have a husband...

Vidar thrust his long fingers into his hair, and sank his forehead onto the steering wheel.

How long would it take her to pack? An hour? Probably less, given she only had one suitcase and would doubtless be in a hurry to get home now she'd come to her senses.

He lolled his head to one side and looked out of the passenger window, up the hill past the Flett farm to the long, low, almost-concealed frontage of *Somerled*. Were they inside, locked passionately together, begging forgiveness, pledging to begin again?

Before a fresh wave of grief overcame him, Vidar sat tall in the seat, restarted the engine, rammed the car aggressively into gear, and sped away from his home as fast as he was able.

He drove aimlessly, recklessly, taking turns at random and wishing for a head-on collision with a tractor. Always ending up back on the main road, he eventually decided to stop wasting time and diesel and drive to where they led – Kirkwall – where at least he could find a hotel room and some measure of sanctuary for a night. Returning to *Somerled* with Grace preparing to depart was not something he had the strength to contemplate. He needed time holed up alone somewhere to give him the courage to stand inside his empty home and face a very different future from the one he'd so enthusiastically conjured.

As he drove into the outskirts of town, he passed so many meandering couples of every age, shape, and size, it started to feel as if the whole world was in on the cruel joke. Did you really believe you could have a normal life, Vidar? Whatever gave you the idea you deserved such a precious gift as a beautiful wife and a nurturing home?

As he drove past the supermarkets and up to the roundabout, an elderly couple decided to cross in front of him. Incapable of much haste, the husband looked anxiously towards the murderous face of the driver glaring down from the large car, hurriedly ushering his unsteady wife onto the opposite pavement, holding up a hand to acknowledge Vidar's patience, and placing a protective palm on the small of her back. She upturned a devoted expression as he helped her negotiate the high kerb with her walking stick. The reciprocity of their interaction ripped at Vidar's insides, and he moaned aloud into the empty car, surging it forward, putting the couple out of sight behind him.

He knew what he was going to do.

He was going to blow seventeen hard-fought years of sobriety and get so steaming drunk he wouldn't remember Grace had even existed, let alone that she'd ever mattered to him one way or another.

He accelerated the car straight across the road and into the nearest 'pay and display' car park, abandoning it messily across two spaces and not bothering to buy a ticket. What did he care about a parking fine? He flopped out of the car on jelly legs, and staggered up the road towards the nearest pub. As he passed the tourist office, head down against the wind, weaving as if he'd already had the drink he was aiming for, Vidar wasn't sufficiently aware of his surroundings to avoid walking straight into a woman who'd just emerged. She was standing in the doorway, hood up against the sleety drizzle, fiddling with her purchases.

"Oh...sorry..." Vidar muttered, about to press on when a small, pale hand on his arm stopped him.

"Vidar, what are you doing here?"

"Son..."

Sonia stared at Vidar in some alarm. He looked terrible; face blotched from recent crying, and something in his eyes she'd never seen before – a sort of unhinged panic, as if the inside of his head was a saloon from a Western, and it was in the throes of a brawl, chairs and tables flying in all directions as intoxicated cowboys threw bottles and punches.

Pulling him by the sleeve of his jacket, she yanked him off the street, through the automatic doors, and into the excessively-heated lobby of the tourist office. Vidar registered their location with surprise, "What were you doing in here?"

Sonia reached into her carrier bag and extracted a six-inch tall puffin toy, complete with felted webbed feet and instantly-identifiable beak, "They had these in the window and I thought I'd get one for the baby…because of the running joke that she doesn't believe their beaks fall off…"

"Who?" Vidar was grimacing as if in agony, squirming with indefinable internal pain, unable to keep still.

"Grace…" Sonia explained, puzzled.

At the mention of her name, Vidar cried aloud, and his legs buckled. Instinctively, Sonia sprang forward and thrust him towards the wall to keep him upright. Vidar curled against the masonry as if craving its protection, beginning to cry again, cheek pressed against the hard, flat paintwork.

Anxious, Sonia put a gentle hand to his sleet-dampened hair, and fumbled in her pocket for a tissue, reaching up and wiping ineffectually at the unceasing flow, whispering, "Shhh…it's ok…ok. Just calm down. Shhh… Don't cry."

She glanced nervously behind her. Sure enough, every eye in the glass-walled tourist office was fixed upon them, "Come on Vid – we need to go. We're the most exciting thing that's happened here this month, and it only takes someone to recognise you, out come the 'phones, and bang goes your anonymity."

That cut through the grief like a hose through a dog fight, Vidar's eyes widening in shocked comprehension. He roused enough to allow Sonia to lead him speedily back outside, across the street, and up towards the centre of town.

Hooking her arm through his, Sonia suggested soothingly, "Let's find somewhere for a cup of tea, eh?"

Vidar halted, stared at her as if she was a total stranger, and tugged his arm free, "Nah...I'm going for a drink...a real drink..." He turned his back and began to stride powerfully away. Horrified, Sonia lunged, clamping onto his arm with both hands and gripping tightly, "Oh no you're not!"

He regarded her coldly, eyes glassy with unspent tears, "Why don't you just leave me the fuck alone? What do you care one way or another?"

"I do care!" Sonia screamed, not giving a damn who heard or saw, "You are not going for a drink, you stupid bastard! I won't let you! Over my dead body are you throwing away everything you've worked so hard for!" Latching determinedly onto his arm again, she held on with all her might, teeth clenched, bright eyes glinting like jewels in the fading daylight. If he wanted to go to the pub, he'd have to drag her dead weight the whole way.

Vidar's bloodshot eyes met hers, at first defiant, then afraid...then defeated...

He sighed, hanging his head. The drizzle intensified, thickening to flakes of snow, scudding past them on the gusting breeze.

Eventually, to her unspeakable relief, he jutted his jaw and looked steadily at her again. In the saloon behind his eyes, the shaken barman was wearily straightening tables and sweeping up the broken glass.

Extending a strong arm, he hugged her against him. The cold of the moisture on the front of his jacket shocked Sonia as it touched her flushed cheek, "Thank you, Son."

"Come on," she pulled at his wrist, "We're going to a boring, middle-aged tea shop, not the bloody pub…and you're going to tell me what the hell is happening…"

****

Sonia slid the laden tray onto the table and looked down at Vidar. He sat hunched over in the wooden chair, coat still on despite the steamy heat of the café, eyes staring with unfocused intensity at the table top, arms hanging limply by his sides. He resembled a huge, stuffed gorilla waiting to be won as a fairground prize. Sweating, Sonia removed her own coat, and put it over the back of her chair. He didn't resist as she stood behind him and eased his coat off too.

Sitting opposite him, Sonia stirred the bags in the teapot and poured two cups from it, placing one in front of Vidar. She gathered up her change from the tray and trickled it from her open palm into her purse. At the sound of the chinking coins, Vidar revived enough to fumble his wallet from his pocket and withdraw a twenty-pound note, which he pushed into the top of her purse.

"What's that for?"

Vidar waved a hand vaguely at the table. Sonia raised her eyebrows, "I know tourism's pushing up the prices, but twenty quid for a pot of tea? This is Kirkwall, not Tokyo!"

Vidar shrugged, barely listening, sliding down in his chair, still staring forward across the table. Leaning over, he plucked a paper tube of sugar from a nearby bowl and rotated it slowly in his fingers, tapping it onto the table so all the sugar slid to one end, spinning it and tapping the other end, spinning, tapping, spinning, tapping –

Sonia reached out, unsure whether to be concerned or annoyed, cupping Vidar's hand between her own small palms, stilling the restless movement, "Talk to me."

Vidar closed his eyes again, face crumpling as if he might resume crying, "Please...I promise not to have a drink, Son...just let me be..."

"No, I shan't! We will sit here all night if that's what it takes! I have never, ever seen you like this...and I can only think of one reason, so, where is she? What's happened between the two of you? Has there been an accident or something?"

"Where is she?" Vidar raised his head and treated Sonia to a hollow, mirthless laugh which made her blood run cold with inexplicable trepidation, "She's at home, Son...with her husband."

"What?"

"She's married, Son."

"She's divorced."

"Is she? It's news to him! He didn't know he was divorced, Son! He just arrived on my doorstep to take her home..."

"What?"

"Yep – not two hours ago."

"But, Grace said – "

"She said a lot of things, Sonia…but it appears quite a lot of what comes out of Grace's mouth is lies."

"I don't – "

"She even lied about her name! She told me her maiden name, not her married one. Why would she do that?"

"Well, if she's divorced…" Sonia defended.

"If she's divorced, Son, she hasn't seen fit to inform her husband of it. He had no idea! He was there to take her home. All those stories about his affairs! What if he isn't the one doing the cheating? What if it's her?"

"What makes you think – "

"Why has it taken him five months to come get her? Could it be because he's only just found out where she went? Apparently, she told a friend of hers. She sure didn't tell him!"

Unnerved by Vidar's conviction, Sonia didn't answer. Her unshakeable faith in Grace wavered. If Vidar, who knew Grace inside-out, was doubting her, surely there must be some basis for his accusations beyond mere hurt or jealousy?

"What's he like?"

Vidar writhed with renewed agony on the rickety wooden chair, crushing the sugar in his fist and tossing it onto the tray. It hit the side of the teapot and bounced onto the floor. Nowadays, bending down only took place in emergencies, as it made her feel so breathless and lightheaded, so Sonia decided, despite the proprietress watching them from behind the coffee machine with undisguised fascination, that the packet would just have to stay where it was.

"He's Ken, Barbie's boyfriend. He's so damn perfect it's like he's moulded from plastic – not a grey hair, not a wrinkle, designer suit, fancy shoes...no contest..."

"But..." Sonia couldn't process what Vidar was suggesting. Every look, every gesture between Vidar and Grace had resonated with meaning. The air around them hummed with the magnetism of their connection, "She adores you, Vidar..."

"Or maybe she does this all the time? Just a bored, rich housewife seeking some amusement...? Perhaps she's got a screw loose? Honestly, Son, if you'd seen him, she'd have to be crazy to pick me over him! He's like an advert for Armani, and I look like some hobo who's spent the last week asleep in one of your Dad's barns!"

"Grace doesn't care about that – "

"Even if you're right, he still kicks my ass in every other department. The guy exudes success."

"Er, Vid...hello?"

"Oh, ok...I don't mean money or anything like that. You know as well as I do any clueless prick can make money if he stands in the right place for long enough. No, I mean I bet he's never screwed anything up in his pristine, crease-free life. I bet he didn't spend every day from the age of seventeen to the age of thirty shoving every chemical he could get his hands on up his nose, down his throat, and into his veins until he was almost dead. I bet he can go to parties without spending all night trying to resist downing the dregs of every glass left on the bar. I bet he can recall names, and anniversaries, and appointments, because his memory's not shot to bits. I bet he doesn't have nightmares, or scars from a million operations to keep him alive. I expect he's never had his stomach pumped…and I definitely know he won't understand the crushing shame of creating a child you know shouldn't ever have been born…"

Sonia didn't understand half of what Vidar was saying, not being privy to the innermost secrets of his past, but the mention of the child hit home, and she put hesitant hands to either side of her swollen belly, as if over her baby's ears, so it didn't have to hear Vidar going on in this hopeless way about things it was impossible to change.

"I've always screwed up with women. I've spent my life treating them as something you use and discard. I'm sorry, Son, I did that to you as much as I've ever done it to anyone else."

"No bother," Sonia reassured, "I used you too, to show off with…like a fancy handbag."

Vidar summoned a weak smile, "Well, at least I was fancy…"

"Oh, you were."

"She was different, Son. From the very start, I knew. It just felt as if I'd known her forever…as if we'd be together always, and I didn't have to think about it. It was such hard work with the others! Oh…not you, of course."

"Of course," Sonia winked at him.

Vidar shook his head, managed another watery grin, and reached across the table to take her hand and hold it gently, "Not you."

"Ok."

"It was easy with Grace. It was natural. It was meant to be…well, that's what I thought. If all that was a lie from the very beginning, I don't know what to think any more! I feel as if I've been cast out into space. I'm just spinning away from everything and I don't know how to stop. I was certain, Son! I know I'm not the brightest guy on the block…but how could I have gotten it so wrong? Who knows, maybe her plastic-fantastic husband's asking himself the same question? Maybe she's got us all on the run?"

"Perhaps it's just a misunderstanding…?"

"You didn't see the look in her eyes. Twenty seconds after he walked through the door, she was eyeballing me as if I was something stuck to the bottom of her shoe. I'm nearly fifty. I've never felt like this about anyone in my life, and now it's over. What are the chances of it ever happening again?"

Optimistically, Sonia suggested, "Never say never?"

"I wanted her so much, Son. I'd lie in bed watching her sleep, and think I was the luckiest son of a bitch on the planet…and it's all gone. She's gone, and she's never coming back." The despair on Vidar's face was chilling to behold.

"You don't know that!"

Vidar wiped his streaming nose with a paper napkin and stared fixedly at the table top. Sonia squeezed his strong fingers with her small, hot hand, and gazed out of the steamed-up window at two lorries trying to pass one another in the narrow street. Grace adored Vidar with as much passion as he idolised her – didn't she?

TWENTY-ONE

Dominic turned his back contemptuously on the Cathedral. St Magnus; I mean, who bloody cared! The trouble with this place was they let too many foreigners in, and had done since the dawn of time. Take the Danes; they were everywhere here, including in bed with his wife, it seemed.

Dominic stomped moodily down Albert Street to escape the persistent wind, which obligingly eased somewhat once he was in the shelter of the narrower streets. He wandered randomly, head down, hands shoved into pockets, scuffing his shoes like a listless child.

It had been good to get out of there with the upper hand, delivering his ultimatum and leaving with his dignity intact, but it meant he was stuck here until tomorrow morning. The dead, damp cold of the April air settled thickly across his body like a heavy, wet blanket. You almost had to chew your way through every breath, it was so sodden with freezing moisture. As he passed the occasional North-facing alleyway, the sharp wind drove a flurry of slushy snowflakes into the unprepared side of his face, the gusts slicing efficiently through his inadequate jacket. London had been a balmy 17°C, with fat daffodils bobbing lazily in what little breeze reached their sheltered courtyard position below his office building. It was warm enough to nip out in shirtsleeves; not like this howling, frigid hellhole off the end of the world. Plodding on, unseeing, killing time, seeking an outlet for the directionless fury flowing through him with a violence to match the constant Orcadian wind, Dominic was once more subconsciously suckered by the flagstone road surface and lack of pavement into the misguided Southern assumption that the tiny lane could not be anything other than a pedestrian thoroughfare. It had caught him out yesterday too, as he continually strayed into the centre of the road and was then roused from his reverie by tooting horns and cars backed up behind his strolling person. Typical of this bloody place that what would be an alleyway anywhere else was the sodding M1 here.

Today, weight of traffic eventually forced him to squeeze himself into a café doorway as two particularly-large vehicles attempted to manoeuvre around each other in an especially-narrow section. He leant sulkily against a window frame as the lorries performed their inching, tentative pas-de-deux. Staring vacantly through the adjacent window, he registered the little shop had only two occupants, and wondered absently how these places made any kind of living. He thought no more about the café's only customers until the man moved slightly, revealing beyond him a flash of distinctive flaming hair, the vibrancy and unique shade of which Dominic had only beheld once before in his life – and far, far away from here. Sensible though it would have been to squeeze down the side of the lorry and jog for the safety of his hotel before she looked up and noticed him staring through the steamed-up window like a kid in an aquarium, Dominic found he was rooted to the spot.

It couldn't be her…and yet, who else could it possibly be?

Who else looked as good as that, with hair such a distinctive and deep red no one would ever believe her protestations it wasn't out of a bottle? No enhancement necessary, with that stunning curtain of fire tumbling across the white of the hotel linen, her alabaster skin brushing his, and those shining eyes luminous in the half-light of a stolen afternoon, blinds drawn against the day, reality suspended for an hour or two of forbidden delight. Something stirred in his memory, the mention he seemed to recall her making about Orkney. He hadn't paid any real attention, just grunting, "Where?" and pulling her to him again. Idly amusing as her conversation might have been in the afterglow, it made no impact on the reality of his existence. London loft living, New York shopping, Monacan posing, Californian fly-drives, and five-star Parisian weekends were the stuff of the life of Dominic Radley and his trophy wife, not this windswept wasteland. What could Orkney offer a man whose entire existence was founded on the pursuit of pleasure? Nothing about his visit here was remotely pleasurable to Dominic. Stepping outside his hotel room door was an assault on his patience, with tireless attempts at unsolicited, cheery conversation from his hosts, when all Dominic really wanted to do was unleash a barrage of complaints regarding the many deficiencies of his accommodation. If you could survive the privations of the lodgings, the banal chit-chat, and the homely food – hardly the haute-cuisine Dominic was accustomed to – there followed the test of survival that was making it to your hire car without either being sliced in two by the vicious Arctic wind, or mown down on what his tarmac-accustomed, pavement-conditioned London mind repeatedly refused to acknowledge was a road.

Dominic wondered who she was with. Was it a boyfriend? The body-language suggested relaxed informality, but not the intimacy he would expect of a couple.

A car horn hooted impatiently, the driver fed up with the delay caused by the thoroughly-wedged trucks. The two glanced over, curious as to what was happening on the street, and Dominic realised her companion was none other than Grace's Viking invader!

Horrified, Dominic staggered backwards across the café doorway, barking his knee on the low sill of the opposite window, swearing under his breath, and limping in erratic circles until the immediate pain subsided.

This was a troubling triangle of monumental proportions!

Grace knew the Dane, rather better than Dominic was entirely comfortable with. More worryingly, it appeared the Dane also knew Dominic's so-recently-discarded dalliance, perhaps not as comprehensively as he knew Dominic's wife, but certainly well enough to shed what appeared to be a great quantity of tears in her presence.

The disturbing discovery placed Dominic's ultimatum to Grace in greater jeopardy than he could ever have imagined! Unnerved, he attempted to reason it out, pragmatically assessing the danger, desperate to keep a lid on his bubbling panic.

Realistically, if Grace knew the whole truth, she wouldn't have been able to resist blurting it out during this afternoon's vitriolic encounter.

If the Dane knew it, might he not have felt it apposite to plug the gap in Grace's understanding as soon as Dominic had arrived on *Somerled's* doorstep?

The answer to both those questions had to be yes.

The Dane had known who he was as soon as he'd opened the front door. If he'd been privy to the truth, he would have used it to make short work of his adversary, of that Dominic had no doubt. The unconcealed hatred in the man's eyes had told Dominic all he needed to know about the nature of the stranger's connection to his wife.

Dominic felt secure in concluding his explosive little secret was safe, thus far. He must hold his nerve.

But all it took was for the Dane to mention his arrival; the evidence before Dominic's anxious eyes suggested he already had. The girl – young, naïve, but no fool – would shortly ask the questions of greatest pertinence, and out would tumble the revelation!

No, no, no – it couldn't be left to chance! Ample time remained for his position to be irreversibly undermined. He needed an effective means of neutralising this threat before it permanently disrupted his future comfort. How, that was the question?

The established pattern of his marriage suited Dominic very well, and he resented its interruption. He'd come all this way to reinstate it, and intended to succeed in his endeavour. Influential contacts who only dealt with Dominic because they'd known and respected Grace's father, were asking questions about Grace's whereabouts he was having difficulty avoiding. Allied to the hurdles at work were the surprising demands of life's practicalities. His girlfriends, whilst deliciously diverting, did not deliver freshly-laundered clothing, finely-prepared meals, or a pristinely-presented home, ready at a moment's notice to receive guests of authority and prestige. He didn't want Grace back – she was a perennial irritation he could happily do without – but there was no one else available who could adequately fill her shoes.

As he watched, the girl reached forward and placed a small, pale hand on the arm of the Dane, a gesture of gentle sympathy and reassurance. He slowly turned his hand over, entwined his fingers with hers, and they remained thus; he staring at the table top with unbreaking intensity, she gazing sorrowfully out of the front window at the continuing chaos in the narrow street.

Grace's lunge of fury, wailing like a banshee, had unsettled Dominic. Five months of separation had wrought a surprising change in her. There was something wild about his wife now, and he wasn't convinced playing on her previous fears of abandonment and vulnerability would be enough to persuade her to return with him. What Dominic Radley needed was leverage…and here it sat, right in front of his frozen, dripping nose.

TWENTY-TWO

When the tea-shop owner had very pointedly started to wipe already-cleaned tables, needlessly straighten chairs, wield a broom dangerously close to their feet, and look very frequently behind her at the large clock on the back wall, Sonia had helped Vidar from his seat like an old man. He'd slipped into a weird, trancelike state, replying in monosyllables, not meeting her eye, retreating inside himself like a tortoise retracting into the protection of its shell.

As they walked down Broad Street, Sonia glanced up at him, "Are you going home now?"

Vidar baulked at the suggestion, "I can't...it's going to smell of her perfume...there'll still be food she's made everywhere. I can't face it, not tonight anyway."

"But where will you go? You shouldn't be all alone – especially not in a hotel room with a mini-bar!"

"No, you are right about that. I'm gonna go to Dr Kirkbride's. He'll keep an eye on me."

Sonia nodded, relieved, "Aye, he will."

Vidar wagged an admonitory finger, "He says you don't go to see him – you miss appointments."

Sonia scowled, retorting sullenly, "What's he going to tell me I don't already know? 'You're pregnant Sonia'. 'You're a bit more pregnant, Sonia.' 'Oh, and a wee bit more...'"

"Avoiding check-ups won't stop the baby coming. The doctor's there to watch over the two of you."

"It's bollocks. Women were having babies long before doctors were invented."

"And they died in droves, Son!"

"Very cheerful, I must say!"

"Here," he pushed another twenty pound note into her hand, "Get a taxi, please." He tapped the note with his finger, "Don't you dare keep that money and get the bus!"

Sonia smiled, "Don't worry, I've already made a profit on the tea..."

"Get your sassy ass home." He stopped her as she turned away, "Hey, Son...thank you."

"No bother. Can't have you falling off the wagon, can we?"

"I didn't appreciate you enough, did I? You used to drive me a bit nuts, actually."

Sonia smiled, "I wasn't as lovely then as I am now."

He took her hand, lifted it to his lips, kissed it, "You're going to be a fantastic Mom, Sonia Flett. You have a big heart."

Sonia giggled, feigning relief, "I thought you were going to say 'arse'!"

Vidar responded with a faint but genuine grin, "Heart...and a perky ass..."

"Will you really be all right?"

"I will. I'm going to Stewart's. I promise."

"I'm on the end of the 'phone if you need me."

"Thank you, darling." Another kiss, and he released her hand, turned his collar up against the wind, and strode away, leaving her standing in front of the Cathedral in the steadily-falling April snow.

****

Sonia trudged wearily across the grass. The larger and heavier her bump became, the longer and steeper the familiar hill seemed. Her ankles were so swollen and stiff she'd had to borrow a pair of her brother's wellingtons, as her feet no longer fitted in her own. If you asked her now whether she wanted this baby, her answer would still be a vehement no. However, enquire what she might like to do with her life instead, and she honestly couldn't say. There didn't seem much point these days in having hopes and dreams.

At the top of Far Field, she stopped at the fence, gazing up at *Somerled*. Copper and Jess meandered over to press their soft noses against her ungloved palms, and sniff at her coat in case it concealed a treat. The ubiquitous packet of mints, security against threatening nausea ever since the ferry all those months ago, proved irresistible to Jessie the Shetland, who snorted in delight, and chewed softly at the outside of Sonia's pocket until she extracted the sweets and gave them two each.

The few windows of *Somerled* that faced the Flett farmland were all in darkness, but that didn't mean the house was empty. From her vantage point, Sonia couldn't tell whether Grace's car was in the garage, or already gone.

Sonia put out her hand to touch Copper's reassuringly warm and powerful neck. If Vidar was right, and Grace's departure was imminent, surely her friend wouldn't leave without saying goodbye?

TWENTY-THREE

Grace awoke with a sharp snort of a snore that made the mucus from last night's tears catch in her throat, and brought on a stuttering, congested cough. She hung off the side of the sofa, spluttering and rasping. The approaching dawn extended from far out to sea, tempting the land with the promise of a fair day. She'd lain here all night!

Disorientated, pushing herself to hands and knees, Grace squinted at the kitchen clock: 5.52am.

She steeled herself to turn her head to the right, towards the Master Bedroom door. It stood ajar, the bed still made, no lump of a familiar, longed-for body rumpled the smooth, neatly-arranged covers. Stock-still, she listened intently, until her ears seemed to roar with the silence in the house.

No one was here but her.

Vidar had left yesterday afternoon, and he hadn't come back…because of Dominic; because of her. He'd trusted her absolutely. He'd shared wholeheartedly, but it seemed she had reservedly picked and chosen. It had never been her intention to give him that impression! She'd simply wanted to forget Dominic and everything to do with him. Would Vidar understand – or would he only comprehend that she had lied?

Grace stumbled to her feet and staggered into the guest bedroom, staring through the window at the driveway of *Somerled*. What was she expecting to see?

Unsure how long she'd stood there, gazing out with swimming, unfocused eyes, a shiver made Grace aware how thoroughly chilled she was after an uncovered night on the sofa. She padded back through the house to the Master Bedroom, deliberately averting her eyes from the undisturbed tidiness of the bed she'd made yesterday morning, shuffling directly into the bathroom, and fully-clothed into the walk-in shower, snapping on the controls and whipping her arm free of the deluge of hot water with a start, as she realised she was still dressed. Retreating a few steps, she stood in the centre of the bathroom, peeled off yesterday's clothes, and dropped them carelessly onto the floor around her. She couldn't tear her stare from her own reflection, because the face that looked back wore an expression she'd hoped never to see again – hollow-cheeked, lank-haired, dead behind the eyes. Her London face. Her married face. Her Dominic face.

Convinced Vidar would return at any moment, despite the fact it was barely six in the morning, she resolved to improve her appearance speedily, displaying the very best version of herself to him. Not wanting to linger longer than was necessary upon such preparations, she picked up toothbrush and toothpaste and stood under the rush of hot water, trying to haphazardly shampoo her hair with one hand whilst brushing her teeth with the other, unheeding the frothy trickle of mingling toothpaste and shampoo that washed from chin to neck, diluting between her breasts to run milkily down her body to the plughole.

She turned and stood directly under the oversized showerhead, eyes and lips clamped tightly shut against the falling force, rinsing herself, desperate to be quicker…quicker…

It was only when she reopened her eyes that the tears came, without warning, until she was unable to do more than kneel in the shower tray, arms clasped around her own body, wet hair plastered across her face, and wail her anguish into the steamy emptiness, eventually vomiting watery yellow bile over the plughole, watching it swirl in meandering tendrils down the drain, distractedly revolted with herself.

At length, the outpouring of guilt and terror finally spent, she crawled on hands and knees from the shower, using the towel rail to pull herself upright, wet body shivering in the chilly air. Wrapping a towel around her as tightly as she could, she leant for a while against the comforting warmth of the rail, eventually rousing sufficiently to rub herself dry.

Making an effort – blow-drying her hair, selecting a pretty blouse, finding some matching earrings – she tidied the kitchen, remade the fire in the grate, and sat upright and attentive on the very end of the sofa, unblinking eyes fixed on the front door as the minute hand on the kitchen clock continued its inexorable progress through another day…and Vidar didn't come.

****

The sharp ring of the doorbell so surprised her that her bottom left the sofa a millimetre or two. 8.45am…and it rushed back like an incoming wave across the sand – it was tomorrow morning! Dominic was here for his answer!

And no Vidar…still no Vidar…

As she tried to stand, Grace realised two motionless hours had made her back ache, and her body as cold as it had been before her shower. Resigned to the necessity of this encounter, Grace stalked stiffly to the front door.

Dominic looked serious and determined. His square jaw worked, grinding his teeth inside his closed mouth. Grace pushed her lips together and said nothing, simply holding open the door to admit him. Dominic looked her up and down as he entered, and Grace considered, with some horror, that he might assume the effort she'd made was for him!

Dominic walked all the way into the living room, down the steps, and across the rug to stand by the window, looking at the beach. At the sound of the hall door closing, he turned to face her, "Sit down, Grace."

Grace folded her arms and instead advanced defiantly down the steps towards him.

Dominic scowled at her stubbornness, snapping, "Sit. Down."

Conditioned to obey, Grace sank immediately onto the arm of the sofa.

"I've come because of what we discussed yesterday."

Grace opened her mouth to explain he was wasting his time, but Dominic raised his hands to stop her, "Wait! Before you say anything, I think you need to be made aware of something…"

"Aware of what?" Grace bit back, impatiently. She just wanted to get this over with. Vidar could be home at any moment, and she didn't want Dominic to be here when he arrived.

"Look, Grace, whatever might be happening here, I am still your husband, and I feel duty-bound to save you from both pain and disgrace if it's in my power to do so…"

Grace felt the knots in her shoulders spasm, the tension pushing tongues of hot agony up the sides of her neck and into her violently-throbbing head. What fresh treachery was this?

"When I left you yesterday, I was pretty pissed-off, to say the least. I tried to go for a walk – to get my head together – to work out how I was going to make you see sense…but the climate here isn't exactly conducive to an evening stroll, so I had to give it up in the end and go back to the hotel to thaw out. I sat in the bar for a while, had a couple of scotches and, I'll admit, my head was spinning. I wasn't particularly aware of my surroundings. All I was really thinking about was how to bring my wife home…"

Here, Dominic paused, and Grace knew he was looking at her, so she very pointedly stared at the stones of the fireplace and counted slowly backwards in her head until Dominic, never known for his patience, tired of waiting for a reaction, and ploughed on, "It got later, the drinkers thinned out and left very few of us in the bar – just the overnight guests, I suppose. My head was starting to ache, as if I couldn't think about it all any more. I couldn't concentrate, so I decided to finish my drink and go to bed. Looking around, to give me anything else to think about but you and I…"

Dominic tried again – another weighty pause, heavy with tacit significance. This time, Grace was more than ready for it, pointing her toes in her slippers, and focusing her gaze on her stretching legs, as if what Dominic was saying was having absolutely no effect on her whatsoever. Dominic's exhalation betrayed annoyance, and Grace felt spitefully satisfied at provoking a reaction.

"I heard a little giggle and a bit of whispering…it sounded a bit saucy to me, and I looked around to see where it was coming from. I noticed there was someone else in the same part of the hotel lounge. There are all these high-backed chairs and you can't really see who's in them, but something seemed familiar to me."

Grace swallowed. Her feet began to ache with the force of the stretch, activated thigh muscles shuddering, stomach tight, neck immobile. She was tensing to absorb the coup-de-grâce Dominic was about to administer.

"It was nagging at me, so I got up for a surreptitious look. I walked over as if I was warming myself in front of the fire, and I saw them…your new fella getting very cosy in his armchair with a striking little redhead. I'm sorry, Grace, but it didn't exactly look as if he'd just picked her up, if you see what I mean. They looked rather well-acquainted, if you ask me. She was on his lap. He had one hand up her skirt and the other on a very prominent pregnancy. We might have had our differences over the past twenty years, but I understand how a man touches a woman he knows intimately. It was a protective gesture, but a possessive one…one of ownership," Dominic finished, flatly, as if he'd just delivered a presentation on the performance of an investment fund, rather than revealing the infidelity of her new lover to his estranged wife.

Grace vividly recalled the three of them sitting and watching a film on the big sofa, fire crackling, conversation ebbing and flowing, Sonia squirming as the baby moved and made her uncomfortable, Vidar reaching a big, warm hand across to gently rub her aching back...

She retched, clamping a hand to her mouth, and swallowing more of the acidic bile from her empty stomach, gasping and exposing her bitter-tasting tongue to the cold air in the room.

Not meeting Dominic's eye, Grace croaked, "I don't believe you."

"No. I didn't expect you to. I can only tell you what I saw; I can't make you accept it. I just wanted you to know, Grace, to understand exactly what you're dealing with...in case it influences your decision."

Grace knew her whole body was shaking. She didn't want it to, because Dominic would see it and know his shot had been on target, but found herself unable to stop.

He was continuing, capitalising on his clear advantage, "I don't suppose he took the time to tell you about his pregnant little redhead, didn't he? Any more than you shared the inconvenient truth of your marriage, eh Grace? You might want to think this is something special, but it's evidently founded on a tissue of lies on both sides. I know I can't prove any of this, but your reaction's persuasive enough. You knew, didn't you? After all, Grace, if I'm lying to you, where is he? Early morning stroll? Working the night shift doing whatever he does?"

He suddenly surged forward, making her recoil, thumping his fists to either side of her hips where she perched on the arm of the sofa, imprisoning her between his arms. She leant away from him as far as she could, stomach muscles screaming from holding her body in balance.

"Tell you what, Grace, I know how to settle the mystery beyond doubt! If he was here with you all night while I assert he was in a hotel room getting cosy with the mother of his child, then you'll know I can't possibly be telling the truth...but, if he never came home?"

Dominic smirked, and moved his face closer to hers. Grace couldn't prevent an exclamation escaping her, and clutched the sofa back, holding herself up.

"Hmmm...it's a tricky one, Gracie, and no mistake. Only you know the answer..."

A howling sob escaped Grace. She pushed against Dominic's shoulders with all her might, jerking him upright with a shout of pain, "Ow! What – ? "

"Get! Out!" roared Grace, as loud as she could.

Dominic rolled his shoulders and rubbed his right hand against his left collarbone, smiling nastily, "He wasn't here, was he?"

"Get out now!" screamed Grace.

Dominic advanced towards her, jabbing an aggressive finger, "Listen, you clueless bitch, if I go, that's it! I'm not coming back. I told you yesterday I've had enough of your bullshit."

Intimidated, Grace scuttled around the back of the sofa, putting the large piece of furniture between them.

"Get! Out!" She screamed again, loud enough to make her own ears ring with the harshness of the sound.

"You're a bit of fun, Grace! A bit of fun with a Trust Fund! Does he know about your money? Especially as in a few weeks' time there'll be nappies to buy..."

"Aaaaaeeeeeaaaaiiiiii!" That noise was coming from her! Grace gripped handfuls of her own hair at the root, and pulled as if she wanted to tear her hammering head in two.

"Go! Go! Go! I never want to see you again as long as I live!"

Dominic absorbed the outburst unemotionally, as was his habit, "I'll be outside, Grace. I will give you five minutes for this to sink in, and you to pull yourself together. Then I'm leaving, and you're on your own."

Grace upturned her dead eyes to his face, "I'd rather be alone for the rest of my life than have to spend even another second with you..."

"Five minutes, Grace."

"Fuck you, Dominic."

The soft clip of his Italian loafers across the wooden floor, the slam first of hall, and then of front door...and the deafening silence of the empty house again.

Moaning deep in her throat, Grace slid down the back of the sofa to crumple onto the floor, curling into a foetal position on the cold wood, pushing her fingernails painfully into her own skin.

Sonia had lived in London for five years. Vidar worked periodically there for months at a time, and had apparently done so for decades. Was theirs a true love of many years' duration, the squabbling a smokescreen; their relationship enduring far from the over-zealous watchfulness of Margaret Flett? Was it such a coincidence that Vidar had chosen to return here now, despite his preference for Californian sunshine, to be present when his child arrived? Had he done exactly what he'd so knowingly implied – paid Sonia to keep her silence? Sonia never seemed short of money, and how much saving could a twenty-six-year-old reasonably have done in her short working life, no matter how astute she might be?

The careless way he touched her! Their unrestrained bickering! The teasing and point-scoring! Did it conceal an urge neither could resist? Recollections of Vidar's hands casually brushing Sonia's body stuttered through Grace's mind like an old-fashioned, fast-forwarding video; a pat of a buttock, a rub of her baby-bump, a caress of her cheek, a finger winding absently into a coppery ringlet. No wonder Vidar had been so confident he understood the circumstances surrounding conception. He'd been there! Sonia's baby was his! How could she have been so blind?

Grace retched again, frantically heaving herself to all fours, and crawling rapidly to the patio door, wrenching it open and staggering out a few paces onto the lawn, dropping to her knees as if felled by a blow, yanking up her hair in her hands, and vomiting over and over until there was nothing left to expel, hollowed out by her own despair.

TWENTY-FOUR

Sonia's wakeful night of foundless fears did nothing to improve her already-short temper, serving only to exacerbate the conviction that her one friend in the world – her rock of stability almost since the start of this mess – had left without a word. It was pointless mooning tetchily about the house and farmyard, getting in everyone's way and hiding from finding out. She just had to go up there, knock on the door, and hope Grace answered it with her usual delighted smile, ushering Sonia inside, parking her on the sofa while she put on the kettle, and tempting her friend to sample whatever it was she'd just baked.

Grace's disarming charm, and Margaret's desperate desire to impress her, had certainly been instrumental in her mother's gradual and grudging acceptance of Sonia's homecoming as a permanent, and perhaps even positive, event. So thoroughly had Grace ingratiated herself with Margaret Flett that an artless suggestion of the wisdom of providing Sonia and her baby with some private space of their own, had instituted an almost-instant directive for the boys to clear out the annexe cottage where Granny had used to live, to deliver Sonia a self-contained home, and the family some valuable breathing-space from the approaching demands of what her mother had taken to describing in polite company as Sonia's 'predicament'. Despite the unforeseen thawing of her mother's manner under the warmth of Grace's irrepressible optimism, there was nevertheless still something lingering in Margaret's expression when she looked at Sonia – disappointment, judgement, perhaps pity? Whatever it was, it caused a catching in the back of Sonia's throat, and a desire to escape her mother's presence as quickly as possible, before she cried with shame.

When she sat around the kitchen table with her own family (without the protection of Grace's civilising presence) and her 'predicament' was mentioned, her brothers tittered as if it was the biggest joke in the world to see their previously haughty, superior smartarse of a sister brought down to size. Lorraine rolled her eyes as if bored-to-comatose by the mere mention of Sonia's baby. Her father shook his head, and attended to his dinner, leaving her mother spooning food onto proffered plates, hunched over the slow cooker like a sorceress over a cauldron, casting portentous doubts upon the future parenting ability of her eldest. Why couldn't her mother and father see how hypocritical it was to pass judgement upon her before her baby had even arrived, when their own child-rearing talents were hardly world-beating? All three brothers remained at home; single, and usually smeared in cow crap. Sonia knew most of the girls here weren't that fussy, given the competition wasn't much better, but surely advising them not to go to the pub to chat up girls in their overalls on the way back from market would be a start? Lorraine, lacking either gumption or ambition, spent most of her time on a buffering YouTube watching make-up application tutorials, and was probably destined for a teenage pregnancy of her own. Their eldest – upon whom the high hopes of the Flett dynasty had rested until so very recently – was now a disgraced expectant single mother, irredeemably forever abandoned to iniquity.

The only place she felt utterly comfortable to be herself, free of judgement and censure, was in the home of her 'adopted' mother and father, where support of her position, and genuine excitement at her impending motherhood had made her feel positive about the baby for the first time since absorbing the bombshell of her pregnancy. What would happen to her sanity if Grace was gone? The pain of his loss would drive Vidar back into the only refuge he had – the punishing push for perfection. He would disappear to Los Angeles, New York, or Nashville, and throw himself into his career with renewed vigour, working harder than ever to keep his mind occupied. He wouldn't return to Orkney. What would be the point? All *Somerled* would do was remind him of what he'd lost, and Sonia would be without the only two people in the world she felt understood her, at the time she needed them most.

Rounding the bend in the drive, Sonia lifted her head to look at the house, and was at first relieved, then intrigued, to observe a head showing above the tufted grass bank. Her first thought was that it was Grace...before identifying it as a man's head. It must be Grace's mysterious husband! He was here early – did that mean he'd spent the night? That didn't bode well for either Sonia or Vidar, but at least it meant Grace was still here now, which was better than nothing.

Sonia slowed her trudge to a tiptoe, and edged across the path to take advantage of the cover of the curved bank encircling the approach to the property. Peeking inbetween the heads of the daffodils nodding gently in a breeze that ruffled her hair and made the long grass bob and ripple, Sonia secretly observed the man who must be Grace's husband. The tall, thin, dark-haired figure felt in his jacket pocket, and withdrew a packet of cigarettes, extracting one with slim fingers, and shielding it from the wind as he touched his lighter to it. His face was turned away from her, so she was unable to make out his features with any accuracy. However, something about the way he held the cigarette, and the mannerisms exhibited as he smoked and paced restlessly on the driveway, stirred recognition within Sonia. Placing a steadying hand in front of her, and easing her increasingly-cumbersome body down to knee and hip against the tussocky grass, Sonia wriggled higher, and cautiously popped up her head like a sentry above a parapet, straining to perceive what it was about Grace's husband that seemed so familiar. Perhaps he was famous, too? It would be just like Grace to be married to a television personality and not think it worth mentioning. Sonia smiled as she thought of Grace's simplistic, almost-childlike approach to life, and how easy she was to get along with. Whatever Vidar had said yesterday, Sonia couldn't believe her friend had lied.

As she waited, motionless among the daffodils, the man eventually turned and began to approach her vantage point once more, head down, deep in thought, eyes focused on the circular pattern of flagstones. As he got within about fifteen feet of her hiding place, Sonia at last comprehended the reason for her déja-vù. His bearing, his gait, the unmistakeable features she knew so very well...

Sinking slowly onto her front, face inches from damp spring grass, Sonia retched as silently as she was able, before vomiting her entire porridge breakfast onto the bank in front of her. Edging down until her feet touched shingle again, Sonia wiped a shaking hand across slack lips, weak arms gradually able to push her heavy body first to hands and knees, and eventually to a standing position. She beat a hasty retreat on juddering legs, back down the drive towards the questionable refuge of her bare, annexe bedroom. How could this be happening? What in a former life had destined her for this kind of punishment? She was basically a good person, wasn't she? She flossed her teeth, paid her bills, said please and thank you, opened doors for people, and gave up her seat on the bus! What had she done to deserve this?

Suddenly convinced she would be sick again, Sonia paused in her tottering downhill pelt, slumping forward as her empty stomach spasmed. Struggling to catch her breath, Sonia staggered sideways, and would have fallen had not two strong hands gripped her upper arms.

Lifting her eyes, Sonia beheld Vidar, face filled with concern, "Son, you ok? Are you ill?"

Opening her mouth to explain, Sonia instead found she was unable to do anything but fling herself against him, and sob and sob as if the world was ending. Wrapping his arms around her, Vidar stroked her hair, and attempted to quiet the hiccupping cries. Gradually, she calmed sufficiently for him to ease her head from his shoulder, "Shall we go up to the house?"

The very idea filled Sonia with such panic that speech was impossible. She shook her head, waved her arms, and eventually managed to pant, "No! No! Not there!" genuinely petrified by the suggestion.

"Ok, ok," Vidar murmured reassuringly, holding her grabbing fists loosely in both of his, "Let's go to the farm…"

Sonia allowed him to lead her along the shingle track, putting his arm around her shoulders and hugging her close to his side. She wrapped both arms around his waist, clinging to his body as if he was a lifebelt in a turbulent sea. Locked together, the two made halting progress back down to the Flett farm.

Outside the kitchen door, Vidar hesitated, "I sure hope your mother isn't home…"

Sonia summoned a smile at his embarrassment. It did strike her as comical that this big, strong man was still terrified of her minute mother, even after all this time, "No…she's out with Auntie Jackie in Stromness."

"Thank God for that!" He eased open the sticking door and let Sonia inside, following her in, and bodily placing her in one of the kitchen chairs. He busied himself opening and shutting kitchen cupboards at random until he discovered the wherewithal to produce a cup of tea. Meg slowly staggered upright on arthritic legs, and came to sniff first Sonia, then Vidar, who reached down to scratch her behind the ears. Satisfied with her investigation, Meg sneezed in approval, and padded back to her cushion in front of the stove. The kettle on the hotplate whistled steam from its spout. Vidar picked it up awkwardly with a tea-towel around the handle, swearing quietly as the hot steam briefly scalded his skin. Placing the two teas on the kitchen table, he sat opposite Sonia, looking with deep concern at the auburn head buried in the crook of one folded arm. The only sounds in the kitchen were the rhythmic swoosh of Meg's lazily-wagging tail across the tiled floor, and the tiny whimpers of Sonia's near-stifled sobs. Eventually, unable to bear it any longer, Vidar pushed a gentle hand into the tumble of ringlets, and whispered, "Son, please. Please stop crying. I can't take it. What's going on? Are you ill? Is it something to do with the baby?"

Sonia raised a swollen, tear-stained face. Pained, Vidar gently cupped her chin in his hand, "Son – "

"Grace's husband is at the house. I saw him."

"Oh," Vidar's hand dropped from her chin, all his strength instantly sapped by the knowledge. It hit the table with a dull thud. Meg stilled for a moment at the unexpected sound. A moment's pause to listen, and the gentle swooshing of tail on tile began again.

Vidar muttered, "So he's been there all night…?"

"I don't know." At that precise moment, offering proof of Grace's sexual reconciliation with her husband mattered very little to Sonia Flett, "It's not about that… It's…ohhh… He's…ohhh…"

Shooting a hand up to her mouth, Sonia lurched off her chair and hurled herself across to the sink, retching emptily. Vidar stood hurriedly, his chair scraping harshly on the tiles, grabbing at the tea-towel and wordlessly handing it to her, one hand gently stroking her back, "It's ok, Son. It's ok."

Sonia briefly ran the cloth under the tap, and wiped the welcome coolness across her burning face. Her body shook uncontrollably, making her teeth chatter.

Vidar's warm hand slid around her waist, and one gentle pull settled her body against his again, "It's like you're in shock, Son. What happened up there? What is it about Grace's husband? Did he say something to you…do something to you?"

Leaning against the safe solidity of Vidar gave Sonia the confidence to whisper, "He's the father."

Vidar, distracted by his own emotional torment, momentarily couldn't make sense of what she was saying, "What? What 'father'?"

"The baby," gurgled Sonia weakly, gripping a fistful of the front of Vidar's jumper and pushing her face against it to inhale the reassurance of him, "His name is Dominic Radley, and he's the father of my baby…"

TWENTY-FIVE

Vidar stood on the doorstep, shuffling from foot to foot and jangling his keys nervously in his palm. If he had the balls, he'd unlock the door. It was his house; he had every right to walk straight in whenever he chose!

He thought of the man – Grace's husband – all slick haircut, square jaw, clipped accent – 'I'm looking for my wife...'

Every time he'd tried to settle to sleep in the narrow spare bed at Stewart and Elaine's, he'd pictured the flatness of Grace's blue eyes, cold as the sea outside the window, and felt such terror he'd had to fight from beneath the bedclothes and struggle to a sitting position, heart hammering, shallow breath whistling. He couldn't conceive of having to exist without Grace in his life; he thought he might just die of a broken heart. What made it worse was that all of this was incontrovertibly his fault. It wasn't only the situation he'd created with Grace, it was what he'd insensitively done to little Son! It was all very well insisting the world was her oyster, but he had the protection of immense wealth, the wisdom of experience, the greased slipway of celebrity to slide effortlessly along. He should have had a greater appreciation of how different it would be to take the plunge when you were barely out of your teens, cosseted by island life, your only knowledge of the wider world a few terms protected by the security-blanket of formal education in a small provincial town not that dissimilar from home. He'd egged her on, fed her imagination, fired her desires and, it seemed all too clear to him now, inspired false hope. Her time with him had been a fantasy, and she'd left for London with grand plans and no idea of the truth of her situation. If only he'd given her a realistic assessment of her prospects as all understood them but poor, deluded Sonia herself. Yes, get the hell off Orkney if you must, but don't believe you'll get any further than Inverness if you're lucky; Glasgow if your ship really comes in. You're unquestionably intelligent, but not as brilliant as you believe. However, your quick wit, combined with your striking looks, will help you attract the type of decent, professional man who will value your verve, enjoy your spark, appreciate your attractiveness, and ensconce you in middle-class contentment to keep his home and raise his children, and you should be more than satisfied with that. Become, in fact, a carbon copy of Dr and Mrs Stewart Kirkbride – educated, respectable, comfortable, fulfilled by one another. Don't expect private jets, secret hideaways, red carpets, and popping flashbulbs. That life, Sonia Flett, is not for the likes of you, however many hours you spend coveting its dubious pleasures. He'd never told her that truth. He'd expected her to know it, as he knew it…but at twenty-one, she knew nothing! She believed what he and every other shark of a middle-aged man has ever told a suggestible young girl to convince her to set aside her reservations along with her clothing. He was no better than philandering Dominic Radley, not really, except he prided himself on always finishing it face-to-face, taking the blame, allowing them the satisfaction of having the last, hurtful word, even when there was plenty he wanted to say in reply. Honourable, gentlemanly Vidar Rasmussen; what a catch for any girl!

Vidar snorted mirthlessly, and pushed an impatient hand through the front of his hair as the wind blew it forward. Angry at himself, ashamed of his conduct, Vidar jabbed his key into the lock, turned it, but hesitated before attempting to push the door. Frozen in indecision, hand on the twisted key, he sullenly reversed the motion, ringing the bell.

When Grace opened the door and stood uncertainly before him, squinting up into the sunlight over his shoulder, Vidar's first impulse was to seize her, crush her to him, and beg her not to go...but it wasn't as simple as that. He had his pride...and then there were the lies she'd told.

"No key?"

"I thought it would be better to ring the bell."

She stood aside, swinging the big door wide, but Vidar remained on the doorstep, "Is he here?"

"No. He's gone."

Vidar couldn't read her expression. It was pinched and tense, her top teeth chewing pensively on her bottom lip. She looked pale, with swollen eyes, red nose, and blotched cheeks, as if she'd been crying. Did she mean gone for good?

He stepped inside. Was it his imagination that she seemed to shrink from him? As he advanced across the hall towards her, removing his coat, hanging it up, she was backing away, through the door and into the living room as if she didn't want him anywhere near her. Unsettled, Vidar struggled to get control of the panic rising inside him as it had last night under the suffocating bedclothes, eventually managing to croak, "Is he coming back?"

Tremulously, she replied, "I have no idea, Vidar. Unlike you, I don't seem to have the innate ability to manipulate everyone who crosses my path into doing exactly what I want them to do."

"What's that supposed to mean?"

"You must have thought all your Christmasses had come at once when you found fragile, easily-led little me in your house! You must've been delighted at the amusement to be had while you passed the time here, waiting it out until the baby came...and nothing whatever poor Sonia could do about you flaunting me in her face. Did you threaten her the same way you did a previous mother of one of your children; keep your mouth shut or the money dries up?"

Trembling, Vidar closed the hall door with exaggerated restraint, and turned to face her, "Why don't you just get to the fucking point, Grace?"

"You were seen yesterday! You can't deny you were with Sonia!"

Vidar looked momentarily perplexed, "No...why would I deny it?"

"You admit it? You were with her yesterday?"

"Yes...in Kirkwall...what's that got to do with what's going on here?"

"What sort of a two-faced bastard are you?"

"What?"

"Well, you weren't discussing the bloody weather!" Clenching her fists, holding her arms ramrod straight at her sides, Grace was close to jumping up and down with barely-repressed rage.

"No!" Vidar retaliated, suddenly countering her aggression, "Actually, we were discussing your *husband*, Mrs *Radley*!"

Ashamed, guilty, Grace was thrown off-balance by the amount of feeling squeezed into that one vehemently-delivered word...all the hurt of having been lied to.

"'I'm shortly to be unmarried', you said to me when I asked you, as if your divorce was imminent. Seems you didn't bother to inform your husband!"

Distressed, Grace felt as if the tears might come again. She didn't want them to, in case Vidar assumed she was attempting to manipulate him. She wanted to show at least one of them had been truthful with the other, "I wanted to make a clean break and start again. I...I...took my rings off and started using my maiden name. I didn't think it would matter... I never expected to see him again! I certainly thought that if he was going to come after me, he'd have done it immediately, not taken five months to make up his mind!"

Vidar rubbed his eyes with the heels of his hands and groaned, "Sweetheart, you lied to me! Not once, but again and again – for months and months! And you lied to him! You didn't tell him you were leaving him, did you? Maybe it's taken him all this time to find you?"

"I told Fen where I was – "

"She might be a better friend than you gave her credit for, huh? Maybe she kept your secret for you?"

Grace hadn't considered that.

"I can assure you I'm not in his Fan Club, by any means, but you have to admit you didn't go about it in the best way. You just left and tried to pretend to yourself, me, and everybody else that your marriage was over, when it obviously wasn't! You can't treat people like that! Did you imagine it was just going to disappear? There had to be a day of reckoning in the end – there always is! You can't just walk away!"

"Says the man who abandoned his sick baby on his first day of life and never went near him again!"

Vidar swayed as if she'd punched him, and growled, "That's low, Grace. That's not fair. I told you that because I thought I could trust you, not so you could use it as a weapon against me. I acknowledged him as mine! I paid for everything for him for twenty-one years! He wanted for nothing – "

"Except a father's love...and now you're about to do it again, thirty years later...and you have the gall to lecture me about the way I conduct myself!"

"What are you talking about?"

"About Sonia!" bellowed Grace, in uncontrollable anger, "About the advantage you've taken of her, of me, as if we're commodities to exploit and dispose of, like you treat all women! About your *child*!"

Vidar gawped in utter incredulity, "My what?"

"Don't come the innocent with me!" continued Grace, gaining in confidence and momentum, "I know she followed you to London five years ago!"

Vidar blinked in genuine surprise, "Did she?"

"She told me! You've probably been keeping her there at your beck and call ever since, out of the range of her mother's antennae. No wonder you're so afraid of Margaret! She's got the measure of you, and you don't like it, do you? In London, miles away from her support network, you could treat poor Sonia however you wanted – a bit of guaranteed amusement whenever you passed through town – until she got pregnant and you rejected her once and for all! No wonder the pair of you are so combative! She's smarting from being used up and cast aside, and you're only here to ensure she keeps her mouth shut, to safeguard your precious career!"

Grace's tirade came to an abrupt halt. She stood, out of breath, facing him boldly with hands on hips and eyes flashing fury, daring him to contradict the damning denunciation.

To her astonishment, instead of the incensed counter-attack she was preparing for, Vidar's eyes filled with tears, before he squeezed them shut and turned his face from her, attempting to control the sudden rush of emotion. "Is that really what you think of me?"

Grace knew if she opened her mouth she would cry too, but head must rule heart. It all made too much sense to ignore! It all fitted too neatly to be coincidence!

"Who told you I was in Kirkwall with Sonia yesterday?"

She hesitated, before stuttering, "Dominic." Why did she suddenly feel so uncertain of her ground?

Vidar sniffed once, and rubbed a hand across each eye, turning back to her. She was shocked at the pain etched across haggard features. He had aged ten years in twenty seconds.

"Ok, Grace...you believe whatever you choose. I would have hoped, with all we've shared and how close we've become, that you might have given me the benefit of the doubt...but I guess now I know where your true loyalties lie."

Grace opened her mouth to reply, but Vidar continued, not giving her the chance, "Just let me say this. I've *never* lied to you, Grace. I've shared my hopes, my fears, my mistakes with you. I committed utterly to you and to the future I thought we both wanted to come out of this. Seems I read it all wrong, huh?" His voice cracked, and Grace's insides turned over.

"I hadn't seen Sonia in years. I didn't know she'd followed me to London. She never contacted me, and I never saw her while I was working there."

Vidar struggled to control the tears that filled his eyes, failed, and Grace was shocked to see them spill unchecked down his cheeks, "As for me being the father of her child...well...if only you knew, Grace! It's not my place to tell you something that's nothing to do with me. There are only two people who can tell you, and I'm not one of them...suffice to say, you probably should be looking a little closer to home."

He swallowed, upturning his face to the ceiling as if that might tip the tears back into his eyes. At length, he glanced back, but briefly; not the lingering, caressing gaze she'd come to know and crave as proof of his desire for her. Breaking the eye contact as soon as it was made, he turned to leave with only the whispered, contemptuous, "Don't let me stop you packing," by way of farewell.

At the hall door, he stopped with his fingers on the handle, as if a fresh thought had just occurred to him, "When you see your darling husband later, ask him how he's managed the last few months at work, without his secretary."

Baffled, Grace took a step forward, anxious there was so much left unsaid. Nothing felt resolved, "Vid – " but the slam of the door cut her off. A moment to collect jacket and keys in the hall, and then the solid, definite thud of the closing front door.

"Ohh…" Grace brought a shuddering hand up to her mouth, touched her lips with trembling fingertips, and stood still for a moment, staring at the door, willing him to step back through it. A trifling thought occurred – where was his car? Why, if he'd gone out in it yesterday, had he not returned from Kirkwall in it today? Before she had time to reason what the answer might be, her whirling head stacked another thought on top of the first like freshly-washed saucers in a hectic café. What had he meant – 'there are only two who can tell you and I'm not one of them'? And what could Vidar possibly know about Dominic's work, about his secretary? Grace remained standing for a long time, palms flat on the cold granite of the counter separating kitchen from dining area, distractedly bouncing the toe of her slipper against the skirting board. Something nagged at her like a fish flicking a line, teasing at the bait but refusing to bite. What kept getting in the way of lucid deliberation was a jumble of memories of Fen dragging her the length of Knightsbridge every three months, looking for yet another outfit to wear to one of Toby's interminable work do's. She was never invited to anything with Dom, and yet it seemed Fen was always attending one thing or another. When she'd asked Dom why Fen got to go but she didn't, he'd explained – impatiently, of course – that Toby was another department, and they organised their social events differently; it wasn't some big conspiracy to exclude her.

He'd made her fears seem ridiculous, childish, self-obsessed, which had swiftly put an end to the questioning, and she'd placidly settle to a DVD while he donned his dinner suit and went out 'entertaining'. Giving the skirting a peevish parting kick at her own gullibility, she decided to get her things together and find somewhere else to stay before Vidar returned. She was finished with placing her hope and trust in men who were clearly unworthy of it. First Dominic and his compulsive infidelity, then Vidar and his arrogant misogyny.

Grace strode determinedly into the Master Bedroom and spread her dressing gown across the bed, tossing items of hers onto it so she could make a bundle and carry it all to her suitcase in the guest room in one trip. Feeling as numb as she had while she'd sat and waited for Vidar, Grace attempted to make sense of the last hour without addressing it too directly – like viewing a scene through a camera-obscura – lest she once again be reduced to this morning's vomiting, wailing mess. Gathering up the bundle in her arms, she staggered across the living room like a refugee fleeing a conflict. Passing the dining table, she extended a finger and hooked up the cardigan she'd leant Sonia a couple of days ago, when her friend had been cold and tired. Sonia always looked poorly now; flushed, feverish, and far from blooming with the final stages of her pregnancy. Perhaps it was just apprehension, as the future loomed ever-larger?

Would Vidar react differently once the child was born? The circumstances surrounding the arrival of his estranged son were a world away from his life now. A young man with myriad personal problems, trying to make sense of immense wealth and increasing fame, versus middle-aged parenthood, with experience and hindsight to direct him. Surely, he wouldn't repeat the mistakes of the past, however unwilling he was to be a father? Grace was reassured by the certainty that, whether Vidar publicly-acknowledged his second child or not, he would see Sonia adequately provided-for; indeed, she was convinced he was already doing so.

Dumping the bundle on the guest bed, Grace retrieved her empty suitcase, unzipped and flipped open the lid, and set about sorting through everything to pack it efficiently.

She picked up the black cardigan to fold it and put it into the case – she would find somewhere else to go and then address such nuisances as getting her laundry done. Several of Sonia's long hairs curled across the knitted fabric. Another incongruous memory swooped to surprise her, picturing herself picking up one of Dominic's discarded jackets, brushing it down, hanging it up. Why was she thinking about Dom, and Fen, and what they wore to work? What difference did that make now; she hadn't thought about her abandoned husband or home any other time she'd sorted through the washing in the last five months? Could it be Vidar's inexplicable mention of the secretary that had connected her befuddled brain to Dominic, work, London, Fen, suits, clothes…?

Grace abstractedly plucked Sonia's vivid hair from her cardigan, and discarded the strands with a wiggle of her fingers. The long, curling trails of copper swirled in the displaced air of Grace's movement, catching the morning sunlight coming in through the window, and glowing like iron in a smithy fire. Another memory stopped Grace mid-fold; a strand of that same bright, beautiful flame cast adrift on a sea-breeze, catching the subdued November daylight as it whirled away from the deck of the Orkney ferry…

The neatly-stacking saucers were suddenly crowned with a steaming cup of clarity.

Dropping the cardigan, Grace shot out to look at the kitchen clock. If she went right now, there was a chance she'd catch him. Not noticing she was still in her slippers, Grace grabbed her keys, and pelted from the house.

TWENTY-SIX

The insistent knocking at the hotel room door didn't stop when Dominic shouted, "Thank you, I'll be right down." It kept going, until he was sufficiently irritated to abandon his packing and stalk to the door to give the inbred cow from Reception a piece of his mind. He'd ordered the taxi for half-past, he still had ten minutes, and it would just bloody well have to wait until he was ready! Snatching open the door and just about to let fly, Dominic was utterly amazed to behold Grace, who shoved a hard palm firmly into his chest and propelled him into the room, kicking the door shut aggressively behind her.

Trying to recover his composure, Dominic leant casually against the tallboy, summoned a sardonic smile, and drawled, "Knew you'd change your mind. Did you know you've got your slippers on? You look ridiculous. Is your luggage in your car, because I've ordered a taxi to the airport now. I can't take two days driving home with you anyway. I've had a call, I've got to be back in the office in the morning – "

"Shut up Dominic," snapped Grace. She'd never spoken to him with such contempt in her tone, and bewilderment silenced Dominic more effectively than Grace could have believed possible. His wife certainly didn't have the appearance of a woman who'd come to her senses in the nick of time. Rather, she wore the expression of someone who's dropped their housekeys in a fresh cowpat, and must now retrieve them without the aid of rubber gloves or implements.

"Beautiful colour hair – red – isn't it, Dom? Flame-haired, they call it, don't they? They're supposed to be very passionate people, redheads, aren't they?"

"Grace...have you cracked?"

"No...I don't think I have. I think I've finally managed to work something out for myself, without Fen trying to throw me off the scent all the time. What is Fen, Dom? A previous conquest who still holds a torch? Or have you got something over her that compels her to do your evil bidding no matter what? Do you know things about her Toby wouldn't like to hear?"

"Grace – "

"Shut up Dominic! I'll give you the chance to talk in a minute...when you answer all the questions I've got for you – truthfully."

Dominic glanced at his watch with apparent nonchalance, but Grace noticed his hand shaking, "My taxi comes in five minutes."

"I'll take as long as I bloody well like! A very distinctive shade of red, the hairs I used to find on all your clothing. Not ginger hair, but more like a polished conker or a brand-new copper coin...so deep, beautiful, vibrant...I'd never seen anything like it before. Well, not until I got to Orkney, anyway."

Dominic shifted from foot to foot, and clasped his hands together. Grace noticed he was squeezing his fingers into one another until the pressure-points showed white on his olive skin.

"You see, I made a friend here; a proper one. A beautiful, lonely, misused young girl, and she had the most stunning hair I'd ever seen. I asked her if she dyed it, but she said it was one hundred per cent natural...and her mother's hair is just the same! Faded a bit perhaps, mixed in with a little grey, but you can see what it would once have been – and my friend inherited that same perfectly-pale skin, loads of darling little freckles across her cheeks, such bright green eyes they didn't look real either...and that hair, masses of ringlets of stunning red like the heat at the centre of a coal fire, glowing and bright...and, what do you know, she'd just left London after five years there! It took months for me to figure it out, Dom, because it was so unbelievable I never made the connection...but I was tidying up at home and I found a cardi I'd leant her. There were a couple of those distinctive, red hairs curled on the fabric and I picked them off. They caught the light, and something leapt into my head! Something from the past...when I used to pick endless long, corkscrew-curling hairs off your jackets – just the same coppery-red, Dom...and so many, so regularly, for so long – as if those beautiful, one-of-a-kind flame tresses had been all over you! I used to idly wonder why I found long, red hairs on your underpants...but now I'm not that sure I want to know. Was she an efficient secretary, Dominic? It's a miracle she found the time..."

Dominic swallowed repeatedly, his Adam's apple travelling up and down his slim throat.

"Did you ever respond to that text message? Did you ever find out why she so desperately wanted to see you...why it was so vital 'for your future'? You can talk now. That's one of the questions I want an answer to."

"Grace...I..."

"And I'm not interested in your weasley little lies, Dominic. I've heard so many over the years you should write the definitive Radley's Anthology of Adulterous Excuses. It'd be a bestseller! Did you discuss your child that day? That's all I want to know."

"What day?"

Nailing him to the wall with a steady stare of pure hatred, Grace stated, "The day I finally grew a backbone and decided I was leaving you."

Dominic's whole body twitched. Unable to look her in the eye, he fixed his gaze on her slippers, and muttered, "Yes, we discussed the...issue..."

"And what happy conclusion was reached, Dom?"

"I...um...I explained I was married, and it would be better all-round if she...investigated a termination."

"And when she refused, how much of my money did you give her to 'seek an alternative career-path'?"

"I don't know why you're being like this!"

"Like what?" Grace's words dripped ice as effectively as Fenella's ever had.

"So...so...flippant!"

Grace couldn't prevent an incredulous squawk escaping her pursed lips, "Flippant! Oh, Dominic, do you have any comprehension at all of the pain you've put me through for all these years? You, and T, and W, and B, and J, and F – was that Fen, by any chance? – and U, and O...oh, and beautiful, unusual, flame-haired S, and her unfortunate refusal to obey orders when the shit hit the fan. Over three years she was on the scene, wasn't she, just ticking along faithfully in the background? Sort of like me, really, except I expect she never had to pick another woman's striking coppery hair off her husband's pants before she washed them! You just discarded her when she wouldn't do as she was told, and – what, Dom – moved to the next on the list? How many times have you done that? How many illegitimate children have you just walked away from? Are all Fen's kids poor old tolerant Toby's, or is that the thing uniting the pair of you? Is kind, gentle, forgiving, decent Toby Dalrymple unwittingly raising a Radley or two?"

"I don't know where you get these funny ideas, Grace, I really don't –"

"Probably from years of disrespect at the hands of my bastard husband. I'm starting to think anything's possible when it comes to you, Dom. How. Much."

The soft buzz of the hotel room telephone distracted them. Dominic stared at the 'phone, but didn't move. Eventually, Grace blurted, "Well, answer it!"

Dominic sprang across the bedroom and snatched it up, "Hello? Oh...oh yes. Look, I'll be ten minutes...I'm just finishing packing... Yes. Yes. Thank you."

He replaced the receiver, and sank slowly down onto the edge of the bed, leaning forward with elbows on knees and palms clasped before him, as if praying.

"Twenty grand. I gave her twenty grand."

"Twenty grand. All your child is worth to you. About a fifth of the cost of your car. You're a piece of shit. I'm amazed you can sleep at night."

Dominic didn't look at her.

At length, Grace continued, "Just a couple more questions to answer, Dominic, and you're free to go. I certainly won't prevent you leaving."

He shook his head slowly, and closed his eyes.

"When you saw your beautiful, flame-haired lover yesterday, did you expect to do so, or was it a bolt from the blue?"

"I never expected to see her again, anywhere, ever…"

"And was she with Vidar, like you said she was…or did you make that up?"

"Oh no, she was with him. They were in a café in Kirkwall."

"A café?"

"Yes."

"Not your hotel?"

"No."

"And what were they doing?"

"They were just sitting in there, opposite each other at a table, drinking tea, and holding hands. He'd been crying. Crying in a fucking tea shop in front of a tart."

Crying…

Grace thought of what all this must be doing to gentle Vidar, "He didn't have his hands all over her?"

"No. Seems a bit of a pussy to me. I don't think he's got it in him, to be honest. Trust you not to want a real man."

Grace ignored him, "They were just sitting in the tea shop together, comforting one another, because you'd shown up and blown all our lives apart. To think, I actually considered believing all that crap you fed me this morning!"

Dominic smirked nastily, "Nice to know I've still got it."

Grace grimaced, revolted, "I know it's been a long time, Dominic, and I understand people can change a lot over the course of twenty years, but I really struggle to remember what I ever saw in you. You are a truly vile human being. I cannot see why I never realised at the start."

"Because you were such an airhead you just did as you were told! Daddy said I'd be good to marry, didn't he? I was in the right job; I knew the right people, and I could milk his contacts for all I was worth. I spent five years kissing his arse to make sure I was in the right place at the right time to make hay. I had to marry you, Grace! I didn't want to – I thought you were a pain in the arse then and I still think you're one now – but it was a sacrifice worth making. I did it for my career…and it paid off, I can tell you! I would never have got half as far without the efficacy of my connected wife…and your Trust Fund came in bloody handy as well. It's nice to have a certain standard of living as compensation for being saddled with a moron."

Grace took a deep breath and held it inside her chest for a moment. Ignoring Dominic's barbs, she made sure to meet her husband's eye and hold his gaze as she beamed as brightly and proudly as she could, "Oh, he's got it in him, Dom. I can assure you he's all man… He's so much more than you will ever be, and I. Love. Him. You can say anything. You can make up anything. For some reason, I can no longer hear you."

Dominic threw himself backwards across the bed, and lay staring up at the ceiling, hands behind his head as if he was sunbathing in a summer meadow. His legs dangled towards the floor, and he swung them briefly back and forth, "Anything else, Grace, or can I go and catch my plane back to civilisation?"

"Two things, Dom. One: you'll be hearing from my solicitor. Desist from making any claim on my personal assets in the divorce. Go after what's mine, and I will use every one of my father's friends, whose approval you need so very much, to topple you off your gold-plated perch and drag you face-first through the mud. Clear?"

"Crystal clear, darling. No need to do the 'hell hath no fury' act."

"Last one, Dominic…again, just for clarity, to ensure I don't humiliate myself with the next confrontation I'm due to have today: the name of your flame-haired Orcadian beauty, please. The mother of your child. The mysterious 'S'?"

Dominic rolled over onto one elbow and regarded Grace equably, "Why were you never like this when we were together? I might not have felt the need to stray…"

Grace snorted contemptuously, "This is who I am, Dom. This is who I've always been…and you didn't like it. You got Fen to bully my personality out of me! As you have sowed, Dominic Radley, so you shall reap. Her name, please."

A shadow of wistfulness played across Dominic's features as he whispered, "Her name is Sonia. Sonia Flett."

"Yes. That's what I thought. Goodbye Dominic. I hope your plane crashes." Turning on her slippered heel, Grace left him.

TWENTY-SEVEN

Grace reversed her car into the empty garage at *Somerled*, turned off the engine, and sat motionless, gripping the steering wheel and staring out at the opposite daffodil-covered bank. The bright spring flowers bobbed in syncopated rhythm as the gusts caught their open faces. They resembled a committee summoned to discuss Grace's quandary, nodding to one another as they concluded it was a catastrophe, no question…

Grace was torn between the desire to march straight up to Sonia, push her flawless face into the Flett farmyard filth, and stamp repeatedly upon it with the heel of her wellington, and the urge to beg forgiveness for every abuse her friend had suffered to satisfy Dominic's selfish lusts.

Why had she chosen to believe Dominic, who lied like other mean breathe, over Vidar, who was nothing if not unflinchingly honest? Was it because, for the whole duration of her carefree Orcadian sojourn, she'd been waiting for the axe to fall?

Grace strode ten yards down the shingle path to the farm before realising her shoes were full of chips of stone. Distracted, head buzzing, she looked down absently and was amazed to behold and recall her slippers! No wonder it was such hard going! Sighing with exasperation, Grace turned and retraced her steps to *Somerled*, letting herself in impatiently and bustling across the hall to swap slippers for wellingtons. A vivid image of the solid boots stamping

Sonia's pale skin into the rich, dark mud made her hesitate, and reach shakily for her trainers instead. She didn't want to hurt Sonia – she'd been hurt enough already – but Grace couldn't help coalescing every one of Dominic's numerous conquests into one nameless entity, and it bore Sonia's beautiful face.

****

Despite her desire to batter at it with both fists and scream herself hoarse, Grace knocked gently on the farmhouse door. There had been no answer at the annexe. Was Sonia hiding from her?

Margaret appeared, smiling broadly, "Hello Grace, how are you today? Will you come in?"

"No Mag, I'm muddy," was all Grace could manage by way of polite small talk, "I'm looking for Sonia, actually. I tried the annexe but there was no answer..."

"Oh...I did see her going for a walk when I got back a wee while ago, but I didn't expect her to still be out..."

Something flickered within Grace, something unhinged – no sign of Vidar, no sign of Sonia... God, Dominic's poison was insidious! She knew it was all lies, yet still she couldn't completely dismiss it!

"Mag, I need to talk to her about something."

Margaret looked Grace up and down thoughtfully as she dried her hands on a tea towel, "She's always been a funny girl...but, these last couple of days, she's been more preoccupied and sulky than ever. I put it down to nerves. There can't be long to go now, she's been complaining about so many twinges."

"Should she be going for a walk on her own?"

Grace tried not to make the question sound too much like a judgement upon Margaret's hands-off parenting style.

"Och, she won't be far! Ever since she was little, if she wanted to go for a sulk on her own, she'd take herself off up the Memorial. It's blowy and wild up there at the edge of the cliff...I think it appeals to the rebellious side of her nature." Margaret smiled in her sometimes-melancholy way, "But it's close enough to home to rebel in total safety..." It seemed Margaret Flett understood all too well why her eldest had returned to Orkney, however unwillingly. Margaret craned out of the farmhouse doorway and peered up towards the Kitchener Memorial, standing tall on the cliff top, "Shame she always wears that black coat, otherwise you'd probably be able to see her."

Grace squinted at the barren hillside, unable to tell if any figures moved there, "Are you sure that's where she's gone?"

"No...but if you asked me to put money on it, that'd be my safe bet."

"I might take a wander up there and see..." Grace tried to make it sound irrelevant whether she spoke to Sonia now or later.

"Why don't you ring her?"

Grace patted her jacket pockets illustratively, "Don't have my 'phone on me."

"Do you want to call her from here?" Margaret was opening the door wider, inviting Grace inside, gesturing over her shoulder to the farmhouse telephone.

Grace shook her head, annoyed at having to explain when all she wanted to do was pursue Sonia as fast as her legs would carry her,

"No point. Her 'phone and purse and everything are on the table next door. I saw them through the window when I was trying to see if she was in. She shouldn't go out alone with no 'phone, Mag, not if you think the baby's imminent."

"Och, Grace, you can tell you've never had a baby! She's a while away yet, don't you worry..."

Margaret's breezy air of self-assurance irritated Grace. Marshalling the kind of false smile she hadn't required since London, Grace forced out, "Thanks, Mag. I'll just take a quick trot up there. I'll probably bump into her."

"Aye, I expect so. Well, in case you miss her, I'll tell her you popped down."

"Thank you."

"See you later!" called Margaret, cheerily, but Grace's departing figure was already half way to the gate, raising a hand in farewell, and making for the beach and Memorial path with determined stride.

****

The track upward was a long, steep, muddy trudge. The wet grass was soft and boggy, and Grace's trainers sank into the saturated ground, causing runny mud to bleed into the canvas uppers, staining the grey fabric the deep brown of the fertile Orcadian soil. Spring was stimulating the patient grass into rapid growth, and long tufts brushed copious moisture across her trainers and jeans until both were soaked. The water seeping into her shoes squelched unpleasantly between her toes, chilling them, and the heavy, wet flap of her trousers around her ankles was uncomfortable and maddening. Sonia better be up here after all this effort. At least the discomfort was hardening her attitude prior to their encounter. She wanted to state her case and place the onus on Sonia to explain herself, without being swayed by any sensation of sympathy for the girl. However badly Sonia had suffered at Dominic's hand, she'd nevertheless had an affair with a married man, and must be made to comprehend and repent of the pain she'd caused.

Distracted from her indignant, self-pitying reverie by a movement in her peripheral vision, Grace looked up the hill and beheld Sonia, creeping gingerly downward, one hand clutching the underside of her considerable bump, the other gripping the wire fence at intervals to support her. The front of her red dress was stained darker in a circular patch spreading from crotch to hemline. Comprehending, just discerning the moans of terror above the gusting wind, breaking waves, and wailing, wheeling birds, Grace broke into a run, trainers sliding with every uphill footfall.

"Sonia!"

Focused on staying upright, Sonia hadn't noticed Grace. Spotted, Grace saw Sonia's shoulders slump in momentary relief, before the crying began with the volume and intensity of a toddler who's dropped their ice-cream at the feet of a delighted Labrador and seen it vanish for good. Heart hammering, breath whistling, thighs burning, Grace slogged on, finally drawing level with the wailing girl, and pressing an anxious palm to the dark patch on the front of her dress. It came away clean.

"Oh, thank Christ for that! From down there, I thought it was blood."

"Noooo," moaned Sonia, "It's my waters…it's happening now! It's too soon…too soon…" Breathless with fright, she gasped, staggered, slipped on the mud, and nearly fell.

Grace grabbed her under her arms, hefting her upright. The two stood for a moment, clinging to one another, recovering their breath. A contraction passed through Sonia. She cried out in pain and alarm, mouth and eyes wide, before clenching her teeth, screwing up her face, and bearing down with a groan of agony, one hand gripping Grace's, the other clutching at the fence.

"Oh God, neither of us has got a 'phone! We've got to get you back to the farm!"

Sonia fumbled a fistful of Grace's scarf, "What if I don't make it?"

"We'll make it," insisted Grace, with a confidence she didn't feel, "Steady steps, just keep going. If you have a contraction, we'll stop, let it pass, and press on…"

Sonia's wide, disbelieving eyes raked Grace's face for reassurance. Grace hugged the frightened girl closer to her, "We'll make it. Come on. Slow and steady. I'm here. I won't let you fall."

TWENTY-EIGHT

Vidar had deliberately left his car at Stewart's. He'd needed the half-hour walk between the doctor's croft and *Somerled* this morning to get his head together, fix his 'game face' to deal with the reality of the reconciled Radleys and Grace's departure.

His sobering encounter with the distraught Sonia, and the subsequent cruel clash with Grace had left him thrashing around seeking a place to deposit his seething rage. Women! They were all the damn same! Grace had certainly seen him coming, fed off his lonely desperation, and consumed him like a female Preying Mantis devours her mate. Diverting while he'd lasted, he'd ceased to deliver for her once dashing Dominic had arrived on the doorstep. All her adorably-selfless care, her gentle caresses, her delighted appreciation of him had been a lie...just look at how quick she'd been to believe the very worst of him, despite everything they'd shared!

He stopped short in his grim trudge, blinking into the sunlight that periodically revealed itself between the swiftly-travelling clouds – how much had they shared? He'd opened himself utterly to her...but what had she revealed of herself and her past beyond a few vague, unsubstantiated allusions to her husband's mistreatment?

That Grace had lied to him was undeniable – about her name, her divorce... Did she make a habit of floating from one affair to the next for idle amusement, playing the abused wife to perfection while her long-suffering spouse footed the bill?

That Radley was the father of Sonia's baby was beyond doubt. Sonia's reaction to his appearance had said it all, but had Dominic sought comfort in the arms of the striking Miss Flett because of his own wife's persistent neglect?

Vidar's most discomfiting reflection concerned his own responsibility for Sonia's predicament. A happy little girlfriend was an attentive, biddable one – all that had mattered to Vidar five years' ago. At the time, he'd never considered what the result of his selfish manipulation of Sonia would be, how unrealistic inflation of her expectations could produce such disastrous results!

What a mess, and he was trapped right in the middle of it, his shattered heart pulsing its pain with the intensity of a lighthouse from a storm-battered brough.

Momentarily, Vidar regretted not callously blurting out every detail of Dominic's shameful little secret at Grace's twisted, angry face. Whether she'd believed him or not, it would certainly have added a frisson of fresh mistrust to their two-day car journey home.

He'd held back for Son's sake. Sonia needed Grace's genuine, unconditional affection, and it wasn't his place to drive a wedge between the two women. Much as he might wish to lash out and be revenged upon the Radleys, he couldn't destroy Son to do it. If the truth was ever to come out, it must be allowed to do so in its own time, without him vindictively helping it along any more than he already had. Grace was no fool. Eventually, she'd work it out.

Reaching Stewart's, he didn't bother to knock at the house, but unlocked the Range Rover and climbed inside, grateful for the respite from the brisk, April breeze. As he drove back, retracing his journey, he allowed his gaze to wander from the deserted road towards the beach. The tide was on the turn, and he decided to go and watch it for a while. There was something therapeutic about standing on the scattered boulders, enjoying the fast waves racing in, every fresh pass surging a little further, concealing more, cleansing each tiny grain of sand.

He parked on the open area where the tarmac road petered out to shingle, and leant his bottom against the bonnet of the car, staring at the water, trying not to think of anything but the inevitability of each wave following the one before. At length, a steadying notion bobbed to the front of his mind like a trail of weed carried on the incoming tide: if she thinks so very little of you that she could accuse you of so much villainy, surely you should be delighted she's gone? If she doesn't care for you, why are you torturing yourself by wasting time and effort yearning for her? Let her go, and consider you've had a lucky escape. Gather up the pieces of your shattered heart, lock them away, and get back in the zone. You've too much work to do to be wasting time on thankless romance. That's the last time you make a fool of yourself over a woman. The older you get, Rasmussen, the more of a buffoon you're becoming. Have some self-respect.

The longest wave yet reached the first of the scattered stones at the rear of the beach, clacking them together like pool balls. The water hissed, fizzed, and bubbled inbetween them, making their previously-dusty surfaces glisten like pearls.

Vidar sighed and turned away from the sea. He needed to go home, remove every discernible trace of Grace from *Somerled*, and start afresh. About to climb back into the car, a panicked scream of "Vidar!" stilled his heart.

Looking across the ridge of rocks towards the other side of the beach, he observed the unmistakeable silhouettes of Grace and Sonia, advancing with slow deliberation. The tone of Grace's shout spurred him to a brisk walk, a jog, and finally a flailing sprint across the loose stones, fighting to keep himself upright as they slid away from his thudding feet. The closer he got to the two women, the more obvious the situation became. Having witnessed the home births of two baby brothers, Vidar well-remembered the sight of a woman in labour. Reaching them, he deliberately didn't look at Grace, but gathered Sonia up in his arms and carried her as fast as he was able, back across the slipping pebbles to his waiting car, Grace scurrying along behind.

At the car, he grunted, "Open the passenger door. Push the seat back as far as it'll go."

Grace complied in silence.

Vidar gently eased Sonia down into the seat, hushing her as she moaned in pain, tucking in her legs, slamming the door, and shooting around to the driver's side, clambering in and immediately starting the engine. Grace hesitated momentarily beside the car, then got into the back before he could tell her not to.

Vidar roared off up the road way too fast, and Grace was surprised when he sped past the farmhouse and continued along the lane. They weren't going to hospital, as that was in the other direction. After a few minutes, they reached a well-maintained croft with a large Audi parked outside. Vidar lifted Sonia out with great care, not uttering a word, and carried her across the driveway and into the house, shouting, "Stewart!" as he fumbled with the latch.

As the three of them burst into the warm cottage, Dr Kirkbride's surprised face appeared around a doorway to their left. One glance was sufficient to apprise him of the situation, "Oh Christ..." He pointed down the passageway, "Get her in there."

Vidar carried the gasping, panting, grimacing Sonia up the corridor and into the Kirkbride's bedroom, placing her carefully on the bed, and propping her up with several pillows. Stewart swung into action with consummate professionalism, "Right, Sonia, let's have a wee look at you. Grace, get her wellies off, please."

Grace tugged off each wellington, which had spread a liberal coating of mud across Elaine's pristine duvet cover. Brows drawn together, Stewart compared Sonia's feet and squeezed her ankles, then lifted both hands and palpitated the palms, wrists, and fingers, before raising her chin and feeling the sides of her face, finally assessing her pulse with neutral expression.

"Right, Vidar, out." Stewart pointed to the bedroom door, "Ring for an ambulance...and then ring the hospital. Explain its on my behalf, and say an ambulance is bringing in a woman in labour...tell them possible pre-eclampsia. Got it?"

"Yes."

"Do it…and then go and watch for the ambulance so they don't miss the driveway – right?"

"Right."

"Go!"

Stewart turned to Grace, "You stay here…I'm going to need you."

Grace removed her filthy trainers, and left them on the floorboards near the door. She felt guilty about the quantity of mud and sand they'd trodden throughout this neat, bright cottage. Taking off her coat and scarf and tossing them over a chair in the corner, Grace rolled up her sleeves and awaited orders.

Stewart looked at her hands, grubby with the mud from Sonia's wellies, "Come in here and wash your hands thoroughly, with soap."

Stewart preceded her into the little ensuite and did the same, taking several clean towels off a shelf above the door and carrying them back into the bedroom, seemingly unaffected by Sonia's continuing cries.

"Ok, Grace, off with Sonia's tights and her knickers, please. Push her dress up and lay one of these big towels across her legs to keep her warm." Stewart jogged down the corridor to his office, returning with a box of latex gloves, "Get a pair of these on."

Stewart held Sonia's hand and looked at her with kindly eyes as she gazed up at him, fearfully, "Sonia, you naughty girl. You should come to your appointments! How long has your blood pressure been high?"

Sonia shook her head, uncomprehendingly.

Stewart elaborated, "Red in the face, swollen ankles, shortness of breath, dizzy spells…?"

Grace gasped, "Since the winter!"

"Oh Sonia! High blood pressure is extremely dangerous for you and your baby! Why did you not come to see me?"

Another contraction saved Sonia from having to reply. Shaking his head, Stewart eased up her knees to lift the towel, "Let's have a wee look here..."

Grace slid both her hands around one of Sonia's, cupping the girl's clammy, trembling palm in her own. Quiet tears of pain and terror tracked Sonia's rosy cheeks.

"Ohh-Kayyy..." murmured Stewart slowly, "Almost fully dilated."

Grace stared at him, horrified, "That means the baby's coming now, right?"

"Aye, pretty much." The doctor's voice was calm, conversational, as if discussing the weather or the test match score.

"Before the ambulance?" hissed Grace.

Stewart sighed resignedly, "I expect so."

Sonia wailed despairingly, and tried to swing her legs off the bed as if to make a run for it, but another contraction prevented her. Whimpering, she sank back onto the pillows again. Grace fussed around her, propping her more comfortably, grateful of a task to dispel the creeping panic. She'd seen births on television. There were doctors, nurses, midwives, machines, drugs, and even then things didn't always go according to plan. However competent and reassuring, what chance did they stand with only Dr Kirkbride in his day-off tracksuit and threadbare slippers?

Sonia's body radiated heat, and Grace managed to wriggle her friend's woollen dress off over her head. Sonia's breasts almost spilled out of her pre-pregnancy bra. Grace unclasped it, frustrated with Sonia. Why hadn't she bought herself any proper maternity clothes? Did Sonia believe actively ignoring the fact of her impending motherhood would make it disappear?

"Dr Kirkbride, please can we borrow one of your wife's t-shirts? We'll replace it."

"Oh, aye," Stewart took a t-shirt from a chest of drawers, and Grace removed Sonia's tight bra, instead sliding on the cool, soft jersey top.

"More comfy, yeah?"

Sonia nodded, smiling nervously. Grace gently pushed her friend's heavy hair from her face. It spread across the pillow like a halo of burnished bronze.

"Just be calm," whispered Grace, encouragingly, "If you relax, the contractions might not feel so bad."

Sonia panted, cross, "What do you know about it?"

Grace smiled, and touched gentle fingers to Sonia's burning cheek, "Bugger all, darling."

Sonia managed a smile, and Grace held her hand tightly, "How long, doctor?"

Stewart examined Sonia again, and beamed at them both, "Another couple of minutes and we might just have a wee go at pushing, eh Sonia?"

TWENTY-NINE

In the rapidly-shortening lulls between the contractions, while Grace patted a cool flannel across Sonia's sweating forehead, and Dr Kirkbride alternately checked her pulse and rate of dilation, Grace found her mind wandering. Was Dominic already on his flight, putting as much distance as he could between his cowardly hide and discarded child?

The rush of icy hatred that had flooded her as Dominic spoke Sonia's name aloud had entirely vanished. In its place lodged an unshakeable determination to do right by mother and child. It comforted Grace to know her twenty thousand pounds was already providing for her friend. Perhaps she could make it a condition of her divorce for Dominic to pay for his carelessness, providing sufficient maintenance to give Sonia and her baby the freedom to live a decent life?

A crushing-together of the bones in her hand, as Sonia weathered another contraction, snapped Grace painfully back to the disturbing present.

Kneeling up on the end of the bed between her friend's bent knees, Dr Kirkbride spoke with cheery encouragement, "Right Sonia, with the next contraction, listen to me, and when I tell you to push, you go right ahead, yes?"

Sonia swallowed, panted, nodded, rolling terrified eyes up towards Grace. Grace squeezed her hand and beamed with as much hope and enthusiasm as she'd ever had to pack into one expression, "Here we go, darling. Not long now, and we can meet your baby!"

****

Vidar stood in the constant, cold wind at the end of the driveway, teeth chattering despite his bulky coat and woollen hat, staring fixedly at the brow of the hill, and willing the ambulance to crest the low rise in the undulating road. He'd been so convinced Grace would be gone. He couldn't begin to understand what it meant that she was still in Birsay!

Mercifully, he was far enough away from the house not to be able to hear Sonia's continued cries of pain, the soundtrack to their ten-minute car journey from beach to croft. It brought back vivid memories of sitting on the sofa in the house in Denmark, opposite his withdrawn, tense, always-distant father; listening to the soft, soothing murmur of the midwife's voice behind the closed bedroom door, the chilling screams of his mother's pain and, finally, the lusty cries of both brothers, healthy and safe. He recalled the feel of holding a warm, surprisingly-sturdy bundle on his lap, gazing at the grumpy, red, wrinkled face of his small sibling, and considering it the coolest thing in the world to have a real-life action figure to play with. The idea of someone placing such a vulnerable, tiny body into his huge, adult hands, and declaring it was not a toy, but that he was responsible for its health, welfare, education, behaviour, and future, filled him with cold dread at the enormity of it. No wonder Sonia would rather pretend it wasn't happening! Caught off-guard, the image he fought constantly to suppress unsettled him – that of his own son, lying helpless and tiny across his thighs, reedy legs and arms purplish-blue with the cold of poor circulation, a tiny tube taped to his little nose, other wires and monitors affixed to his hollow chest, every minute rib visible through paper-thin skin, every vein a wavy-blue line like the tributary of a river marked on a map. He'd thanked the nurse, who'd lifted the boy gently back into the incubator. Before she'd closed the lid, he'd touched one finger to the back of a tiny hand no larger than a ten-pence coin, and said a prayer that, when it soon came, death would be quick and painless. Not for the first time, he wondered where his boy was, what he did, who made him happy…and whether he'd had the courage to do what his selfish, cowardly father could not; willingly take responsibility for the love, care, and nurturing of his offspring. He hoped his son's life left him fulfilled and, above all, that he wouldn't end up middle-aged, betrayed, embittered, and alone.

****

Stewart bustled in and out, cleaning up, grinning with magnanimous satisfaction at a job well-done. Sonia sat propped up in the bed, strands of sweat-soaked hair standing to attention amongst the tumbling ringlets, staring in utter amazement at two towel-swaddled bundles, one in the crook of each arm, as Grace pushed pillows underneath to support the weight of the twin girls.

Dr Kirkbride paused at the bottom of the bed, putting his watch back on, "No sign of that ambulance." He smiled indulgently at Sonia's bent head, drinking in the overwhelming sight of her tiny, perfect, miraculously-healthy daughters, "As they're clearly still in the canteen, I think we'll join them. You wouldn't say no to a cup of tea, would you Grace?"

"I'd say 'Yes please!'"

"Right, I'll do it now."

Grace sat on the bed next to Sonia, extended a gentle finger, and eased aside the edge of each towel to better-observe the baby's faces, surrounded by coronas of thick, dark, curly hair, "No wonder your tummy got so big."

"Aye. I was scared I was eating too much. Cake, you know."

Grace was unequivocal, "You can never have too much cake! You are a complete idiot! If you'd been to your appointments and had regular check-ups, you would've known you were having twins…"

Sonia rolled her eyes, for a moment exactly resembling the teenage Lorraine, "All right! I know! It's a bit too late to go on about it now, isn't it?"

Grace shook her head, exasperated.

Sonia continued, "Anyway, there's a bigger problem…"

"What?" After the last couple of days, Grace wasn't sure she could take on any more and retain a fragile thread of sanity.

"I've only got one of everything! One cot, one high-chair, a single buggy instead of a double. I'm going to have to take half the stuff back to the shop and start again."

Grace chuckled, flooded with relief, "As problems go, Sonia, I think that's a nice one to have."

Sonia laughed, gazing from one baby to the other, "I can't stop looking at them."

Grace stroked each little rounded cheek in turn, "They're beautiful, Sonia, why would you want to stop?"

A sudden bustle down the hallway, doors opening and closing, thudding footfalls, male voices. Grace looked up, "Ambulance, at last! You won't have time for your tea."

Stewart marched in, "Ambulance. I had a whinge about how long they've taken...just got a lot of shrugging. Vidar's gone for your Mam, Sonia. He'll only be a minute and then we'll get you all off to hospital."

"My Mam?" There was a fearful edge to Sonia's voice.

"Aye. Vidar suggested it, and I think he's right. Your Mam needs to go with you to the hospital."

"Not Grace?" Sonia looked uncertainly from the doctor to her friend.

"No Sonia."

"But – " Sonia looked worried, as if she thought Grace might be offended.

Grace sought to reassure her, "Dr Kirkbride's right, Sonia. Your Mum should be with you. If they keep you in, I'll come up to the hospital later and see you all. I can bring you some bits up."

"But – "

"They need to check the girls, make sure they're ok. They need to monitor your blood pressure. You haven't been taking good enough care of yourself. You have to do that now...you've got two little girls relying on you."

Sonia opened her mouth to protest again, and Stewart wagged an authoritative finger at her, "No arguing, Sonia! Do as you're told for once. It's for your own good."

Stewart nipped outside the door. They could hear him having a low-voiced discussion with the paramedics.

"I'm not offended, Sonia. You need to involve your Mum in this. You can't come home, throw yourself on her mercy, and then shut her out of your life at every turn because her opinions don't chime with yours. You said yourself you had to patch it up...and you've done very little to do so..."

"I thought I'd have more time!" blurted Sonia, fixing Grace with wide, frantic eyes.

"More time for what?"

"I thought if you were coming to the hospital, we'd have...time. To talk..."

Grace rubbed her temples rhythmically. A headache was forming behind her eyes. She wanted to lie on the sofa at *Somerled* in the warmth of the evening sun as it streamed through the window, close her eyes, feel Vidar's arms slide gently around her, rest her aching head against his chest, and fall asleep to the steady rhythm of his breathing.

"Are you leaving, Grace?"

One of the babies clucked gently, a little sound like a duck's quack in the sudden pindrop silence of the bedroom. Grace felt tears threaten, and swallowed repeatedly, confessing, "I don't want to...but I don't think I've got a choice. My husband..." Her voice failed her. She stopped, collected herself, began again, "My husband came. I...just...ran away from him! I never told him where I was going, or that I wanted a divorce. Vidar realised I'd lied to him. I didn't do it to hurt him, I did it to forget what I'd come from...but he didn't see it like that. I said some horrible things! I realised my mistake...but...too late... It was all already out there and I couldn't take it back. He pretty much told me to pack my bags and get out. I have to leave, Sonia. I don't want to – I'm falling in love with this incredible, wild place – but how can I stay here when there's a chance Vid and I might keep running into one another? I don't think I could take that pain...the pain of knowing I had it all and just threw it away!"

Approaching sounds of shoes on the creaking hallway boards made Sonia gabble frantically across Grace's explanation, "I have to tell you something!"

Grace looked very directly at Sonia's flushed face, "No you don't...because I already know."

What Grace stated with Dr Kirkbride-style unflappability was the earthshattering, "They even look like him...all that curly, black hair..."

Sonia gaped, tried to talk, but couldn't make any noise come out.

"How long did you work for him?"

"Huh?"

"You were his secretary, weren't you? Did he ever tell you he was married?"

"He didn't act like a married man!"

"No, I'd agree wholeheartedly with that statement," muttered Grace, drily.

"I never knew he was married until the day I told him I was pregnant. He all but scoffed in my face, said he had a wife so he didn't want me, and he'd give me twenty grand to keep my mouth shut and bugger off back where I came from." The sides of Sonia's mouth pulled down as if she was about to cry. Grace extended a gentle hand, and squeezed her shoulder, "Don't give him the satisfaction of spilling even one tear on his account. I'm certainly through with doing so. You indubitably should be!"

Sonia breathed a shy laugh into the greater understanding between them.

"I worked for him for four years. I thought it was the best thing in the world when he wanted me."

"So did I," said Grace ruefully, "but I swiftly realised what he actually wanted were my Dad's investors…and I was the way to ensure his job security, so my well-connected Dad passed the baton to his son-in-law upon retirement. I was a commodity…like you were. You were for entertainment. I was for financial security. He didn't love either of us. He didn't love any of them. I'm not sure Dominic is capable of love, or even of mild regard. He might be a sociopath."

"An arsehole is what he is," stated Sonia, flatly.

"Amen, sister!" Grace laughed, a jarring sound in the quiet bedroom.

"Don't go," begged Sonia.

Grace stroked the nearest baby's hair gently, "So soft… You realise I used to read all your text messages?"

Sonia blushed, "I never would have done it if I'd known he was married! I thought he'd hung the moon! I thought we had a future! I thought I'd struck gold finding such a fantastic, well-to-do, handsome, unattached man, who wanted me as much as I wanted him! What a stupid cow, eh?"

"That twenty grand he gave you…it wasn't his to give. It was mine."

Sonia hurriedly gasped, "If I'd known, I wouldn't have taken it! I felt like a piece of crap taking it anyway, but I thought it would hurt him, because he cares about money, doesn't he? And I thought I'd probably need it. I've not spent it all, not by any means. I'll give it back!"

Grace soothed her, "No, no…I don't want it back. I don't need it back. I inherited a massive property portfolio, stocks and shares, an invested Trust Fund…I'm the original rich bitch. I don't need that money, Sonia. I want you to spend it on your babies, and I can help you with more if you need it."

"No…I can't take it – not after everything…"

Grace sighed, "Don't be a silly girl! It's all very well being high-minded with twenty grand in the bank. What happens when it's down to twenty quid? Be practical, Sonia! This isn't about pride, it's about security."

"I'm sorry for all of it, Grace."

"So am I. If I'd had the courage to divorce him fifteen years ago, when I first wanted to, none of this would have happened, I'm sure of it."

"What do I tell my Mam?"

Grace shrugged, "Whatever you want. No one has to know anything if you decide not to share. Only you and I need ever know the truth – and if you keep it to yourself and I leave Orkney, who can tell?"

"Vidar," breathed Sonia, "Vidar knows…because I saw Dominic at *Somerled* this morning. I was coming to see you and there he was, on the driveway…and Vidar found me…and it all came out…"

"Ah, I see. I did wonder how he knew about Dominic and his secretary. He tried to tell me without coming out and saying it, because he knew it wasn't his secret to divulge. I don't believe he would ever put you in a difficult position, Sonia. He's very fond of you…"

Sonia was about to reply that Vidar was fonder of Grace, when the sound of Margaret's near-hysterical arrival captured her full attention. Stiffening, she fixed her eyes on the white rectangle of the bedroom door, hugging her babies closer.

Stewart opened the door and admitted a pale, visibly-shaken Margaret, flanked by two grinning paramedics. One of them eased politely past the obstacle of Mrs Flett in the bedroom doorway, and approached Sonia, "Well, it all looks mighty cosy in here! I think your Mammy might need us more than you do, eh?" He winked at Sonia, "My name's Allan, Sonia. I'm just going to take your blood pressure and pop a wee monitor on you, and then we'll get you and your bairns in the ambulance and off to hospital for a check-over, ok?"

"Ok." Sonia was quiet, biddable, submitting to the kind attentions of Allan without complaint, bright eyes fixed on her mother's shocked face. Grace stood, took Margaret's arm, and gradually eased her into the bedroom, "Come and see your granddaughters,

Mag. They're beautiful. Sonia was so brave…" Margaret extended a carrier bag in one trembling hand, declaring, "He" – even in her distressed state, she succeeded in packing a considerable amount of contempt into the word – "suggested I should bring some clothes and things for you. There's a tracksuit and a nightie and things…some shoes…undies…"

The second paramedic stepped forward, "Margaret, I'm Alastair."

"Oh…" Margaret looked around slowly, surprised, as if she hadn't noticed him, smiling up into the handsome, friendly face, "One of my boys is Alastair. He's a twin, you know…"

"Ah, you'll be an expert, then! Perhaps you could give me a hand with the babies while Allan takes Sonia's blood pressure and just puts a couple of monitors on her for the journey…?" He leant forward and smiled into Sonia's eyes, wordlessly persuading her to allow him to lift one baby from her arms, looking over his shoulder at Margaret, encouraging her to participate. Grace took the carrier bag and placed it on the bed, edging backwards and allowing the new grandmother to occupy her space. As Alastair carefully checked over the first twin, and Margaret wonderingly cradled the second, Sonia fumbled in the bag for something to preserve warmth and modesty. Surplus to requirements, Grace was shuffling, unnoticed, to the door as Alastair asked, "What are their names, Sonia?"

Sonia looked up, realised Grace was nowhere to be seen and queried, tremulously, "Grace?"

"I'm here." Grace was by the door, inching on her coat.

"Do you have a middle name?"

Puzzled, Grace replied, "It's Jeanne, after my sister..." She was going to elaborate with 'the one who died', but stopped herself just in time, realising how inappropriate it was to mention death in a room containing two such new-born babies.

Sonia nodded once, decisively, and pointed with authority at her children, "That one's Grace, and that one's Jeanne."

The eyes of the two friends met across the bobbing heads and bustling bodies, oblivious to everyone else in the room. Grace's vision blurred, awash with tears of love, confusion, regret. Suddenly, more than anything in the world, she longed to stand before Vidar and tell him how sorry she was, how wrong she'd been.

She struggled out, "I'll see you later, at the hospital," blowing a kiss at Sonia, "Safe journey."

"Thank you for...well...you know..." Sonia's voice caught, and Grace thought she too would cry if she didn't escape immediately.

Snatching up her dirty trainers, leaving a drying muddy outline on the floor, Grace flitted silently down the passageway in socked feet, heart hammering in anticipation of encountering Vidar in the living room, but he wasn't there. She checked the kitchen, office, downstairs toilet.

No Vidar.

Frantically hopping around pulling on her trainers, trying to stay on the doormat and not spread any more mud, Grace yanked open the front door and pelted onto the driveway. Only Stewart's Audi and the parked ambulance remained. There was no sign of the Range Rover.

Grace ran up the slight incline to the road and turned around repeatedly, straining to see as far as she could in both directions, but there was neither sight nor sound of any vehicle.

Vidar was gone.

THIRTY

Stewart watched from the front door as the ambulance edged out onto the lane, and rattled off towards the main road in a cloud of diesel dust.

Closing the door, he turned back into the living room. Grace sat by the window looking as if she was trying to take up as little space as possible, perched on the edge of a dining chair, ankles crossed demurely, knees pressed together, hands cradling an empty mug in her lap, shoulders hunched, head bowed. The index finger and thumb of her right hand rubbed persistently at the ring finger of her left, massaging the skin as if it itched.

"You were a super nurse today."

Grace jumped, "Oh!"

"Sorry…"

"No…I was miles away…"

"Sonia couldn't have gone through all that as calmly and smoothly as she did without you here."

Grace shook her head incredulously, "Twins! Premature twins…with no pain relief and barely time to catch her breath! I knew she wasn't right, you know. She's been pink and tired, huffing and puffing around the place for ages…but I kept telling her to go to the doctor's, and she kept saying she'd been and it was all fine…"

"I didn't see her once," Stewart revealed.

"My God – her whole pregnancy without as much as a check-up! She can be a little sod, can't she?"

"Oh aye...always has been...and hanging around with Vidar probably didn't help with that, fond as I am of him. He's used to people dancing to his tune, and he infected wee Sonia with a touch of that, I reckon..."

Even thinking of Vidar made her want to cry, so she changed the subject, "I haven't seen Mag look so bowled over since I met her!"

"Yes..." Stewart considered the most diplomatic way to frame his response, "It was...refreshing to find her so...acquiescent..."

Grace laughed softly, "I suppose Sonia must get it from somewhere!"

"They're two peas in a pod...which is perhaps why they rub up against each other a wee bit."

Grace nodded at the perceptive, kindly man, and stood to take her leave.

"I can give you a lift home if you like...?"

"I haven't got a home." That was an odd thing to realise. From her parents' plush country manor to an expensive boarding-school. From University digs to her marital home. From there to *Somerled*...and now, nowhere to go, and no one to go with.

Stewart frowned, "Where are your things? Where's your car?"

"*Somerled*."

"Well, I'll take you there. It's up to you after that."

Grace protested in her middle-class way, "I wouldn't want to put you to any trouble – "

"It's half an hour or more to walk it, it's freezing, getting dark…ten minutes in the car and you're there. Go on, Grace, I'm just looking for an excuse to drive it."

Grace raised a quizzical eyebrow.

"Smartest car I've ever owned," confessed Stewart, "I've had it months but the novelty still hasn't worn off!"

"Well," smiled Grace, "Far be it for me to stand in the way of your enjoyment. I'd be very glad of a lift."

"Excellent!" said Stewart, gleefully, "I'll get my coat."

****

As the big car surged powerfully from driveway onto darkening lane, Grace agreed, "This is very nice."

"I know! I can't quite believe it belongs to me."

"Will Sonia be all right?"

"Oh aye…it's a precaution…check the babies over, monitor her blood-pressure, at least overnight. One or two days in hospital and she'll be home, I'm sure."

"That's good."

A beat or two of silence. The car radio played quietly. Grace watched the ribbon of headlight streaming ahead.

"Grace…you can tell me it's none of my business if you like, but Vidar's been my friend for fifteen years, and I don't know a better man, I truly don't. He's clever, he's kind…he's loyal…and he's open with those he trusts. The reason I say that is to explain Elaine and I have his trust, and he came to us yesterday evening distraught. I've never seen him so upset. Usually, he's a positive, optimistic guy. He can find fun and good in everything…but this…! He told me your husband had come, and you were going home to London with him. It was destroying him, Grace. Is it true?"

Stewart kept his eyes fixed on the road, to give the tense woman next to him some space and time to answer.

Grace rubbed cold palms across her hot face, "I've made some huge mistakes. I lied to Vidar. I didn't do it to trick him, but it was still a lie, and it undermined his trust in me. I implied I was getting a divorce, when what I'd really done was run away from my husband without resolving anything. Since I've been here, with Vid, life has been so perfect...maybe too perfect? I didn't think I needed to come clean, I just pretended none of my past had ever happened and threw myself into the here and now, because it was so amazing! Yesterday afternoon, my husband arrived on the doorstep, and I think he gave Vidar to understand my return to London with him was a done deal. He's a manipulative bastard, so perhaps he even implied I'd requested it? Whatever happened between them on the doorstep, I'll never know. You understand how chivalrous Vidar is – he let my husband in! If only I'd answered the door! I would have just slammed it in his evil face!"

"You do know he invested all of himself in you, don't you?"

"Yes!" Grace cried out in anguish into the dark car.

"The shock and hurt was a bit too much for him to bear. He had an early life full of rejection. That's why he works so hard for awards and fans and recognition of every kind...because he needs affirmation all the time. He appears confident, but he's very insecure in that way. His parents were young when they had him, I think...and he was a wee bit of a neglected child, from what I understand. By some things he's said in the past, I get the impression his Dad used to whack him as well. Whatever happened, when the two wee brothers arrived, the parents obviously favoured them over Vidar. They were kept at home with the Mam and Dad, and Vidar was sent away to Music School. I suppose it was the making of him, but it left him with a lot of hang-ups, to say the least. He slogged his wee arse off to make everyone love him, which meant he became incredibly successful – a child star – but he had no one to keep an eye on him, no one to care what happened to him. It's small wonder he ended up with a serious drug problem in his teens that it took him the best part of fifteen years to shake. That's why he doesn't let his guard down with just anyone. Everyone sees the public face – 'showbiz Vidar' – and not the real guy."

"So, what did I see? It felt real enough."

"Oh aye. He worships you."

"Worshipped. Past tense. Now he can't stand me."

"I wouldn't be so sure about that."

"Do you know what I said to him this morning?"

"No...?"

"I accused him of being the father of Sonia's baby – *babies*," Grace corrected.

"He *can't* be!"

"No...and he isn't. I made a mistake...another mistake...but by then I'd said all these hurtful things, as if I thought so little of him I considered him capable of doing that to Sonia; abandoning her to struggle alone! Believe me, I know how much I've hurt him, because I'm hurting just the same. It feels as if someone's reached inside me, ripped my insides out, and let Euan's cows walk all over them – but there's no going back from what I said. He pretty much told me to pack my bags and get out. I was doing just that when everything kicked off! That's why my things are still at *Somerled*, because I found Sonia staggering from the beach in the advanced stages of labour! I don't really want to go back and face Vidar, but I know I've got to. Before I leave for good, I need to stand in front of him and apologise to his face for what I said."

"He loves you Grace. This is torturing him."

"Loved. You don't seem to understand, it's finished. I've messed it up beyond redemption!"

"He arrived here before Christmas a frightened man. He could see his old age stretching away, devoid of any love or care. Gold disks don't smile when you walk through the door. Awards don't put their arms around you. A big bank-balance doesn't keep you warm at night. He was craving the dull, boring life the rest of us take so much for granted we barely notice it. Someone to talk to every day, someone to nag you into getting off your arse, someone else to think about, another warm body in the bed beside you, nicking all the covers and putting their cold feet on your shins in the middle of the night…"

Grace managed a weak smile.

"All those things we say drive us potty but we'd be lost without. Those things that anchor us and give us purpose. Vidar's only purpose has been the pursuit of fame and fortune, and he has both in abundance, so much so they're losing their appeal the older he gets. He's lived his life at a thousand miles an hour – and he won't admit it, but he's getting tired. He wants to slow down, but he knows if he does he'll never be able to speed back up again…and if he slows down too much, he'll start to notice there's nothing else in his life but his job. If he stops working, what's he got left? When he got back here in December, I picked him up from the airport and he was verging on the suicidal. Within two days, you'd given him everything his starving soul was crying out for. How could he not fall head over heels in love with you from the very start, when you made all his dreams come true?"

Grace shook her head slowly, regretfully, whispering, "I've ruined it all…"

"Being a GP in a place like this, you see a lot of people going through challenges no one should ever have to face…but they do, and they get through somehow, because they have hope that things can change. That's the thing about life – every moment it's changing, and you can do something different from the moment before to make your existence just that wee bit better! Nothing's ever set in stone, Grace. If you want something badly enough, it's within your power to make it happen. Look at Vidar, he's living proof of that."

Stewart brought the Audi to smooth halt outside *Somerled's* front door, and smiled generously at his companion, "I think it would be a great shame if you left us. We're all just getting to know you…and Sonia's girls will need an Auntie."

"You're very kind."

"No, I'm very honest. I'm an Orcadian."

Grace chuckled, "And they're the best sort of people, aren't they?"

"Without a doubt!"

"Thank you. Sorry for the mud on your floor at home."

"No bother. I think it was worth it, don't you? Shall I see you inside?"

"This bit I must do alone, I think."

"Well, best of luck…whatever happens. You might be surprised, you know."

"Thank you, Stewart."

"Bye, then."

"Bye."

Grace slid out of the car and closed the passenger door with respectful care, waving briefly as Stewart drove away.

Turning to the front door, she placed both palms flat against the cool wood, counted to ten, and let herself in.

THIRTY-ONE

Leaving her trainers on the floor and her coat on the hook, Grace tiptoed to the hall door and pressed her ear against it.

No sounds…and no light shining from beneath the door into the unusually-dark hallway.

Unnerved, Grace opened the door as quietly as she could, and peeked in.

The whole house was completely dark.

She stepped inside, inching the hall door closed behind her. If Vidar wasn't at Dr Kirkbride's, and he wasn't here, where had he gone? What if he'd decided to leave Orkney, instead of waiting for her to do so? He made instant decisions, and acted upon them. She had easily been absent for long enough for him to pack and depart. What then?

The Master Bedroom door still stood ajar. Nothing seemed disturbed. The kitchen remained as tidy as she'd left it. Glancing to her right, she could see the chaos of the guest room as she'd abandoned it, her jumble of unsorted clothing across the bed, empty suitcase next to it, black cardigan that had started it all puddled on the floor where she'd dropped it in her haste to confront Dominic. It all seemed like another lifetime!

The interior of the cosy house was unusually chilly. Grace was sure she could feel a draught coming from somewhere, eventually noticing the patio door standing slightly open. Instantly on the alert,

Grace tiptoed towards it, glancing around apprehensively. It seemed foolish to consider such a thing in this sleepy place, but were they being burgled? Reaching the door, she peered cautiously around it, out into the evening garden.

Bundled in his winter coat, Vidar sat on the flagstone steps leading from patio to lawn, gazing down at Marwick Bay. The setting sun stained the sky burnt orange at the horizon, fading through yellow into rich cream, pink, lilac, and finally surging upward towards the infinite navy of the approaching night, pinprick stars beginning to emerge as the cloudy sky cleared. The door creaked as Grace pushed it open, padding out into the cold in socks and jumper, already shivering.

He inclined his head at the squeak of the door, but didn't turn to look at her, "Is she ok?"

"Stewart seems to think so…they just want to monitor her blood pressure for a while. Did you know she hadn't been to one check-up for her entire pregnancy?"

"I had my suspicions, but…"

"You should have stayed to see the babies. They're gorgeous."

"I hope you took plenty of pictures to show their Daddy…" The contempt in his tone shocked Grace. She was gripped by panic, retorting before she could stop herself, "That's not my fault! I didn't make my husband do what he did to Sonia, or to any of those girls! Are you suggesting if I'd been a better wife…? I did everything I could! Who I am wasn't enough for him! No matter what I did, it was never enough!"

"It's none of my business." His usually-rich voice was frighteningly flat, devoid of any warmth or animation, "Your marriage, Sonia's affair...none of my business..."

In a way, that was true...but it wasn't that simple, and both knew it. If it wasn't for her marriage, if it hadn't been for Sonia's affair; Grace would never have fled to Orkney. They would not be at this impasse.

"Why are you sitting out here in the cold?"

Vidar's icy voice dropped the temperature further, "Why do you think, Grace? I'm waiting for you to finish your packing. I don't want to get in your way. Make sure you take everything. Don't leave anything behind because I won't...I can't..." His voice faltered, and stopped. Grace heeded his agony, and her heart began to pound, fragile hope awakening, Stewart's encouraging words uppermost in her mind.

Vidar muttered, "I'll stay out here. I won't interfere."

Grace shuddered with the cold, "Vidar, we need to talk about this."

"I thought you'd said everything earlier...?"

His pain reverberated through every syllable. It made Grace feel braver.

"Well, I haven't. I need you to hear me out. Can't we go inside? It's bitter out here!"

Vidar's voice remained quiet, but he was back in control of it now, "No, Grace. I can't go in there. Your stuff is everywhere. It smells of your perfume. The kitchen is full of food you've made. I can't go in there," he repeated, rubbing a hand across his eyes, "You go inside if you want."

"But I need to talk to you."

He shrugged, "So talk."

Grace took a deep breath, and began before her nerve failed, "I'm sorry. You'll never know how much. I know Dominic's a liar, he's been lying to me for twenty years, but I still took his word over yours and I was wrong to do that, I know I was! I just couldn't believe what we had could happen to me. I was waiting for perfection to turn to shit. By believing it was going to go wrong, I ended up assuring it! I'd been so miserable for so long I genuinely didn't believe I could ever be happy, and then you walked into my life...and everything changed! I've never felt as precious, as valued, as respected, as vital, as desirable, as empowered, as free...as content with myself and my lot as I did with you...and I doubt I ever will again. I know what true happiness is now, Vidar, and I'm convinced nothing else will ever come close. I know I betrayed your trust. I know you want me out of your house, out of your life. I promise you I'm going. I just wanted you to know how much I will miss you, and long for you...every day."

Grace's own voice wobbled. Tears threatened. She didn't want to cry. She wanted to get out everything that had been churning inside her since yesterday afternoon.

She breathed, swallowed, blinked rapidly, pressed on, loathe to squander her only chance, "I'm sorry for ever doubting you. I'm sorry for the horrible things I said. I'm sorry I never told you my real name. I wanted to start again without any reference to my detestable husband or my sham of a marriage. I felt if I used my maiden name, it was as if those twenty years with Dom had never taken place. It took him five months to come here, not because he didn't know where I was, but because he was hanging on as long as he could before having to fetch me. He told me he didn't want me back, but I had to return to 'fulfil my obligations'. Naturally, I told him he could stick his 'obligations' where the sun didn't shine... I know I've made a million mistakes. I know I've screwed it all up by being a clueless fool. I don't expect you to forgive me for what I said or did. I just want you to know I never lied to hurt you. I lied so I could feel free! I lied because I wanted to forget everything apart from how wonderful life is when I'm with you..." Grace's voice petered out to a whisper, and the tears began, tipping from her brimming eyes, and skimming across her rounded cheeks, hot against her cold skin. Teeth chattering, body quivering, hugging her arms around her in a vain attempt to keep herself warm, she hopped from foot to foot on the flagstone patio as the extreme chill penetrated the thin fabric of her socks and made her feet ache.

Vidar raised his head, turned, and regarded her steadily. Grace realised how much she'd missed him looking at her these last couple of days...*right* at her, as only he could, "Are you done?"

Grace's chest heaved, and she nodded weakly, pressing her lips together, trying to stop the sobs escaping.

"Ok. I've got something to say now."

Grace steeled herself to weather greater pain before a word had been uttered, crying openly.

"Get your ass over here."

"What?"

"Are you cold?"

"Yes."

"Well, come here."

Distraught, confused; Grace's instinct was nevertheless to obey. Extending a hand, Vidar slid his fingers between hers, and pulled her towards him. At first wary, Grace resisted, but he tugged insistently until she yielded, allowing him to draw her down to curl onto his lap, his warm forehead touching against her frozen cheek.

Vidar reached up and brushed the streams of tears from her face with his long fingers, rocking her gently against him, trying to soothe the uncontrollable sobs that racked her shivering body. He inhaled the scent of her, now so familiar to him – perfume, shampoo, the cream she put on her skin – fragrances that pervaded his home and made his heart race when he opened the front door and detected their hint on the escaping rush of air. The feel of her was becoming second-nature too, caressing the softness of each curve, sensing the underlying strength in every limb, knowing her physical form as well as his own. The idea that she could go, and he would never touch her again, was as inconceivable as it was terrifying. What would he do for the rest of his life if stupid pride were allowed to carry the day now?

"The stuff I've done, and expected everyone to give me a second chance! I did truly terrible things and demanded forgiveness I didn't deserve, without a shred of remorse. I thought because faceless fans thought I was amazing – strangers, who didn't know me, and didn't understand what an asshole I was – then I must *be* amazing! In their eyes, I could do no wrong, no matter how much wrong I did. I treated the people I was supposed to love like total shit, and never even tried to make amends. I never faced up to anything I'd done. I still haven't, really, a lot of it. I just threw money at every problem and ran as fast as I could in the opposite direction, before it caught up with me. Once I knew my son was going to live, I should have been a part of his life…but I was too selfish, too stupid, too much of a coward to take responsibility for what I'd done. I was incapable of being the bigger man. My loss, I guess. I don't have the right to judge anyone's behaviour; not you, not Son, not your husband, not Margaret Flett, even! You had good reason to want to escape your old life, and the guts to stand in front of me and lay yourself emotionally bare…you didn't have to do that. It's my fault if you felt as if you needed to, as if you thought you owed me some sort of apology simply for wanting to be true to yourself after you'd been repressed and controlled for so long."

"What I said…about you and Sonia's babies…it was cruel! That was wrong of me."

"You were mistaken! Anyone can make a mistake! It's no wonder a lingering suspicion got into your head about Son and I. I should have moderated my behaviour towards her! The way I talk to her; the way I still touch her! I shouldn't do it like that. Maybe your husband made some insinuations based upon seeing Son and I together? I guess he did it for his own reasons, but he's a pretty perceptive guy, right? Why shouldn't his assertions have nourished a seed my thoughtless conduct had already sown? When he saw us in town, he must have known what was left of his marriage was on a knife-edge! Who can blame him for grasping whatever advantage he could get? I'd have probably done the same. You always try to trash the opposition if you can, don't you? I don't want Sonia, Grace. I never even wanted her when we had a relationship. She was young, attractive, available…and persistent! It was easy to give in and enjoy myself. In my head, I knew it was nothing…I knew I'd be gone in a matter of months, and I'd never think of her again. It never crossed my mind Son might have a different opinion. I just thought she'd do as she was told, same as everyone is supposed to! I'm not good at relationships. I'm close to my brothers now, but I didn't see them for a long time when they were kids…and I've barely spoken to my parents in thirty years! I try to protect myself from everything that hurts, and that means not committing, so nothing touches me deeply. You took me totally by surprise, you know. I wasn't expecting you, and I certainly wasn't prepared for what you'd do to me! You're lonely if you deliberately isolate yourself in a little bubble where no one can touch you. I blamed fame for that…but I let it happen! I made it happen! And you were right earlier, I do treat women like commodities. I extract what I consider useful to me, and I discard the rest – and abdicate responsibility for that too, by blaming them for not being 'good enough' to keep me interested. How arrogant is that? It's no wonder I was on my own! I thought I'd come here for Christmas, process the loneliness, find a way to cope with it, and get on with my life…and there you were, the other side of the door when I'd made up my mind all hope was lost. You could have taken away all the money, the awards, the notoriety, the adulation…it wasn't important; I had you. The feeling when I thought it had all been snatched away, when I thought you were leaving with him…and there was nothing I could do because he was your husband! I was lying in bed at Stewart's last night, thinking I was gonna die. I couldn't breathe! I thought my heart was just going to stop beating. I had no fight left in me, because there wasn't anything worth living for if you were gone."

Grace shivered involuntarily, and Vidar slid his hands up her back to her shoulder blades, pulling her against him, pressing his lips against her neck, whispering fervently, "I can't let you go, Grace! If I do, I know I'll regret it for the rest of my life. The pain of being away from you will kill me. The idea is already destroying me, and you haven't gone yet."

Grace couldn't speak, so she clung to him.

Vidar wrapped the sides of his padded coat more tightly around her, endeavouring to cover as much of her chilled body as he could with the insulated fabric, cocooning her in the protective warmth of his embrace, seeking to comfort and calm her.

At length, as her tears lessened, he whispered, "Are you getting a divorce?"

At last able to articulate her relief without crying, Grace breathed, "Oh yes, I'm getting a divorce all right! As fast as I can!"

"Has he put you off marriage forever?"

Grace smiled faintly, "Marriage has put me off him forever, not the other way round."

She felt his brushing lips smile against her tingling skin, and the gentle tickle of a warm sigh as he relaxed against her.

"So, you wouldn't be averse to the idea of it?"

"Certainly not…I'd just choose much more carefully next time."

"Define 'more carefully'."

"Well," Grace pretended to take her time considering the criteria, "Any future potential husband would have to meet a very exacting list of prerequisites before I'd even entertain them."

Vidar drew in a sharp breath, "No pressure. Give me an example or two."

"Let's see," Grace ticked off each specified requirement on her fingers, "He'd have to be tall, handsome, muscular, Danish, musically-gifted, polyglot, kind, gentle, endearingly-flawed, as all true heroes always are...anything else? Did I mention handsome? He's got to be that, oh, and Danish..."

Grace cupped her cold hands around his warm face and uptilted it to hers, fingertips tracing reverently from cheekbones to chin, savouring him.

Vidar smiled at her touch, and closed his eyes, "Your hands are freezing."

"Well, you insisted on doing this out here. You always accuse me of choosing to be out in the freezing cold, but it's evidently you!"

"You've woven yourself so completely into my life that even standing inside the house was making me feel as if I was gonna drop dead. It's the scent of your perfume, your sketchbook on the sofa, your purse on the table, food you've made on the side! It's the reality of you in my home, it's the feel of you on my body, it's the melding of you to my soul. I didn't know how I was going to undo all that. I couldn't face it...so I hid out here, and just hoped you'd take most of it away with you – otherwise I might've had to sit out here forever."

"I never meant for any of this to happen, but I don't regret that any of it did. Without Sonia…without all the affairs, I would never have come, and we wouldn't exist. There'd be a you and a me, living our empty, lonely, horrible lives somewhere in the world…but there wouldn't be an us."

"I can't even begin to contemplate that."

"So, you see, the way it turned out was exactly the way it was supposed to. Sometimes you just have to trust to luck, to Fate…and let life happen. I found that out by coming here. I never would've known otherwise."

"Is there anything else you need to tell me, Grace?"

She stroked her index finger across his forehead, down his straight nose, catching gently on his lips, skimming the slight cleft in his chin, running the length of his throat and over his Adam's apple, hooking under the collar of his t-shirt, and rubbing gently across his collarbone, "Only that I love you, and I always will…"

Vidar slid his hands into her hair and drew her face close to his, lazy grin creasing his features as he murmured, "That's plenty good enough for me."

He pressed his lips slowly against hers, tasting the tears that lingered on her skin, and they curled together, securely wrapped in his coat, sheltered by the stone wall, forehead to forehead, nose to nose, feeling the gentle warmth of one another's breathing.

The Orcadian breeze ruffled their hair as the velvet darkness gradually chased all colour from the endless sky.